BEM LE HUNTE was born in C̲_____ _____, and grew up in India, London and Cambridge, and is now living in Sydney with her husband, Jan Golembiewski, and their two children. Her first novel, *The Seduction of Silence*, was published internationally to critical acclaim.

Visit Bem Le Hunte's website at
www.harpercollins.com.au/bemlehunte

Also by Bem Le Hunte

The Seduction of Silence

There, Where the Pepper Grows

Bem Le Hunte

FOURTH ESTATE • *London, New York, Sydney* and *Auckland*

The writing of this book was assisted by the New South Wales Government Ministry for the Arts.

Fourth Estate
An imprint of HarperCollinsPublishers, Australia

First published in Australia in 2005
by HarperCollins*Publishers* Pty Limited
ABN 36 009 913 517
A member of the HarperCollins*Publishers* (Australia) Pty Limited Group
www.harpercollins.com.au

HarperCollins*Publishers*
25 Ryde Road, Pymble, Sydney NSW 2073, Australia
31 View Road, Glenfield, Auckland 10, New Zealand
77–85 Fulham Palace Road, London W6 8JB, United Kingdom
2 Bloor Street East, 20th floor, Toronto, Ontario MW 1A8, Canada
10 East 53rd Street, New York NY 10022, USA

National Library of Australia Cataloguing-in-Publication data:

Le Hunte, Bem.
 There, where the pepper grows.
 ISBN 0 7322 7991 7.
 I. Title.
A823.4

Cover and internal design by Gayna Murphy, Greendot Design
Cover images by Getty Images
Author photograph by Niki Zubrzycka
Typeset in 12.5/17.5 Centaur MT by Helen Beard, ECJ Australia Pty Ltd
Printed and bound in Australia by Griffin Press on 70gsm Bulky Ivory

5 4 3 2 1   05 06 07 08 09

For Tally and Rishi, my darling children.
This book is my prayer for your future, and for the future of
the world, from the bottom of my heart.

PROLOGUE

I suppose I could start this story with Adam and Eve, if I were to start at the very beginning. Better than starting with the sons of Abraham, Isaac and Jacob, because that is the story of my people and we would be travelling along tributaries that take us upstream, instead of to the oceans we all share.

I could start with the explosions here in New York last week. The planes, which I saw from uptown, colliding with the World Trade Center. Or I could tell you about the planes I saw back in Warsaw, swastikas painted on metal, like angels of death in the sky.

Wherever I start, please be patient, because there is so much to tell and it may come out clumsily at times. By the end you will have a fuller picture, believe me. Life is not a painting we can see all at once. It is a story, which needs time to tell. A jigsaw puzzle whose pieces start to fit together only once you've finished playing.

So where should I start?

Yes, I will start this story on a boat ...

We are sailing down the Hooghly River, inland towards Calcutta. I am a younger man, and I travel with a group of Polish Jewish refugees. Our lives are cheap and our pockets are empty, except for a few coins that we may as well throw overboard, because they will be no use to us here in Calcutta.

I have two women in my life, and they are both on the same boat: Ewa, a Catholic, whom I have loved since I was a little boy, and Rivka, who is Jewish, to whom I am married. I do not know what the future will hold for any of us. I do not know when we will be able to stop wandering, like our ancestors, and find a shore that will give us refuge. I know nothing and I have surrendered myself to the possibility that we will ride these oceans indefinitely. And even that will be better than the prospect of going back to Poland under Hitler. At least we are alive. At least we are together. Who cares where we are, really?

Near the jetty where we land, an Indian holy man is carrying a statue of a goddess into the waters of the Hooghly. The man carries her respectfully, as if she is an elderly mother and he is laying her down to rest. But the goddess is neither weak nor elderly. She is strong and beautiful, with many arms to add to her power. Her chariot is a tiger and she smiles charmingly up at the sky as her face is immersed in the water and red dust floats to the surface.

If I were to remind myself of Abraham's idol shop, I would know that this statue has no power. But I try not to think such things, because I am here as a stranger and it is not my right to impose ideas of where God's power is to be found. Already, you see, my faith is challenged and I have a choice: to believe that I am right, or to believe in the God of us all. The One God.

We don't have much to take ashore. A bedroll each, courtesy of the American Jewish organisation that helped us in Vladivostok. A few clothes kindly donated by the Russian Jews in Japan, who gave us shelter after we had crossed the whole of Siberia by train. I have a prayer shawl I was given by a man in Singapore, where our boat, the *Asama Maru*, stopped on its way here.

We are told that we must disembark here in Calcutta and find our own accommodation, as our boat has engine failure. Our experiences have taught us that the best way forward is to find our own. It is always possible to rely on the kindness of strangers, and believe me, there has been no shortage of that type of kindness in my life. But a hounded animal will always seek out its own lair before that of another. We are too exhausted to try to convince some kindly Bengali gentleman of our plight. However, the Jews in this city — they will understand. We can rely on shared sentiments, shared ancestors and common knowledge of our duties. There is no doubt about it — we have to find some of our own people.

So we go to a nearby office and ask to make a call. In the telephone directory we turn straight to 'J' for Jew, Jewish, Judaic. To our relief we see the words 'Judean Club', and so skip through some other relevant letters. We look under 'C' and sure enough there are a few Cohens. Then we look under 'L' and find a few Levis. We put a call through to the Judean Club, and a man by the name of Isaac Hellen, the Honorary Secretary, tells us to stay right where we are, he is coming to get us. We are so excited that the people in the office must think that we have been reunited with long-lost kin, and perhaps they are right.

Nothing could have prepared me for that first ride through the streets of Calcutta. We climb into a line of taxis and soon we are looking out at the strangest land I have ever seen. There are rows of buildings like palaces; mansions with columns and large windows, framed with European shutters. Horses and carts, bicycles, an elephant and a herd of goats in the middle of the city! A few buttoned-up English ladies and gentlemen walk the streets next to rickshaw-pullers with their vests rolled up above their nipples, exposing their brown bellies. The locals are fiercely industrious by the side of the road, chopping up tobacco, selling coconut slices, newspapers, baskets of trinkets, pumping water from the roadside wells, haggling with the men who sit in their cubbyhole shops, legs folded amidst a pile of goods.

We are strangers here, and in what a strange land! Yet I do not feel unsafe, perhaps because of this feeling that nothing could be worse than where we have come from; nothing at all. So far we have had the safety of HaShem's protection and so I am thinking — there must be some reason why we were brought to the end of the world. Yet at the same time I am wondering what could possibly be here for us in this crazy place?

We are taken to the Jewish Girls' School and given the rooms upstairs to sleep in. My wife, Rivka, starts making arrangements for Daniel, her son, rolling out a bed for him, with Ewa's help. This is the way the two of them have managed so far — always focused on Daniel. I suppose I have done the same, because there is not much I can give either of the two women in my care. Rivka pretends she is not my wife, more of a fellow traveller; and Ewa acts as if she has known Rivka and Daniel far longer than she has known me, which is her way of dealing with the uncomfortable situation we find ourselves in. Together they make the beds for the four of us, and Rivka lies down next to Daniel to stroke his forehead. Eva curls up to Daniel on the other side, and the three of them form their own unit of resistance, leaving me with the other men, to make plans for tomorrow, here in this land where pepper grows, so far from Poland that there is little way of imagining a day or way that we could ever return.

We are a group of thirty if I count all the people who have disembarked the *Asama Maru* with us. We have lived through everything imaginable, and now we are in Calcutta, of all the places on God's earth.

Jankel and Zalman, two men who made the journey from Japan with us, are in the corner of the same room I share with my family and Ewa, because the privacy of a married life is a luxury of the privileged. Lewek and Mosze, who crossed Siberia with us, are squeezed in on the other side of me. Nobody complains about these arrangements, because we are lucky to have somewhere safe to put down our heads for a night or two. Lucky, as well, to have food, and people who are concerned about our welfare.

This is our first night in Calcutta, and nobody is quite prepared to go out and explore the city, but we hear it, in the lanes behind the Jewish Girls' School and the streets beyond. A prayer call from the nearby mosque reminds me that we haven't yet given thanks for the place where we find ourselves today, or recognised that it is God's will that has brought us here. So I close my eyes and recite the Shema, and we talk in whispers so we do not wake Daniel, the only child in our midst. We talk softer than the conversations of the cars outside as they honk at each other into the night, slowly silencing themselves as it gets late, until just a few horns blow, remembering something they forgot to say earlier. Rivka tells me to go to sleep, as she rolls over and cuddles Daniel, but I am too alert to even close my eyes.

I have not really told you about Daniel yet, because that takes a lot of explaining. This little boy is my son, and he has the makings of a rabbi. In truth, he is the son of a rabbi who died before all of this happened, yet I am his father. Work that one out if you can. Nothing in this life of ours is simple. From the outside, yes, maybe: we don't look as if we have many possessions, and surely that should make our lives simpler. But it doesn't, because there is nothing simple about a man who has no home. Some say that if you have nothing, you have nothing to lose, but what about memories? How can you get rid of the photographs in your mind once they have been framed and hung there — photographs of things you should never have seen? How can a man be simple if inside his head is a pool of memory so thick that no spoon dares to stir it?

So no, I cannot explain Daniel in a way that is simple. I see him sucking his thumb sweetly, and he seems to sleep peacefully in this place, his new home, with its high ceilings and wooden floors, yet his other hand is outstretched and he is touching his mother, Rivka, to make sure that he doesn't lose her when he loses grip on reality and surrenders to his dreams.

I must be the last one to sleep. Something about this place keeps me awake; something here makes me feel alive, for a change. I sense the warm breath of the city occupying our room, travelling around the heads of us all — Calcutta's latest refugees — and through it I feel the world outside as a living place, full of people who are sleeping only temporarily, waiting till dawn to start another day. There was a time, just a few weeks ago, when there was no guarantee of anything, least of all the assumption that we would be alive at the break of dawn.

We were on our way to Jerusalem, and the boat stopped here. Why? What has God planned for us in this place where pepper grows? What is happening to Poland? What is happening to this world of ours? What is the reason for any of it, and what lies ahead for Rivka, Daniel, Ewa and me?

A car honks and Ewa startles, sitting bolt upright in her bed on the floor. When the first flush of panic subsides and she realises she is not in the Warsaw ghetto, no longer in Poland, she takes a deep breath and smiles at me with the relief of a child. It doesn't take much for me to remember her as a child. We were together when we were children, and thought we always would be, for the rest of our lives.

CHAPTER 1

In my memory, Ewa and I are sitting in my childhood home. It is as Polish as can be, apart from the *menorah* on the table, the Star of David on the wall and the *mezuzah* on the outside of the front door. There is a wooden staircase that creaks up to the first storey, oak parquetry the same as you'd find in any other part of Warsaw, wooden tables, bowls and basins to wash in, wide mirrors over the fireplaces and small lamps in every room. One distinctive feature, however, is the small patch of plaster missing from the ceiling in the dining room, to symbolise the destruction of the temple in Jerusalem.

Poland had been an independent nation for only a few years and there were already wars, this time with Russia. 'We are the bones for other nations to pick over,' my father used to say. 'One day we should finish off our business here and go to Palestine.'

Tonight I am reading from the Haggadah, while my father continues with his politics. He can never stop himself, and this time he has to bring up Marek's conversion to Catholicism.

'So, Yudl, tell me something. Now that you have converted, are you going to help stop all of these rumours? You know, of Jews taking communion wafers and stabbing them till they bleed? These stupid rumours. Yes, of course, we use Christian blood in sacrifices! What do you think of it? Come, tell me seriously — does it make you feel as sick as I do, Yudl, this ignorance?' My father could never call his best friend by his new Catholic name, Marek.

My mother kicks him underneath the table, to distract him from his probing, yet still my father cannot stop himself from being so direct. He is close enough to Ewa's father to feel he can demand some answers, demand that Marek speaks up for everyone who shares his new chosen faith. Yet this is no time for politics. There should be no bones to pick over at Passover except the customary leg of lamb. All bitterness at this festival of ours should be restricted to the bitter herbs! But this year? This year is different of course, because we have invited politics to Passover. It is the first Passover that Marek has spent with us since his conversion to Catholicism and his marriage to Kasia. My father cannot accept it. So many times I have heard him say, 'Scratch a Pole and you'll find a Jew. He can be a Catholic, but he'll always be a Jewish Catholic.'

'A friend is a friend,' my mother says. 'Marek is still Jewish; we all know that. He's just trying to fit in and make a future for Ewa. Jewish Shmewish, what does it matter anyway?'

My father is informed enough to know that it does matter. He knows what the Endeks are saying. He knows that those anti-Semitic parliamentarians only regard Jews who have been Catholic for three generations to be full Polish citizens.

Marek says to my father that he is not alone in converting. 'Everybody is doing it.'

And I remember the words of my father, which I cannot repeat now without feelings of great sadness.

'Converting? Ha! Indeed! The synagogues and *cheders* are still full in this country, and they always will be.'

Later in the evening we fill a cup for the mysterious Elijah from our own glasses and walk to the front door to open it and welcome in the prophet of burning chariots, fire and redemption. My father always told me such wonderful stories from the Tanakh and Midrash about Elijah. I remember him holding my hand at the front door that Passover and telling me, 'You know, every day Elijah comes to the world waiting for a simple act of love and kindness. One such act from one kind heart could trigger the freedom of the whole world, so if ever you have an opportunity to give kindness in life, Benjamin, you must give it.'

That night we look out at the stars and my father says, 'How many of our ancestors, be they Catholic, Jewish or Muslim, would have lived in the desert under these same stars?' By this stage of any Passover feast he is always flushed with the red warmth of kosher wine. 'We are all children of Abraham, and we must all hope together for the future of the world, for we have seen the seas split and we know what things are possible.'

Then we all walk back to the dinner table, the adults a little clumsily, starry-eyed, ready for the fourth cup — the Cup of Praise.

The Passover candles shine warmly, putting lights into the tears in Marek's eyes. My father notices that this temporary return to his old faith is making Marek nostalgic. He hugs his friend and tells him in all earnestness, 'You know what the Torah says, Yudl? It says you must accept the truth from whatever source it comes. This is sound rabbinic doctrine. The Jewish path is not necessarily the easiest, but it is my path and the path of my ancestors. It is where I find a home for my heart and soul. I cannot do what you have done, but I respect your decision and, no matter what, my home is always your home.'

With these words he takes Ewa off Marek's lap and puts her on his other knee, facing me. We exchange smiles and hold hands.

That night, when my father tastes the saltwater from the bowls, he cannot help but taste the tears of Marek, too. 'Don't grieve, my friend,' he consoles. 'You can come to my house whenever you miss Jewish food!'

Marek wipes his tears and laughs. He puts his arm around his wife, Kasia, and says, 'One day we'll have to take you to the church for midnight mass. So many candles, Solomon, you have no idea.'

'Who knows if we can join you? Who knows where we will be? Who knows, who knows ...?'

'Are you going somewhere?'

I come to the end of the reading and the women raise their glasses towards the ceiling. 'Next year in Jerusalem!' they chorus.

My father raises his glass, too, and looks up to the ceiling, to the patch of missing plaster. Yes, one day he will take all of his family to Jerusalem, and there will be no more worrying about what is going to happen to Poland. No more worrying at all.

CHAPTER 2

The accommodation we have at the Jewish Girls' School is a blessing, but still there is no understanding of this world we have found ourselves in. As for me, I have no understanding either of how I am supposed to make a family that includes Ewa.

God created the world, and if we are to do the work of God on earth, we, too, have to create the world. But it is not easy when you have to create your world from scratch. It's a day-to-day business, and the foundations are still new and untested. What weight can they carry? How long will they last?

You must remember that we had been in exile from the land of our birth for many months. I am not complaining. There were many millions of other refugees like us within a few years. It was the same for all of them, I'm sure. I'm just telling it to you as it was.

The hardest part of it all is the fear. Once fear has become a habit you cannot shrug it off. You can dine in a land of plenty, but you cannot forget your hunger. You can look into the eyes of a saint, but you still see the dark side of humanity. A simple act of kindness will bring you to your knees and make the rivers flow from your eyes.

Imagine us then, me, my wife Rivka, our little boy Daniel, and Ewa. We have been invited to pray at the Maghen David Synagogue in Calcutta. Ewa is a Catholic, but we all remind ourselves that she has Jewish blood, if indeed the blood of a Jew is any different.

A man by the name of Elias Shalom has come to take us to pray. He tells us that we will not want for food, because one of the patrons of the community, Sir David Ezra, will be providing all the sustenance necessary. 'Please do not even think about repayment. You are our honoured guests and it is our duty to take care of you,' he states plainly. As I say, this brings tears to our eyes, because it speaks of a humanity we did not dare to expect so far away from our homes. Being an honoured guest does not come easily to any of us. We are too humble and grateful to be the bearers of any such honour, but we accept it nonetheless, because we have no choice and these people have large and generous hearts.

Maghen David Synagogue is magnificent. We enter through the grand wrought-iron gates, past the bearer whom I am told is Muslim and has served the community here for years. Another Muslim man with a small white hat and square white beard gives us water to wash our hands and a clean towel to dry them.

He ushers us into the temple, gives us our books and makes us welcome, showing Ewa and Rivka the stairs to the women's gallery upstairs and guiding us men into the packed main hall. Hundreds of faces under the fans and chandeliers turn to greet us and smile. Word has gone around — not just about our boat and its engine failure, but about the journey we have made from Poland, through Russia to Vladivostok, and from there to Japan. Word has gone around, too, about the treatment we have received from the Nazis in Poland, and I can see from looking into the eyes of those Calcutta Jews that they are curious about how such things could happen.

Let us make no secret of it: we are here in the magnificent Maghen David Synagogue to give thanks for being alive. We feel different from the men around us and yet profoundly united with them. Our ancestors shared the same exodus, the same revelations and the same promises, so these people must understand in principle what it feels like to be persecuted. But we are the living reality of all that this world is capable of dealing out. There are Jews in this synagogue who have never truly experienced war in their lifetime. God bless them, may they never know it.

The chorus of voices starts, some seeming to lag behind, others jumping ahead. Then Zalman, one of our group, is asked to get up and read, and his voice sounds more abrupt, less melodic. He sways in a different direction and I see the congregation become more alert, introducing themselves slowly to the differences. It seems as if somewhere, somehow, a little piece of Polish Jewry is manifesting here in a synagogue in Calcutta. In spite of all odds, it

has survived and transported itself across the world, and we feel
at home for a moment, showing our fellow worshippers
something of ourselves, our former lives. This is the way we have
done things for many, many years, since the tribes were parted.
Really, the exchange is truly beautiful, and I am beginning to feel
hopeful that there is some way we can return the extraordinary
generosity of our hosts.

After the service there are so many people to greet. So many
offers of help it is overwhelming and even embarrassing, because
we will never remember all these names and faces.

We are invited by Sir David Ezra and his wife, Lady Ezra, to
a grand mansion some distance away, with a private zoo in the
grounds. Giant turtles stroll among the guests and I am told that
there is even a black panther, which is taken around on a lead
every morning by one of the servants. One fellow, Moses, tells
me that if I can find a single weed on this perfect lawn I will be
given one hundred rupees by the proprietor! It's been a long
time since I have played such games, or felt so free to pursue
such a quaint and trivial challenge, but I humour him by
looking around and trying to find these weeds.

Amongst the crowd I can hear the voices of these Jewish
men with Indian accents, in this place I'd never even located on
a map before there was a need to land here. I catch the eye of
one of the young men, a few yards away, talking to Ewa.
Meanwhile, someone else is talking to me: 'You must try one of
these treats — they're a speciality of the Baghdadi Jews here in
Calcutta. Jumping Potatoes we call them. Cut them and they'll
jump away from you!'

Without being rude, I am trying to listen not to him but to the man who is talking to my Ewa. She throws her head back and laughs, and he moves closer.

'I have Saturday afternoons off and I can show you the Victoria Memorial, if you like. We can go for a walk on the Maidan — you'll love it.'

'I will have to ask Benjamin if that's alright,' Ewa says.

'Who's Benjamin — your father?'

'Well, er, no, he's actually more of a . . . a brother.'

The Jumping Potato I ate is starting to jump in my stomach! I feel winded as I hear these words, but I know that I have no right in the world to stop Ewa from seeing a strange man this Saturday. Even though she gives me the respect of her guardian, I am not that. The love that I feel for Ewa will never be that of a father, or even a brother, for that matter.

I can think of Ewa only one way, and I remember her best from that time in our teenage years, when we went up to the Tatra Mountains, another lifetime ago.

We are in the mountainous borderlands that separate Poland from Czechoslovakia, in Zakopane, our two families together. Ewa is thirteen and I am a little older. We are picked up by buggy from the station at the edge of town and dropped at one of the many picturesque *gural* houses made from interlocking logs. A small path wanders past the front door and up through the mountains, swerving purposefully around pine trees as it wends its way up to the peaks. So much fun we are going to have.

As soon as we have settled into the house where we are staying, Ewa and I manage to free ourselves from our parents to go on a bear hunt. That is her idea, not mine. I am not interested in bears. There is only one creature on my mind.

She makes me carry her up the mountain, I remember, until my leg muscles are cramping and I am about to collapse, but I don't want to stop carrying her, because I so like the feeling of her body against mine and her hair across my face. I continue walking and walking like this, and because I cannot see where we are going, before long we are lost in the forest but neither of us cares about whether or not we will ever find a path home.

'Let's go down one more path and then stop looking,' I suggest, because I want to make a place to lie down together, on a blanket in the snow. But no, Ewa doesn't want to stop looking, so we go further and further into the woods until we are lost under a dark canopy of pine needles, and she turns to me and says, 'Do you think our parents can find us here?' I put her down and shrug and she leans forward to thank me for carrying her, and we start kissing each other in secret, in the woods, like brothers and sisters should never do.

Then, of all things, Ewa says, 'You know, I've always wanted to roll in the snow without my clothes on!'

'It's far too cold,' I object.

'How do you know until you've tried it,' she says, and she takes off all her clothes except for her underpants and jumps onto a patch of snow between some pine trees. What a sight! Ewa is shivering and screaming with joy as she rolls about in that snow, and I don't mind watching because she is just a little older than a small child, really.

'You're crazy,' I call out.

'You'll love it,' she yells. 'Come and roll with me.'

How can I refuse? It looks as if she is having so much fun, and I so want to join her, so I take off most of my clothes and together we roll in the snow. Over and over, holding hands and kissing, until I am sure I will die of frostbite. Then the two of us put our clothes back on and run out from under the dark woods, laughing and holding hands, into the bright sunlight, towards a river, and eventually back towards the house where we are staying in Zakopane. Only then do we stop holding hands, as we knock on the door.

Later, I remember wondering whether my father will mind if I marry Ewa. She is not Jewish, but she is Jewish enough. Yes, we could marry. Papa will allow it if it takes place under the *chuppa*, no questions asked.

That night, Ewa comes to visit me in my room, to tell me that she can't sleep. I can't sleep either, but am I going to tell her these things?

'What were you dreaming?' Ewa asks.

'I was dreaming about climbing,' I lie. In fact, I can dream of nothing but rolling in the snow with Ewa.

Then she gets under the covers next to me. Of course, I am worried about what her parents will say if they find her in the bed with me. What will *my* parents say, for that matter? So I send her back to her room, on the other side of my wall, where she starts talking to me through the wood, saying, 'Benjamin, I wanted to say that I love you so much. As much as I love my papa.' I don't say anything, so she continues, 'Are you asleep yet, Benjamin?'

'No!' I whisper, but I don't know whether or not she can hear me from the other side of that wooden wall.

I cannot sleep that night, because I am daydreaming, on and on, about when we will be together as adults. With my eyes open and my body alert I try to imagine the day when there will be no more walls between us. When we can be married and hold each other always, just as we did earlier that day.

CHAPTER 3

After our visit to the Maghen David Synagogue and the Ezras' mansion, we go back to our quarters above the Jewish Girls' School and once more we roll our beds out onto the floor.

There was a time when Ewa and I slept near one another on the floor, back in Poland, when we were escaping the tyranny of our own people — long before the war started — on that same trip to the Tatra Mountains.

Marek, Ewa's father, had brought us to Zakopane at his expense, but there was one ridiculous condition: all of us had to pretend we were Catholics, because we would be staying with a woman who was an anti-Semite of the most preposterous order.

'I would not do anything quite this silly for any other person, Yudl,' my father tells his friend.

'Please, remember — I am Marek. This woman knows me as Marek and if you start giving me another name she will be suspicious.'

'Okay, Yudl, okay,' my father says.

'And you will be Michal, alright? Benjamin, you can be Marius.'

'Yes, yes,' my father says. 'We will have so much fun with this game, I can tell. It is truly ridiculous, Yudl — I mean Marek.'

'Good. Now practise. Marek, Marek, Marek. It's not so hard. I've been Marek for fourteen years and you still haven't got it right!'

Mrs Cebula, our landlady, opens the roughly cut door and welcomes us to Zakopane. She has an awkwardness about her, and small blue eyes under thin lids. We all feel uncomfortable to be there under false pretence. How much easier it would have been to have a Jewish landlady for our holidays. The only solution is to conduct as few conversations with her as possible, to go upstairs as soon as we have finished eating. 'Everything will be alright,' my mother tells us, and I know she is glad to have my father's *kippah* and prayer shawl safely hidden at the bottom of their case.

I remember our first adventure, climbing Kasprowy Wierch. My father and Marek lead the way, carrying small bags full of food. I am blessed with a memory that can bring back whole conversations from years ago, so I will tell you something of their discussion.

'Marek — see, I called you Marek,' my father says to his best friend, 'what do we do for Sunday mass when everyone disappears to church? You'll have to teach me how to do confession; there is so much I have done wrong. The priest will be there all day and the following day listening!'

'I think we'll avoid mass. We'll say that you're sick.'

'Do you ever feel like one of them, Marek?' my father asks. 'Tell me, in all honesty. Does it feel different going into a cathedral? No *dovening*, no prayer shawls?'

'To tell you the truth, Michal, it feels much easier. I have my own arrangements with God — we all do — and, you know, there are none of those complicated rules. I don't have to employ a Shabbas *goy* to turn on the lamps on Saturdays. I can drop a coin in church and there'll be no shocked faces. I can take transport to the service without feeling guilty — actually, I do feel guilty about that. After all these years I haven't rid myself of that guilt. But no more six hundred and thirteen *mitzvot* — there's only one all-important commandment: Love thy neighbour. Think about that.'

'Hmm, neighbours ... that's what Mrs Cebula needs. A few more Jewish neighbours. It would help her and all the other Poles practise their most important commandment.'

'Keep your voice down,' Marek says. 'The hills have ears.'

The following morning, from the top of the stairs, I hear my father and Marek talking together over breakfast in the dining room.

'Here we have it, from Cardinal Krakowski himself: "A group of rabbis went to plead with the Cardinal to help combat anti-Semitism in Poland and he was unable to help, saying that the Jews were to blame because they propagated atheism, hurt Christian feeling and published pornography." What do you say, Marek?' My father passes the newspaper over to his friend.

'He's been set up by the Endeks. It is nowhere in the Catholic faith ... He is not to be trusted ...'

'The fact remains that this Cardinal of yours is inciting the country to violence. If the church in Poland thinks like this, who on earth is going to put the morals in place to stop the killings against Jews in Vilna, in Kielce?'

'But this is not the work of the church. It's this one man who is to blame —'

I hear Mrs Cebula coming down the passage rattling her plates, and so I run down the stairs as swiftly as my legs will take me to silence the two men, who seem to be permanently stuck in the same debate.

'Mrs Cebula is bringing the breakfast,' I say, putting my finger to my lips to explain this announcement.

'Ah, Mrs Cebula, maybe you can help us,' my father continues. 'We were reading the paper and wondering why our Cardinals are not stopping the anger against Jews here in Poland. As Poles, shouldn't we be living in a peaceful society with respect for different people, be they Poles or Jews, Armenians or Ukrainians?'

'You people in the cities all think the same,' she says, slowly. 'You come out to the country more often and you'll see how the Jews have taken over Poland.'

'But they're not all bad. I know some fine Jewish people in

Warsaw,' Marek says, a little embarrassed. 'They would do anything to help you.'

'Yes, they'll help you if they have some interest in the matter. The Jewish moneylenders are a fine example. Look how they bleed us Poles.'

'Marek, do you have anything to say about that?' my father asks. Ewa's father is stuck at that moment. He himself took a loan from my father to buy an apartment before he was married. If it weren't for my father's generosity, he would still be paying that apartment back now.

'Well, I think there are two sides to every story ... and we should try to see the side of those who are oppressed. These are the teachings of Jesus.'

The air inside our cottage is icier than the air at the top of the mountains. Mrs Cebula's eyes flicker and I can tell what she is thinking as she turns for the door. I run after her to help her get the breakfast.

'Where did you say you live in Warsaw?' she asks me.

'Pawia Street,' I answer. I am not thinking fast enough, otherwise I would have lied.

'That's in a Jewish neighbourhood, isn't it?'

'Ummm, I don't know ... there are Catholics there as well. Everybody together, like it should be.'

'I see,' Mrs Cebula says flatly.

I feel uncomfortable so I go back to the dining room to sit down with my father.

'You've really upset her, Solomon,' Marek starts.

'I'm not Solomon, I'm Michal, remember.'

'Yes, yes, but you have to be careful of what you say. Let's not spoil our holiday, okay?'

'Spoil it? Spoil it? I was just starting to have some fun! Come along, Marek,' my father says, 'what can this little lady do to spoil it? We'll go out and have another fine day in the snow. You wait and see what fun we'll have.'

My father is right, to a point. Until nightfall, that day is the most blissful one that I can remember in all those years in Poland. First we go to a photo studio and have pictures taken of all of us together, the beautiful mountain scenery behind us, smiles on our faces. Then we go outside and the snow is still crisp and the sun still shining. That day, instead of climbing the higher mountains, we stroll along the gentle slopes of a river bed in the pine forests above Zakopane.

Later we go home to the quaint little chalet in the hills and the strangest thing happens. Outside Mrs Cebula's chalet is a policeman with his typical highlander's curly moustache and dimpled chin, watching out for passers-by.

'What do you think she's done?' my mother asks.

'Nothing,' Kasia replies. 'She's a widow, you know. There's no crime in loneliness.'

Marek tips his hat as he approaches the front door. 'Good afternoon, officer. I trust you are here in an unofficial capacity?'

'Are you the Michal Zagorski who is renting an upstairs room in this residence?' the policeman asks.

'No, that's my friend here, but can I help?'

'Mr Zagorski, you are under arrest.'

My father is taken aback, and Ewa's mother starts up in his

defence. 'Please, Mr Rahabi is the most upright citizen you could possibly find.'

'Mr Rahabi? Mr Rahabi? I thought you were Mr Zagorski?'

So you can see how the whole farce comes unstuck.

'Well, only when I'm on holiday,' my father laughs, and then stops. 'I'm sorry, I didn't realise there was any crime in being Jewish.'

We are all ushered upstairs and into my parents' bedroom. There, hanging on a hook behind the door, are my father's prayer shawl and *kippah*. Seeing them hung up on public display, my mother says, 'Somebody has been through our bags'. I can see fear in her eyes, even though she challenges Mrs Cebula with her head held high.

'And somebody has been hiding Mrs Cebula's silver crucifix, along with her silver shoe horn, in their bags,' says the policeman. 'Who knows what else your husband may have to hide, Mrs Rahabi. First his name, then his clothes, then the silver.'

'Good lady, I assure you,' Marek interrupts, 'there is absolutely no reason for Mr Rahabi to steal your silver. I'm sure we can clear this up in no time. Mr Rahabi has no requirements for such items. He is a man of substantial wealth and a few pieces of silver would not make him any richer.'

'Sticking up for the Jew will get you nowhere,' the officer replies. 'Mr Rahabi, will you please come with me down to the police station.'

So we all follow my father and the police officer out of the door, with our bags in our hands. I take one look at Mrs Cebula as we walk out and she looks like nothing but a small onion of a peasant, with her small thinking and devious antics. When we are outside nothing is the same as it was. Gone is the romance of the snow-covered mountains, the bear hunt, the sun, the picnics, the wooden chalet with its pretty curtains, beautiful carved beams and conniving landlady.

We all sit on the hard bench inside the police station and I hear my father's hoarse, broken voice repeating again and again, 'I do not know what I have to say or do before you will believe that I am innocent. Please let me go. I have my family waiting outside. We will leave and we'll be no more trouble to you.'

I feel sick hearing this. I feel like punching the walls and screaming back at them, so I leave the police station and go outside for a walk, kicking the virgin white snow until it turns to black slush. Everything about this quaint little town seems ugly now. The snow is melting, the night is dark and it is painfully clear that our holiday is over.

Ewa runs behind me and I tell her to go back. She runs faster to keep up with me and is so sweet, you cannot imagine.

'I know your father could never do such a thing, Benjamin. Please don't be cross. We haven't done anything to hurt you. Please don't punish us.'

And then she says something that I pretend not to care about, but which touches me very deeply.

'Benjamin, I will become Jewish like my father was. I promise. I can't bear to be different.'

'You're not being different, you're being stupid.'

'I'm serious, I'll become Jewish.'

'You'll never be Jewish — your mother is a Catholic.'

'So I'll convert.'

'Still you wouldn't understand.'

Through the streets we hear my mother calling us. My father has been released, without a *zloty* in his pocket, sent out into the night with his shoulders hunched and his spirit broken.

All of us walk with our bags down to the railway station, ignoring anybody who looks at us. When we reach the station, Ewa's father talks one of the local peasants into taking us to the *shtetl* where he grew up, some three hours journey by road from Zakopane. Before long, all six of us are huddled up like country peasants in the back of a farm cart. We travel through the night, along roads lined with dark fields, home to scarecrows and pumpkins, wheat sheaves and sparrows. Down from the mountains and away from the snow, past farmhouses and a bordello, mills and more of the traditional *gural* houses. Ewa soon falls asleep on her mother's lap and my father is silent, but Marek uses this quiet moment to approach the subject of full integration into Polish life.

'You know, it wouldn't be such a bad thing to get used to the name Michal Zagorski and start using it sometimes.'

Neither my father nor my mother reply; only Kasia comes to my father's defence.

'No, why should he? I would never change my name just to please someone else.'

'That's ridiculous. You know your situation is not the same.'

My father is still deep in silence and remembering his humiliation.

'What do you say? It's not such a bad name, is it? Hey, you had fun using it earlier on —'

'Marek,' my father says slowly and deliberately. 'Marek,' not Yudl, as if he is emphasising the difference between the two of them, 'in the time of Egypt the Israelites kept their Hebrew names, through thick and thin. Through slavery, through exploitation, through all kinds of hatred and prejudice, they kept their names … and their style of dress. This was their means of survival. And you know, through all of this that happened tonight, I had this feeling that my strength was in my traditions … the traditions about which the average Pole does not even bother to enquire …'

'That's where the ignorance comes in.'

'Unfortunately there is ignorance, or fear, or whatever they say it is, but I still believe one thing — the God that established all the extremities of the world has made room, too, for some differences.'

'You've had a hard night, Solomon. You'll feel at home in my village. God bless you.'

We arrive at Marek's *shtetl* after taking several smaller paths through the pine forest. I am exhausted, but too excited to sleep, because I have never actually stayed the night in a *shtetl* before. There is some romance in the idea, for I am still a young boy and I have heard stories, so many stories, of this *shtetl* life.

It is almost midnight when we arrive. To anybody else, the sight of dark hats and dark coats in a rundown village in the cold black night might be disturbing, but I find it deeply reassuring, even as we pass the communal garbage disposal at the village entrance which heralds our arrival with a stench of rotting food. Really, it feels as if we are trotting into a former era of Poland.

The country was full of these villages in those days, believe me. Now, not one, I am told. A few graves, maybe, if you can find them under the grass, that's all.

As we draw close to some small houses a man comes up to our cart, shines a lamp and asks us to state our business.

'We have no business,' Marek says. 'I am Yudl. Don't you remember, Szmul?'

As soon as this old man recognises Marek, he says, 'I can't believe it. I heard that you'd converted: you can't keep any secrets from an old *dziadek* like myself. I'm coming to your parents' house for some vodka whether you like it or not.' Then he tells us that Marek's brother is also at home. 'He's left Lvov University and he says he'll never return. Who knows if he'll ever reach the same station in life as you have, Marek?' And then this man adds with some force, 'Mind you, he's still a Jew.'

The man leads the horse and cart through the dark streets to a small single-storey wattle-and-daub house with a thatched roof and small windows. He knocks on the door and we wait for some gaslights to come on.

'Hurry, hurry. It's Szmul. I need some vodka!' he calls out from outside the door.

'Go away, Szmul. This is an unholy time.'

'But I have some friends. All *goyim* from the city.'

Kasia is shaking the sleep from Ewa and my mother is passing down bags. The men are at the door, awaiting their welcome, and the horses are eating some rotten cabbage that someone has left by the road. Marek's mother opens the door whilst fastening her headscarf. With Szmul's lamplight in her eyes she is almost blind to the sight of her son, his wife, his daughter and goodness knows who else. But a mother is a mother and she soon sees that it is her son standing there in the middle of the night. She must be thinking, why now? What is he doing here and who are these people? Instead she says, 'Yudl, you know how to make a mama happy. My darling, come inside. All of you, come inside, my friends, you're very welcome. Even you, Szmul. I'll wake up my husband. He would so like to greet you all.'

When Marek's father comes down, he is equally warm. 'And who have we got in our house now?' he asks jovially. 'Did you all go for a walk in the streets of Warsaw and end up here?'

'These are my friends, Papa. Remember, I always write of Solomon, who lent me the money for our apartment.'

'Ah yes, the Jew who isn't ashamed to be Jewish. We've heard nothing but your praises. Please, make my home your home. Where there is food cooked for two, a third can also eat — or a fourth or fifth for that matter.'

Marek's mother brings out some plaited bread and pickles, places it in front of us and pours some vodka for the men. I take a few sips from Papa's glass, and I feel warm and sleepy. As we stay up late into the night, my mind drifts in and out of their conversations about the politics of the land, the discrimination and the pogroms. These are my father's favourite subjects, so I have heard it all before. Marek's father listens solemnly as

Marek tells him what happened to us in Zakopane. He thinks for a minute and then breaks out in a smile. 'Well, well,' he says, 'I promise not to search your bags if you promise to stay here with us for a few nights, alright, my friends?'

My poor father. He is laughing, but he still feels the shame, still nurses the insults that were thrown at him in Zakopane. Marek's mother notices and tries to change the subject.

'I'll tell you what's new,' she says to Marek, 'that brother of yours. He's come back from Lvov and refuses to go back to his studies. You know, they were printing leaflets there telling the students to break the teeth of Jews with iron bars. Is he telling the truth, my darling, or just trying to get out of his studies?'

'What do you think?' my father says. 'You can ask a group of Poles if there's any anti-Semitism in Poland and most of them would tell you there isn't, but they've never had any experience being Jewish, have they? That's the difference. Send your son to school in Switzerland. That's my advice.'

They talk until it is almost light and when they are all too tired to speak any more, mattresses are rolled out onto floors and all the spare quilts in the house are gathered and thrown over us. There are no spare rooms, so we all sleep in a row. My mattress is next to Ewa's and we hold hands under the covers. The vodka I have drunk makes me feel bolder than I am, and more of a man. I hold Ewa's hand close to my stomach and she doesn't pull it away. I am in love, and feel the moment should be frozen forever as it is, but love does not survive under ice. It changes, and through the years, so too has my love for Ewa changed.

CHAPTER 4

You must forgive me if I talk so much of Poland. It is hard to be
free of memories, especially when they are your only true
possessions. They will be taken with me to the end, and then be
either erased or recorded, depending on what the truth is on
this matter.

Let me talk instead about the city of Calcutta. Let me tell you
something of the first British settler, a man by the name of Job
Charnock, who came in 1690 as an employee of the East India
Company, established a settlement in Sutanuti by the Hooghly,
and started to trade. I can tell you, too, of the first Jewish settler.
A man by the name of Shalom Cohen, who arrived in Calcutta
in 1798 from Aleppo, in Iraq. He also arrived as a trader, but
unlike the British never turned into a conqueror.

I must tell you also about Farha and Aaron Isaac, direct
descendants of Shalom Cohen, who took us into their lives in

1941. It is the story of a beautiful friendship that still exists to this day.

Farha is a young woman, the wonderful mother of two small twin girls, as well as Ezekiel, Daniel's friend. She works for the Women's League in Calcutta and helps see to the needs of every widow and pauper in the community. Now we, too, have come under her care and she has taken on our cause in her effortless charitable spirit.

The Isaacs have an apartment in South Calcutta's Free School Lane, and Farha has taken us home to eat with her and the children regularly since she first heard about the *Asama Maru* landing at the Kidderpore Docks. Whenever she comes to the Jewish Girls' School to drop off food or clothing for our group, Ezekiel, or Zek, as Daniel calls him, tags along as well. At first Zek holds on to Farha's skirt and follows her around our rooms as if he were her tail, while the maidservant takes charge of Farha's twin daughters. Zek notices Daniel and smiles. Daniel speaks some words in Polish; Zek laughs and buries his face in his mother's skirt. Then one day he comes with some toys for Daniel, and suddenly Farha has lost her tail. All at once the boys are dealing out playing cards and throwing them up into the air. They blow up balloons that Farha has bought in China Bazaar, and parade around in the clothes that have been brought for the men in our party. It is the start of a great friendship, this much is easy to see, and Daniel is already learning a few words of English, Hindi and Bengali without even realising it.

Meanwhile, Farha talks to Rivka and Ewa, the only two women in our group, about Poland. She asks them about their lives before the war. 'Life was normal,' Rivka tells her. 'My father, he doctor.' From their conversations Farha makes out that our rooms here in the Jewish Girls' School are humble quarters. 'We lived in big white house, in Piaski. No problems until the Russians came, and then the Germans.' From the fragments of information that Rivka gives about her life in Poland, Farha tries to understand what chaos has prevailed to bring Rivka and Ewa to this situation they find themselves in. 'It was so terrible,' Ewa says, with just enough English to touch the surface of what faced us back at home. 'So terrible.'

How can Farha and Aaron know about our lives, really? How can they know anything about the world we have come from, when our activities here are so restricted? None of us work, except for Jankel, who has been offered employment in an accountancy firm. Instead, we spend our time trying to familiarise ourselves with this new city, waiting for news of the *Asama Maru*, which has now been taken upstream to be fixed, given the lowest priority imaginable by engineers, because it is not a military vessel. Our lives, it seems, must be lived in Calcutta for longer than we had anticipated, and so our need for friendship has become even greater.

Then Farha comes round one day and says, 'Why not come with us on our family holiday to Madhupur?' I cannot believe my ears. We all look at each other, a little embarrassed, because, to tell the truth, a 'family holiday' is not something we have on our minds. Without consulting the others I say, 'No, we cannot trouble you.' Yet Farha persists. 'What trouble could you possibly be? You need a holiday far more than we do, and if you don't come with us I'm not going either.'

So a week later we board the train at Howrah Station with Farha's husband, Aaron, and Aaron's father, Jacob, an elderly fellow who used to trade opium with China. The station itself is unbelievable. Howrah is the place where the whole province of Bengal enters the city, it seems, and I am fairly sure there would not be another station in the world quite so crowded.

Farha has organised us in a single file, with four coolies at the front carrying her crockery and cutlery, bed and table linen, pots, pans and more clothes than I have ever owned, even back in Warsaw. Tied to one big bundle there is even a cane potty for the two little girls. Daniel holds Ezekiel's hand some way ahead of us on the platform, and I walk behind Rivka and Ewa to make sure that we are all together. Staying together has become an obsession on our travels, and even here, among the crowds of Howrah Station, my instincts serve me well. I know that the two women who walk ahead of me have the same associations as I do with train journeys. When we crossed Siberia in our escape from Poland, we travelled as inconspicuously as we could, and it seems so strange now to walk freely in broad daylight and with such an ostentatious bundle of luggage.

The coolies help place our heavy loads onto netted luggage carriers and we settle down for a journey that will take us to a sleepy railway town in Bihar, which they say is run by Anglo-Indians. Rivka and Ewa each sit down with a small girl on their lap, while Daniel and Ezekiel monopolise the window seats. Jacob, Farha's father-in-law, quietly prepares himself for the journey by opening a tin and popping some small black balls of opium under his tongue.

The coolies finally climb down and the train starts its heavy departure, leaving hawkers hanging on to windows as they exchange their last coins. Before long I am looking out at Bengali villages with their thatched mud huts, ponds and paddy fields, carefully demarcated by mud ridges and sheltered by banana palms, acacias and bamboo. I am thinking: wouldn't it be nice to have a little house like that, away from the world? What if we don't climb on board the *Asama Maru* when it's repaired? Could our lives be like those of our friends in India, so undisturbed and so charmed?

I sit next to Farha's husband, Aaron, a dark-skinned man whose face is soft and round like a child's. It is a running joke in Aaron's family that he takes after his children, not the other way around.

'How does India suit you after Poland?' he asks me.

It's a hard question to answer after only a few weeks here, because I have not known two places more different. To this day I wonder how God could make the West and East with the same flick of the wrist. I puzzle, too, about how God could have placed Poland between Germany and Russia, or made the Israelites and Egyptians neighbours. All I know is that we are meant to learn to live together and understand each other, as Aaron and I are now starting to do.

'India is my Palestine,' I find myself telling him, without really knowing the full meaning of my words.

'You feel at home here then?'

'Now that we cannot go back to Poland, my home is with me, on my back like a turtle.'

'On your back?'

'Well, inside.' I point to my chest and wonder how much more I am truly capable of fitting in there next to my heart and lungs.

'But won't you consider staying in Calcutta? We can find you work, no problem. B N Elias & Company has agreed to give jobs to everybody. Maybe you can work in the tobacco factory ... and we can find a school for Daniel, as well.'

It sounds too simple and I am unaccustomed to seeing such an easy future prepared in front of me. In fact, if this future of ours is laid out in such a straightforward fashion, it seems as if it doesn't quite belong to us, like the simple lives of Bihar's rural people that I see through the train window.

'If anything is going to persuade me to stay in Calcutta,' I say, 'it is the hospitality of people like yourself, Aaron. I do not know if we would be so well received anywhere else in the world, including Palestine.'

I look over at Ewa and Rivka and wonder if they would be happy to stay in India. We are all blessed to speak a little English, although Rivka's isn't so good, and what's more we're thriving here in these few weeks with the support of such kind-hearted souls. Perhaps Aaron is right? Perhaps I should take a job here and let the *Asama Maru* leave without us? Put an end to this feeling that we should always be elsewhere, always moving.

'Once you are working you can rent a place very cheaply,' Aaron says. 'Since the war started you can't imagine how fast people have left the city; in fact, there are beautiful apartments and houses lying completely empty.'

The idea of having a home is pleasing. It is a thought that stays with me as we disembark at Madhupur and make our way to a grand brick bungalow called Willow Lodge. I stare up at the columns and arches above us as the mountain of possessions is unloaded from four *tongas* and the women start to make the empty house into a home.

Throughout the reorganisation of our holiday house, Ezekiel talks to Daniel about the potters of Madhupur as if they are the local magicians. The magic they offer the children is a basketful of small clay toys for only a few *annas*. I have to remember that these things are important for small people, no? It has been such a long time since Daniel was able to play with such an abundance of toys, and even longer since I did, so I translate some of Zek's promises for Daniel, and his eyes light up.

'If you're going to town, don't forget to buy some papaya,' Farha says. 'Benjamin, you have not lived until you have tried papayas from Madhupur.' I do not tell her that I have never tried papaya anywhere, let alone Madhupur, so I would be an unworthy judge. 'Oh, yes, another thing ... please get some vegetables and salt, also. I forgot the salt.'

It is hard to imagine that anything has been forgotten, as Farha has literally packed the entire contents of her kitchen. Nonetheless, on her instructions we follow Ezekiel and Daniel down the dusty road to buy instant toys and freshly grown produce by the basketful. Throughout this trip I am acutely aware of the fact that I will be unable to fund any of the expenses that lie ahead of us, just as I was unable to pay for our train fares. 'Don't ask for anything,' I tell Daniel in Polish. 'It sounds rude,' and he nods as he runs ahead with Zek.

Sitting watching the potter in town, Aaron tells me about three German Jewish sisters in Calcutta who have been given asylum in India thanks to a Bengali gentleman who lived with them in Germany as their tenant. Aaron is not too sure about their story, because they don't like to talk about it, but he believes that this Bengali tenant of theirs watched them being persecuted during Kristallnacht and a sense of duty led him straight to the Indian Consulate, where he applied for immigration visas on their behalf. According to Aaron, these three ladies are in a British camp in Darjeeling now, so I can't meet them, but really, what is so different about their plight? I feel as if I know them already, and within a few minutes of Aaron's story I am wiping from my eye a tear that is rightfully theirs.

While we talk the children squeal and the potter shapes a miniature spoon and then a rolling pin with his nimble fingers. 'I'm sure you will look after your toys better than Zek does,' Aaron says to Daniel, oblivious to the effect his story has had on me. 'Every year Zek gets a new basket and by the end of the holidays they're all destroyed.'

My heart goes out to Daniel, and I thank the Lord that he is alive and well and free to shed tears like other children over small losses like broken toys. When the potter hands over a new basket of toys, Aaron gives him the money and once again I am forced to accept that I am here at the mercy of God, unable to offer even a few coins in gratitude. Instead, I make myself the bearer of the toys, placing the basket up on my head like the Biharis do.

Zek runs on ahead, dragging his father with one hand and Daniel with the other. 'Pleeeease let's have a *tonga* ride, Papa,' Ezekiel insists. 'I want to take Daniel to the Dak Bungalow by horse.'

So once more Aaron opens his wallet, this time to pay a *tonga wala*, and we climb into a horse taxi, with Zek at the helm, and drive to a government building in the middle of a playing field. To me, it feels as if we are exploring a place that the world has forgotten. Perhaps we are even dreaming this place into existence, because there could be nowhere on earth that has banished noise quite like Madhupur. My eardrums are straining for sounds, because they are unaccustomed to such empty spaces. Apart from the delights of the children running around the government bungalow, the only other noise is the hypnotic hum of crickets, which seem to be communicating from another layer of existence beyond all of this.

Ezekiel and Daniel climb onto a merry-go-round that has just been constructed on the lawns up ahead, and Aaron and I sit down to talk some more about the events of a distant continent. It seems so strange to talk of Hitler in a place such as this, but I feel I owe Aaron some stories, because there is nothing else that I have to repay his generosity. There is no doubt that these stories are what he wants. He has been following the war news carefully, and I can tell that my presence here is useful, because I can provide him with a first-hand account of Hitler's army in Poland. Aaron senses, though, that I cannot talk easily of some of the things I have witnessed. Describing the Warsaw ghetto in a place like Madhupur is virtually impossible; all the adjectives are useless. I am thinking, how can I tell him how the Germans are treating the Jews? It's an insult to him. So instead I tell the facts, and describe the way I felt on September the 1st, 1939, when we all knew for sure that Poland had been invaded by the German army. 'I was a soldier,' I tell him. 'Nobody, not even children, was going to let Germans take our country that day.'

As we stroll back home, I tell Aaron about how I left Warsaw during the war to go and practise medicine with Rivka's father in Eastern Poland. 'In that village, Piaski, many of the Jews left for Russia, or left to live in a mine outside of town. One woman I know placed her baby on the doorstep of a childless Polish couple. God knows if any of them are still alive now.'

Ezekiel and Daniel are up a tree, throwing down guavas for us to catch. We couldn't be further from the tragedy of Europe, but somehow Aaron has connected with this particular story and he puts down the guavas and grabs my arm. 'There must be something we can do. Something we can send your people.'

How do I tell him, standing under a guava tree in Madhupur, that not a day has gone by when I haven't considered what we can do to help the friends that we've left behind?

'There's nothing we can do,' I tell him, lamely, and he looks at me as if I have let down my whole country, my family and my friends. I feel uncomfortable, until he smiles, and then I feel relieved to have shared some of the burden of my experiences with someone who has the same strong emotions about these things.

By the time we get back to our bungalow the sun has set and even the crickets have silenced their hum, leaving no sound in the vast and open world except our feet and breath and the slow chug of a train that can be heard from far away as it pulls up at this station in the province of nowhere. We arrive home to a simple first meal of dahl and rice and a bungalow lit with kerosene lamps. Although we have the option to visit some of the holiday-makers from the Calcutta community, we decide to stay at home and spend some time getting to know each other a little better.

After dinner, when all the children are fast asleep, making the night quieter still, Fahra says, 'Rivka tells me her English isn't good enough to describe how you met. Why don't you tell the story, Benjamin?'

I look at Rivka for permission, and she nods. I see Aaron's face smiling like a child's at the anticipation of a good story. I only hope that he is ready for what he is about to hear. I look at Ewa, and hope that she does not mind the retelling of this tale. She shrugs, so I begin, slowly at first, because this story deserves to be told with tenderness, not with fear, even though the two are inseparable in the way things really were.

CHAPTER 5

In 1939 marriage is not at the top of my agenda. I have just graduated in medicine, and I have already swapped my academic gown for a military uniform. Every man old enough to fight is being called up for service and so I also go into the field for military exercises, just outside Warsaw. I have never felt so proud to be Polish, and even my father shares this pride, which is unusual, because he is the one who keeps telling us how we will never be truly accepted by the Poles. Nonetheless, right now he is more Polish than I have ever seen him. He is proud, too, of the *shtetl* Jews who are marching to the city in lines of black coats and hats, with spades over their shoulder, to help dig trenches to defend their capital. 'The Jews of Poland are every bit as loyal to this country as the Catholics,' he tells me. 'Just see them now. Nobody can ever say anything otherwise.'

At this time there is this feeling of anticipation and fear that prowls through Warsaw. There are anti-Semites, too, who walk the streets at night, preparing Poland for Hitler by forcibly cutting off the locks of old Jews with their razors and leaving boot prints on the faces of their victims. What's more, some say there are around 15,000 Polish Jews at Zbanzyn, at the border with Germany, who are not being allowed into Poland by our government, even though they have Polish passports. So you can imagine how nervous the Jews of our neighbourhood are feeling — not just about this German Führer, but also about the situation in Poland itself.

In the midst of all this, I have to say goodbye to my family and Ewa, to go and join my unit. My father does not find it easy to say goodbye to me and I have never felt so heavily the weight of being an only child, believe me. Once I am gone, there will be nobody for my father to control. My poor papa — anything could happen if he takes his hand off the wheel that turns the world, and if he cannot control the people and circumstances around him, why, he is discovering he has no power at all. There is nothing he can do about the situation we find ourselves in, and being deprived of the power to act, he is left only with the power to react. To weep as he watches me walk down the street, not knowing if I will ever return.

The war starts without any announcement on the radio, without any mention in the press. It's an ordinary Friday morning in autumn when the short-lived peace of our nation is shattered by the German army in the north. There is no doubt about it — this is the day that we have all anticipated and feared and hoped would never come. Before long the thunder of the German cannonade approaches Warsaw, where my unit is stationed, and as the noise gets closer, we all realise that the time has come for us to fight for our country. I cannot tell you what this does to your body, that first realisation. How it pumps fear and excitement so fast around your heart and brain that you can only capture moments of awareness. I am acutely aware of the fact that I am not with my family, especially by the time this day ends and dusk falls. I know my mother will be lighting the Sabbath candles, trying to bring some peace, if not to the whole nation, then at least to our home. I sense my parents' thoughts; see them as they face the inevitable future of war, with their son goodness knows where.

Our unit is building a ditch in Aleje Jerozolimskie, which we will use to defend one of Warsaw's main districts. However, we are told to take cover at regular intervals — whenever Warsaw radio broadcasts another air-raid alarm. Planes with swastikas painted on them fly over us, and the people all around us cheer whenever one is hit by a Polish anti-aircraft gun. There is this feeling of disbelief, but also a feeling that we will be able to get rid of the invaders quickly. A blind ignorance of what is to come. Why, there are even children playing in the streets, wearing gas masks, swords in their hands, shrieking with excitement. Attics all over the city are filled with patriotic supporters, field glasses up close to their eyes. 'We'll finish off the Germans in no time,' I hear someone say. 'Just take a look at the spirit of the people. Every child, every adult is going to save this city. The Germans cannot stand up to such resistance!'

A butcher nearby comes and helps me dig the trench I am working on. When the siren goes off, he grabs me and another soldier and we run into his shop to stand under a solid doorframe for a few minutes. Alongside us, in the front window, is a row of animal corpses hanging from their feet. Just my luck, I am thinking. To be waiting out the battle with corpses. I try not to breathe in too deeply, concentrating on the city outside, where the shrieking continues, followed by cheering. We stay in this man's shop for a while, and help him tape paper strips across his window to prevent the glass from shattering. Everybody is doing this. The city is beginning to look eerie — as the homes of the Israelites must have looked in Egypt, when they were painted with a cross of blood to allow the angel of death to pass over and move swiftly elsewhere.

We go back outside, and when I first see them — those tanks — I am filled with the impossible realisation of what we are up against. We have defaced our city by building ditches and barricades, but we may as well lay down our arms and make this whole operation bloodless, because we have no hope — no hope in the world against all that metal. The tanks rumble along the street, heavy as prehistoric creatures, but with the most modern instruments of death, you have no idea. A small boy is running across the road. A gun fires and misses him. I am thinking: we have to stop them. We have to help them see reason. I see it all — this boy, the bullet. I am utterly helpless in the knowledge that a shot from my gun would bounce off the metal tank and cause more harm to our side.

I cannot explain what I do next, even to myself, so I find it hard to tell you about it, in case you think I am truly a little crazy. Remember, I have no bullets that are worth firing and, admittedly, I am not entirely in control. A lot of thoughts are shooting around my head all at once, in different directions. I am in the butcher's shop, crouching behind the meat in the window, looking at all the people running into homes and shops, deserting the streets. In one second, the tanks trample over the ditches we have spent days digging, and I turn to the man who owns this shop and tell him, 'We've got to stop them.' He looks at me as if I'm suffering from shell shock, and the next minute I am standing in front of the German tanks. Yes, I'm afraid so, standing there in the middle of the street while everyone else is taking cover. I am like an idiot, really, alone and weaponless, facing them with only my life in the hope that my humanity will speak to them. It is insane, you might say, to try and stop a war single-handedly, but there is no logic or reason present at that moment, believe me.

Someone shouts, 'Get back or they'll kill you,' but it is too late. I hear bullets whistling through the air and I fall down on the street, from the force of the bullet alone, and someone comes to drag me away. I watch the tanks go by, their business done. I am bleeding from my shoulder and it is painful, but not quite as much as you might imagine. No doubt I deserve the bullet that has lodged in it.

The tanks have passed. I am lifted by one or two other men, I cannot remember, and carried into a corridor, where I continue to bleed on the floor and my wound becomes more painful by the second. A short while later the butcher comes running in with some clumsy bandages made for me out of bed linen, and he shakes his head in disbelief but does not say anything. Everybody else is asking me why I walked in front of the tank, but thankfully they appreciate that I am too shocked to talk. Besides, I have no answers for them. How could I have any answers? I don't know why I did this any more than they do. I know of no reason for any of this insanity.

I am given a makeshift bed in that home, and it is only a few days later, as I make my way back to my parents' apartment in Pawia Street, that I realise our city is in a state of mayhem beyond recovery. There are no taxis because they have all been commandeered by our army, so I have to walk, constantly ducking for shelter. Moving through the main streets is virtually impossible because of military traffic, blockades, ditches and craters left by the bombing, so I take the side streets back to Pawia Street. In the doorways, I see people who have been hurt, and others who look as if they have nowhere else to go. One man in uniform calls out to me and asks what unit I am from. 'My unit no longer exists,' I tell him. He looks across the street and says, 'My home no longer exists, let alone my unit,' and I feel absolutely dreadful for him, and worried, too, about whether or not my home has survived.

When I get back I discover that our apartment was partially hit, but not too badly. My relief is nothing compared to my mother's. She takes one look at me and starts wailing, holding me as if I have just come back from the dead, taking off my bandages so that she can inspect my wound and wrap it up again with her prayers and protests as ointments.

We spend all that afternoon listening to the radio. Our home is filled with people who have come in from other apartments, and our maidservant is providing makeshift food for everyone. Every now and then the mayor of Warsaw gets onto the radio and says in a hoarse voice, 'Everybody must remain calm.'

The minute my mother hears this, she starts wailing again. 'Oy, oy, oy — the Germans are walking into our city and he tells us to stay calm!'

My father tries to soothe her where the mayor has failed. 'My darling, he is just talking about the way we should be conducting ourselves. What good is all this panicking? Your fear is not going to help our soldiers.'

There is much discussion amongst the group of neighbours in our apartment about how long it will take to get the Germans out of Poland and who will come to help us. Then everybody falls quiet as a man's voice speaks out from the radio: 'If you are able-bodied, if you have a love for your country, if you want to see an independent Poland, the government has requested that you travel east immediately to join a unit and protect our borders.'

A few people in the room gasp, and my mother turns to me and says, 'You can't go, Benjamin. You'll be no use to anybody with that arm.'

Later still, there is this one devastating piece of news: our government has already left Poland and is now in exile. What hope is there left for us, really, with no government, no nothing?

Then, before too long, Warsaw falls.

The Germans tell us to get on with life as normal, yet we have lost all sense of what normal is. Everything about our city looks different. One day I am out walking, for example, and I see that our Ministry of Religious Beliefs and Public Enlightenment is a headquarters for the Gestapo. On the walls are all these ridiculous declarations telling us to step off the streets and give way to representatives of the Third Reich. In this horribly formal tone, there's this statement: 'The Streets Belong to the Conqueror, not the Conquered'. Really, this is no longer the city that we knew. We are all just dogs on the street which these so-called civilised soldiers have to tolerate.

Not only are there piles of rubble on every street corner and damaged buildings everywhere, but the Germans have managed to destroy the spirit of us Varsovians, too. You can see the defeat in people's eyes, and this feeling goes so deep that I am beginning to believe I have no power at all to start my life. To make anything happen in this country of ours, which is now occupied by Germans, Germans, Germans. Everywhere, Germans.

We are lucky to have lost only a few walls in our apartment. I have seen people trying to clear debris from buildings that have been completely destroyed, so they can find their dead and give them a suitable burial. There's one man, Wlodek, who lives further down Pawia Street and has lost his whole apartment, so my parents have given him some money and asked him to help rebuild ours. This man goes into the streets and collects bricks from the debris to rebuild the outside wall of my bedroom, which is exposed to all the elements.

My father keeps telling me to help him with what strength I have in my good arm, but I am thinking: why do any of it? None of it is ours any more. I am now living in the German capital of Poland, and I try to carry on with life as normal in this city, but it's impossible. My mother tells me to be more positive. She says, 'You should help with some of the rebuilding, because you're the one who will inherit this place one day,' but no amount of optimism can make me imagine a situation where the Germans will just get up and leave.

But what has any of this got to do with meeting Rivka? Let me explain. While all of this is going on in Warsaw, I have this stupid idea that things will be better elsewhere in the country — maybe in a smaller town. So I start making enquiries, and I receive an offer to practise medicine with a man called Doctor Hirsh Ruben, in a small town called Piaski, near Lublin. I know nothing about this place, but I don't care. All I can think of is leaving Warsaw. Anywhere will be better than here — especially somewhere far from the centre of things.

Of course, Ewa and I have been close all this time, and everyone in our two families expects that we will marry and be together always. However, when it's time to leave I feel so disheartened that I am even thinking a small separation from Ewa will be good for me and allow me to become a stronger and better person. Still, when the time comes closer for us to say our goodbyes, I start to go to pieces and it is Ewa who has to reassure me that I have made the best choice, given the circumstances.

'Should we get married?' I ask her. 'Do you want to come with me?'

And you know what Ewa says? She says, 'I can't come with you, because this is something you have to do on your own.'

I think my parents are quite relieved to see me go — they have this idea that I'll be safer elsewhere, studying under a sensible Jewish doctor. 'Be careful,' my mother sobs. 'Work hard,' my father says. These are my two parting blessings and I remember them to this day — simple words that have acquired layers of meaning for me with the dust of the years. And so I leave the apartment cheerfully, really. I remember that happiness, in the ruins of Warsaw. Yes, I am cheerful as I leave our home!

Catching a train out of Warsaw is easy enough, even with the Germans crawling around the city. I have my letter of invitation, I have work, and that is something they respect, so I am permitted to go about my business and travel comfortably by train to Lublin. When I arrive in Lublin I take a horse and cart owned by a Jewish transport firm called Lejzor to travel on to Piaski with some other folk, who all seem to know Rivka's father.

'What is it like in Piaski?' I ask. 'How do the Germans treat the people?'

A fellow on the cart answers me: 'I think they'll be better than the Russians. The Russian army came with their guns held together with pieces of string, dressed in rags, and rode around the streets yelling "Give us your watches!" One week the Russians were in Piaski, next we get the Germans. Now the old German commandant is back from the last war. Same man, quite kind. Not so bad. These Germans are much more elegant than the Russian army, you know. I think they'll be more civilised. We'll have to wait and see.'

This is what he says or something like it. I find the information hopeful, and I am already imagining a situation in this village where the invading army will live peacefully alongside the local people. What a fool I am to think that life in a country village could be quite so simple.

Our horse and cart turns the corner by the Piaski cemetery and comes to a halt in front of some ordinary white limestone buildings. Rivka's father, Doctor Ruben, comes running up the street wearing his stethoscope, just as he wrote me he would be.

'Doctor Ruben?' I ask as I get down, offering him my hand. He greets me like an old friend, with a warm embrace, and I know instantly that I am going to like this man.

CHAPTER 6

This is how I meet Rivka and find myself living in the home of her father, who has agreed to be my mentor in my early days of practice. We live together in an old limestone house with a small courtyard out the back and balconies overlooking Piaski's main street. There is no sense of any tragedy looming, even though the Germans are moving into the house of the wealthiest Jew, just down the street — a man called Hochman. They are also vacating the school for the troops. Through all of these interruptions, everybody continues to talk about this amiable German fellow, Ernst Kresse, who is meant to be a kindly commandant from the last war. Things will be just the same as they always were — so we are assured by the elderly of Piaski.

Doctor Ruben is quite a character, and it soon becomes obvious why he wants me to live with his family instead of in some back lane of Piaski. One night at dinner, when there are just the two of us at the table, he tells me, 'She's so beautiful, my daughter, don't you think? Too bad she is alone.'

I try to change the subject, because to me it is obvious that she is beautiful, and obvious, too, what Doctor Ruben is trying to orchestrate. 'You are also alone, Doctor Ruben. How did you lose your wife, if you don't mind me asking?'

'Rivka lost her husband from heart failure. So young. You know, he was a perfectly healthy man. So unusual.'

'I'm so sorry.'

'Oy, oy, oy, it was a terrible tragedy. Terrible tragedy. And of course Daniel has no father now.' He looks over at me to see if I am moved by his lament.

'Now this is really terrible,' I reply, and Doctor Ruben continues to examine me with his gaze, stroking his long beard and searching my face for any hint of loneliness.

Rivka knows what is going on. 'Do you think I found my own husband?' she asks me. 'He can't stop himself. He introduces patients to each other in the waiting room. Some of them are stupid enough to listen, would you believe it?'

Of course, I have not come to their house to find a bride or a son, but to learn with Doctor Ruben, who is the best teacher imaginable. He is one of those doctors who does not need to heal people to make them love him, and there's a great lesson in this. People come to see him when they are in perfect health — just to talk, to listen to his advice and to make some small offering. In the few months that I work with him in his clinic I am given more gifts than I have received in a lifetime, believe me — every type of farm produce available, watches, herrings, bottles of vodka, black bread, Tanakhs, clothes, furniture, everything. Actually, Doctor Ruben is much more than just a doctor; he is the hub of the village roundabout. One time I sit in on a consultation and what do we talk about? Whether or not the patient should marry a certain doctor in Lublin!

I am far too involved in what I am learning to be interested in marriage. Nonetheless, I like Rivka from the moment I meet her, because she has the heart of her father and a mind of her own. I am even a little nervous of her, because she is strong-willed and full of instructions. I must remember that I am not her son and therefore do not need to listen to all of them.

Of course, I notice her beauty, because, no doubt about it, she is beautiful. Her eyes are large and dark, her hair is long and curly, and her body is strong and curvaceous. Really, she is very seductive if you allow yourself to look at her in that kind of way. Yet, I am the sort of person who can admire beauty without feeling any desire to possess it. This I do not tell Dr Ruben, because he has different plans for me. In fact, whenever Daniel is asleep, he leaves Rivka and me in the room together and goes off to bed early. I know he does not sleep, because I can see the gaslight from under his door. He is waiting, maybe, for some sign that we are lighting a flame together downstairs.

So we spend many evenings talking, but there are no wedding canopies in sight, because I have given my heart to a girl in Warsaw and the world is at war. It is not a good time to be thinking of marriage, and besides, Rivka never gives me any indication that she is interested in me. No, it is Daniel whose charms seduce me.

Let me tell you this story about Daniel, who comes to me one day really confused about whether he should become a rabbi or a doctor. He is so sweet: he fixes my elbow, though it is perfectly healthy, ties bandages around my ankles and takes my temperature, making me bend down for him to reach my mouth.

'You will be a very good doctor one day,' I tell him. 'Just like your grandfather.'

'Would I make a good rabbi, too?'

'Why, yes, of course you would. Different books, same profession,' I tell him, but he doesn't believe me. He is much too wise.

'They are the same, only doctors look after bodies and rabbis look after souls,' Rivka points out. 'Both need looking after, of course.'

'If my father was alive, he could teach me how to be a rabbi,' Daniel says solemnly, his large brown eyes looking out from under his curls.

'So you will have to be a doctor instead,' Rivka replies. She is surprisingly matter-of-fact, I soon discover, and always thinking about practical solutions to even the most intensely emotional problems.

'You will teach him how to be a doctor, won't you?' Rivka looks me directly in the eyes. 'That's if you're still around when Daniel is bigger.'

Her comment takes me by surprise, and I promise you, this is the only time that I realise I have any long-term role in Rivka's life.

'How will I know if I'm around?' I say, and I see some disappointment spread slowly across her face, so I add, 'His grandfather will teach him medicine and I will help in whatever way I can.'

This is how we leave the situation, until everything starts changing in our world and we also have to change to make our lives again in circumstances that are entirely new.

CHAPTER 7

I suppose our troubles start when this teenage girl, Rebekah, comes to our surgery with broken ribs. The German army has just commandeered her school, sent home the teachers and burnt all the books and maps. Her only crime was to stay and watch it all happening. There is to be no education in this town, we are all told, and this young girl is the first victim of the different types of lessons that we now have to learn. So what about this kind commandant? This is what I am thinking. Why is this happening if he is so compassionate?

This is the first time I have ever seen Hirsh Ruben angry. He wears a reassuring smile but beneath it I notice this anger of his and see his hands shake a little as he feels the ribs that are exquisitely tender in one place and causing some breathing difficulty.

'My darling, you will have to stay in bed for a while, because this will get worse before it gets better — and please, no more going to your school to see what is happening, alright? Good girl.' This is what he says to Rebekah, but later, when our patient has left with her mother, he cannot hold back his outrage.

'How dare they do this to a young girl?' he says. 'She is not a soldier. She is nothing. What can she do to them? Nothing, absolutely. They are never going to get the support of the people if they treat us like this. Never. They will never be able to rule, because we will not accept them!'

Rivka's father is hardly able to contain his anger. He pleads with me for reason, but I cannot give him any. Instead, I make the biggest mistake I have ever made in my life: I agree. Then I tell him about how I stood in the street in front of the first German tank that I saw back in Warsaw, and unfortunately I can tell he is impressed.

'If we are going to resist the Germans, we must do so peacefully, with our humanity, like you did,' he says. 'We must show them what is acceptable and what is not. The leaders of the community must stand up to them.'

Rivka's father then goes about writing a letter. The first few drafts he tears up, because they sound too angry. Later he settles down to write two copies of a letter worthy of a great statesman — someone the Indians might call a Mahatma. It reads something like this:

To the representative of the German Reich, here in Piaski

The people of our town have accepted that the Polish administration is now in the hands of the German state. It is not a situation of our own making, but we have no choice in the matter and are obliged to continue our lives under a different command. We entrust, therefore, that you will take full responsibility for the role that you have taken upon yourselves, because power cannot come without responsibility. We cannot give you our service unless you show us your compassion. We cannot follow your rule unless you lead by example. We cannot believe in your administration unless your treatment is fair and your judgement is reasonable. We wish the lives of all citizens to resume as normal, and call for the end of all violence against civilians.

For and on behalf of all the people of Piaski,

Doctor Hirsh Ruben

Physician

I can still hear his voice as he reads this letter out loud. I can still see him nod approvingly, his anger, together with his sense of responsibility, urging him on. Certainly he has expressed the sentiments of his fellow Jews and Poles adequately and feels satisfied that the letter is ready to send. I do not know what kind of response he is hoping to receive. We continue our lives and await it.

The next few days are ominous. Kresse, the curiously kind commandant, has hired a Jewish cook, who is the wife of his friend, but this act of charity does not last long. Kresse is called unexpectedly to Lublin, and when he returns one of the soldiers working for him has 'dealt' with her. She is no longer employed for the commandant, and only some time later do we find out that she was killed in Kresse's absence.

During this same period, a soldier working for Kresse, called Schultz, has arrested one of our patients for whistling while he was having a drink at Jadlodajnia, the bar down the road. It's hard to imagine how whistling could be a crime, but perhaps this man was doing something else he shouldn't have been doing. This is what we are all hoping.

But then something shocking happens.

A man comes running to bring us news about a family in Piaski who have just lost their child. 'Dr Ruben,' this man says, 'you must go and see them immediately, because they have collapsed.' He tells us, 'In front of the parents they chopped off that poor child's legs! In front of the parents ... Oh God!' and he starts sobbing, hardly able to utter another word of his story.

To this day I can feel my shock at hearing these words. Later, through other people, we discover that the German soldiers responsible for this vile act had also made the parents watch as they threw the poor innocent child off the balcony.

The village is silent for many days after, and people only leave their homes for basic errands. This horror has frozen our limbs. There is no reason, no sanity, in anything we previously took for granted. None of us feels safe.

'We must try and reason with them,' Doctor Ruben keeps insisting. 'Every person in this town is willing to slit those soldiers' throats in revenge. They know they have to start behaving properly or their lives are at risk here.'

All true in theory, yet there is this sickening, sickening

feeling of losing control, losing sense, losing everything, because there is no way to negotiate with them. Believe me, once people start venturing out again, everybody is coming to see us for one problem or another — there is a plague of fear spreading around Piaski that is turning people's bones to jelly. We know now that we are dealing with something inhuman and completely unknown. There is no gentle commandant able to help any of us.

Daniel is not old enough to go to the underground school that's been set up by the townspeople in various houses, so he is at home the day that the Wehrmacht come to take his grandfather away.

Doctor Ruben and I are attending to a woman who has an injury from treading on a nail. I am given the task of opening the abscess and draining the pus, but before I finish cleaning the wound we hear German voices outside the door. I turn around and there are three soldiers in the room. They ask which one of us is Doctor Ruben.

Rivka's father recognises his name among the harsh tones of this military language. He is not ashamed to admit to his crime of writing a letter on behalf of the people of Piaski, but if his fear is anything as strong as mine, some part of him somewhere is shaking as he looks down at the long black boots. His face is absolutely still as he shuffles out of the room. He says goodbye to his patient, courteously, and to me he says, 'Please look after Rivka and Daniel.' That simple.

'*Kommen Sie bitte,*' one of the officers says, and Rivka's father walks to the door with them. From the upstairs balcony, Daniel is asking where they are taking his grandfather. Nobody answers, so he runs downstairs and grabs his grandfather's coat, but his hand is twisted and thrown off by one of the soldiers. Rivka's father holds Daniel's head and kisses it, before he is taken away. He doesn't have time to give a kiss to Rivka and she doesn't expect one.

That evening I feel so sick that I hadn't stopped Doctor Ruben from writing that letter. Rivka cooks the dinner for all of us, but I cannot touch a piece of food and neither can she. We don't want to talk about what could have happened to her father in front of Daniel, so we talk about other things — the noise from the bordello, the people in the market behind our house, the sick farmer who grows hops just outside town — things that don't matter to anyone, just so that Daniel doesn't start worrying. But later on, when Daniel is asleep, Rivka's brave face crumbles and she wraps her arms around her father's chair, the chair he used to sit in as he humoured his guests and family over the years. I hold her in my arms and weep with her, knowing that I should have taken his letter and thrown it in the bin. I, of all people, with a bullet wound in my shoulder to prove the futility of such resistance.

'Please, Rivka, don't cry. He'll come back once they've finished questioning him,' I say, but as soon as these words are out they sound like fantastic lies. 'He's done nothing but write a letter. What can they do?'

Rivka continues weeping and no amount of consolation can slow her tears. She is shaking in my arms, and I know then that

I will look after her and Daniel, just as her father requested, till the end of our days together. I will be her father and her husband. We do not need to talk about these things. They are already written down.

The next day I see the patients alone. Everybody asks questions, because they come here hoping to see Doctor Ruben and I am a poor replacement for him. I know where all the necessaries are kept, but there are so many medical questions I want to ask, and there is nobody who knows the answers. Any healing skills I have learnt from Rivka's father, it seems, are taken away from me in these days of absolute loss. By lunchtime I have to let everybody know that Doctor Ruben is unavailable and may no longer be in practice. I look into the eyes of the people who come to the surgery and I know they are all thinking the same question: what is going to happen to Rivka? Are you going to take responsibility for her and Daniel or not?

It's as if everything in my life, all my desires up to this point, have become irrelevant. The person that was Benjamin Rahabi has just been sacrificed so that life may continue as long as it can in these circumstances. As for Ewa? Well, somewhere in my heart I wonder if I will ever see her again, because Warsaw seems as far away as any hope of peace, and in some way I am glad of the distance, because it protects me from my own betrayal. Nonetheless, when I allow myself the luxury of a few minutes remembering our hopes to be together I feel so raw it hurts my insides. I should at least write to her, I know, and I always plan to do this, but somehow there is nothing I can say. Saying sorry to Ewa would be like apologising for the sins of the whole world. Really, I feel beyond sorry, beyond any hope of reconciliation with my past. I cannot even start feeling sorry for myself, because if I do I know I will lose the battle and start to crumble, so I stay strong, and whenever these thoughts of Ewa approach me, I ward them off, because I know I can never be the person I was; not for her, not for anyone.

So, now you understand something of the circumstances that bring Rivka and me together, in marriage. I will spare you the nuptial details; just let you know that we decided to marry after mutual discussions rather than any proposals as such. Of course I love Rivka, but it is not love that dictates we should marry. I simply write a letter to Warsaw to let my parents know, and receive no reply, which probably means they never received the letter. Our wedding day comes and there is no great ceremony. It's a simple marriage with only a few guests. The Ketubah is read, the wine is blessed, and afterwards a glass is given to me to crush. Rivka looks away. This is to symbolise the temple in Israel, I say to myself as I feel the fragile glass shatter. This is not going to happen to us.

Yet things are not looking good for any one of us in this part of Poland as the winter sets in. Nobody knows what has happened to Doctor Ruben. Piaski is freezing now, colder than it has been for years, I am told. Nobody goes out unless it is absolutely essential, because the snow is stacked up thick along the white limestone houses and grey blizzards blow through our small town. Even so, nothing seems to stop the force of the occupying army. Their black boots crunch in the snow and their huge vehicles draw tracks in the roads as they go about their business. You hear German voices everywhere, and you could almost believe you were in Germany, or some place in the middle of nowhere, a million miles from Warsaw. Really, I am starting to miss my home town.

Through this freezing winter, out of the snow, the German soldiers march rows and rows of German Jews into our town.

One day I hear German voices outside our house and a knock on the door. Rivka opens the door with great hesitation and a gust of icy wind whistles in, along with two soldiers and a small party of people. The soldiers don't even ask if they can look around our house, but start walking up and down the corridors. Who are they looking for? This is what I am thinking, but it soon becomes clear that they are not looking for anybody. Rather, they are deciding on how they can change our living arrangements, would you believe?

Rivka and I are left facing two German Jewish families, the Schreibers and the Kaufmanns, who have been forcibly billeted in our house by the Wehrmacht. They look absolutely sick and exhausted, too afraid to even talk to us, while the soldiers decide on where to put their charges, as if they are baggage to be transported and dumped anywhere. After a few minutes of consultation between themselves, they shove Marian Schreiber and her baby, Ferdinand, into our waiting room and Immanuel and Ida Kaufmann into the surgery.

Our 'guests' stay locked in their rooms for some time after the soldiers have left. When I tap on the doors they come out, as timid as mice — so nervous they make me feel like I could be one of the soldiers. I ask if I can move some of the equipment out of the rooms. 'We will make you comfortable,' I assure them. 'There's enough room in the house.' And Rivka takes the little baby upstairs so his mother can bathe.

Then Rivka makes a modest meal for our visitors and we try to behave decently, without showing our annoyance at what has happened, because this situation is no fault of theirs. That night, our first supper together, I will never forget, as Ida Kaufmann tells us about their march from Germany.

'We had no idea where we were being taken,' she says. 'Only a few minutes to pack our bags and then we had to start marching. So many days we were walking, it seemed as if we had reached the end of the earth. Honestly, when we first made our way through this snow we thought we had arrived in Siberia.'

She finishes this alarming story with the words of one soldier on the march who was a little friendlier than the rest. 'Get out of Poland,' this man had told them. 'They're going to kill you — every last one of you — if you don't escape.'

CHAPTER 8

One night, while we are all fast asleep, there is a light thud on the door. I wake and get up, quietly stepping past the rooms of our guests, and look through the window to see if it is a German soldier. In the dim light I can see someone familiar, but I cannot place the face. I open the door and a man pushes his way in.

'I need you to pull a tooth. You can pull teeth, can't you?'

I may be sleepy, but I know immediately that this is one of the men who have taken to the forest. I have heard some of my patients talk about this partisan. He used to be the baker, but now he is working in the underground resistance. His skin is hard and cracked in places with dirt, and he looks as if he's been sleeping rough for several months. It takes no intelligence to realise why he has come at night. Still, even in the darkness there is a chance that he was seen coming, or will be seen leaving, and then we'll all be dead. You know, you just cannot trust people in this war. One person talks, another doesn't. One person feeds the soldiers, another fights them. Everybody is saying one thing and doing another. Can I even trust him?

For a minute I am thinking: shall I tell him I can't do it? Send him off with some morphine? But then I think: how can I leave the poor man in pain? He is fighting this war of ours for us. So instead of resisting, I signal for him to come upstairs.

'I don't need any painkiller, just pull the tooth,' this partisan says.

I listen to him without saying a word. I do not worry about asking for his name and neither do I take a patient history; I just light a small candle in the hope that it will be enough for me to see into the darker regions at the back of his mouth. Holding the candle close to his lips I say, 'Point to the painful tooth,' because there is not enough light to see if there is any abscess in the gum area. I am working in a cave of darkness but I don't really want to be able to see what I'm doing, in case other people see as well.

I do not have the right equipment, but I find an implement that I think will work. 'I am not a dentist, so please bear with me,' I tell him, knowing that there is a serious risk I will leave the roots inside, making the condition even worse. However, I am under pressure to pull the tooth, so I do, pushing it down as I've been taught, praying that my patient will not scream.

Of course he does, but at least I have the tooth.

I blow out the candle and we wait a few seconds. I hear his rapid breath in the dark, together with an agonising rasping sound. My eyes adjust to the dimness and I see him holding his cheek, his mouth wide open as he lets out another scream, this time virtually inaudible. I am thinking: please, please be quiet. For the sake of our Maker, keep quiet. For both our sakes, keep quiet.

The man gives himself a full five minutes to recover. Time I would never usually begrudge any patient, but now I am hoping that he leaves the house as swiftly as he came in. I am praying that Marian Schreiber has not woken downstairs, and also praying that her soldier friend is not visiting. I cannot stop myself from saying, 'It should be better soon. Sitting here is not going to help either of us. Please go now, if you can.'

The partisan stands and hugs me, leaving some of his strong smell on my clothes as evidence of his visit. As much as I would like to offer him hospitality, right now I just want him out of the door. 'Thank you, my friend,' he says, and walks downstairs, out of the front door and into the shadows thrown by the cemetery walls. He disappears into the cemetery and I never see him again.

By the time I return into our bedroom, Rivka is waiting with a terrified expression, not knowing what is happening right here in her father's house. 'What were you doing?' she asks. 'Who on earth came to see you at this time?'

'The baker,' I tell her, and she knows immediately why I was so quiet. 'He's gone now, don't worry,' and I hold this wife of mine, who is a gift of this war we are living through.

The next day nobody says anything about strange sounds in the night. There are no rumours of screams coming from the doctor's house. Nobody tells us that they saw or heard anything.

If they did, then we will know soon enough.

Not long after the partisan incident, Rivka, Daniel and I are taking an early morning walk in the forest near Gardzienice to pick some mushrooms and talk about what we should do now that the Germans are building a ghetto for the Jews in Piaski, and another in Lublin.

'At least we're not being marched to another country like the Schreibers and Kaufmanns,' Rivka says, as if it's not such a bad idea to go and live in the ghetto after all.

I need to express my objections to this plan more privately, so I tell Daniel, 'Go look for some mushrooms under those pine trees, my darling, you'll find lots there.' As soon as he's run off I say, 'Why do you think they want us to move from our homes, Rivka? Think about it! They're rounding us all up like animals.'

'Where do you suggest we go?'

'I don't know. Maybe first Warsaw, and then out of Poland.'

'Without papers? Without permission? Where exactly are you planning on taking us?' she asks.

I have no idea where. All I can say is, 'Out of here. Anywhere. Some place far away from all of this.'

As we walk, I am thinking about the partisan who came to the surgery and wishing that I had asked him about his whereabouts in the forest, just in case things get too difficult in Piaski. I am thinking, too, about the Jews who have already left to live in the stone mines in the forest. There is no doubt in my mind that we have to get out of town before our lives are made unbearable.

We are still thinking about our options when we hear footsteps crunching along the forest floor behind us, together with German voices asking, 'Wo gehen Sie?' I don't know much German but I know that these men want us to stop, so we do.

Daniel is searching the ground some way ahead of us, fully absorbed. I yell out, 'Daniel,' trying not to sound too afraid.

The soldiers are wearing the same Wehrmacht uniforms that the soldiers in Piaski wear, with swastikas on their armbands. One of them is my age, yet I can see that we have nothing in common. The other — an older man with a moustache — grabs my arm, waves his gun around and starts signalling that we should take our clothes off. There is no time to think. I look around quickly to see where we can run to, but there is nowhere to go, nothing to do but obey orders, so I yell out to Daniel to come and listen to everything we say. I try to avoid looking in the eyes of the soldiers as I start to unbutton my shirt slowly, because I know that once we are naked we will share the fate of the others who have been shot before us. This is how these people like to kill their victims — always naked, because it's easier to search through pockets, I am told, if there is no body weight lying on the clothes.

Daniel runs up and we tell him to take off his clothes, like we are doing. He needs no help, which is unusual. He is being the perfect child, listening to everything his mother says, because he knows that a stupid move could kill us all. My heart is beating so fast I can hardly breathe. I am trying to think of something I can say or do to stop this from happening, but I cannot think of anything except the gun that is pointing down at the ground, not directly at us, giving us a few moments to feel the fear of facing our end.

Rivka is talking rapidly in an odd mixture of Polish and German. She says over and over, 'Please, please do not do this to us. I have a child. I am a mother, can't you see?' She is looking to me for protection, for support, for anything, but there is nothing I can do to help her. She is so nervous she can hardly carry out the task of undressing, so I try and help unbutton her, but the tip of a rifle separates us. Rivka continues undressing slowly. All five of us are silent, poised for the quick pull on the trigger that will kill the three of us and leave the two Germans standing.

'*Schnell*,' a voice instructs, and then two other soldiers appear further ahead in the forest where my eyes are failing to focus. Maybe, I am thinking, these two soldiers will be distracted and we will be able to escape. My mind is telling me things I cannot understand, in garbled signals. The fear is so sharp and fast you wouldn't believe it. I am unable to open my mouth. I cannot think.

The older soldier lifts his gun. I hold my breath and I put my hands over Daniel's eyes. Then this five-year-old boy says something that I will take with me to my grave. 'Mama, Papa,' he says, 'don't worry. At least we are all together.'

Up ahead one of the soldiers calls out, '*Halt! Halt!*' The barrel that was pointing directly at me a moment earlier turns down to the ground, and the choking feeling in my throat releases, setting off another wave of rapid heartbeats as we watch the soldiers talk. Rivka's eyes are beseeching me with her fear, but she sees me naked and helpless. I wish I could say or do something to console her, but language is not ours to use. It is the sole property of the Germans, who are not even looking at us as they discuss our fate. The soldier who has just arrived is telling them that I am a doctor. I cannot follow the other words they are saying. All I can see in front of me are Rivka and Daniel, both of them naked and vulnerable and more important to me than the whole world. We are waiting to die, this much is clear. The adrenaline running around my veins has already prepared my body for a bullet. I know what a bullet will feel like, from that time in Warsaw; this is what I tell myself. It will be fast and too sharp to be painful. We will feel nothing. God, please let Daniel be the first to go.

The gun that was pointing to the ground lifts again, and I hold my breath, but this time the barrel is being used to lift our clothes off the ground. The soldier who has just arrived is telling the others about a place where they need doctors and is indicating that he wants us to put our garments back on. Still not thinking straight, I pull on my clothes as fast as I can, as if they are some kind of armour, and hold Daniel's trousers for him to step into. They are so small and I cannot believe that somebody so young, who has just been threatened with a gun, can be looking so calmly and directly into my eyes at this moment. My hands are shaking and my teeth are moving on their own. Rivka is pulling on her clothes rapidly, shivering, as unprepared to be dressing as she was to be undressing a few minutes earlier. Nothing makes sense. We are living in the moment and it is the most terrifying instant of judgement imaginable — without even time for a goodbye, should it be needed.

We are ordered into the back of a truck and driven for what seems to be the whole day, but is probably no longer than a few hours. There is very little light inside, and nowhere to sit, so we get down on the floor and hold hands. In the darkness Rivka says, 'If that ever happens again, I want us to remember what Daniel said.'

'It won't happen again,' I say. 'See, they need doctors. We're going to be alright, aren't we, Daniel?'

Daniel cuddles up between us. Rivka holds him now as if for the first time, showering him with her affection. 'Such a brave boy I have never known,' she tells him. 'You are so precious to me, my darling. Always remember how much I love you. You will, won't you? Wherever you are and wherever we are?'

I close my eyes and I try to talk to God, hoping for help and consolation, but there is no God anywhere, no feeling of any holiness, just an instinct that it is the people that matter in all of this. I search again for a sign, for some sort of reassurance that God is with us, but I feel God's presence only through the temperature of Rivka's body and the sweat of Daniel's palms. Yes, these are the only signs of the strange type of divine grace we have just experienced. I am painfully aware of how much love I feel for the two people who are crouching down in the darkness next to me, being thrown from side to side whenever there are rough patches in the road.

We are experiencing these moments together as if they are our last. We are still here and we are still together — this is the bizarre miracle of it all. I don't think I've ever felt so grateful to be alive in all my years, and yet I know that we are hanging on to life from a piece of thread, because we are going into German custody, just like Rivka's father.

Farha has had her face turned away while I am telling this story, and she turns it back now and I see some heavy drops fall onto her lap. She sits absolutely still, but her hair is trembling, still covering her face. Aaron is holding the cane chair below him as if it could fall away at any moment, his face as distressed as a child's. Ewa and Rivka too, look as if they couldn't stand another second of this story, so I stop, and the large room falls silent except for the soft rattle of crickets in the fields beyond and the chatter of a group of servants who have gathered outside our bungalow to enjoy a happy reunion in Madhupur's pleasant night air.

CHAPTER 9

In Calcutta people always ask me if I will ever take Rivka and Daniel back to Poland, and I try to explain to them that I go back often, as a hostage to my memory, which tricks me into enclosed spaces like that truck; into places where the air is hard to breathe and my eyes are always searching for the light. When I'm trapped like this, everything that happened then happens again in the present, before my very eyes, as real as a knife in my stomach. But really, there is no reason even to think of that place again, because now we have India and the past is behind us.

Here we have been lucky enough to get real jobs that pay real money. In fact, within a few weeks of arriving on the *Asama Maru* most of us have been placed in some sort of employment, however humble, either in the jute mills or tobacco factory. I am one of the luckier refugees, thanks to Aaron, who has found me a job as an export manager at a paper factory in a back lane of China Bazaar: a market with cobblestone lanes and small shops selling paper, chinaware, pots and pans. My office is on the fifth floor of one of the old buildings, towards the back of the market, overlooking a mosque and some simple roof gardens, as well as the narrower laneways with their tiny shops selling paintbrushes, balloons, lacquers — everything you didn't even know you needed.

So you must be wondering how it feels to work again? And as an export manager, of all things. Ha! A businessman, if you please. There is no doubt in my mind — I only have this position because Aaron Isaac runs the jute mills for Ravi Bose, the owner of this and many other companies. Our company is the least profitable business in his group, so he entertains himself by employing me, of all people, to run it for him.

Working for me is a man we call Nayar Babu, who is such a fast typist you would not believe. He is responsible for the management of the office and all of the accounts. He has showed me his filing system and tried to explain where everything is kept — some of it in four steel cupboards we call the *almaris*, and the rest stacked up in piles on the floor. This man Nayar Babu is completely aware of the order of things, and I know that I must pray for his good health on a daily basis, because if anything happens to him I will be responsible for retrieving pieces of paper that have been filed away goodness knows where.

Thankfully, Nayar Babu has never had other employment, so he will most likely retire in this same job. When he came to work at the company he was a young, slender clerk I am told. Now he is a grandfather, with a small potbelly, grey rims around his eyes and a toupee, which he readjusts as inconspicuously as possible in between typing these letters and telexes that we send.

'You people from Poland are doing things so differently from the British people,' Nayar Babu tells me one day at work.

I am wondering if I am doing something wrong, so I ask him, 'What's so different about us?'

'Nothing is wrong with you people, sir. That's what I'm saying all this time. The Polish people should have come here to run India instead of the British!'

How funny this man is. If only he knew what struggles we go through ourselves. 'We understand what it is like to live under occupation,' I tell him, although in my mind there is no comparison between India's struggle and our own.

Nayar Babu wants to make every effort to get to know me, I can tell. He is always asking me questions about my family. I show him an old photograph I have of my parents and myself, taken in a studio in Zakopane — the one that I have carried from Warsaw to Calcutta, and even showed to a policeman at Minsk, to prove that I have family, people who will care about me should I disappear. Then Nayar Babu wants to know about my wife, and about the others I have travelled with. When I tell him about Ewa he says, 'Ah, so you have two wives!'

I try to explain that she is just a friend who travelled with us. 'What could I do? Leave her behind?'

'No, you must marry her, too. Doesn't your religion allow this?'

'Religion, religion, what of it? It is my wife who will not allow such a thing,' I tell him, and we laugh.

'Where I come from down south the women used to have many husbands,' Nayar Babu tells me, and his whole body seems to light up as he smiles over his small metal typewriter. 'They lived through times of war, and in these times a woman must be having more than one husband in case the first one was killed.'

And so these conversations between Nayar Babu and myself continue, and I do not take his advice on matters of the heart. Much more important is the advice he gives me on running the office. 'This broom,' he tells me, 'is actually the most important piece of equipment we have.' I watch carefully as he shows me how I can poke the fan back into operation whenever it is stuck, using the broom's long stick.

I watch Nayar Babu as much as I can, because there is so much I have to learn. I listen to him speak to understand everything I can about India, in every waking minute that I am lucky enough to spend alive here. I watch how he eats, using his whole hand. I watch how he nods his head sideways, dismissing everything I say as 'no problem'. He is my adviser in all matters of adjusting to life here, but there is one area where we simply do not agree.

'Why don't you practise medicine here in Calcutta?' he asks me. 'You were in service in your home country, so why are you doing business here instead?'

'I am not a doctor any more,' I tell him. I cannot explain to Nayar Babu how inadequate I feel as a doctor. What a hopeless doctor I was in the camp, hardly able to look after myself, unable to cure anybody. How can I tell Nayar Babu of the horrific memories that rush back when I see somebody sick, or somebody waiting to die? How I promised myself I would never practise medicine again; never again be trailed by sickness or disease or death. But do I tell Nayar Babu any of this? Of course not. Instead I say, 'How can I treat patients when I only have Polish qualifications?'

'You know, if you're from overseas, you will have people lining up to see you here in Calcutta,' he tells me.

I find this hard to believe. I cannot think of anybody who would want to see a refugee about any medical complaints. Who knows what they could catch from their doctor? I am thinking: I have a job. I can support my family, and I should be thankful for this much.

Yet with all my explanations, Nayar Babu cannot stop thinking of my terrible downfall from service to business caste, and insists that we talk about practising medicine some more. He explains his plan to me over many hot gingery cups of *chai*.

'I'll tell you one thing,' he says, 'if you let me bring you some patients, I won't take commission. At my age you know so many sick people, and I will just be doing this thing to be helping them. Sir, everybody is sick in India!'

There is no doubt about it, Nayar Babu would be able to find me sick people.

'Sir, take me for example,' he says, 'I am having this amoeba trouble, like everybody in this country. Please find a solution from your people in Poland.'

'I cannot see patients,' I tell Nayar Babu. 'This work suits me better.' I am thinking: the only worry here is whether or not we'll deliver all our products, and even that is no big worry, because who will kill us if we don't?

And so we go back to the work at hand. Nayar Babu types up letters, and I watch his fingers move over the small round keys faster than any male or female typist I have ever known. Next to him I am a slow paper-shuffler, making my phone calls, trying to be methodical but getting hopelessly confused with this business of ours. Nayar Babu helps me send telegrams. He helps me find addresses for clients. He tells me what I have to say to the banks and to the shipping companies. He helps me so much that I wonder why Ravi Bose does not give him my job.

One day Nayar Babu surprises me by saying, 'Really, you are wasting your time working here, Mr Rahabi. You must be doing your practice, no?'

'As a doctor?'

'Yes, sir. This work is not so interesting for you.'

I am thinking: how could he have noticed that? What have I said or done to give myself away? But to tell the truth, I've never thought about whether or not my job is interesting. The main thing has always been to get the work done. There is no doubt about it, I have greater difficulty in sending a telegram than I do in performing some minor surgery, but I blame it on my written English.

'Nayar Babu, I'm telling you, I cannot practise as a doctor in Calcutta. I don't have the same qualifications as your doctors. I know nothing about tropical diseases.'

'Someone will be teaching you these things.'

'But how much time do I have for learning? I have a job here in this office, remember.'

'You haven't given me your signature here, please,' he says, changing the subject.

We continue working and no more is said about these things, but the next day an elderly man comes into the office. The first thing I notice about him is the thinness of his legs under his *lungi* and oedema in his ankles.

'Mr Rahabi, please be meeting Mr Menon. He is my cousin brother and is having "this thing", whatdoyoucallit, very bad trouble with his thyroid. Do one thing — at least tell him what else is wrong.'

I am taken aback by Nayar Babu's surprise tactic, but I play along, as if this is a game of no consequence.

'Please sit down, Mr Menon,' I say, and no sooner are the words out than I feel as if I am back in the surgery at Piaski, only next to me is Nayar Babu instead of Rivka's father. The process is so familiar. I look into the patient's eyes, his mouth. I feel his stomach and then feel his neck, where my hands instinctively help me find part of the diagnosis. The room seems quieter. There is no clacking of typewriter keys. Just the fan, the sound of our breathing, and the world outside. Then I press his ankles and notice the pitting oedema. I take his wrist in my hand and start feeling for arythmia of the pulse, and the diagnosis becomes even clearer. I am not thinking about whether or not I want to get involved. I am simply thinking: this man has atrial fibrillation, and I don't even know if we can get digitalis in India.

'He has problems with his thyroid and also congestive cardiac failure,' I tell Nayar Babu. 'Mr Menon, you should see a doctor about it as soon as you can.'

'But can't you prescribe something?'

'I don't know anything about the medicine available here. He needs to have some tests done. The medicine I would use is very strong, and his pulse and breathing must be monitored properly or he could get very sick and start seeing strange colours. Really, I am not the person to be treating him.'

We have had this conversation before and yet Nayar Babu insists on having it again. We are sitting in an office, not of a doctor, but of an export company, in the back lanes of China Bazaar. There is no running away from the facts.

'I will write down the tests you need to have done, and once you have the results you can come back and visit, alright?' I hear these words come out as impatient. Listening to myself sounding so irritated I remember something that Hirsh Ruben taught me: that a doctor's main task is to leave the patient smiling, no matter what. 'Please come back. I want to help, my friend,' I add. It only takes one second to say these words and there's a look in Mr Menon's eyes of total relief that touches an instinct in me to be humble, above all else.

He is smiling now, this Mr Menon, and in that smile I remember Rivka's father and his devotion to his patients. 'Thank you so much, doctor,' he says, and Nayar Babu smiles at me, as if to say that he has won. 'Thank you, doctor,' Nayar Babu repeats, emphasising my qualifications.

I feel as if I should be thanking them, because Mr Menon, my first patient in Calcutta, brought to me by an office clerk, has just helped me to remember what few skills God put into this head of mine. How hard it is to see our own future unfold, or to recognise the people who unwrap it for us as the angels they actually are.

CHAPTER 10

We have been to look at some grand apartments in Bow Bazaar, Lower Chitpur Road, Kyd Street and near a marble palace made from stone imported from Italy. Rivka and I have seen so many apartments and houses, and every one of them is adequate for our needs. There's no doubt about it, they are all better than the dormitory we currently sleep in above the Jewish Girls' School, but Farha is not satisfied with a single one we've inspected. I would be pleased to just settle on a place and end the house-hunting, but Farha flaps her fan incessantly and climbs into her car yet again to instruct the driver to take us to our next destination.

'You can get such low rents since the war started, you may as well go for a place in South Calcutta,' she tells us. 'And if we're looking in South Calcutta, we may as well try and find a place with verandahs facing the right direction so that you can catch the nor'westers.' She explains how one gust from these great north-westerly breezes and their wild thunderstorms can cool down the entire house in the evenings around March. 'You'll die of heat if you don't have some breeze in the evening,' she tells me, with such authority I have to remind myself that these are details, not life or death issues.

'What for to have wind in the house?' Rivka says, and I tell Farha that surely the north-westerly winds should not make any difference if we have fans.

'Trust me, I know what is available in Calcutta,' she announces matter-of-factly. 'After everything you have been through, you deserve a bit of luxury.'

I cannot even start to explain that the Jewish Girls' School is more luxurious than any other place we've stayed in for a long time. Yet I know that my family deserves to feel safe and comfortable, so I decide to leave the final choice in Rivka's hands.

We continue on our rounds. Farha takes us to Karaya Road and we look at a grand run-down mansion, where the water has stained the columns and rising damp has bubbled up the paint on the inside walls. I like the place, but Farha says, 'This is not such a good area — too many prostitutes, too much rubbish on the streets. We made the mistake of setting up home in Free School Lane, and look at us, we still haven't moved!'

So we go to look at a house where both she and Rivka are happy, in a back street called Rowland Road. It's a long distance from the synagogue apparently, but nobody here worries about these things — if we're happy to take transport on the Sabbath, what of it? 'Just get the servants to pay the *tonga*,' Farha suggests. 'We're very relaxed in Calcutta.'

A tattered old guard with a long stick opens the gate and lets us inside this disused house. It's been painted in faded yellows and has two pillars at the front, holding up a porch with marble stairs leading up to double doors. There are three huge rooms downstairs, and three more upstairs, with ceilings that tower over us, bearing low-hanging fans. The windows are enormous, some of them broken, and instead of doorways between some of the rooms there are curtains made from sheets that hang down in a single flap and flutter with any passing breeze. In one corner of the house is a pile of old metal trunks that the previous tenants have left, along with a few pieces of elaborately carved black teak furniture: chairs with swirls for legs and sideboards with carved black crowns placed on top of mirrors. Where can the previous owners have gone, I am thinking. Perhaps, like us, they had to leave at a moment's notice. What disasters in this part of the world could possibly make people leave their homes?

Out the back are the verandahs that Farha has been seeking and, thankfully, they are facing the right direction. She opens the door onto the back garden, then inspects the water tank and the outhouses for the servants.

'You've got enough space here to keep lots of help,' she tells us, satisfied at last. I should hope so — I'm sure there are enough rooms above these three garages to house the Russian army!

I look at Rivka, who seems absolutely satisfied. 'This is perfect, no?' she says, and Farha smiles. A quick paint and it could become a grand home, and Rivka deserves one, I keep telling myself, repeating what Farha wants for us. I have learnt now to trust the will of God, especially when it manifests through the wisdom of women. We will sign the contracts and I will do my utmost to satisfy the needs of all the people in my care. This is what I feel.

'Ewa can move in with us,' Rivka says to me, in Polish.

'Of course,' I say, 'but she will feel uncomfortable, because we are married.'

'So you would rather leave her in the Girls' School?' Rivka asks, indignantly.

'No, that's not what I meant. I was thinking about you.'

'She will stay here, and we will live as one family,' Rivka tells me, with some force. 'It is our duty to look after her.'

'But she should be thinking about her future,' I say.

'Which one of us can think of the future right now?' Rivka laments. 'Who knows where any one of us will be in this future of ours?'

Rivka's attitude to Ewa wasn't always this positive. How could I forget the time on the *Asama Maru* when they refused to talk to each other? Believe me, that time was so hard for the rest of us that I wonder how easy it will be for us to live together now. But what choice do we have, really?

Ewa sees our house for the first time when she moves in with us a few days later. The first thing she says is, 'I cannot believe the size of it,' then she asks me, quietly, 'Are you sure you don't mind me living here with you?'

'It's enormous,' I tell her. 'You said it yourself. There's plenty of room for everyone.' But I know that Ewa is not referring to the size of the place, so I add, 'Rivka insists that you stay with us.'

Of course the house needs a touch of paint, but it seems like yet another thing to organise, and why go to the extra trouble of creating a grand residence? We should be grateful for what we have, no? A house that is grander than any we have lived in before — either in Piaski or Warsaw.

At first the place is a bit bare, but soon Farha organises some beds she calls 'cots', and a dining table with chairs. Once we have these we seem to have a life again. I am thinking: how strange that we feel alive again only now that we have these possessions.

Yet here, in this grand house and haven of safety, Daniel has trouble sleeping, would you believe? The reason, I am sure, is that his room is so large and empty, and he's unused to sleeping separately. Every night Rivka has to reassure him that he is safe. 'Don't worry, darling,' she tells him, 'I will sleep with you all night long,' and she lies down next to him until his breathing becomes heavier and she knows he will not notice her tucking in the mosquito net and making a little tent for him, and him alone.

So we settle down as best we can, Rivka, Daniel, Ewa and I, and Farha visits us often to tell us about the various people she is lining up to work for us.

'It's so difficult to find good household staff,' she tells us with great authority. 'Once you've got hold of them, you have to keep an eye on them and make sure they work hard.'

Rivka looks at Ewa and I can see they are wondering which one of them is going to make sure that the staff work hard.

The following night Farha brings round a cook called Tariq who used to work for another Jewish family that have just left town. She explains to us how important it is to employ someone who is 'known', and tells us that we should ask him some questions about his cooking. Neither Rivka nor Ewa know how to interview an Indian cook, so Farha takes over for them. 'Will you learn how to cook the dishes from their country?' she asks him, and he says, 'Yes, memsahib. I am cooking some English tiffin.'

'These people aren't from England,' she tells Tariq plainly. 'You must learn to cook some Polish food, alright?' To us she says, 'You must get his accounts from him regularly to make sure that he doesn't cheat you.'

I am shocked and embarrassed that she is already accusing him of cheating, and in front of us! 'No, no, that won't be necessary,' I tell Tariq. 'We trust you.'

'He knows how to cook kosher food, Baghdadi style, so you'll dine like kings,' Farha explains. 'He makes good chicken masala, too, and lamb cutlets. All kosher.'

'I'm so glad we have a kosher cook,' I say for Farha's benefit, knowing that this young man with his hollow cheeks and small square beard will be his own master, and will be able to cook any food, kosher or not, without us knowing the difference.

We watch Tariq work for a few days, as Farha has instructed us to do. He always squats on the floor, peeling his vegetables and sifting through the *dahl* to pick out the grit and other creatures that get into the sacks at the market. The food here takes a long time to prepare, because Tariq has to refuel his brick stove all the time, and when the water runs out he has to go down the street to fill up the old goatskin and bring it back. Farha has also told us to see that he boils all the water before leaving it for us in the pitcher, so the poor man is working hard all day, and very soon we are wondering how we would ever be able to manage without Tariq's help.

The next person that Farha brings to see us, a few nights later, is a young Christian girl called Mary, who is an orphan raised by some European missionaries. More than anybody else I meet here, Mary is the one who takes me by surprise. How can a Christian have such dark skin, I ask. Darker even than the Muslims or the Hindus whom we've met.

'They taught you very good English, didn't they?' Farha says to Mary, and then to us she says, 'I've been looking for people that you can instruct properly, and it's not been easy. The Biharis and Orissans that we employ here sometimes don't even speak proper Bengali, let alone Hindi.' Farha sounds quite scandalised by this fact and I try not to laugh.

This young girl, Mary, is dressed in an old white sari, two thick silver chains around her feet and a thick silver belt around her waist. Apparently she is seeking work here as an *ayah*, whatever that is — something about looking after Daniel. 'Hello, little boy,' she says. 'How are you, little boy?' Daniel doesn't know quite how to respond.

'We are looking after Daniel ourselves,' Rivka says in her broken English, as politely as possible, but Farha takes me aside. 'You know in Batanagar, it is company policy that every employee with children has an *ayah*. Over here it is necessary to keep an *ayah*. The girl will be very helpful; give her something to do, you'll see. How much will it cost you really? Nothing.'

I look at Mary and she looks down, a little embarrassed. She seems like a very gentle soul. Her hair is oiled and pulled back off her face in a small bun. She is almost a child herself, and she has no parents; how could we not employ her? More importantly, Mary speaks English, so we have a language other than Hindi or Bengali that we can struggle by in together. Yet Rivka is looking a little overwhelmed at the thought of having somebody to help her with Daniel. I look back at Mary and I can see how eager she is to get a job, so I cannot bear to say no. 'She is an orphan, Rivka.' I speak in Polish, so that Mary doesn't understand. 'Please, let's take her in.'

'Just let her take Daniel to school and make sure he comes home safely,' Farha insists. 'She can help the ladies in the house, too — just wait and see.'

The deal is quickly finalised, and our household seems to run even more efficiently with a cook and an *ayah*. Next Farha comes round with a sweeper. She has noticed how hesitant we are to employ servants, so before even introducing him she says, 'He lives in the *bustee* just around the corner, so he doesn't have to live here, just come in the mornings and evenings to dust and swab.'

I am shrugging my shoulders and looking at Rivka.

'Well, I don't want to spend all my time cleaning if I don't have to,' she says quietly in Polish. 'Every time Ewa and I sweep up, the dust just falls again.'

'You cannot get any of your other servants to sweep,' Farha tells us. 'They just won't do it. Girish is from the sweeper caste, so he will; you're lucky.'

Yes, we are indeed lucky. Probably more lucky than anybody else in Poland. Now we not only have a palace to live in, but we're running a full court, complete with these courtiers. For people who were living in a bunker the size of one of our rooms just a few months earlier, we are fortunate beyond belief.

CHAPTER 11

After a long time the truck comes to a halt and the door is opened by the same soldier who saved us back in the forest. We see light for the first time in over five hours. I am relieved, although I still do not know the full implications of what lies ahead.

We are taken straight from our truck towards some sheds, each one painted black with bitumen, and I cannot tell you how much they stink. It is spring when we arrive at this camp, and the weather is quite warm, but there is no sense of spring here.

We are shown inside our shed, which is unlit, and a few of the prisoners stare at us as we are allocated some hay to sleep on. Next to our hay lies a sick man who hardly moves. I am told later that he used to be a schoolteacher in Kazimierz Dolny. Thinking that I will be required to treat this man, I ask if anybody knows what's wrong with him, but none of the prisoners answers, and the soldier who has shown us inside kicks the man for not responding. His body moves in the same way that a sack of flour moves, lifeless absolutely, and the soldier mutters something in a language I cannot understand. Only later do I find out that most of the guards here are Ukrainians, and the other prisoners say they're even crueller than the Germans.

These soldiers tell us to wait outside the hut and we see more prisoners marched into the compound, carrying logs cut from the forest outside. They stand around, waiting for goodness knows what. Within an hour of our arrival the night sets in, and we are sunk into an unholy darkness before a fire is lit. Some soup and bread are served, which we take next to the fire and eat sitting on the ground. It is thin potato soup, and looking around at the other prisoners I can see that this nourishment is responsible for most of the illnesses I will surely be treating here.

In the firelight, as we eat our soup, I notice a gypsy woman reading palms. Her hair is in two buns on either side of her ears. No doubt she has examined the fortunes of everybody at least a dozen times. Daniel is keen to have his palm read and I can't see the harm, but Rivka disapproves, whispering to me that these gypsies have already made a fortune from Jews who are desperate to discover whether loved ones are still alive. Still, I am thinking, what can she take from us, really? What can she take from anyone here?

After our miserable supper everyone goes to the sheds to sleep and it's pitch dark again. At first nobody wants to talk to us, as if we have spoilt some great camaraderie that was happening before. Daniel is the only person talking in this eerie, dark silence, all the time complaining about the hay that we have to sleep on. It is a week or so before we discover why they are so wary of us.

The next day I am looking for Gunther, the soldier who brought me here to work as the camp doctor, but I cannot see him anywhere. The whole family is allocated work: Rivka in the kitchen and I with a man called Itzick, who is a carpenter by trade. Stupidly, I tell the guard that I'm meant to be working as a doctor, not a carpenter, and he laughs and pokes me with the tip of his gun, as if I haven't got the joke.

So, we are taken to one of the other sheds and at first a guard stands by while Itzick makes me saw wood. Then, without saying a word, we construct more bunks for the other 'criminals' they will no doubt collect for this new prison. It is a farce, I'm telling you, because I do not have the muscles that Itzick has, or any of the talent. If I had been trained as an orthopaedic surgeon, yes, maybe, but I have been trained to lift a stethoscope, that is all. We work in silence, which means Itzick makes no comments about my incompetence as a carpenter, and I feel that somehow he protects me in this way. I like him, even though we cannot talk.

One day when we are left alone in the shed for a few minutes I look behind the hay and wood to see if anybody can hear me if I say a few words. At first I ask him about the wood, in case the soldier walks in to check up on us, but then I start asking about his background. Cautiously I whisper, 'Where are you from?'

I cannot believe it when he says that he is from Warsaw. I tell him that I used to live in Pawia Street, and he cries in hushed tones, 'My friend, I lived in Nowolipki!'

I am so thrilled to meet someone from Warsaw, really, in spite of the circumstances we now share. He tells me that he escaped the ghetto, and then left the city altogether because it was crawling with Polish blackmailers who were turning in Jews for five hundred *zlotys* and a bag of sugar. 'I could not walk down a street without worrying about the footsteps behind me. It was terrible, so terrible. If you're Jewish it's safer to be in the ghetto in Warsaw, I'm serious.'

'So the people in the ghetto are safe, you think?'

'Nobody is safe,' Itzick says. 'Not even the Germans. Someone attacks them, and then a hundred of us have to pay with our lives. I am telling you, they don't care who they take.'

'And if the people there have some money?' I ask, hopefully.

'How can you buy things in the ghetto?' Itzick says, lifting his head from his work and looking at me as if I don't understand a thing. 'A fur coat for a loaf of bread, a violin for a small bag of potatoes — this is how they are buying things now. The peasants have taken all the money in Warsaw. They come into the city with slabs of meat hidden in their clothes, and go back to their farms with a fortune.'

After talking to this man I cannot stop thinking about my parents, about Ewa and her family and our other friends in Warsaw. I feel a constant agony, wondering what could be happening to them, let alone worrying about what is happening to us here in this hellhole. I cannot stop these thoughts, and, worse still, I cannot stop Ewa coming into my mind again and again, uninvited, always with this feeling of guilt. I try telling myself that I am married, but I can't stop myself wanting her, going back in my mind to our times together. The happy times.

Sometimes I hear myself talking out loud, which Rivka complains about, telling me that I've become like an old man already, letting this experience break me. I don't know why this happens. Maybe the thoughts have more room when they are out of my head, but I know this is dangerous, because sometimes when I start talking to myself a gun points at me. Other times I find myself thinking about Ewa, and Rivka asks me why I keep mumbling her name. I have to tell her the truth, that I cannot stop thinking of my family and everybody I love in Warsaw, that's all.

'For me it's easier,' she says, and at first I don't understand. Then she goes on, 'The other person I love is dead.'

When she says this I feel reassured, really. I feel as if somehow Rivka understands the situation I find myself in and I don't have to explain that she shares my heart with someone else. Next time I start mumbling about Ewa, Rivka makes no comment; instead, she instructs Daniel to give me a hug.

So our lives continue like this, and still there is no hope of working here as a doctor. We are prisoners like everybody else, except for some reason the people in our shed are more suspicious about us, until slowly one man befriends us — an engineer called Herzl, who tells me he has a son the same age as Daniel back in his village. There is this slow breaking of ice and then a few others start talking to us, including a man called Berl, and others still.

It is soon after this that I hear noises in the night, and I walk over to the corner of the shed and see that the prisoners are removing a plank of wood in the darkness. Under the plank is a deep hole, big enough for a grown man to stand up in. Herzl sees that I've realised what's going on and immediately starts explaining. 'We have to construct a lateral corridor next,' he says, 'and then a vertical tunnel for the other side.'

It doesn't take much to work out that the people in our hut have been planning this for several weeks. One of them is digging the pit a little wider with a spoon, and the others are carrying away the dirt by placing it in their clothing. 'Not a word of this gets mentioned to anybody,' Herzl tells me. 'Even to the other prisoners.'

The sensation that sweeps my body is of thrill and dread mixed up together. 'Maybe it's not worth the risk?' I say, hesitantly.

Herzl rolls his eyes as if I have come up with the most stupid objection. 'You want to stay?' he says angrily. 'Then stay.'

'And if we want to come?' I whisper. 'Are we all going to do this thing together?'

He doesn't say anything, which makes me feel uncomfortable. What if we're left behind? What sort of future will we have, sitting out the war in this camp with a five-year-old boy?

'I'm serious,' I repeat. 'Are we all going together?'

I want to know if we're welcome to join their escape party, because we haven't been part of the planning operations. I know, too, that if we are left behind, they will kill us for not telling the guards about the escape plan. I take one look at the old schoolmaster, who has hardly lifted his head since we arrived. What will happen to him if we all go through that hole in the ground? What will happen if this escape plan is discovered between now and the time fixed for the break-out? Then this absurd sense of caution strikes me and I am thinking: we can't be part of this escape. We can't risk Daniel's life.

The men continue digging with their hands and a couple of spoons. There is no room for me near the pit, but I ask if there is anything I can do to help. Nobody replies, so I just take some earth and put it in my pocket to sprinkle out the next day amid the sawdust and hay of the shed where I'm working. Rivka comes over and helps me put more dirt in her pockets. After an hour the night's work is done. When the men move away, I lower myself into the pit. As soon my feet touch the bottom I feel sick with the conspiracy. It is so close to the wall. We only need to dig three metres more before making our way upwards and out to freedom.

The next night, around the fire, Daniel gets his way and places his small palms in the hands of the gypsy. We gather around him and she asks to see ours, too. 'Only tell him something if it's good,' Rivka requests. The gypsy takes no notice of her request. She says nothing at all to Daniel, but grabs my hand instead. She is squeezing my hand and looking down at my palm, then into Rivka's eyes in the firelight. Before she says anything to us she turns around to some of the other prisoners and says, 'This family here will survive. They will survive, along with this engineer. Nobody else,' and she tosses my hand away with great finality, as if that is the only piece of information we need to know.

I want to ask her more. I want to know about my family in Warsaw, and about Ewa. I present my hand to the gypsy once more, and she takes it, this time looking directly into my eyes. 'How much do you want, eh?' she asks me. 'How much do you really think you can get?' I am puzzled by this statement, but she continues, 'Isn't it enough that you will remain with your family?'

'But my family is in Warsaw, too,' I tell her, and her reply is so odd: 'You have two love lines on your palm. Two women who love you.' She points to the line that crosses along the top of my palm, just beneath my fingers. 'See?'

I look, and to my amazement there actually are two lines there, and immediately I start convincing myself that the whole of her prophecy must be true. If she knows about Ewa, the bit about our survival must also be true.

Herzl tells me, 'It's a load of nonsense. Don't take any notice,' but I find myself thinking of her again and again throughout the following day as I also think about that tunnel. I ask myself: how is Daniel going to grow in this place? There is no option for us but to go with this escape party. We must escape when everybody escapes, or we will never survive this camp. I feel more determined than ever, no matter what the consequences. How can we deny our freedom? The Israelites were given their freedom — it was a Divine gift — did they refuse it? What are our options, really? Am I to stay around here and await instructions for my job as camp doctor?

After breakfast one day Daniel is taken away from us by the guards at gunpoint and we have no idea why. No idea whether he will even survive until the end of our work day, let alone to the moment when we could make our way through that tunnel that Herzl and the others have been digging all this time. He looks back at us and his eyes are wide open in terror.

Rivka and I look at each other in desperation, without saying a word, and then we too are separated. All through the day while I'm working with Itzick I can think of nothing except where they could have taken poor Daniel. I am so frantic with worry that I can hardly hold my tools.

It is only when Daniel comes back later that evening, and we find he was simply assigned the task of picking mushrooms outside the camp, that I stop wishing that we had all been shot in the woods outside Gardzienice, because then, in the words of Daniel, at least we would have all been together.

CHAPTER 12

One evening I try to help dig the pit, but one of the men, Berl, asks me not to, as if I'm some kind of *schnook*. Herzl is also not his usual friendly self. He tells me they have decided that we should not join the escape party, would you believe.

'Your boy, he's too young,' Berl says.

'He will cry,' Herzl explains, as sympathetically as he can.

Rivka is indignant. 'How can you say that my son will cry? How dare you!'

Daniel is hearing all of this and says, 'I won't cry, Mama. I won't.'

'You can come with us,' Herzl tells me. 'Your wife can come, too, but not the boy.'

'I cannot go anywhere without my wife and son,' I say, and believe me, I am as offended as Rivka at their suggestion. There is no way that I would consider leaving Daniel, absolutely no

way. Both Rivka and I would rather die than leave him behind
in the camp; this much I know. Why do we have to go with
them, anyway? This is what I am thinking. Maybe the gypsy
was right — maybe their escape is doomed. But then I start
worrying about staying behind. What else can we do, really? If
we don't escape with them there will be no second chance, and
we will surely go insane.

Rivka is talking to Daniel on the other side of the room and I
can see his brown eyes, large and serious for one so small. His
mother is whispering in his ear and he is looking directly at
Berl, who keeps talking to the others about the stupidity of
taking such a young boy.

Rivka takes Daniel's hand and brings him back to the centre
of the room. 'We have to test whether or not my son will cry.
I can promise you he will not. He will never give us away.' I am
nervous listening to her. She speaks the following terrifying
words: 'Please, torture him if you must, you will never make
him cry.'

There is a discussion among some of the men and women in
the group and then one of them says, 'How can we make sure
that he won't cry? You tell us.' They talk some more and then
the path of action is decided, along with Daniel's fate.

'We will throw these chairs at him,' Berl says. 'If he cries,
then he must stay behind. You can come or stay, it's your choice,
but if he cries he has to stay behind. If he doesn't cry, then he
can come with us.'

I myself am already crying, such is the hopeless dilemma that
Rivka has created. Of course Daniel will cry! He's a young boy.

Rivka talks to him, explaining everything, and Daniel, once more, looks straight ahead with great intention and resolve. His face as he listens to his mother is another of those images that will stay with me forever. I don't think I have ever felt so nervous, except when we were facing those soldiers in the forest. Rivka kisses Daniel and walks him to the centre of the room. I am fighting hard to control my instinct to protect Daniel, so I can only guess at Rivka's feelings. After she has placed him in the correct position for the 'test,' I go and talk to him as well.

'Daniel,' I say, 'you must think of something else. You mustn't think of how much it hurts, alright? We are doing this to you because we love you. You must not cry. You must not, my darling. Think of a strong rock that will never break; think of something nice. Close your eyes. It *is* going to hurt, but you must not cry or we'll never get out of here.'

Daniel nods. I cannot imagine what is going on in his small mind, but he is showing a lot more composure than I am. Meanwhile, Rivka is signalling me to walk away. She does not want to drag this out, that much I can see. She wants them to throw the chairs and then stop. Finish.

Herzl is the first to throw a chair. He throws it timidly. I cannot even blink, because I am watching Daniel with my heart squeezed in between my clenched teeth. I squeeze Rivka's hand as the chair hits Daniel's arm. 'Don't cry,' I tell her, 'stay strong for him.' I see Daniel and he doesn't have even a single tear in his eye. I look at Rivka's face and it is frozen, looking ahead to a future moment of time when all this is over. It is the only way she can survive the torture of her son, even though her eyes are virtually popping out of her skull with anxiety.

Berl picks up a chair and throws it, this time more roughly to prove that he was right about their decision not to take our boy. It catches Daniel in the middle of his short body. He bends over the chair that's fallen to his feet, and clutches his stomach. I cannot bear to watch this; I cannot bear even to be a part of it. I am holding my stomach in the same place that Daniel is hurt. I check Rivka. Still she is not crying. When Daniel lifts his head again, there are no tears in his eyes.

Herzl goes up to Daniel, ruffles his hair and picks up a chair. He gives it to me to throw.

As I hold the chair, I am acutely aware of Daniel's size. I am also fully aware of Rivka watching me. If I throw the chair, I betray the trust my son has in me. I betray Daniel's father and his grandfather. Yet if I don't throw it, I show no loyalty to the people who are going to risk their lives with ours to escape the camp. This is such a dilemma, you have no idea.

Rivka whispers in my ear, 'Just throw it, you idiot. Don't drag it out.'

Her words are a blessing, because they break my deliberation. I throw the chair with just enough force to show that I mean it, and it hits Daniel on the head. He makes a face and I want to run to cuddle him better, but then he straightens and stands fully upright with his chin high, still undefeated. I turn my back to him, because I cannot stop the tears flooding from my eyes, even if the tiny boy before me can stand up fearless like a man.

Then Herzl hands Rivka a chair. I wipe my eyes and turn around, because we are willing Daniel not to cry and we need all of our powers at work to carry us through.

'Good boy,' Rivka calls, and throws the chair without any hesitation and with greater force than I had previously put to the job. She draws blood across his eyes. But still, it is only blood and no tears fall.

'Is that enough?' she asks, slowly, with only a hint of anger, and Berl says, 'Enough, please. Enough. He can come with us.'

Rivka and I run to Daniel and hold him between us. He is shaking as he tries to smile. 'I didn't cry, Papa,' he tells me. Rivka wipes his eyes with her skirt and kisses the bloody cut that she has made across his face. We are all shaking and talking fast. I feel like a hero and a traitor. Rivka tells me to dry my eyes, because it will make Daniel start crying. 'I'm not crying,' Daniel says. 'Look!' And he makes me look into his eyes, which are dirty and bloody and large and childlike.

One or two of the women come and pat Rivka and Daniel on the back, but the rest of the people in our shed reach for their blankets to set up for the night, hardly interested in our huge victory. We are the last to get into bed. That night my heart paces rapidly for an hour or so before I go to sleep with Daniel in my arms. It is a relief to hold him with such tenderness after everything he's been through. I have never held him so carefully before. I feel like covering him with kisses for being such a hero, but I do not want to wake him. He is an angel in my arms. He has saved us all.

CHAPTER 13

The tunnel is now ready to pass through. The lateral corridor has been dug and runs to the other side of the fence, except for a foot of earth that Herzl has supported with wood from the benches, to make certain that soldiers who walk over it do not fall through. He calculates that we can create an exit within ten minutes on the night of our escape.

Now that the whole affair is settled, I am thinking: we should go. Just get out of here as quickly as we can before this plan of ours is discovered. Before they find some earth in our pockets. Before we collapse from hunger and exhaustion.

There are many quiet discussions about procedure over the next few nights. 'As soon as we get to the other side, we split up,' Herzl instructs. 'Everyone in random directions to improve our chances.' Then there are discussions about what time of night we should make our escape. Too early and we could wake the soldiers. Too late and we do not leave long enough to make a good distance away from the camp.

We work out that it will take no more than forty minutes at the most to get everybody out. Nobody is to wait at the exit, even if they're waiting for family — they must take shelter behind some trees on the other side. Apart from that, what the outside world will hold for any of us is unknown. I am thinking: just worry about getting through the tunnel. Don't think too far ahead. God willing, there will be life beyond all of this.

The time is fixed for one o'clock in the morning, when the digging usually takes place and we know all the soldiers will be asleep. Everybody will be in their beds by nine, in case the Ukrainians come and check on us. There will be no lights, no conversations beyond that time. Any discussions about the plan have to be completed before we all go to sleep. Everything must seem normal. Nobody is allowed to suspect a thing.

Throughout the day of our escape I live every detail of my life in full consciousness. I record the faces of the guards and commit them to memory, in case this information is ever useful to us. I look at the other prisoners, too, because I want to remember them. I want to say goodbye to the carpenter, Itzick, who has taught me a few skills with wood, but I know that if I do I will arouse his curiosity, so I say nothing. Will he even survive till the end of the war? Believe me, it makes me sick to think about it.

That night I say goodbye to the old schoolmaster on the floor, but he says nothing. 'The war will end soon,' I tell him, as hopeless consolation, but he does not register. Perhaps he is making his own escape, the only way his failing body knows how.

Our escape takes place exactly as planned. We lie in our beds with our eyes open, not saying a word, in that shed that stinks of bitumen. Nobody comes to check on us, but even if they did, they wouldn't see anything out of the ordinary. None of us sleep that night, except Daniel. We just lie there, looking at each other — shapes in the darkness, waiting for Herzl to check the watch he's kept under his mattress.

At one o'clock everybody in the shed knows that the time has come for the escape, because Herzl rises and walks towards the tunnel without saying a word. We wake up Daniel, but remain lying down, in case anybody comes in, and we watch Herzl and Berl lift the planks covering the pit. Then Herzl climbs down into the hole, still in total silence. A few minutes later he passes some planks and board back through the hole, and then some handfuls of fallen dirt. That's all. He gestures for the rest of us to come through behind him, and he's gone. That's the last we ever see of him.

My ears are straining for any sound, any movement, any sign, but no noise follows; no shouts, no guns. Not one of us makes a single sound, listening in expectation, in hope, in fear. Still, no noise. All we need to do now is escape from here as quietly as Herzl has just done. One of us is already free, on the other side of the camp wall. This is what I am thinking as we wait our turn, knowing that anything could change in a flicker of an instant.

The man from Krakow lowers himself through the pit, and is followed by his wife, and then Berl, exactly as planned. After a dozen people have passed through, in absolute silence, it's finally our turn.

I go first, praying that there is still time for all of us to make this exit. I lower myself down into the bottom of the pit and move, crouching, along the lateral corridor, which is clad with wooden planks I helped saw only a few days earlier. I am praying to my Maker as I go through the hole in the ground, and as I pray I am acutely aware of Daniel's presence behind me. He follows every move I make; so perfect he is, without making a sound, let alone crying. Even his breathing is quieter than mine. Together we crawl along this short corridor, my heart beating so frantically I can feel it colliding with my ribs.

A few feet more and then I feel the air above my head, and you know, somehow it feels different from the air inside the camp. I touch the loose earth that Herzl has pulled down to make the opening and I reach upwards towards the rim of this pit, first with my fingers, before raising my head. I cannot describe that feeling of pulling myself out onto the other side. We are not so far from a small, roughly constructed observation tower, and I dare not even think about looking in that direction in case my curiosity awakens the guard. Instead I look straight ahead, where I see trees, thank God. There is absolutely nobody out on this free side, it appears, yet I feel as if someone, somewhere, is watching me and my instinct is to move away fast, but first I lie on the ground and reach down through the earth, with my arms outstretched, to help Daniel. His small hands grope for mine and I pull him up through the hole with all my strength, as quickly as possible. I can hear Rivka, following behind him. Another few minutes and her head appears, and I hold my breath, because I just can't believe that this is really happening, without anybody trying to stop us. I am thinking: Rivka, for God's sake, be quick. One breath too many and they could find us.

As soon as we're all out, I pick up Daniel and we run into the forest as fast as we can. We do not know where we're going, what direction we should follow, or what lies ahead. All we know is that we must stay awake and not stop until daybreak. Then, and only then, will we think about hiding some place. There is no time to feel pleased with ourselves about our successful escape, or marvel at the fact that we haven't woken any of the soldiers. There is no time to think about anything but putting as much distance as possible between the camp and us.

After running for about an hour, we hear them — the inevitable bullets, at a distance, and the howl of dogs. By this stage Daniel is asleep in my arms and without his conscious mind alert he feels heavier. I want to stop for just two minutes to recover from the ordeal, but Rivka doesn't let me. She picks up Daniel as if he's as light as a small bag of turnips and continues marching over the dark ground, using her spare hand to steady herself against the trees.

'Rivka, let me carry Daniel again, you must be exhausted,' I say, but Rivka does not allow me to help her. 'Why the hell are you talking about exhaustion?' she says. 'I can't believe it! Do you want to have us all killed?'

So we carry on walking, deeper into the forest, until the first light starts to lance its way through the highest birch leaves, piercing holes in my confidence even though the guns have silenced. I am starting to feel dizzy, but I don't want to stop to drink or eat, because I will only be reminded of how little we have and how long it must last. I don't want to tell Rivka that I'm too exhausted to go on, but I have to.

'Rivka,' I say. 'Stop. I've got to rest. You've got to rest, can't you see? We can't go on.'

How does she think we can continue like this? Whether Rivka is willing to accept it or not, we are completely worn out. So we agree to lie down for a few minutes, but even the wind that cries around the trees can't stop us from falling asleep. I close my eyes and I am unconscious within a few numb seconds. The camp, our escape, the cold — none of it can penetrate my skin. I sleep like a dead man until I am stunned out of my dreamless sleep by someone whispering into my ear.

It is Daniel saying, 'Where are we?'

For a few seconds I can hardly remember who we are, let alone where we are. Rivka is still fast asleep and snoring loudly, concussed almost with tiredness. She deserves her sleep more than anyone, but I know that we're too vulnerable lying here in broad daylight, so I touch her gently and she wakes up with a deep breath of panic.

'You should have woken me earlier,' she wails. 'Why didn't you wake me?'

She is desperately searching my face for answers, but I have none. What can I say? Please do not forget — we are human beings, even if the world is trying to force us to believe otherwise. Looking at Rivka's determined face, I can see that the time for being human has been postponed. Within seconds she is standing fully alert and helping Daniel to his feet. 'We shouldn't have gone to sleep,' she keeps saying. 'We could have gone much further by now if we hadn't slept.'

So we continue walking and eat a few stale pieces of bread that we've saved. Daniel is no longer asleep, so our burden is lighter now. We are walking ahead with no destination, just to make distance between ourselves and the prison guards. There is no doubt in my mind that the Ukrainian soldiers have already found some of us, and I try not to think about it, because when I do the sound of the crunching forest floor sets off these rapid heartbeats. I try not to think about what will happen even a few minutes into our future. Meanwhile, Rivka is talking and thinking through a survival strategy that will see us into the next day, before we collapse from hunger and exhaustion.

She is the first to notice a narrow forest road to one side of us. 'Let's go to the nearest village and find some food,' she says, with such confidence, you wouldn't believe it. What are we supposed to do, I am thinking. Just walk along the road as if we're on our way to Mass?

'And when we get to this village,' I say, 'who are we going to visit? Who is going to risk their life to give food to some escaped prisoners?'

It is obvious to me that her plan is naive. We cannot go walking into a village looking like this, asking for food. There would be too many questions. There are too many people in this country of ours who would turn in anybody suspicious. All they have to say is *Zydzi*, Jews, and we will be sitting once more on the skewer we have just jumped off.

'Then we must find people like the baker in the forest.'

'Do you want us to shout out his name? Maybe he will hear us and come to help! Think about it, Rivka. Please, just think about it.'

There is only one way forward I can think of and that is to pray. We are free, but we are not safe. The God who has brought us this far is still able to hear another request or two, surely? Is it too much to ask? I have never before had to pray for shelter or food, but now we are all by the side of the road, praying for these things. There are no *tefellins* to lay, no prayer shawls to wear, no candles to light, but we are praying, more desperately than we have ever prayed before. We are hidden from the road, hidden from the eyes of man, but not from the eyes of God, so I pray. I plead: God, help us now. Please God, we beg of you. It is not such a big request. Look at us! See where we are. Just take one look. Are we so undeserving?

There is nobody on this road through the forest, but the morning light filters through the leaves and branches above us, and I imagine that there is a presence that travels with us. As we walk, I think about the other people who escaped the camp last night and I wonder where they are right now. Maybe Herzl is nearby in the forest, or in some village by now? Maybe some of the people who pulled themselves out of the earth with us are already back in the camp, who knows? No doubt those who are still in the forest are facing the same stark reality that we are. No doubt they are looking for strangers who are prepared to give them food and shelter. Maybe some of them have already found someone to help them? Who knows what will happen next to any of us? Who can we trust? As I think about having to speak to a stranger I panic, imagining the blackmailers and collaborators out there, like crows. Yet I feel angry not with them, but with my father, would you believe, for filling my head with suspicion of fellow Poles. We have to trust someone; we have no choice. How can we condemn a whole nation because of a few unscrupulous people? All we need is the help of one person. One single person. We are in this together. This is how I reason with myself. Surely there is enough goodwill in this world of ours? Why this mistrust? If someone came to me desperate for food, I would give it, no matter what.

We are walking along as silently as possible when we notice an old peasant coming down this forest track on a horse and cart, and we hide behind a nearby oak. It is not I but Rivka who jumps out from behind the tree to approach him.

'Good sir,' she blurts out, before I can stop her, 'we are desperately hungry and we've run for our lives throughout the night.' I hold my breath and she continues, this wife of mine. 'We are looking for some partisans,' she says. Can you believe it? Listening to Rivka, all I can think is: don't say we, say I. Daniel is right next to me, we are hidden behind this tree, and I am making certain that neither of us moves an inch.

'We have escaped from a camp some way back.' She points behind her.

Please, Rivka, don't tell him any more. I am waiting for the worst, but what can he do, this old peasant? I am thinking: he has no weapons. There are no Germans nearby. He is old, what's more. Even I, in this condition, could fight him.

'Why do you want to go to the partisans?'

'Because we have helped them in the past.'

'I can take you to them,' he says slowly, and my first thought is that this man is going to take us straight to the Gestapo to receive his bag of sugar and five hundred *zlotys*.

I look closer at him and try to settle my panic. I am expecting cruelty, and yet this man does not look cruel. Do not carry your father's fears: this is what I am thinking. The man is safe. He has to be. Around his grey eyes are lines that have been carved out from a million smiles. He is probably a grandfather, I tell myself — someone who helped to fight in the last war. I am imagining as much of his history as possible, because I need to know something about him. In my mind I need to turn this stranger into a friend, so I tell myself that he is a good man. In peacetime I would have no trouble befriending him, but now, when I so badly need to trust this man, all I can hear is my father telling me: you should never judge people by their appearances. But what then can I judge them by, Papa? Their smell? For goodness sake! I say a quick prayer to relieve myself of the suspicions I've inherited, and then I move forward, just as the man is asking, 'How did you escape?'

'Good morning,' I call out, as we come out from our hiding place. I catch his eyes and see that this man is obviously a peasant — as we say in Poland, he has straw sticking out of his shoes. Daniel's presence is reassuring. I am a father, and with my son on my hip I share something in common with all people, be they Germans, Russians or Poles. I look innocent and harmless with Daniel, surely, even if I am jumping out from behind a tree.

He startles when he sees me. 'How many of you are there?' he asks a little crossly.

'Three of us, but around thirty others who escaped with us.'

'In this forest?'

'In every direction.'

'God bless them.'

His blessing reassures me. He is a God-fearing man, and if there is one God, we must share him.

'You're Jewish?' he asks.

Why, for goodness sake, does this question always leave me so uncomfortable?

'I'm a doctor, too,' I say, hoping to balance this certain disadvantage with my qualifications. Being a doctor has already saved my life once, this much I know. 'If you can take us to the partisans, I will work for them,' I say, knowing full well that there is no energy left in me to heal anyone, let alone myself.

So we are standing there, Rivka, Daniel and I, and this man, Mietek, who is driving the cart, tells us that he will have to blindfold us. 'I'm not going to hurt you, so stop looking so scared,' he says, as if that is going to stop our fears. But as the Jews say: he who rides on somebody's wagon, sings his song. So what can we do? Go back to the camp? This is the only human being who is likely to help us find food, and Rivka is willing to go ahead with this plan, so how can I object? She even helps Mietek cover up Daniel's eyes, and holds this old peasant's hand as he leads us through the forest.

With my face covered I feel completely vulnerable. What if he takes us somewhere to kill us? This is what I am thinking. But what for to kill us? We have no money. We have nothing.

Daniel trips over and I pull him up, even though I have very little sense of balance myself, and we walk some more, guessing at where the ground will rise and fall and scraping alongside the bark on the trees. It seems like a very long time before Mietek takes the rags off our eyes and tells us to continue walking.

Behind some trees we hear a child singing an old gypsy song that I learned years earlier myself. Her notes are quiet and sorrowful and her presence here seems unreal, because there is no sign of life. The bunkers of these partisans are almost invisible. All we can see through the leaves on the forest floor is smoke coming out from the ground in different places, so thin that it could be our imagination.

The girl sees us and runs towards the entrance of one of the bunkers, followed by the old man. I am thinking: Mietek didn't lie to us; there are partisans here, this much is true. Waiting at the entrance to this camp, I try to remember as much as possible about the baker who came to see me in the middle of the night with an aching jaw, in case this story will buy us some time here, or at least some food.

A man of about forty comes out, with his hand on a gun, and he's introduced to me as Commandant Jacek. This man has stubble on his square jaw and heavy-lidded eyes. If my reading of eyes alone is accurate, he is sympathetic. He is in the uniform of the Polish army — the same that I wore, until it became bloodstained and useless in Warsaw. I salute him and tell him about my unit that fell in September of last year. Already, we have shared ground: we have fought the same enemy, in the same clothes. 'But you have no weapons,' he says, and I feel helpless. How could we have weapons in the camp, I feel like saying, but I know it is hopeless. He is going to turn us away, because we have no weapons, no ammunition, no nothing; just a five-year-old child. We will be a useless burden on them, no doubt.

'I am a doctor,' I tell him, starting again with the most relevant fact. 'I may have no weapons, but I can make myself useful.' I pull down my shirt to show the scar in my shoulder, which is still red. 'I have sworn to defend my country and I was injured while fighting for Poland. I will lay down my life to get the Germans out.'

Rivka turns her head to look at me. She knows that we have been concerned only with the simple task of survival; fighting enemies has never come into it.

'We don't have any special arrangements for Jewish people,' Jacek tells me, and I am thinking: he's going to accept us if we can prove we need nothing from him.

'What do we need? A synagogue? All we want is to stay together,' I say.

'You can stay for a while, because you have to, but don't expect it to be any better than the camp you were in. We are living on the point of a needle here. It's not just the Jewish people who are suffering in Poland, you know.'

I am not about to try to defend my people. I do not want to compete in a battle over who has suffered the most. I've had enough of these squabbles, believe me, they are no use to anybody.

'You will find my wife Rivka and myself to be the most loyal Poles in your service,' I interrupt him. 'We will not require any special facilities, so don't worry.'

Jacek goes into the bunker and comes out again some time later with confirmation that we can stay, for a short time only. 'But if you can't fight you have to leave. And you,' he points at me, 'we have sick partisans who need immediate attention.' His hand is on the holster of his gun as he continues telling us our obligations. 'No walking in the forest alone. We had to shoot someone we didn't know earlier this morning. He could have been one of your people from the camp, who knows?'

Imagine how I feel hearing this? We are most definitely on the outside of their elite group, this much is certain, and if I understand anything it is this: we will have to work extremely hard to gain the trust of these people.

But we have been accepted for the moment, it seems, and we are shown into one of the underground bunkers, through the tiny entrance above the ground. There are about twenty bunks around the walls, but we're told they belong to the other partisans, so once more we'll be sleeping on the floor, this time on hay that looks much cleaner. Most importantly, though, we are out of sight, even though we have almost as little freedom as we had yesterday.

I look around this new refuge of ours, with its low ceilings, its wooden beams and walls that disappear into the darkness on every side. Only a few people are inside right now, and the fire has not been lit, but it feels remarkably warm. Whatever they say, this is comfort compared to what we have experienced in the prison camp.

'Do you feel safe?' I ask Rivka. 'Will you be alright staying here?'

'Yes, yes,' she says, impatient with me for even asking, and I feel like such an unworthy husband, forcing her and Daniel to sleep in a hole in the ground, like forest creatures. How different things would be if we were in Warsaw, and this occupation had never happened.

'I'm so sorry, Rivka,' I say. 'If there was anything I could do to change any of this, I would do it,' and I know as I say these words that if we're going to survive — if the Almighty who has brought us this far helps us get through all of this — Rivka will live like a queen when the war is over.

CHAPTER 14

So this commandant of the partisans, Jacek, returns to the bunker, holding his gun, and says he wants to take me to see the 'hospital'. Rivka is clearly not welcome, and I see her brow knot with concern as I turn and say goodbye.

Our walk to the hospital takes us through the thick forest, over trees that have fallen like Polish soldiers, and around thickets that form landmarks and signposts. All the while, Jacek tells me how he likes to spread out his fighters to improve their chances of survival should the Germans come into this part of the forest, and it is quite some distance before we arrive at the entrance of my place of 'work', marked by a large birch tree and a few old logs covered in moss and fungus.

Of course, I do not recognise this hospital when I see it, because there is nothing there. Only when Jacek starts fumbling around in some leaves do I see a small burrow-like entrance, big enough for a man to crouch down and climb through. I follow him down this hole and then we are in a dark, wooden-clad chamber which we can walk across in eight or nine strides. Lying in that semi-darkness on the floor are two unshaven, neglected young men. The only light is a dim lamp.

'Can you remove shrapnel?' Jacek asks me.

I look around the dark bunker for surgical supplies before I even consider an examination of the patients. There is nothing, of course, except a metal contraption with all these tubes, which I don't recognise from any surgery I've ever visited. 'What's this?' I ask, and Jacek smiles. 'That's for making the vodka. These boys get first shot,' he laughs. My face must be giving away my concerns, because Jacek adds, 'Look, if you really don't think it's possible to help us, then you may as well get out and go back to your camp.'

What can I say? 'No, of course I can help,' I state firmly, sensing that I may be as useless to the partisans as these wounded fighters — absolutely useless if we can't get our hands on some basic equipment. Yet when I ask Jacek about equipment he says, 'We don't have any, so you'll have to improvise. You're the doctor, not me,' and he leaves me in my new hospital to perform whatever miracles he commands.

Of course I try to be as professional as I can, considering the circumstances. I turn up the lamp and examine these two young men as thoroughly and gently as possible. First I take a look at the older of the two, Bogdan, who has shrapnel in his back and shoulder, some of it only under the surface of the skin, but mostly deep in the muscle tissue and, most worrying, near his spine. The younger boy, Filip, has shrapnel in his leg, his arm and also, unfortunately, in his eye. I lift the cloth that sits on top of this eye and can see that it has already formed an abscess that could affect the optic nerve and the brain. Immediately, I know that this patient needs his eye enucleated urgently if he is to survive, but how? I have never performed this type of surgery, only read about it in medical textbooks. Of course, if I tell this to the patient he will panic, and if I tell it to Jacek he will set us marching off into the forest.

'I will need to remove your eye,' I tell Filip cautiously, wondering how on earth I am going to do this operation.

The boy must be reading my mind, because he says, 'How are you going to remove it? With a spoon?'

We talk for some time and I explain the dangers involved in the surgery. He listens and then starts crying out loud and saying, 'Pull out your own stupid eye if you want one, I'm not giving you mine!'

I try to calm him down and keep explaining that there are worse things that can happen. 'Do you want a brain abscess?' I ask this new patient of mine. 'I will not be performing this surgery for the fun of it, believe me.'

Just then a boy, hardly six years older than Daniel, comes down into the bunker with some potatoes for these sick partisans. He tells me to follow him back to the base camp, which is fortunate, because I would never have found the way back on my own. When I arrive there, Rivka and Daniel are still sitting in the bunker, just as I left them, grateful to have this new kind of prison under the ground.

We are there together for just a while before Jacek comes down and tells me, 'We'll go to the local doctor this afternoon. What should we bring back?'

Is he going to ask politely for some free provisions, I'm thinking. Hardly. There is no doubt in my mind that Jacek is going to steal anything I order, so I try to keep it simple. Some iodine for antiseptic, some dressings, scalpels, artery forceps, a retractor, needles and glass syringes, some catgut for sutures, a lamp, a few ampoules of morphine, some cocaine distillation for the eye, and a few other necessaries. Of course, I would like to ask for a book on some of these procedures, but I am not willing to give away my inexperience. I hand over this 'shopping list' as confidently as I can, slightly guilty that we'll be stealing from another doctor who's probably struggling to keep up with the violent demands of this war. What to do? We have sick people here, too and there is no way we can risk surgery without these supplies.

It is surprising how quickly these men come back with the surgical equipment. The same afternoon, in fact, just as if they had indeed been shopping. Of course I don't ask whether or not they paid for these things, but when I ask to see the 'purchases' Jacek says, 'Look at them down at the hospital bunker. You'll be operating there in half an hour.'

So he commands me, just like that, to go and perform surgery down in that pit, and you can imagine the tension I am feeling.

'I need an assistant,' I tell him, and Rivka offers her services, hoping that this will give us an opportunity to stay together. What about Daniel, I am thinking. I know you can handle anything, Rivka, but this will not be a pretty sight for him.

Jacek offers to come and be my anaesthetist, and I have to say I am grateful, because I know his nerves are made of something far stronger than steel, and I know, too, that the patients will respond to his command. So we go back to the hospital and this commandant of ours takes full control, as if this were a military exercise, an operation of attack.

'Filip, you close that one eye of yours, boy, and drink some vodka. We want you out by the time we finish off Bogdan,' he orders. And so we begin.

Now, I have often heard the expression that in an emergency the wise doctor takes his own pulse. This day I have every reason to check my own pulse, because I am operating in the dark, quite literally. No books for guidance, hardly enough light, and a maniac for an anaesthetist who combines vodka with morphine for double the effect. However, I am grateful for one thing, and that is the resilience of this commandant who assists me. We remove the shrapnel from near Bogdan's spine, which I was concerned about, then from his back and shoulders, and I can tell that Jacek is impressed. Of course he knows nothing about surgery, but he congratulates me on my skill nonetheless.

The next surgery we perform is on the younger boy, Filip. 'Let's do it quickly,' Jacek says, and Filip, poor fellow, is absolutely silent in the face of Jacek as he prepares himself for the morphine. When the patient is out, I place the cocaine distillation into the damaged eye, prepare the area properly, and scoop the eye out of its socket as swiftly as I can, without dwelling too much on its gelatinous consistency.

The eye lies in a bowl on the floor of the bunker and I am trying to breathe normally as I pack the patient's orbit with antiseptic and gauze, before placing a head bandage around the eye cavity. 'He can take this off in three days,' I say, as confidently as I can. 'Then the cavity will fill up with granulation tissue in the hollow. He'll be alright,' I say, trying to convince myself.

Jacek congratulates me once more. 'He's got one good eye, and he's young,' he says, picking up the bowl. He prods the removed eye and flops it over to see the piece of shrapnel that has cuts its way through the iris. 'You're not so bad at this work, Benjamin,' he says, totally unperturbed, as if he's assisted surgeons all through his life. Then, like a true commandant, he orders me to go and bury the eye outside the bunker before my patient wakes up and gets a chance to look at it himself.

My hospital bunker remains empty for a few days, but I am sent to sit there and 'work' even so. Really, the only work to be done is to check how the vodka is going, but this is not my line of experience, so I sometimes go for short walks in the forest instead, to get some air and look for bushes that would be good for hiding in, because I know this much: if the soldiers come for me again, I don't want them to find me trapped under the ground.

Just when I am getting used to this 'freedom', Jacek comes into the hospital bunker with two other men, carrying Tomasz, his second-in-command. At first I am grateful to have something to do, but this changes once I notice that Tomasz smells of vomit and is rolling around in severe agony as the men lie him down on some high planks I've constructed for examination. He looks dreadful, really — 'like he's just been pulled off the cross', as the Polish say. I feel his abdomen, which has a board-like rigidity, and ask him to speak to me, but he is quite delirious, this man, moaning through all of this, quite unable to speak properly. These symptoms are distressing and my first suspicion is that Tomasz is suffering from peritonitis, caused by a sudden rupture to the appendix. We are in for big trouble now, there is no doubt about it, because if this is the case his chances are not good. Not good at all.

While I'm making my diagnosis Jacek keeps telling me, 'We've got to get him back on his feet as quickly as possible,' and I am thinking: if only this hadn't happened to Tomasz. Any other partisan, but not him. Meanwhile, Jacek says to this semi-delirious comrade of his: 'Don't worry, if he cares for his own life we'll have you back in working order in no time at all.' You can imagine how I am feeling, no?

So we put this poor man out, and I am thinking: we've got such little hope, really, but this has to work. Dear Lord, make it work. After a few seconds of hesitation I open the abdomen at the McBurney point, just as I learned, and see, as I suspected, a necrotic appendix with large quantities of free pus surrounding it. I clean it up as best as I can, sucking out the pus with a straw I make from paper, would you believe. Then I pack the wound with swabs to absorb the rest of the pus and when it looks clear I remove the stump of the appendix. All through this I am acutely aware of Jacek, and I am thinking: if only I hadn't trained him up as my anaesthetist. Benjamin, if anything goes wrong now you must let him know why. 'This is not a good sign,' I keep saying. 'There is so much pus, can you see?'

When I start putting the purse-string sutures into the friable tissue of the caecum I ask Jacek to take a good look, explaining to him every step of this procedure. Then, as I tighten the knot, the stitches start to pull out of the repair and I have this sinking feeling that we are all doomed now. Why did I add to this poor man's suffering?

'Can you see this?' I ask Jacek, pointing to the stitches. 'I have to tell you now that the outlook is grim and I don't hold out much hope. We can only do our best and make sure the patient is comfortable.'

Then this commandant of ours starts yelling at me that Tomasz is not just a patient, but our best fighter and the person most responsible for making sure that I'm fed. He watches me finish off the surgery, threatening me the whole time, then leaves, saying that I shouldn't bother coming back to the base camp if I don't arrive with good news.

Can you believe it? What hope do I have, really? Somewhere I am thinking: this is what I deserve. This was my fault. Even though I know that I am not the person who gives life or takes it, I feel so responsible, so guilty — it's horrible.

I cannot tell you what it feels like to sit in virtual darkness next to a man who is struggling to die. There is nothing I can do after I have administered more morphine, except place small quantities of water into this poor man's mouth and sit by his side, listening to him groan. During those hours I decide that if I survive this experience I am never going to work as a doctor again, because I could not bear to do another operation like the last few I've done. I decide, there and then, that it would be a crime for me to continue in this profession, because I have failed as a doctor. I try to forget about the surgery I have just performed, but the image of the stitches falling out keeps coming back to me and I feel helpless, knowing there is nothing I can do to change what has happened. Nothing I can do but wait. So I stay exactly where I am, underground, and nobody comes to see me with food. I stay there the whole night and by the morning Tomasz has died.

I walk back to our bunker, carrying the burden of this news in my stiff shoulders. The first person I tell is Rivka, who immediately starts looking around the bunker frantically. I ask her what she is doing and she says. 'We've got to leave here, Benjamin, can't you see? The minute Daniel comes back, we've got to be ready to go.' She looks under some of the other bedcovers for things she can steal, tossing back her long wavy hair defiantly. 'You know what they're going to say, don't you? They're going to say that it was the Jew who killed Tomasz.'

I am thinking: thank you for telling me this, Rivka, this is just what I want to hear. This is what you'd call consolation, no? I tell her to calm down, but she takes no notice of anything I say and I feel as if she's angry with *me* for what's happened.

I sit her down and say 'You know that it wasn't my fault, don't you? Please believe me, Rivka, I did not kill Tomasz, and if you don't believe me, who will?' But Rivka is beyond hysterical and I know then that I will have to continue carrying this burden alone, because there isn't a human being in sight who will have any sympathy for me whatsoever. All Rivka wants is to leave, without thinking through any of the problems we will cause for ourselves by taking such action.

'We have to find a safe home away from these people,' she keeps shouting, but who am I, the good Lord, that I can conjure one up for her?

CHAPTER 15

We are now living in a palace by any standards, Polish or otherwise, and paying so little for the privilege of it. We even have a pet parrot, Tota, which we bought from New Market for Daniel. In the past few months, Daniel and Ezekiel have become the very best of friends. Like the Poles say, they are such good friends they could steal horses together.

Daniel tries to impress his new friend with his outrageous behaviour that he learnt from the partisans, and Zek impresses Daniel with his cheeky command of all the servants, his understanding of the language, the life here, everything. They have a beautiful friendship and that makes me happy, because it's helping Daniel to settle down in Calcutta and he's learning to speak good English, Hindi and bits of Bengali.

Whenever Daniel wants to play with Zek he starts making demands on all of us, just as he has seen Zek do with his *ayah*.

He commands Mary to take him to visit Zek in Free School Lane, and then off he goes to make mischief there. At our home they spend hours teaching Tota to fly, which is a little unfair because her wings have been clipped. However, they also teach her how to speak, with great success. Now she can say, 'Hello, I'm Tota', and 'The Germans are coming', as well as, 'Daniel is a good boy'. Whenever Tota says anything, the boys fall about laughing; then Tota laughs and the boys start laughing all over again. Between the three of them they have a fantastic circus.

Daniel is getting spoilt; there is no doubt about it. Mary takes him hot meals in a tower of little bowls every lunchtime at St Xavier's. Like all the other servants who attend the boys at school, she lays the table for him, fills up his water glass, puts on his napkin and watches him eat. After his food, Daniel runs off to play with Ezekiel, leaving poor Mary to clean up and bring the tiffin carrier home.

Rivka tries to teach Daniel to fold up his clothes and dry himself after his bath, but Mary always does these things for him so it's useless trying to retrain him, really. If he is going to stay here in India, let him become like the other Indian boys — little maharajas that they are from the day they learn to speak their first instructions.

One day Daniel and Zek are particularly naughty. They go into the kitchen and trouble Tariq, making him give them lumps of dough to play with and then throwing around the flour. Tariq finally sends them out of the kitchen so that he can get on with cooking the evening meal, and what do our boys do? They go and swing on Mary's sari instead, until it is torn, and Mary starts crying. Then, of all the stupid things, Tota starts chirping, 'Daniel is a good boy!'

'Tell that parrot to shut up!' I yell.

'No, you shut up,' Daniel screams.

What rudeness! Just hearing him makes me regret ever having landed in India. We have to get rid of all our servants immediately, or at least get Daniel to start wiping his own face after his meals! We must do something to stop him from becoming such a spoilt brat.

'Give him a slap,' Rivka instructs me.

'No, don't hurt him,' Ezekiel says, but I am too furious. I pull Daniel by his shirt and raise my hand. Yes, I raise my hand for the first time, but it doesn't come down on him.

'What are you waiting for?' Rivka asks me, and seeing my hand immobilised in mid-air she takes Daniel from me and smacks him once, twice, three times. Daniel does not cry, and I can't help but remember why.

'Rivka, STOP IT!' I call out, and she stops, but not without giving me an angry look for intervening. 'Now say sorry to your father!' she orders.

Daniel looks at me from under his curls and says in the sweetest possible voice, 'Sorry, Papa,' and everything is forgiven. How could an angel be anything but an angel? How could such a *bubee*, such a darling, have a wicked thought in the world? This is what I am thinking.

'You must remember what he's been through,' I tell Rivka later. 'It's not fair to hurt him. He's such a good boy.'

'Who told you to say that? The parrot?' she says, and we both end up laughing about our naughty boy. He will grow out of it, I know, and he'll become the most charming young man imaginable. He has it in him, so I don't worry about Daniel. 'He's just a bit unsettled at the moment,' I tell Rivka. 'We're all trying to adjust. We all have our difficulties.' The main thing is that we continue to have faith in him, just as we always have.

Throughout our early adjustment period, Farha continues to come around to check up on the servants to make sure 'they are not misbehaving'. For me, it's strange to think of them misbehaving — they are, after all, adults. Then, just when we feel that Farha is finally satisfied with the number of servants we have, she suggests that we get a *mali*.

'What's that?' I ask, wondering what other tasks she can imagine need doing in this house where we are literally tripping over all the servants.

'A gardener. You could have such a lovely garden out the back here.'

I start to laugh, but take the smile off my face as soon as I see that Farha is serious, looking back at me with her concerned light brown eyes. Only a woman — a Calcutta-born woman — could think of this. It's true, the garden is just flat dry earth surrounded with brick walls, but we haven't got to the stage yet where we are worrying about looking good. We haven't even got used to the idea of having a home, for goodness sake.

'We'll manage,' I tell her, but does she listen? No. Somebody comes round a few days later, and he's badly in need of work, so I tell him he can plant some things and try to keep them alive if this is what he wants to do. What will it cost us, really? I am earning so much more than he is. What's the difficulty in sharing some of it?

To start off our garden Farha gives us a myrtle plant. 'Let the servants cut sprigs from this and you can give blessings for the fragrance on the Sabbath.' Very nice, I am thinking. All very nice. But is this the end of it? No, certainly not!

A few days later a *dhobi* arrives, who wants to clean our clothes for us. Mary is delighted and says to me, 'Madam Rivka and Madam Ewa won't have to be cleaning the clothes themselves.' So what are they going to be doing? This is what I'm thinking, while Mary continues with her convincing argument. 'Everybody has a *dhobi*,' she says.

'We are becoming like everybody,' Rivka laughs.

'That's not so bad.' This much I can recognise. Isn't it better to fit in?

So we hire the *dhobi* to come twice a week to hand-wash and wring our clothes in the back bathroom. Sometimes he takes the clothes away to clean them, and we see all our laundry hanging out on the streets not far from our home in Rowland Road!

Nowadays we have so many people working for us, Mary has become their supervisor, and Farha is quite right: she has proved herself invaluable as our translator and adviser. She is so much more than just an *ayah* for Daniel.

Farha tells me it takes a lot of energy to run a household, even with this much help. Can you believe it? Then there's all the shopping. Not just for food, but for everything. For some reason my presence is always required for all the major shopping trips, so I have to leave my work at Bose Paper Mills and get from China Bazaar to New Market before everybody closes down for the day.

When Rivka wants me to come shopping to choose a new cane sofa, or bed linen, or the rugs that they sell here, she always insists Ewa comes along as well. There is nothing that will separate the two of them, so I have to bring the two compartments of my life together at all times. I feel so sorry for Ewa, but I cannot explain these things to Rivka. Why on earth should Ewa choose the bed linen that we will sleep on? But Rivka says, 'We mustn't make Ewa feel left out,' so what can I do? Mostly I just let the women make their decisions, and I agree with whatever they choose. Whatever makes them happy is fine. I do worry, though, about Ewa's happiness. She talks so much less than she used to, and when I come home from work she is often in her room alone, learning her English, trying to stay out of the way. Ewa has always been so good at speaking through her feelings, but nowadays she talks very little about the things that matter to her. It's so hard to know what's going on in her heart and mind, really.

One day, when Rivka is out with Farha, I ask Ewa if she is alright living here in Calcutta. 'Are you happy here?' I ask, and as soon as these words pass my lips I feel as if I am putting pressure on her to feel a certain way. How can we expect happiness from anybody? What right do I have to ask?

'I don't want to get in your way,' she tells me, without answering my question, and I have to remind her that nobody can get in anybody else's way in such an enormous house.

'Do you ever think about how things were in Warsaw?' I ask.

'I think about Warsaw all the time,' she says.

'Do you ever think about our holidays together as children?'

'How can I think of holidays, Benjamin?' She sounds a little cross, but I know by looking at her face that the memories are still there. I see it in the flinching of her eyes, and the water that's collecting in them now. I should stop here, this much I know, but I don't.

'How do you feel about Rivka?' Really, there is no stopping me now. 'Have you forgiven me for marrying her ... for breaking my promises to you?'

Ewa is silent, so I continue. 'Ewa, I need to be able to talk about these things with you, because it feels so strange if we don't speak. If we pretend that we never had any expectations ...' The water in her eyes is forming droplets now, and falling down her cheeks. 'I know that this is difficult for you, but we need to talk. I need to know. Are you angry with me for marrying Rivka?'

She is too choked to reply at first, and then she tells me, 'No. How could I be angry? You did nothing wrong.'

'But it wasn't right by you.'

'She's just lucky. What can I say?'

'I don't think that Rivka would ever say she was lucky. I don't think I would ever consider myself lucky, either.'

'Then we've all lost,' Ewa says, wiping the tears from her eyes and trying to smile.

I take her hand and kiss her cheek, and a feeling of closeness comes back. Ewa feels so familiar, yet so far away, so distant.

'None of us has lost,' I say. 'You'll find someone else — much better than me — and you'll be happy that things turned out this way.'

Her smile goes in a blink, and again she is crying.

At this moment Rivka walks in. She takes one look at Ewa and says, 'What have you been saying, Benjamin? Why on earth are you upsetting Ewa?'

'He wasn't upsetting me. I was already upset,' Ewa says, and Rivka glares at me as she goes and puts her arms around her friend. From behind Rivka's arm, Ewa smiles at me again, and even though her face is wet with tears, I allow myself to believe that she is happy living here with us.

After this, Rivka says to me all too often, 'I hope you're being nice to Ewa; she is such a good person, you know.' Of course I know! Of course I'm nice to her! I'm doing everything I can to make sure that everybody feels comfortable in this house where we're living, all of us together. But Rivka keeps saying, 'She's not comfortable about staying with us. Are you sure you haven't said anything to her, Benjamin?'

How can I tell Rivka that under no circumstances on God's earth would I ever ask Ewa to leave? How can I tell Rivka that Ewa stole my heart in a way that nobody has ever done either before or since? How can I tell Rivka that sometimes I find it hard to share a house with a woman I still love? But would I ever even hint that Ewa should leave? No, how could I? With all this going on, I am thinking: maybe I should move out of this house. Rivka and Ewa are friends; maybe I am the one getting in the way.

Now, we have everything. Yes, everything we could possibly want and more, but it doesn't make our lives uncomplicated. Whenever I start worrying about Ewa and Rivka and our living situation, I remind myself of our circumstances back in Poland, and I cannot help feeling that the good fortune we enjoy here is at the expense of the family and friends we left behind. Really, we are *so* lucky, and we should be doing something to share this luck. I keep returning to this one thought: how can we help the people back home? How can we get more Jews out to India? I think so often about this, but I wonder — is it still possible to cross the borders? Will some of the guards still turn a blind eye when a Pole presents a train ticket paid for in rubles? Do the refugee committees still operate in Japan?

One night I cannot sleep because of these thoughts; I keep remembering the different people we've left behind, and they haunt me. Rivka is fast asleep under our mosquito net and a fan spins its low hum through the air, but I cannot even close my eyes, so I get up and write a letter to an old friend from university. I write to patients in Piaski, including the postman and one of the schoolmasters. I describe every single detail of our journey overland and by sea to India. I tell them about our new home here, the Jewish community, and Daniel's new friend Ezekiel. I even tell them about Tota, our parrot.

I send all of these letters off personally at the post office and then we wait for several weeks, checking the mail every day. Daniel is already halfway through the year at St Xavier's when the letter that I sent to my university friend, Samuel, is finally returned to us. On the envelope in neat Polish handwriting are written the words: no longer living at this residence. How can that be? Samuel's family have lived in the same building for generations. Who could be there now, for goodness sake? Billeted guests?

'There's no point in even sending letters,' Ewa says one day when we're all having tea. Sitting enjoying the north-westerly winds on our verandah in Calcutta, watching our garden bloom with flowers we have planted I cannot help but feel the desperation of my people back home, still facing the persecution and fear that we knew only too well before we escaped from Poland. I feel helpless and even guilty to be enjoying the luxuries we now enjoy, when the people we grew up with hardly have enough to eat. I spread jam on my toast and I remember how the partisans craved bread. I watch the *dhobi* whisk away our clothes to be washed and I remember the fear we felt going down to the river to wash our own clothes at night-time in the forest. I lie down on my soft bed and remember the itchy straw I slept on in the prison camp. I feel so incredibly guilty, and yet I know that going back will not solve the problems of a single person in the world. There is no doubt about it: we should stay where we have a home, here in Calcutta.

'Do you feel as if Calcutta is your home?' I ask Rivka, soon after that letter to Samuel comes back.

'Yes,' she says, and looks at me with surprise at her own answer.

There is nothing we can give back to the people who helped us. Being here, having a home, is like having a debt, and I know that if I don't give something back to somebody we will be laughing in the face of our Maker. There is only one way to give thanks and it is in offering our services to God; allowing the Almighty to redistribute whatever we can give of ourselves.

'If we can't help people in Poland,' I say to Rivka, 'let us at least do something for the people of Calcutta.'

'To the best of our abilities,' Rivka says, and when she talks about abilities, I am forced to think of my training as a doctor. Nayar Babu is right: I should practise medicine again. Regain my confidence, forget about my earlier experiences, forget about my promise to never practise again, and start having some faith in myself, in God, and in our future. No matter how much we have suffered, we are lucky and must give what we can of ourselves. Whatever we do, though, we must do soon. Time is running out, it seems, to help this world of ours.

CHAPTER 16

It is not Nayar Babu, but Mary, our maidservant, who propels forward this idea I've been having of a free clinic on our back verandah — only in the evenings, of course, because I have a job, which must come first.

She tells me one day, '*Saab*, there is one Hindu man who is very much wanting to help you in the evenings. He is offering his services to the Sisters, and he is a surgeon.'

I look at Mary and congratulate myself on taking Farha's advice and employing her. She is worth her weight in gold. How strange that the One God is sending me, a redundant Jewish doctor, a Hindu surgeon via the blessed Catholic nuns! How this God strides through the various religions of man in order to operate in this little world of ours.

We meet this man, Doctor Mitra, one evening when he comes around to look at our house. He is a short man in his late thirties, with spectacles that magnify his eyes, making them the focal point of his entire body. He wears the traditional *dhoti*, clutches a brown leather case and shakes our hands vigorously.

'Wah! What a beautiful place to set up a surgery!' he says when he sees our back verandah, ignoring the peeling paint and looking only at our small frangipani shrubs which hope one day to grow. I offer him a chair and Mary goes to bring some *nimboo pani*. I ask him about the sort of clinic he hopes to set up.

'To start with, just a charitable surgery. I hope that we are under the same understanding that we do not charge the people who come to see us in this evening clinic?'

I look around and wonder who would possibly want to pay to come and see us on the back step of our house, out in the open air. 'Of course there will be no payment,' I assure him, and then I start to ask him the many questions I have about tropical medicine, including Nayar Babu's amoebas. I ask him about the disease profiles I can expect to see in Calcutta, and how to differentiate between the different types of fever. We talk about malaria, cholera, typhoid, diphtheria, tuberculosis and polio.

'Very serious problems,' he keeps saying, 'very serious problems.' And then his serious side gives way to a special Bengali glee as he says, 'In Calcutta when we tell our patients "one at a time", we're always referring to their illnesses, not the queues!'

He is laughing, this odd character who has just come into our lives, and I like him. His magnified eyes make him look like a wise owl, and I know I can learn a lot from this Doctor Mitra, because he is so gentle and open-hearted — a real *mensch*, as we say — an honourable, decent human being.

'Everybody in my house will be able to help us,' I tell him. 'My wife's father was a doctor, so she is used to having these things going on in her home.'

Rivka smiles at Ewa and the two of them look like they have accomplished a secret plan as Doctor Mitra and I discuss which nights we will start our free clinic, here on the back verandah.

We've only been in Calcutta a few months before the clinic is ready to start. Just as we make these preparations, and it seems that we made the right decision to stay, we receive the worst news imaginable.

The air is cooler, and on this day I leave Bose Paper Mills early and pick Daniel up from St Xavier's. We take a walk near the Victoria Memorial, a white marble building in the centre of a huge park, near an ugly statue of Queen Victoria. I've just bought Daniel an ice candy and we're walking past a Bengali family — a few boys in school uniform and girls, too, with their pink puff-sleeved dresses.

Then the father of these children turns to me and says, 'Are you from England?'

I say, 'No. Why do you ask?'

He gives me the news, straight out, just like that. 'Did you know that Singapore has just fallen?'

I cannot describe the feeling of hearing this. How could it be true? How could the British lose such a stronghold? How could the Japanese have beaten them and driven them out?

I tell this man, 'It's not possible.' And he says, 'Listen to the radio. Wait until the newspapers arrive. I'm telling you, Singapore has fallen.'

But what will happen to Poland if the British are no longer able to fight this war? What will happen if the Japanese take hold and start bombing us here in Calcutta? What will become of the wonderful Jewish people who looked after us in Japan? All these questions race at me from all different directions and I try not to let anything show, because I don't want to worry Daniel. Instead I change the subject, turning to this stranger and asking, 'Do you really want the British to leave India? Who will protect this country once they've gone?'

This man shrugs his shoulders and says in his soft Bengali voice, 'It's better they leave. Then the Japanese won't be bombing us. We're not responsible for any of the mischief in the world.'

I look at the aeroplanes that peek out of their hangars along Red Road, which runs through Victoria Maidan, and I wonder how long it will be before these planes will have to protect Calcutta. I am thinking: the war has followed us to the ends of the earth. Why is this happening to us all over again? Is there nowhere in this world that is safe?

Daniel isn't playing with any of the other children, which is unusual. Instead he is looking up at me with his concerned eyes, listening to adults talking of fighting once more. I tell him, 'Don't worry, darling, we don't have to run away. Nothing bad will happen here. We'll be safe. Look, there's a nice *tonga*. Let's take a ride around the park before going home.'

That night we three adults in Rowland Road hear the news confirmed on the radio. Ewa says, 'Maybe I should go to Jerusalem with Mosze and Lewek when the *Asama Maru* is fixed.' And I tell her, 'Do you think there's going to be any less fighting there, with the British controlling Palestine? Wherever we go there'll be fighting, no? The minute we're born we risk being killed.'

'Maybe we should leave India,' Rivka says, after the broadcast.

'I am not leaving,' I tell them. 'I'm going to start our clinic in the house, just as we all decided. How long can we carry on changing our plans, running for fear of our lives?'

I look at their distraught faces and I realise that I cannot make plans for all of us. If they want to go, then we'll all have to go. 'We'll leave as soon as they start targeting us here in Calcutta, alright? We'll go the minute the first bomb falls.'

CHAPTER 17

The summer comes, and still no bombs have fallen on Calcutta, but the people in my life continue talking about the possibility of elsewhere. For me, the only thing that would make me leave now is the weather. Really, it can be unbearable under this sun, with nothing but a solar topee for protection. As the heat intensifies further it feels as if the *dybbuks* are boiling their cauldrons under the streets of Calcutta. Outside, the crows squawk slower and more decadently, and the lizards grip the walls, immobilised by sloth as they observe us poor suffering humans who share their homes. I am thinking so often nowadays: is the heat this bad in Palestine? Maybe we should try to go there, after all? And I often wonder how the people on the streets manage to survive without fans. I ask Farha if Calcutta is always this bad and she says, 'Yes, always.' Then she adds, 'The summer would be tolerable this year if the mangoes hadn't failed as well.'

It is the height of summer the day we go to the Kidderpore Docks to say goodbye to Lewek, Mosze and a few other friends who are leaving for Palestine on the repaired *Asama Maru*, and in spite of the heat, we all know in our hearts that we have found something of a home here in Calcutta, and it is too precious to risk on another venture into the unknown.

Rivka doesn't want to go with us to the docks and I don't think it's just the heat. The truth is, she doesn't like to say goodbye — not to anybody. So just the two of us, Ewa and I, go down to the tram stop, where a Bengali gentleman passes her a newspaper to use as a fan. When the tram arrives I don't sit down next to any of the other passengers, because I don't want to add somebody else's body heat to my own. Really, this dry heat is so unbearable I find myself wondering again whether we should be getting on this boat, too, along with Lewek and Mosze.

Just as I am thinking this, the sky explodes and, would you believe it, the monsoons begin. These are not raindrops like we know in Poland. They are the size of cups, and warm, too — rain that no drizzle in Poland could ever match. How the sky collapses! The Indians on the tram cheer and congratulate each other as if they were the ones to organise the downpour, and outside on the streets near the market we see children dancing in the rain.

'Let's get off here and buy some gifts before going to the boat,' Ewa says, and so we get off to feel some of this warm rain on our skin.

No sooner are we off the tram than the hawkers and coolies run up and start to tap Ewa on the shoulder with their wet fingers.

She takes my arm and walks faster through the rain. We have learnt a few words of Hindi from Farha to get rid of them, but neither of us can use these words with the same effect she does. So the coolies continue following us as we take shelter in the meat section of New Market. We hold our noses as we pass the chickens that hang slaughtered in rows, with flies instead of feathers. We walk past the slabs of randomly scattered animal parts on the tables which create an unholy stench in this heat.

Next we walk past the fresh-food sellers — all men squatting down in front of their fans of fruit and vegetables, with the odd light bulb hanging above from a bundle of loose wires. They shout their prices loudly and beckon us over as if we're old friends. How could we refuse them? Ewa buys a few pieces of fruit which Farha would call 'donkey mangoes', as well as some other delights like papaya which we had never even tried before we arrived in the East. Then we go through the main market, past the shops selling clothes, wigs, shoes, fabrics, ivory, jewellery, silks, toys, kitchenware, flowers, perfumes and handbags, to get to Nahoum's, the Jewish pastry shop which has become our favourite place in the whole of Calcutta.

Nahoum, the owner, sits at a desk in one corner, writing out receipts and making sure all of his customers are happy. 'Are your friends leaving today?' he asks. He knows everything there is to know about the Jewish community here in Calcutta. He knows who's a gossip and who's to be trusted, who is generous and who is miserly, which family goes to which of the two battling synagogues, and which families don't go to any synagogue at all. He knows who does well in business and who doesn't, who eats kosher food and who doesn't, and he knows that today the *Asama Maru* sets sail again to Palestine, having finally been repaired at a workshop nearby.

'Not so many of them are going,' I reply. 'We've decided to stay.'

Nahoum congratulates us on our decision and tells us about the shipmates we have lost touch with. 'Those two tall men — they went to Bombay,' he says. 'And do you know, some other Poles have just arrived there who escaped your country and came travelling by raft down the Tigris!' As he tells us these facts I marvel at how this man is able to know so much. Sitting at his desk here in this shop in New Market, he is at the very crossroads of Jewish life in India, exchanging information as fluidly as money.

So he tells us all the news and we buy a bagful of pastries to give to our friends who are leaving, and receive another two bags for free from Nahoum. 'My choice is better than yours, actually,' he tells us confidently. 'These *namkeens* will last long enough for them to eat in the Holy Land!'

Taking the extra gifts I am moved, and I know that our friends on the ship will be, too. They will take the taste of India's hospitality away with them, along with their memories.

Outside the market the rain is still pouring and the streets have turned to swimming pools. As we wait for our bus, Ewa's attention goes to the women. She is watching how they pull up their saris to save them from the floods at their feet; how they dodge the floating vegetables that have escaped their baskets. And while she is looking at them, I am watching her, soaked through in the rain.

'If this is what it's going to be like every summer, maybe we should get on the ship with the others!' she laughs. 'How about it, Benjamin? We'll jump on the ship in the clothes we're wearing!'

I know that she doesn't mean it, but I think of Daniel once more, and Rivka, my wife, who doesn't like to say goodbye.

'Could you really start again, Ewa?' I ask. 'Without knowing anybody?'

'No, of course not. I would rather be with people I know,' she tells me. Then she adds quietly, 'I want to stay with you, Benjamin. If I got back on that ship it could just as easily be bombed, and then we'd all die anyway.'

'There could be bombs here, too. Whatever time God has planned for us to go, we will go, be it on the *Asama Maru* or here in the monsoons of Calcutta.' This is all I can say.

We get off the bus at the Writers' Building, which is full of clerks creating records, files and other such bureaucracy, together with reports on the natives and their agitation for Independence. Ewa wants to walk from here to the docks and enjoy the rain. She slips her hand into mine as if we were teenagers again, and once more I think about Rivka, at home. I remind myself that Ewa is my childhood friend, and a sister to me. It is a practised thought. My memory is not so easily fooled, but it plays along, because it needs this kind of discipline to stop my imagination from taking the reins.

'I might have to start a life again,' she says. 'You have your life here, with Rivka and Daniel. How can I ever be a part of that?'

'How can you say that? We have survived this far because we've stayed together. We can't separate now.'

How can Ewa be thinking of leaving, just like that? Separation is so final, yet I know that she is right — eventually she will have to find someone and live elsewhere. Surely she deserves more than a family of refugees as her life-support system?

As we walk past the high courts we see the judges in their silly wigs and Ewa laughs like a child. Really, if I think of her as a child, just a few years older than Daniel, then I feel as if I have the most appropriate relationship possible with her, but it is hard to remember to do this, because every bit of her is a woman. She looks as elegant as the Indian ladies in their beautiful saris.

We walk through the Eden Gardens, taking our time to get to the docks so we can enjoy the lush monsoon air. Believe me, I have never smelt earth so sweet and fertile as the Calcutta soil drenched by the monsoon rain. Taking in a deep breath I think about Palestine and wonder how it could be more colourful or rich than this place we have found ourselves in.

By the time we catch a *tonga* to the docks, the boat looks ready to go. On board are just a few of the people we arrived with, ready to relocate, on their eternal journey. They stand on the deck, looking back at the city they arrived at by accident.

'Still time to climb aboard, Ewa,' Mosze shouts in Polish, laughing. 'We won't have to pretend we're married just for the sake of the train guards — we'll get married. Go to Jerusalem together. Have a family!'

I notice that Ewa has let go of my hand now that we're near the boat. The rain has stopped and there are no clouds in the sky, because they have exhausted themselves. Instead the sun shines as powerfully as before, making the steam rise from her clothes, together with a light smell of Ewa.

We go on board and we hug the people we have travelled with and give them bags full of delights from Nahoum's. We may never see them again; who knows even if we will ever feel the need to stay in touch? Does the sharing of hardship make somebody into a best friend? Certainly, speaking for Rivka and me, we would not be together if it weren't for the suffering we've shared. But does it have to be suffering that always binds us? Are the people that we struggle with the only people who will truly understand us?

'Look how few of us remain on the boat,' Ewa says, interrupting my thoughts. It's true, the numbers of Polish Jews on the *Asama Maru* has dwindled. Thirty of us arrived and now eight are leaving. Not all of them stayed in Calcutta — some went to Bombay and elsewhere. We are being randomly scattered around the globe, it seems, and again that instinct to stay together comes back to me. Who knows if we should be leaving on the boat with them? Who knows if the place we're choosing to put down our roots is the right one? We are like seeds being thrown around the world. Do seeds ever have to make such decisions? Isn't it just a question of survival? If there is soil and air and earth and water, then that's all that's required. Here in Calcutta, we have everything we need, so what's the point of worrying about where we've landed?

Lewek gives me another big hug. 'This one is for Rivka,' he says. 'Tell her we're going to miss having a mama with us on this next trip.'

'She doesn't like to say goodbye,' I say, to explain her absence, 'but she'll come and say hello to you one day in Palestine.'

Then Lewek gives Ewa such a long hug it's hard to miss the feelings that he must have had for her all this time. I don't feel bad watching them. Ewa and Lewek are never going to be together. This much I know.

The fishermen squat down on their long, thin hooded boats, watching Ewa and me hug our friends one last time. Then the horn blows and we go ashore. The boat leaves without us, and we watch it glide over the waters of the Hooghly without any of the strange noises it made on its entrance into Calcutta.

'Good luck!' Ewa shouts at the top of her voice. 'Goodbyyyyye! Do Widzenia!'

As she yells out these words that Rivka hates, I remember a goodbye that we said to each other in another life. I am no longer in Calcutta as I hold Ewa's hand and watch the boat float off into the distance. We are back in Warsaw on a warm spring day, sitting under the chestnut trees and dreaming about how we will be together, some time in the future. A future that neither of us could have anticipated a few long summers earlier.

Minutes later, the boat that brought us to India through some twist of fate unties that knot and disappears from view, leaving us to negotiate not the cold expanse of the Indian Ocean but the warm monsoon puddles at our feet.

CHAPTER 18

We have to leave the partisans, there is little doubt about it. Since Tomasz died after his surgery, Jacek often looks at me and says, 'Get out of my sight.' Of course, I do as I am told because I don't like looking at him either, but I am not nearly as upset by these insults as Rivka, who keeps saying, 'That pig wants us to leave, can't you see?'

If there is one incident that pushes us into leaving the partisans, it is this. One day Daniel and I are walking along with a group of partisans, and we hear some noise ahead of us. Getting closer we see a German soldier, with some of his uniform scattered around him on the forest floor, lying on top of one of the women who lives with the partisans. I start to walk away, but within a few seconds Jacek is lifting his gun to shoot and there is no turning our backs on what is about to happen. I try to cover Daniel's eyes.

The bullets fire, the soldier's body convulses and blood spills over the poor girl, who is still lying underneath him. Then Jacek kicks the German to one side as he holds his gun up to the female partisan who has just had sex with the enemy. I still have my hands over Daniel's eyes as Jacek starts shouting at her, '*Kurva*, what the hell do you think you were doing?' She is looking at his gun, screaming, 'Stop, don't shoot,' but Jacek pulls the trigger and the poor woman falls back dead, covered now in her own blood as well as her lover's.

Daniel pulls my hands away from his eyes and says, 'Why didn't you let me look?' I am thinking: what has got into this young boy's head? Does he think he is some kind of great soldier to be witnessing such horrors?

When Rivka hears that Daniel saw one of the partisans being shot by her own commandant, she says once more, 'We are leaving, we have no choice in this matter. I am not going to watch my son turn into a murdering *goy*.'

'But he's not unhappy here,' I tell Rivka.

She says, 'Of course he's not unhappy, because he's out all day on this ... this adventure. If we were not living this pitiful existence, Daniel would be in *cheder* by now, studying the Book, learning the *mitzvoth*.'

I am grateful that Daniel is not unhappy, but I, too, cannot help thinking about the damaging effects of this life on our child: not just the kind of education he is receiving here, but the food — eating potatoes, potatoes, potatoes, and drinking the sap from birch trees for nourishment. There is nothing for him here, really, but he seems to love it. For example, the partisans have this game that they play every night as we drink tea. A cube of sugar hangs from a piece of string in front of us, to help us imagine that our tea is sweet. At the end of every week, one of us is allowed to eat it. When it is Daniel's turn, he is so happy you would think that it was his birthday or Chanukah.

On the one hand I am glad to see his joy: it shows he can still experience happiness. But the problem is he learns nothing whatsoever. We don't teach him anything that will make him feel different from the others. We don't even teach him 'Thou shalt not kill', because what's the point, really? He is only six, but he has already helped to kill goodness knows how many people, because the partisans take him out with them for good luck! Last time they took him along with them to explode a train. But what sort of a lucky mascot is he, I ask? He is a little boy who thinks that he has nothing more that he needs to learn about the world, that's all.

Rivka is going crazy living here, really. Living with all these people eating at her intestines; these people she hates because they use her son in their battles and separate all of us without a thought for our safety.

'What if you're caught and I'm left to live out the rest of my life without either of you?' she says. 'What if the Germans find this bunker when you're out?' she asks. 'There'll be nowhere I can run. I'll die in this pit all alone.'

I don't tell her that I've been worried about the same things. I just say, 'It won't happen. We're far too deep in the forest for them to come looking for us.'

One day, though, they will come, that much is sure. They have caught one partisan in town and hanged him as an example of what will happen to the rest of us. Do you think they would do anything different to us, Jewish partisans?

A few days ago some Jews arrived looking for shelter, just as we had, but they had no weapons so they were told to stay elsewhere in the forest. 'Let them stay,' I insisted, but do you think that our commandant wanted to listen to me? 'We can't keep providing for people,' Jacek said. 'The more people we take in, the more we will have to steal. The villagers will hate us even more than they already do. They'll turn us in.'

When Rivka hears about his reaction, she tells me, 'We're leaving. I don't care where we go, we're leaving.' She is almost frantic with anger.

I try and calm her down. 'No,' I say, 'Jacek is in a difficult position. How is he supposed to find food and shelter for everybody?'

'He's taken in Poles — Poles without weapons, Poles without provisions.'

'But if we go, what would we eat? Where would we sleep?'

I've realised one thing about Rivka and it is this: in a fit of passion she doesn't care about anything. No consequences, nothing. It's plain that there is hardly enough food to feed the partisans already living here, so how can Jacek take in any more? His hands are tied, no?

In her frustration at being trapped here Rivka somehow gets it into her head that Daniel has to have a proper bath, of all things. Now, we have not even seen soap for months, it seems;

washing in the stream with running water at night seems to have worked so far — but no, Rivka wants soap to get all the *schmutz* off Daniel. She has been to the village on one or two occasions and she knows the way now, but this time she goes on her own, with a shotgun, if you please. She waits until I am out at the hospital, so I cannot stop her, and then she goes, no doubt with her head held high, to one of the farmhouses on the way to town. These farmhouses are quite well protected, I'm telling you — they have high wooden fences around their small courtyards to stop people stealing their produce. There's no way that she could climb over the thatched roof of the house itself.

Goodness knows how Rivka does it, but she comes back with soap and corn, some cheeses and a small pile of money. I ask her how she managed to get all of these things and she tells me, 'At gunpoint. If they can't give anything to help us, then we have every right to take it from them, no? We're doing their work, Benjamin. We're doing their work.'

I say nothing.

Daniel is bathed in the river that night with soap as well as running water. He thinks it smells funny, but at least Rivka is satisfied. She is doing her best for her little boy, and is prepared to risk her life for him, this much is obvious, even to her. Nonetheless, this bravery doesn't make her any more sensible. After washing Daniel with the soap she says, 'Let's leave,' just like that. Of course I am thinking: she must be joking, but then she says, 'Our lives are terrible here, no?'

'And you think that life will be better anywhere else?'

'We'll go and visit your family.' She is so convinced by this idea that I hardly dare to talk about the risks of travelling right now. Her solo raid has filled her with a sense of determination and confidence I cannot match. 'Next time they bring in some provisions, we'll just take some and go.'

'To Warsaw?'

'Yes, to Warsaw.'

'You're crazy.'

'I'm not crazy. I just want to live in a home. A proper home. We can stay with your parents until we find something.'

Indeed? And what about the ghetto everyone talks about? This is what I am thinking. What about the walls they've built around the streets where I grew up?

I think about my parents, and about our home in Pawia Street. Yes, a home would be wonderful, if it were a safe one, but what safety will we find in the heart of German occupation? And is a home worth risking our lives for? I don't know the answers to these questions. I have lost all certainty about life. All I know is that Rivka wants a home and she will get one. Knowing her determination, sooner or later she will get one.

We end up leaving the partisans during the night, so that we're not noticed, and our journey to Warsaw is surprisingly uneventful. We travel by horse and cart with a peasant family as well as making one train journey, during which nobody even asks for our papers.

When we arrive by buggy in the old city square, I try to muster some confidence. The place is crawling with the 'blue' Polish police as well as the 'green' German gendarmes — more so than anywhere we have been in the countryside. I tell myself, surely we look just like anybody else living in Warsaw? We have recently washed and the clothes we 'borrowed' from the partisans are not too old. We certainly don't look as if we've travelled far, because Rivka and I are carrying only one small bag each, and Daniel is carrying nothing but the weight of my nervous hand.

Yes, we look like innocent Varsovians, locals, on our way home, but that doesn't stop my heart racing as we pass one of the 'greens'. All of us, as planned, walk without looking anybody in the eye, because it is our eyes, always, that betray us. So we look straight ahead, as if we are simply going about our daily business, but this one man turns his head and notices us. I can tell this without looking at him. It's as if I can feel the heat in his body, even though he's a few yards away from us. I can sense his curiosity, not with my eyes, nor my ears, but through this heat. Maybe it is just the heat of my own anxiety, but it's burning me nonetheless, and I hold Daniel's hand tightly to remind him that he must not look up either. Daniel senses my fear and walks faster, but I pull him back. We cannot walk too fast, because that will draw attention to the three of us. We have to walk with purpose, confidently; not a drop of fear is allowed to show. Rivka and Daniel have to look as if they're as familiar in these streets as I am. We must walk as if the Germans are just holiday-makers visiting our capital city.

I lead the two of them away from the town square as quickly as possible, towards a tram that will take us to Pawia Street. We get on this tram and I am expecting it to stop very near our house. I don't know what is going on in my head, but I am actually surprised when the tram stops at the wall I was told about, the wall around the streets where I grew up. The driver yells out that the doors are about to lock while we go through the ghetto. What are we to do? I look at Rivka and quickly take Daniel's hand, at the same time pushing past passengers to get out of the tram. What a shock this is, I'm telling you. This is our first attempt to reach my home and we cannot even enter the neighbourhood.

Once we're out of the tram, looking at the high wall ahead of us, Rivka asks, 'How do we get inside?' Of course I have no answers, but I say, 'The same way as everyone else — through the gate.'

We walk around the wall for a few moments and I read a poster saying that the police have the right to shoot any person or animal on either side of the wall. Rivka asks, 'If they're guarding it with guns, who will let us out again?'

'What do you want us to do?' I say. 'Come all the way to Warsaw and leave without seeing my family?' I'm raising my voice; I must stop myself. This is no place to start getting angry. 'I'm sorry, my darling, but we have no choice,' I say, more softly this time. 'Where will we stay if we don't get through to the other side?'

So we walk around the wall for a bit, but not too close, because we don't want to look as if we're interested in the other side at all. We are Catholic Poles in this moment. Imposters, supposedly with no interest in the Jews that have been locked up behind the wall. Already I'm regretting our decision to come back here.

An elderly couple walk past us, away from the wall, with bundles piled up on top of an old pram that they wheel along. Both the man and woman are wearing black and their faces hardly lift from the cobblestones. I approach the old man and ask him, 'Do you know Solomon Rahabi in Pawia Street?' I do not want to mention who we are, in case they get too curious.

'How would we know them?' the man asks. 'There are thousands of Jews living in the ghetto now.'

I am thinking: this man is a Catholic — I should ask if he knows Ewa. But instead I find myself asking about her parents. 'Do you know Marek and Kasia Jacubowicz in Smocze Street?'

'They have a daughter?' the woman asks.

'Yes, yes. She's called Ewa.'

'I don't know them personally, but I was told that the mother was taken to Pawiak Prison.'

'That can't be right,' I tell them. 'Are you sure you have the right family? They're not Jewish.'

The old woman lifts her head up to me and says, 'Neither are we. Do you think that helps us?' Then she carries on, without another thought for us, and pulls her husband and luggage with her.

We watch them for a few minutes, wandering down the street with their pram to go and set up in the Polish district, and it makes me acutely aware of the fact that we're not moving and soon anybody could approach us. If everything is true about the blackmailers, that old man himself could inform on us. So I take Daniel's hand and Rivka's arm and we walk around the walled area. When we get to Gesia Street there's a gate and I go up to one of the 'blues' there and find the courage to ask if my family can go in.

'This area is only for Jews now,' he says. 'Are you Jewish?'

'No, but I have friends inside that I want to see. Polish friends.'

'They must have left by now. Where are you from?'

'From Piaski, a small town near Lublin. I'm supposed to be helping some Polish friends move out.' As I say this I give the man some of the last coins that Rivka stole from the farmhouse. This gendarme doesn't even look at me, just signals me to go in. 'Say nothing, or you'll find yourself in trouble,' he says, and believe me, just one look at Gesia Street on the other side of the wall is enough for me to know that there is nothing but trouble ahead of us.

CHAPTER 19

I cannot describe the feeling of going back to the place where I was born, because there is no joy, only shock and repulsion mixed with fear. Nothing could have prepared me for this: no descriptions from Itzick, the carpenter at the camp; nothing even in my imagination. The beautiful old buildings are still here, of course, but the whole place has been turned upside down, like a refugee camp. It has become a hellish, over-populated prison. Before, this area was always well kept, but now the streets are squalid and the smell is horrible, worse than any place I've seen in Calcutta. Worst of all, there are all these desperate faces looking back at us.

I am anxious to see my parents, all the time thinking: how could they have put up with this? Now we are walking swiftly, and I am so distracted that I almost walk into a dead man whose body lies across the pavement. This man's body I will never forget. His eyes have sunken so far into his skull that his sockets seem empty, and his bones poke out of the little clothing he still wears. Instinctively, I cover Daniel's eyes to protect his innocence, but then a group of street children, sitting on the kerb, stare at us, and I pull my hand away, because if these children can see these things, then so should Daniel. What else can I do? Am I to take this son of mine blindfolded through the streets where I grew up?

I hear Rivka whisper in my ear, 'Benjamin, we have to get Daniel out of here.' I squeeze her hand and start walking again, even faster, pulling them behind me, because I have this instinct to get my family into a safe house as quickly as possible; inside a home, any home, for protection from this stinking hell. 'Things will be different at my place,' I tell Rivka and Daniel, and I walk faster still, hoping that Pawia Street will look a little more decent.

As we rush through the ghetto, occasionally a face looks familiar, but I cannot be sure that I know these people. Mostly they are strangers, many of them trying their best to look respectable, given the conditions. Virtually all of them wear these blue and white armbands, which we don't have. It's all so strange, I feel as if I'm in a dream: some place that I know well, but everything around me has warped and twisted. Stranger still, nightfall is approaching and not a single streetlight comes on. The electricity has been turned off, it appears, and the entire area slips into an unearthly darkness.

We are walking in the direction of Smocze Street. It is on the way to my family home, but it's also the street where Ewa lives. We could easily walk past her place and go to my home directly, but I am feeling the panic that this darkness brings and I think: whether she likes it or not, Rivka is going to have to meet Ewa.

When we come to Ewa's apartment I go up the stairs and knock on the door. Daniel knocks a few more times before I stop him. It takes a while for her to answer, but after a few minutes we hear a very timid voice asking, 'Who is it?'

I can hear fear in her voice, so I immediately announce myself: 'It's only me, Benjamin.'

The door flings open and Ewa rushes at me, holding me so tight it feels as if she'll never let go. 'Benjamin, Benjamin, Benjamin.' She is repeating my name and we are both crying in each other's arms and kissing each other, until I stop her, because she hasn't taken any notice of Rivka and Daniel, who stand next to me patiently waiting for an introduction. I try and pull myself back from her, and once we're no longer in each other's arms I say, 'Ewa, this is my wife, Rivka, and this is Daniel.' It is my only way of telling her that I can no longer be hers, but as soon as I say these words I wish that things could be different. I cannot tell you what happens to her face. She cannot say anything, so she just stands there watching them, absolutely frozen.

'Can I come in?' I say, and she walks us inside, still not speaking. It is pitch dark inside the living room, so Ewa lights a carbide lamp and says in a strange, formal way, 'Sorry there's nothing to warm us. There's been no allocation for coal.'

When we're sitting down I start to mention her parents.

'Please don't talk about them,' she says and bursts out crying. 'I wrote to tell you about them, but you never wrote back to give me any comfort.'

'Ewa, I've been living in the forest. I never received any letters,' I tell her as gently as I can manage.

'Did they tell you what happened to your parents?' she says, crying again now so hard I have to hold her arms to get her to talk to me. But all she can say through her tears is, 'You were going to come back within a few months, but you just left. Everybody had been waiting so long for you to come. Why did you keep us all waiting?'

'You don't know anything of what's happened to me, so please, Ewa, put me out of my misery. What has happened to my parents?' Again I am raising my voice and it doesn't feel right to be shouting at Ewa. Not now; not here in front of Rivka.

'I thought you were the police,' she says, sobbing again. 'You were knocking so many times.'

'What happened to them? Please tell me. We were on our way home to Pawia Street —'

'No!' she shouts at me, and her face is crumpled and twisted with tears. 'They were shot … they came in the night and shot them.'

'I don't believe you,' I say, and then I look at her face again and know that she could not be lying. Not my Ewa. Why would she ever tell me such a lie?

I am sitting there in stunned silence when an absolute stranger walks out of Ewa's parents' bedroom and comes into the kitchen, nodding and apologising for his presence. 'I am so sorry,' he interrupts, 'I'll be quick,' and then this person proceeds to boil milk for his baby, would you believe it? Really, I am not given even a second to try to understand what has just been said to me.

Rivka is standing behind me with her arms around my chest. Underneath her palms my heart must be thumping, but I cannot weep for my parents, because I don't believe that they could have been shot, just like that. How could something so impossible have happened? I am completely in denial of the fact that anything could have happened to them, believe me. I am going to go to Pawia Street tomorrow, and I will discover that Ewa has somehow got this information wrong.

Only when we have settled down for the night on the kitchen floor, and everybody is fast asleep, do I allow myself to weep for my parents. I scream for them, silently, inside my head. I pull at the blanket until it tears at the corner. I pull on all my muscles until there are knots in my shoulders and my arms are cramping, and then I weep some more until my shoulders drop with exhaustion and my eyes are so swollen I can hardly open them. I want to go out and shoot every German soldier in this ghetto. Every soldier I see, I want to gun down.

I imagine myself with a gun. I am walking and shooting it loudly into the sky. But when I point it at another human being, I cannot pull the trigger, so I thump and beat the floor instead, until my fingers are so clenched that my fists have squeezed shut into a spasm of hatred. And then through all of this I hear my mother in this dark room, saying, 'Thank God you're alright, Benjamin.' Maybe I imagine these words, but I hear them and this is how I know that my mother is alive. That I am right. That my parents are safe and well at home.

CHAPTER 20

The next day I go alone to our home in Pawia Street. A strange man answers the door and when I tell him that I am Benjamin Rahabi, he is pitifully apologetic, saying, 'I'm so sorry . . . we had no choice . . .'

'Where do you come from?' I ask him with as much friendliness as I can muster, and he tells me, 'I'm so sorry, I'm Frimet. We're from Otwocko. We were sent here when they made the three different districts.'

'Do you mind if I come and look around my apartment?' I ask him. How stupid it sounds, to ask to look inside your own home. He invites me inside and there is nothing that I recognise of my own, except for a photo of my family in Zakopane, which I take out of its frame and place in my pocket. This is the only picture of my family that I have to this day.

When I'm in the living room I feel like asking about my parents, or at least telling these people in our home about them, but I feel so uncomfortable. Worse still, this man, Frimet, carries on apologising. 'If we only had the money for rent I would gladly pay it.' This is what he says as he takes me down the corridor and into the room on the left, my bedroom, showing me where he's living with his wife and three children. When he opens the door his wife and the children look up to see the stranger who is standing above them. I see some repairs that my parents must have made before they were taken away, but I can't bring myself to actually go inside my old room. This room is not mine any more. This is what I am thinking. None of this is mine any more. I cannot tell you how strange this feels.

'Did you hear anything about how it happened?' I ask this man.

'How they were killed?' he replies matter-of-factly, and as soon as he says these words I am crying, just like I used to cry in this apartment over trifles when I was a young boy. It is as if my worst nightmare has just become a reality.

'I am so sorry. Please, sit down,' Frimet instructs me, and I do as I'm told, sitting down in my old kitchen as if I were a child once more and he the adult. He puts some corn coffee on to boil over the lamp and then he starts to tell me everything he knows.

'They came looking for the Rahabis. They said it had something to do with an escaped prisoner. Your parents said they didn't know any prisoners, although they must have, because everybody knows someone who's been taken away to Pawiak or elsewhere. They should have at least made up a name ...'

When I hear Frimet say this I feel numb with the realisation that I could possibly be responsible for this disaster. I am looking directly at this stranger, and I can see myself sitting there, from his point of view. I am acutely aware of myself as he tells me the plain facts. The corner of my mouth is twitching and catching a few hairs that have grown longer and rough on my face. I am no longer crying, just listening, half dead myself, because things like this could not happen in the world of the living.

'They were lined up in front of a grave at the Jewish cemetery. There were some children from the ghetto hiding in the cemetery and they saw what happened ...'

'No, please stop,' I tell him. I cannot bear to find out how they were shot, or hear anything more about it. My father is alive for me and I can hear him talking in this apartment of ours. HaShem, how could I have arrived here too late to see them, to even say goodbye? How many times I hoped for all of this to finish, so that we could be together again as a family. If only I could see them walk in the door. My God, where are they?

As I leave our apartment I have this feeling that I need to kick everybody out, just for an hour or so, and spend a few minutes there alone.

'When would be a good time to come back here?' I ask this man, Frimet, and he says, 'This place is your home. You must come back whenever you want.'

It's no secret that many people in Poland bury gold as an insurance measure, and my father had once told me where some of his was hidden, behind our old stove. So the next day I return to my apartment, and I ask Frimet to leave me alone for a few minutes in my old kitchen. Once this man Frimet has closed the door behind him, I pull the stove forwards and feel around for one brick that is slightly looser than the others and moves out easily. I pull the stove out further to take the brick out, then I put my hand inside the small cavity left by the brick and reach for the box. It is there, untouched, exactly as my father described to me some years earlier.

I sit down and I am shaking as I open that box, because what is inside is beyond sentiment for me, to this day. Yes, there are five gold coins, as he told me, but with them are the sidelocks that my mother told me he cut the day I was born. Believe me, the box in my trembling hands is so precious — I am so overwhelmed with a feeling of love and loss, melting together, that I can barely comprehend what I have just found. It is beyond a gift, really; beyond even a sacrifice; and through my tears I can almost see him smiling, knowing that he has given me more than just a few coins in case of an emergency. He has given me a part of himself: his hope for the future — for our future as a family.

When I go back to Ewa's apartment, I sew these sidelocks of my father's into the hem of my coat, and I feel that he is with us and can never be taken away. He will come with us across the world, and my mother, too, and their memory will live on as long as mine does, and past my lifetime, too, in this precious heirloom that he knew I would find one day.

Having these locks of my father's, I cannot help but think about the circumstances that led to him cutting them. My father, Solomon, knew that his strength lay in his tradition. Yet at a time when the Haskalah movement insisted that Jews integrate into Polish life, he also knew in his heart that it would be dangerous not to adapt. That the time would come when he would have to cut off his beard and sidelocks and conform to the Polish norm.

My birth was that time.

'He did it for you,' my mother always said. 'For you, my darling, your father would do anything.'

I used to ask myself how this man who argued with his friends, like Marek, who had made similar compromises, could do such a thing for anyone. My father always felt that the Haskalah movement was misguided. 'We can be Polish and Jewish,' he said. 'Why not? Nobody can dispute either. My ancestors came here long ago. We sing the national anthem in our synagogues. We never stop the Catholics from keeping their customs, so why can't we keep ours?'

So why did he cut off his locks? My guess is that he must have realised that the situation for Jews in Poland could only get worse. Still, he could never have imagined how bad things would get.

'We are a free people,' he'd say. 'We've been free since the time we left Egypt. Nobody can take my religion from me. I am Jewish. And to hell with it, I am Polish, too.'

That much was a fact. My father could trace our Polish ancestry back more than a thousand years, to a time when one Rahabi had arrived in a band of terrified refugees, escaping the violence of the Crusades to the east. In his ancestry were Jews who had arrived seven hundred years earlier, taking refuge in these lands after the Tartar invasion in the lower Volga. On all accounts he was Polish! For goodness sake, some of our forebears had even been invited to the country to help manage the wheat trade and bring economic fortune. Who else was going to do that? The Polish aristocrats with their clean fingernails and *kontusz*? *Feh!* Not likely, I'm telling you.

But how would he have felt when he cut his sidelocks? I often wonder this. Shame, or even fear? Yes, as my father walked back to the apartment in his Polish tweed trousers and shirt, devoid of sidelocks, he must have felt as naked and shameful as Adam after his disfavour with God.

And my mother? Apparently there was never any comment from her about my father's decision. Not even a mention. And as for me, I was too young to have known any better, for my eyes were closed when he kissed me in the morning, wearing his locks, and still closed when he kissed me at night, with his face softer and bare.

However, I know that Ewa's father was shocked when he saw the concession that my father had made.

He would have said. 'My good Lord. Has the world come to an end? Solomon, you of all people should have taken those locks with you to the grave.'

I know, too, that Marek tried to convince my father not to go ahead with my circumcision. Of course my father would not hear a word of it, but my mother often used to repeat Marek's advice.

'Now that Poland is a nation,' she said, 'we must be careful, for every nation needs an enemy. The Germans are no longer our enemies. Nor the Austrians nor the Hungarians. The enemies of the Poles have gone, so they will have to find some new ones. Believe me, no nation is possible without enemies. We don't know what we're fighting for unless we know what we're fighting against. They're going mad outside with patriotism. It's dangerous for Jews, Solomon.'

But my father, would he listen? No! 'Ach, let them say whatever they like. Tomorrow the *mohel* is going to come and we are going to have a grand circumcision.' This is what he would have said.

Tomorrow, tomorrow. You wouldn't have received a straight answer from the gypsies back then about what was to be expected tomorrow. But my father, he had a straight answer. 'Tomorrow is the eighth day, the *mohel* is coming, and make sure you bring your whole family, Yudl.' That is what he would have said.

Besides Rivka, there are three people who make me want to leave Warsaw more than anything else in the world. The first is Daniel, with his large, concerned eyes. He is a helpless prisoner in this place of Ewa's, because we hardly ever let him leave the building. I see those eyes when I leave the house and again when I return, and whenever I look at him I know that we must stay alive for him, not for ourselves. It is our duty to make sure that we never leave him an orphan in this world.

The second person is Ewa, who goes out to work in this wretched factory for long hours, coming back with the most terrible stories you wouldn't believe. For example, one day the crèche has been emptied of all its children. The next day an employee has had her fingers chopped off for not working fast enough. Yet she is still worried about leaving this place because her spirit has been broken. Ever since the Germans announced on their yappers that the ghetto would be sealed, she has given up all hope, believe me. 'What use is there in trying to leave?' she says. 'If they find you, they'll shoot you.' Then at other times she asks me if it's alright for her to come with us. She is crazy, really. What the hell is she thinking? That I would let her stay here? That I would betray her parents and mine by leaving her behind?

'You have no choice in the matter. You're coming with us whether you like it or not,' I tell her.

'I won't be any trouble,' she says, and she sounds so pathetic that I have to say, 'Shut up and listen to yourself, for goodness sake.'

This is not the Ewa I know. How could they have reduced her to such a person? But then I see the rings around her eyes and her sallow skin and I know that none of us can truly be ourselves right now.

'If you don't come with us, Ewa, I don't know what I'll do. I will not be able to live knowing that I left you behind. Not knowing whether or not you've been picked up and taken off like the rest of them.'

Ewa takes my hand and says, 'Benjamin, you haven't changed,' and I am thinking: neither have you, and neither have my feelings — fortunately or unfortunately. You knew my family, Ewa. You knew my parents. How can I leave you behind?

The third person who insists that I leave is my father. I cannot explain how he manages to convince me of this, but he is still here with me, in my head, and he wants us to leave Poland, as a family, all of us alive. My father's locks are inside the hem of my coat like a living memory: a sign telling me that we should leave this place. Get out as quickly as possible. He was the one who always had some inkling of what could happen to the country he so loved, and his worst fears have already become our reality.

Truly, the only thing stoping us from leaving is our fear. We have the money now, and Ewa has managed to get some papers for us all through a priest at St Augustyn's Church. So I take everybody to Sztuka for some coffee, to discuss how we are going to get out of the ghetto and go somewhere far away from Poland. On the way we see some soldiers forcing a small group of street dwellers to wash in the gutter. While these poor people carry out their orders, the soldiers prod them with rifle butts, enjoying the sick joke. I am thinking: how can we stay in this place? How can we possibly stay here, watching these things happening?

That day at Sztuka everything becomes clear, and I learn for the first time about a man who has received an entry visa for Japan from a diplomat called Chiune Sugihara in Kovno. Hearing this I am thinking: Kovno is where we must go. The sky is lit up with signs. We have to make our exodus as soon as we can, otherwise we could be washing ourselves in the gutter to provide entertainment for soldiers who have been briefed to kill every last Jew in Poland. This small island on the other side of the world, Japan, sounds far enough away for us to start up our lives from scratch. And from there, maybe to Palestine, who knows?

CHAPTER 21

This is not the first time I have experienced emigration hysteria. There was much talk of leaving Poland and going to Palestine back in 1935. I was studying medicine, I remember, at the university. Sitting at the back of the lecture hall on the 'ghetto benches' which were reserved for the reduced numbers of Jewish students allowed to take up places in the universities after laws were introduced to reduce our numbers. Some used to stand, ready to make a quick exit should one be necessary. So what if standing up was uncomfortable? That's how these boys thought. Better to have tired legs than broken ones. But me, I never stood up, because I had won my place there and, as far as I was concerned, that included the seat beneath me.

I remember what we were studying that day when my father started panicking about leaving Poland. I remember, too, leaving the lecture theatre and seeing two grown men embracing outside the university gates, in tears. Farther down the street a small group of female students were looking at each other in disbelief. One of them told me as I was passing, 'Pilsudski has died.'

I couldn't believe it! Pilsudski, the great liberator of Poland, hero of Jews and Poles alike, had died only hours earlier, and the news was already sending tremors through the capital. I remember joining this group of strangers to talk about the prospect of a Poland without Pilsudski, because I knew exactly what it meant. The man who gave us our Independence, the friend to Jews, was no more on this land to offer us his protection. From dust he was made and to dust he would return, along with all Jewish hopes for equality in this country we had inhabited for so long.

I knew what my father would say, even before I arrived home.

'If we don't leave for Palestine now, we might never leave, I'm telling you, Sarah. Now is the time to go — can't you see?'

'Where will I get an education in Palestine?' I asked. I was just like Daniel, I'm telling you. 'I'll have to start again over there,' I pleaded. 'It'll be such a waste of time. It's hard enough being a Jewish student, without having Jewish parents,' I told my father. 'Let me finish my studies. I have enough troubles at the university, without yours to add to them.'

'Things may not be easy for you, but do you think they are any easier for us?' my father scolded me. 'Do you think I enjoy having to display my full name at the front of my business? To display my name while the Jews are being thrown out of shops and markets all over this country! Do you think I enjoy listening to the likes of Bishop Pradzynski talking about accelerated deportation of this ... this tribe of an alien race? We have to go and go now, Benjamin, and you will come with us, because you were my son before you were ever a student.'

A man may plot out his course, but it is the Lord who directs his steps. This is what our proverbs say, and at that time I thought I should let my father dream on. I knew that nothing could happen in a rush, because no progress was easy at that time. My father would have to wait for the sale of his property in Ozarow, and of another in Kampinos. He had been trying to sell them for some months, ever since there was discussion of confiscating Jewish property and redistributing it amongst the peasants. I remember, too, one of our parliamentarians at that time, Lupacewicz, said that the Jews shouldn't just have their assets confiscated, but they should be incarcerated in camps and given one *zloty* each per day to live off! I never took any of it seriously, but my father had some idea about what could happen; he really did. He was one of those people who anticipated the need to leave well before Hitler arrived in our homeland.

'If we don't go to Palestine,' he told me, 'they will send us to Madagascar, Uganda or Abyssinia, and what on earth would we do over there? What strangers we would be. And in what strange lands.'

'Don't worry the poor boy,' my mother always said. 'You settle your business here first, and let Benjamin finish his studies.'

A few months later, in 1936, the properties were still unsold and my father had fallen prey to the worst kind of emigration hysteria. At that time there were also plans for a great march from Warsaw to Palestine, and nearly two hundred Jews all over the capital had designated a date when they would leave.

'We can come back and sort out the properties another time,' my father insisted. 'Nobody else can possibly take over the deeds. We can leave them in the hands of Marek and Kasia. They can try to sell up and send the money to us in Palestine. I would trust the two of them with my life.'

This march to Palestine was much discussed amongst a few people we knew in our area. There were regular meetings in a room at the Great Synagogue in Tlomackie Street. Several Jews who had fled pogroms in places like Minsk and Mazowiecki had come to Warsaw, but were eager not to rest too long, lest they lose their determination to escape the violence while they still could. They told stories of Jewish children being killed; stories that not even the Polish papers were allowed to publish. Stories of successful pogroms being celebrated in the churches. Yes, in the churches, believe me.

'Just listen to them,' my father said to my mother at one of the meetings. 'You cannot agree with that son of ours and allow this to happen to our family? Surely not.'

At these meetings, lists of things to be brought and things to be left behind were drawn up, and my father made friends with a few other people who would be going on the march to Palestine, as well as the leader of this adventure, a man by the name of Wilhelm Rippel. Mostly the band of travellers were much younger than my father, but he had the intrepid enthusiasm of a twenty-year-old man, and such a strong desire to see Jerusalem that any sensible objection to this quixotic plan was instantly sidestepped.

My mother, however, saw all the obstacles that could lie ahead between Warsaw and the Promised Land. She came back morose and uninspired from those meetings.

'I'm too old to go sitting on a cart and carrying all our things to another country. Do you know how far it is to Palestine? I can hardly march from here to the *Rynek*. What help will I ever be to you once we get there?'

'We'll take a car if you'd prefer,' my father told her. 'You mustn't worry yourself with details. Let me organise everything. You know what the Proverbs say: Trust your affairs to the Lord and your plans will succeed. You have nothing to fear. If this journey fills you with uncertainty, think about the uncertainty that remains here in Poland.'

'But what about Benjamin? He has to finish his studies. How will he feel about leaving everything he's worked for all these years?'

'Hush, Sarah. You speak as if there will be no life after this one we are living here. As if there will be no joy in Palestine when we arrive there. Just imagine. A new world. Freedom from all these absurd rules. No more people telling us that we cannot work in our own country.'

'I know, I know. It's just that I can't see us there. I ... I don't have the imagination.'

'Well, I have enough imagination for the three of us. Just let me be your imagination and think nothing more of it. I can imagine everything. I can organise everything, my darling.' This is how they used to go on, my parents.

I remember their long discussions and all the planning. The date was set for our departure, some time in the spring, and all those who had put up their hands for the march were to gather at the Market Square early in the morning. People all over our area who were coming on this party prepared for the great pilgrimage over the next few weeks. Mattresses and quilts were folded, ready at front doors. Horses and carts were claimed from country properties, and so on. Around this time there was also a law — passed by the Poles, not Hitler, I might add — that all large Polish enterprises were to dismiss Jewish employees. Can you believe it? Naturally, the numbers of people joining our small party swelled.

The only emotion I felt at this time was this sickening fear — not just because I would have to leave my studies, but because I would also have to leave Warsaw, the only town I had lived in for as long as I could remember. Even more importantly, I would have to leave Ewa, and it was this thought more than any of the others that put out any small flame of excitement I could have felt.

A few days before our departure for Jerusalem, I went to her school and waited outside the gates with a large bunch of violets.

'What's this I hear about your family going with this silly exodus party? Is it true?' she asked me.

I also remember her saying, 'You'll forget about me as soon as you leave the country, and you'll find a nice Jewish girl and never come back.'

Of course I reassured her that I would never find someone else, and that I would come back for her, no matter what. Then I asked if she would be able to leave Warsaw after her studies, and come to live with us in Palestine, and she said, 'Why not? After all, I'm Jewish, aren't I?'

These were her words, I promise you. Even back then I used to wonder how Ewa could identify so strongly with our people on the strength of two grandparents in a *shtetl* she hardly ever visited. Was it love of danger or her obstinate sense of justice that gave her these sympathies? I never worked it out.

We spent that afternoon as a young couple in love, walking our beautiful city together. Ewa clutched her violets and school bag and we strolled arm in arm down cobbled lanes under the chestnut trees to find a nice bench to hold each other. I remember it so clearly. Through a nearby window, from behind lace curtains, came the long notes of somebody playing a cello. Even the music of that day comes back to me.

When the day came for the great march to Palestine, my father woke early to check our bags and prepare himself for the adventure. It was raining outside, which made him nervous. He knew that my mother and I would be the first to use the open heavens as an excuse to stay behind. 'I promise you that it will rain on this journey. If not today, in a month's time. We cannot afford to let these hardships weaken our spirit,' he told us.

'Benjamin, wake up and get into your clothes,' my father called out from his room. I can still hear him today, telling me, 'Say your prayers and we'll be off.' He was wringing his hands together and circling the bags in anticipation that morning. He was very enthusiastic, I'm telling you. 'Hurry, hurry, Sarah or we'll miss the others!' he shouted, and I could tell that in his mind he was already some miles away from Warsaw.

Rather than taking a car and standing out from the other travellers, my father had organised a special cart and two horses. Built into the cart was a secret box, where he kept some gold coins to help us continue our journey should we come across any difficulties and need to travel alone. 'Who has bread, finds a knife,' he told my mother confidently. 'A golden key will open every lock.' She, of course, was not so convinced.

I remember my father giving our maidservant a generous tip as we bade her goodbye and climbed into our chariot with its two fine horses. He'd planned everything, this father of mine. By the time we arrived at the Market Square to meet the others, quite a few travellers had already gathered; a small army of pilgrims, actually — some foot soldiers, some horsemen — leading the way back to Palestine, with Wilhelm Rippel like Moses at the helm. The rain had settled and the sun was emerging hopefully. Everyone was warming to each other, introducing friends and offering words of encouragement. A rabbi was there to offer his blessings, too, giving this mission a feeling of religious importance, and already food was being shared.

'Even if we never get there, I would not have missed this adventure for the world,' my father said.

'Who says we're not going to get there?' my mother objected. Already, you see, she was taken by the spirit of it.

'We will get there, and we will arrive in a grand procession, just watch us,' my father said confidently. Meanwhile, I was thinking of one of King Solomon's proverbs: Do not boast of tomorrow, for you do not know what the day will bring.

At last the first horses started moving ahead of us and the voyage began. The long line paraded at first through the streets of Warsaw, before starting to head into the woods beyond. By the time we saw the forests outside the capital, it seemed to my parents as if the Promised Land was just a stone's throw away. Why, they had enough energy between them all to fly there if need be! Already we were in fertile lands. Fields were ahead of us, and before too long we would surely be surrounded by orchards full of the fruits that were brought to the synagogue at Shavuot in temple times. We would soon be able to pick the grapefruit off the trees that lined the roads into Jerusalem, and harvest wheat to make unleavened bread, just like they did in the old days.

Up ahead they were singing Yiddish songs, and the music floated down the convoy so that everyone was singing the same tunes. Everybody but me sang about this mythical place we were heading to. Singing the words of the Hatikva:

So long as still within the
inmost heart a Jewish spirit sings

So long as the eye looks eastward
Gazing toward Zion

Our hope is not lost —
That hope of two millennia,
To be a free people in our land,
The land of Zion and Jerusalem.

How could any song, however hopeful, make up for my sense of loss? While my parents sat facing forwards, I sat at the back of the cart, looking in the direction of Warsaw, which was fast becoming my Jerusalem, the place to which I must return. Already in my imagination, you see, my home town was the most beautiful city in the world — a place with golden light shining through the green leaves of the chestnut trees. In my mind I had left behind my personal history to follow the history of my people. Worse still, nothing and nobody would be able to replace my Ewa. That's how I felt back then.

'Why are we doing this?' I asked when we stopped for lunch not so far from Warsaw. 'We don't have papers, nothing. Even the older Jews in Muranow thought it was a crazy idea.'

'We'll never get visas as long as the British have Palestine,' my father said. Then he added, 'Don't worry, darling. Once we're inside, everybody will know we're living there and we won't need papers.'

'I hope we never get there,' I told him.

'Hold back your thoughts,' my father said, and I remember thinking: as a sparrow must flit and a swallow fly, so a gratuitous curse must backfire.

'Your thoughts are capable of cursing this whole party,' my father told me. 'You are the only one here, I am sure, who nurses these thoughts of Warsaw. Even if you don't want to go, lift your spirits, please, for the sake of those who do.'

'Leave him alone. He'll cheer up as soon as he makes friends with the other boys,' my mother said.

'I wish I could beat this moroseness out of him,' my father said, making me feel really happy to be on this journey.

We continued forward in a kind of rhythmic progress. It was dusk already and our clatter on the roads was regular and hypnotic. It seemed as if the distance we had covered could be repeated effortlessly over the days ahead until we had made up the required miles. So easy. So, so easy it would be.

You can imagine our surprise, then, when the pilgrims ahead of our cart stopped, forcing us to stop, and so too the groups behind us. My father jumped down from the cart to walk to the front of the convoy and see what was happening. There, up ahead, was a group of policemen, who were shouting and gesticulating madly in the direction of Warsaw. Barricades lay across the road, some as tall as a horse. How were we supposed to climb them?

As my father approached the front of our convoy, a fight started against the police as some of the younger boys in our party tried to push down these barricades. Inspired by this defiance, some of the older men also started to dismantle the obstructions that stood between our party and the Promised Land. Believe me, I was beginning to feel nervous. The men were grabbed and handcuffed and dragged off down the road, in the direction of Jerusalem, but as powerless as slaves. Mounted policemen were now coming down the long line of travellers saying, 'Turn back right now. Go back to your homes.'

'We have no home,' shouted one man out of the darkness.

'Well, go back to Warsaw and sleep on the streets. We have strict instructions to stop this party from proceeding. You step over the barricade and you'll all be arrested. Just try it and see what happens. You're acting against our authority and against the authority of both the Polish and British governments.'

'What do we do now?' my father said to the old Jew in the cart behind him. 'We go back and we are told by the likes of Colonel Beck that Jews can no longer be employed and therefore must go and live elsewhere. We go ahead and we are told that there is no "elsewhere". Where on earth do they expect us to go? What exactly do they have in mind for us?'

'Who am I to answer this question? The Messiah? If we leave now we can get back to Warsaw by daybreak tomorrow.' That's exactly what the old man said.

'But how can all of this come to nothing?' my father said. 'Daybreak today I was taking leave of our home and our maidservant, and before the sun has turned full circle we will be returning? How stupid we are going to look.'

'Papa, don't be so proud,' I said. 'We must go back. This is a sign.'

'Sign, sign. You *schmuck*! Who sent this sign? You?'

'Alright, it was a sign telegrammed by the police in Warsaw. Everybody was looking a little too happy to be leaving, no?'

'Except for you.'

'Yes, yes, it was all my fault, now can we go back home? You sleep and I'll guide the horses.'

Oh Lord, you did wonders we dared not hope for.

I felt so happy, I cannot tell you, but I tried to hide it as we turned around and began our journey back to the familiar cobblestones, chestnut trees and apartment blocks of Warsaw.

'Rest, Mama and Papa. You both lie down in the back on the mattresses. Make yourselves comfortable. I will make sure you both arrive back home safely, by tomorrow.'

And so began the first of many night journeys that I've taken in my life since. But what made this night different from all the rest was the lightness in my heart. The joy of knowing that I was travelling closer to happiness, instead of away from it. Closer to the warm heart of everything I knew, not farther away into a dark night sky with nothing but a distant notion of Jerusalem to guide me.

CHAPTER 22

Everybody we know in Calcutta seems to feel as if the war will come upon us at any minute: they still talk about the fall of Singapore, as if the same thing could happen here. But really, nothing has changed in the daily lives of Indians living in this city. The artists still stand on their bamboo scaffolding to paint posters for the Hindi movies, and people still go to see these movies. The Chinese are still cutting hair in the beauty parlours, the hawkers are still selling their ties and pens and buckets on the sidewalk in Chowringhee; you'd hardly even guess from looking at Calcutta that the world is actually at war. What's more, people are still being born, people are still dying, people are still falling sick, so it doesn't take long for a clinic like ours to succeed. After all, our patients don't have to pay to see us, and often they even take home free medication, thanks to the generosity of Doctor Mitra.

The night comes for our clinic to start, and still no bomb has fallen on Calcutta.

Doctor Mitra is already waiting out on the verandah when I get home from the office, and we sit for some time talking about world events. Not a single soul has come for treatment, or so it seems, and we are chatting for some time before we notice that a man is waiting at the darkest edge of the verandah to see us.

'Doctor *saab*,' he says eventually, and we both jump up as if we didn't believe a real patient would arrive. Our poor patient is so shocked at our reaction that he is about to run to the gate. Really, Mitra has to force him to come back and tell us his complaints.

'Come, come,' he tells our patient, sitting him down in front of the two of us.

Then this kind Bengali surgeon asks the man some questions and starts translating for me the details of an incontinence problem. The poor patient, no? He's nervous enough to see even one doctor, and here he is telling two about the dysfunctions of his bladder.

And all through this first consultation, I can see that things will have to change. How am I ever going to diagnose the problems of these people if I can't speak their language? I am thinking: if I am to practise medicine again I will have to go back to Poland and practise when the war is over. How else to do it?

Mitra sees the problem immediately and suggests that I find a translator. Mary, who is hovering just inside the house, quietly offers her services. 'You won't be shy?' I ask. She says, 'No, *saab*.

I'll be very interested to help.' And so it is that Mary becomes my translator.

The number of patients increases with each clinic we hold, and soon we are dividing the verandah and seeing our own patients. If I need any advice or a second opinion, I simply put my head around the divide and Mitra helps out. Of course there is no privacy in any of this, but the patients don't seem to mind. There is no more privacy in any of their *bustees* — the makeshift dwellings where they live — and our working conditions don't seem to stop any of them from wanting to see us. In fact, they tell everyone about our clinic, so we get patients who come all the way from the other side of the Hooghly to stand in our queues. Sometimes there are so many of them that I don't get any sleep until midnight. Then I'm up at six to go back to the office in China Bazaar, where I continue to work hard to keep up with Nayar Babu in our attempt to increase the sales of Bose Paper Mills. How strange life is, really. To think that this clinic is the last thing I wanted to do just a few months back, and here I am now, enjoying every minute of it.

There is no more talk of leaving Calcutta, or maybe there is, but Rivka and Ewa keep these conversations from me. I don't have any time to talk to either of them nowadays, it seems. I work from dawn to dusk, at the office or at the clinic. I don't even have time to hear the news on the radio, so I feel as if this war is going on without us, somewhere else.

Maybe I am too preoccupied with my own adjustment to Calcutta, and with this new clinic that I have started with

Mitra; too preoccupied to spend more time with the people who have crossed the world with me to get here. Really, this is a recipe for disaster, and maybe I deserve to be shaken out of it by the call I receive from Ewa — the call that tells me that my whole world is about to change once more.

'She's been vomiting since the moment you left this morning,' Ewa says, trying to sound calm. Of course I am thinking: I must be to blame. I've hardly seen them for weeks. This is all my fault.

'Don't worry,' I say. 'I'll be home early and I'll take a look myself.'

When I get home Daniel is absolutely distraught. He grabs my hand and makes me run to the bedroom, saying, 'Is Mama going to be alright? Is she going to die?'

'Don't say such things,' I tell him. 'She's just eaten something bad.'

I try to sound as composed as possible, but when I see Rivka lying on the bed, hardly able to smile back at me, I can understand why Daniel is in such a state of distress. There's a strong smell of vomit in the room as I kiss her, hold her wrist to feel her pulse, then put my hand to her forehead. My poor darling. She does not deserve this.

'I'm so glad you're home early today,' Rivka says weakly, and I hold her.

'I asked Doctor Mitra what to do,' Ewa says. 'He came and took some blood. He's prescribed water, with salt and sugar mixed in, until we get the results.'

'What's his guess?' I ask, but I suspect I know the answer.

Ewa turns her head away as she says, 'Maybe typhoid. He says there's an epidemic on.'

Hearing her voice break, I say, 'More likely to be something she's eaten, that's all.'

This is still a reasonable assumption, I am thinking. But, I wish I could do something about this smell of vomit; it's making me feel like retching myself, and it lingers, like the smell in the hospital bunker in the partisans' camp.

We all sit with Rivka, and I put ice on the calves of her legs while Ewa puts cold flannels on her forehead and Daniel holds her hand. Rivka falls asleep through all of this, because she is so weak from vomiting, and soon Daniel curls up next to her and falls asleep, too, in her sick bed. It's getting dark, but there's a 'brown-out' in town so we don't turn on any electricity, just in case the Japanese planes fly over us and see the lights of some Polish refugees from the sky. The darkness is making me panic. I cannot stop thinking of Poland. If we have to repeat our experiences, we will never survive them. How could we escape from Calcutta with Rivka sick like this? This is what I am thinking. How much longer can we trick the Angel of Death? Yes, I feel as if we're being punished for the little luck we've had, and that this luck is running out fast, because I have not been concentrating on the things that matter, on the people I love — the most important gift that God gives us during our few short years on this earth.

Farha comes round often during that first horrific month of the illness, always hoping to see progress. I tell her, 'An illness comes in hundredweights and goes away half an ounce at a time.' This is what the Jews of Poland say.

'Nonsense. Give her more coconut juice,' she insists, and she sends Mary down the road to get some.

I am thinking: coconut juice? She can drink the milk from a hundred coconut trees and she'll still be exactly the same. It's not that I don't want Rivka to get better. I have been praying for her to get better all this time, so we can have some hope in our lives once more. I've tried everything, believe me, but nothing seems to help and I know that a few more coconuts are not going to make any difference. Nonetheless, this is not something I tell Farha.

Once Mary is back with the coconut juice, Farha announces the real purpose of this particular visit. 'You know, Benjamin,' she starts, 'we were surprised to see thirty of you people coming from Poland.' I am wondering why she is saying this, but I listen carefully as she continues. 'Now there are literally thousands of Jews arriving in Calcutta.'

'From Poland?' I ask hopefully.

'No, Burma,' she says. 'All Baghdadi Jews, from the same part of Iraq as us. Actually, many of them have family here, so they don't need homes, but the rest of them are crowding out the Jewish Girls' School. There are so many now they're being asked to vacate, poor things, and we're hoping to put them up through B N Elias & Company. Some of them are so sick, Benjamin, you have no idea.'

'How can we help?' These are the first words that come to my mind.

Farha starts to tell us about the people who have arrived in Calcutta with septic wounds, with raging malaria, with exhaustion and malnutrition, having suffered the long trek overland through the Tammu Pass.

'Benjamin, I feel so sorry for them. We've got to help. Everyone is doing something to lend a hand. I've been going down to the docks with my sister, Leah, almost every day. You know how the boats have to stop at the Ganges Delta, before they're brought upstream by the harbour master — there are poor fishermen out there coming aboard with food for these people, would you believe?'

Listening to her stories I feel despair that this war is continuing indefinitely, ripping us all away from our homes, tearing apart our lives and scattering us around the world.

'Farha, you can send me any amount of people. I promise you I will help them to the best of my abilities.' I say these words with confidence, but inside I am shaking at the prospect that there are thousands of people who need help, perhaps all of them coming to our back verandah here, and how to treat them all, what with Rivka sick?

Over the next few days Farha and other members of the Jewish community here spend many hours organising the new refugees, and I keep my promise to help. I have taken two weeks off from my work at Bose Paper Mills, because this is obviously an emergency. I have to put aside any remaining hesitation about starting up my medical practice again, and believe me every minute of my day is used up helping these poor people. At first, before it all gets too much, I am very happy to help, because here are people who are arriving in Calcutta like we did, with nothing, relying on the kindness of strangers. But then there is such a flood of illness I feel as if I am drowning in their vomit. This whole stupid business is repeating itself: this is what I am thinking.

Rivka is not well enough to help me, so Ewa and Mary do most of the work, seeing to the patients in our living room where they wait to see me, and Doctor Mitra as well, when he comes in the evenings. One man was sick with jaundice even before he left Burma, I am told, and had to be carried by six coolies in a *dhoolie*, with all of his baggage on an elephant's back. Really, I am wondering how he made it to Rowland Road in his state, and there is not much I can give him that will help, except for Farha's suggestion of coconut milk and plenty of sugars. Another woman I treat has severe dysentery from the conditions in the temporary camps that were set up in the jungles. She has bruises all over her body, from the bamboo bunks they slept in, as well as marks from the leeches that sucked her blood. 'What to do? There was no fresh water to bathe the wounds,' she says. This same woman tells me about how they were given only one cup of water to drink every day, and even that was filled with chlorine. What's more, with her stomach condition she couldn't eat any of the chilli *dahl*, so she spent what little money she had buying bananas, potatoes and salty tea from the villagers. Sometimes she even drank elephant's milk! So many stories I am hearing from these refugees, you wouldn't believe it.

I treat a lot of people for *kala azar*, or jungle fever, which ruins the spleen and leaves the patients completely exhausted. I see people with bilharziasis, trypanosome and nematodes. I am becoming so familiar with the anti-helminth medication available in Calcutta, because almost every patient requires some. So many refugees with more serious conditions didn't survive, I am told. Every day there were dead bodies collected in the camps, and dead bodies, too, floating in the River Chindwin. But the ones who made it — they are the lucky ones. When they arrived in Calcutta they were met by the poor people of this city at every stop, all of them shouting 'Rangoon *walla*' and offering food! How strange, I am thinking: here I am, a refugee myself, offering treatment to other refugees. What on earth is going wrong in this world of ours?

There is very little time to spend with Rivka or Daniel throughout this period. No time for anybody except the refugees that keep arriving, and the tension must be showing, because Farha comes round one day with more people for treatment and says, 'You need a holiday, Benjamin. You need to get out of here. Just look at the circles under your eyes.'

'And where exactly can we go?' I ask.

'When Rivka gets better you should go — all of you — some place like Madhupur or Gopalpur. Get away from Calcutta, in case they bomb this place, too.'

'Yes, yes. When Rivka gets better,' I say, knowing that Farha is dreaming up this possibility of a happy future. Even after several weeks of illness Rivka still spends most of her days in bed and finds it hard to walk to the bathroom. And even if she did get better in the near future, where are we going to find time for a holiday?

Our lives are too much to handle at the moment. The weight of misfortune is too heavy — not just ours, but of all the people who come and visit this clinic, day and night, many of them with no homes, no money and no happiness. It is rubbing off on me, this much I know. I feel like I did before I got back into medicine — with this thought that I don't want to look at another sick person again for the rest of my life — but how can I make that choice when my wife is sick and so many people here are looking to me as their only hope?

At the end of my two-week 'holiday' from the office, we are all exhausted. It's Shabbas, and for once there are no patients, no servants, nobody. Rivka and Daniel have gone to bed, and Ewa and I have just finished cleaning up the surgery. Both of us are sitting down on the sofa in the living room where our patients usually wait. I am too exhausted even to speak, and too exhausted to get myself to bed, either. I am alone in my thoughts when I notice that Ewa is crying. This is the last thing I need, because whatever helplessness Ewa is feeling, I am feeling the same, only ten times worse. I move closer to her and she leans on my shoulder, saying stupid things like, 'Please don't you fall sick. Nobody else, please, I couldn't bear it.'

I let go of Ewa and go to the cabinet, where I find some whisky that the Isaacs have procured from Mr Mazda, who owns their building. I pour us both a glass, and we drink whisky for a good hour, but the drinking makes neither of us feel better.

Then Ewa comes and sits next to me, holding me close. I can feel her blonde hair against my face and somehow it lifts my spirits a little. I feel as if I am holding my old life in my arms. Somehow — don't ask me how or why — we end up kissing on the lips, like we did when we were teenagers. It must be the whisky: this is what I am telling myself, as I lie down and pull her head down to rest on my chest. I can feel her tears falling on me, and I kiss her eyes to taste her tears, and then her lips again, one last time, or so I tell myself. I am thinking: Ewa, stop me, I am going crazy. What in God's earth are we doing? Ewa, we should stop this now.

'Benjamin,' she says, 'I'm so, so scared,' and I feel her fear as if it's my own. I feel terrified at what I have just done, and my heart is pumping because I am not stopping. We keep kissing each other and I am thinking: I have to stop this, but how? My body doesn't want me to stop anything. It is in its own fantasy of the past. We are kissing under the chestnut tree on our favourite bench in Warsaw and a cello is playing. Ewa is lying on top of me on the bench and it is dark, so I am taking her clothes off. Nobody can see. The cello still plays and we are both naked, lying close. I am drunk and this is not an excuse. My wife is in the next room, and she is sick, with our little boy holding her, but Ewa is not stopping and neither am I. What on God's earth is going on? Why can't I stop this disaster from happening?

I have never felt Ewa so closely before, but somehow there are no surprises, because this is how things would have been. Of course I feel a love for her, but this emotion races through my body with a sense of fear, of everything we lost: our families, our future together, our country. Surely we deserve some consolation. This is what I am thinking as the inevitable happens.

If making love can ever be a punishment, this is how it feels. Any enjoyment is drowned out by the guilt. I feel as if a levee has broken and the floods are pouring out with such force that there is no time to think about what they could do. In this moment I am swept away, and my conscience is not even a small voice at the back of my head. In this moment there is nobody in the world but the two of us, allowing this meeting to take place. This meeting that we had planned and dreamed about long before. For a few seconds it feels good enough to outlast any punishment, any amount of guilt. For a few split seconds. Yet no sooner have we finished this unstoppable business than I whisper, 'I am so sorry, Ewa.' What more is there to say?

She says quietly, 'Please don't feel sorry,' and we kiss. Then she starts crying again and says, 'I'm so sorry, I'm so sorry.' Just like that, crying and crying. Can you imagine how guilty I feel now? I feel so bad. So bad. I stroke her hair and kiss her. 'It's nobody's fault.'

'Nothing will be the same again,' she says, and I feel like weeping now, too. I feel like saying: it's true that nothing will ever be the same again, but it wasn't just because of us.

I help her to pull on her dress and I feel unbelievably evil, because I have this thought: I always wanted this to happen. Even after my marriage to Rivka, somewhere I wanted this to happen.

'Don't be sorry,' Ewa says again, and kisses me once more. 'It was my fault. I always wanted this to happen.'

So there — she said it: it was both of us making this take place.

Now we are both crying about our mistake of thinking we could be together. I offer her a few kisses that are less needy, and she kisses me back on the cheek, like a brother. I put on my clothes and we kiss some more — these kisses that are like small consolations. There is an understanding that this had to happen, and for this I am relieved. There is an unspoken understanding, too, that we will always love each other, but this can never ever happen again.

I am so shaken and yet relieved that she is pulling away from me. Ewa goes to her room to sleep, and I go for a bath. All the time I am remembering one of our sayings: you wash the outside of your body in vain if something sticks to you inside. That night I go to sleep on the sofa. I do not even think to disturb Rivka and Daniel. Tonight I want to sleep on my own, to belong to nobody, not even myself. I want to forget about everything in my life. Forget my past, my future and my present. Forget any commandment, forget to pray.

I sleep that night not for rest, but to erase the memory of anybody I have ever known or cared about. To escape not from enemy forces, but this time from the forces of my own creation.

CHAPTER 23

We haven't been living in Calcutta even for nine months when Farha starts talking about a 'war' that will take over the streets. Having just escaped the war in Europe I feel tense even at the mention of this word.

'It is essential that you escape from Calcutta for the festival of Holi,' she tells us. 'The whole place is turned upside down, absolutely. It's a festival of hooligans.' At once I start wondering about what kind of dangers will be involved. 'Stay at home, or come to Agarpara with me if you don't want to have colour thrown on you by some *goonda* on the streets.'

Rivka still hasn't recovered from the mysterious exhaustion that has come in the wake of her typhoid, so she insists that Daniel, Ewa and I go to Agarpara without her. 'I'll have more rest if you're all gone,' she says, like an injured fighter who is braver by far than the healthy ones who are free to escape.

So we're waiting for Farha inside the house, nicely behind the gates, and all this singing and dancing starts up from the *bustee* nearby where our sweeper lives.

'Please, Papa,' Daniel pleads, 'let's go and play Holi. Zek says he's playing at his cousin's today and I'll never get a chance if you don't come.'

So I agree, and I have to say I feel like I am breaking one of the ten commandments, because Ewa is too scared to join this war and Farha has warned us not to go outside for fear of our lives.

I hold hands with Daniel, in case anybody tries to hurt him, and as we turn the corner of our road one of these so-called *goondas*, or crooks, comes up and dabs some red powder onto Daniel's cheeks and then onto mine. This is nice and gentle, I am thinking. Red powder, not red blood. So far so good. Then a few more people come and throw colour on us, and they are much more enthusiastic, hugging us and spreading their colour on our clothes before they run away. I'm expecting knives to come out, the way Farha has been talking about this festival, but everybody is so friendly you wouldn't believe it.

We walk down to Ballygunge Circular Road and watch a group of people standing around singing and dancing. How happy they look as they toss green, pink and yellow powders up above them into the trees, onto each other and onto the passing cars. What was Farha complaining about? Alright, our clothes are a bit spoilt, but everybody is having fun and nobody is hurt.

'I want to buy every single colour on that table,' Daniel says, pointing to a young boy selling bags of green, yellow, red and orange powders, and I buy him all of the bags, because Daniel is allowed anything he wants from us nowadays. The young boy gives me the change and smears our faces in pink powder before we leave. This is what Farha calls 'misbehaviour', I am thinking. Let these people misbehave to their heart's content. What harm will they do, really? The only weapons are a few purples, pinks and blues. There's not a gun in sight.

Before long we're throwing the colours back at the people who come up to paint us. Yes, we're the hooligans now and I can only hope that Farha doesn't drive past and see us! We're thoroughly misbehaving ourselves, joining in their war games. Nothing can hold us back now that Daniel has his ammunition. His bags are ripping open and colour is pouring everywhere. I am thinking: never before have I seen anything like this. If this is war, let the world continue fighting! What a celebration.

Daniel is squealing with laughter as he throws colours on complete strangers. 'You look so stupid!' he laughs, and throws some more of his powders on me. I don't have a mirror, but if I did I would show him how stupid he looks, with his yellow eyebrows and his huge pink mouth. I shout to him, 'Look out!' but it's too late. A bucket of green water gets thrown on him and all of his colours run together, into a kind of military khaki.

By the time we arrive home, the street party has only just begun, but we have an appointment to meet Farha, who's already waiting for us behind the safety of our gates in a black Ambassador that's been lightly dusted with pink and green powder on the bonnet.

'What did I tell you?' she says. 'Now you'll just have to come looking like *junglees*.'

'We'll wash first, if you can wait ten minutes,' I say.

'Wash? Wash? You'll be washing that colour off next week, I'm telling you.'

Nonetheless, we have a quick bucket bath, which only fades the stronger colours and mixes the lighter ones into a pallid brown. Then Farha, Daniel, Ewa and I drive for about half an hour or so through the north of Calcutta and into the paddy fields beyond, towards Agarpara, where large numbers of the Jewish community live and work near the tobacco and jute factories of B N Elias & Company. Farha has helped to organise a picnic at a place called Riverwood, an elegant house by a river, with gardens running along the waterfront — the house of the plantation manager, she tells me, which the Agarpara community use for holiday picnics.

When we arrive at Riverwood I meet some more Jewish refugees, who have found work in the tobacco factory: someone from Lithuania, whose name I can't remember, and another young man from Czechoslovakia, who made his way here by crossing Hungary and travelling towards the Middle East, where he constructed a raft and travelled down the River Tigris for some of the way to India. I sit and talk with these men before meeting anybody else. What is it that attracts us to each other? Again, this search for similarities — for stories.

I do not remember the names of any other refugees, but I still have a photograph that Farha took with her Brownie camera. In the background are some ladies in front of a picnic cloth loaded with cucumber sandwiches, potato chips, cheese pakoras and samosas. It's a lovely day in March, with a perfect reading on the thermometer: sun with cool breezes on the banks of the river. It would be an idyllic day, except that Ewa is distant, and of course I am blaming myself and thinking about what happened between us a few nights back. While the others are down by the river she whispers, 'Should I try to get a job here at Agarpara?'

'What will you do?' I ask, and before she can answer me, I say, 'Don't feel that you have to come here and work. You have every right to stay in Calcutta, with us, for as long as you want. I'll support you.'

'But you have your own lives there, and what with Rivka sick —'

'If you want a job so badly, I can employ you to look after her. Is that what you want?'

My goodness, I've made Ewa furious now, that much I can see. 'Don't you have more respect for me?' she is almost shouting, and Daniel is looking back to see what's happening. Really, I wish I hadn't said something so stupid.

'I just don't want you to go. That's all.'

'Well, I have to, Benjamin. Can't you see?'

She's wiping away a tear and I'm wondering how I can change the subject. If I ask her to go for a walk, Farha will wonder what we're doing going off together.

'Please, Ewa, let's just enjoy ourselves today. Don't get upset. Just look around you.' A group of monkeys are chasing their leader into a eucalyptus tree. The sun is shining.

This was meant to be a glorious day out. 'We're so lucky to be here.'

'I wish I felt lucky,' she says, and again the water pools up in her eyes.

I take Ewa's arm, and together we leave Riverwood to wander for a while down a narrow lane, past the paddy fields.

'What shall I do if I never find another man that I love as much as you?' she asks, looking into my eyes so directly that I am almost ashamed of this question. What can I say? I can't imagine her with another man any more than she can.

'You will, I promise. There are millions of men better than me.'

'But I'll miss you,' she says, like a little girl. 'And Rivka and Daniel...'

'Don't talk about leaving. There's no need for you to go anywhere.'

'I have to, though, can't you see? I feel so bad about what happened.'

As soon as she says this, I start feeling guilty. So guilty, believe me. Still, I am thinking: stop this crying, Ewa, otherwise we'll both be back at the party with red rims around our eyes and everybody will be talking.

'I should try to get a job here at Agarpara. Really, it would be better for both of us, and for Rivka, too.'

'Don't worry about Rivka,' I say. 'I am doing enough worrying for the whole world,' and in this moment I'm sure that there couldn't be a person alive who has as many worries as I do. It feels as if I am pinned to my past and to all my mistakes and worries. I am thinking: what hope is there for any of us if we can't accept that there are parts of ourselves that we will never want to own up to?

As these thoughts go round my head we pass a dog with droopy eyes and patches of purple and green fur. Ewa starts to laugh and so do I.

'Imagine seeing this dog in Warsaw,' Ewa says. 'They would think it was a new species!'

We laugh some more and I am thinking: what is this love, really? There is love and there is just living, and the two have to take their place side by side. We are just living, and we should be glad to be alive. To be laughing now, in this beautiful place.

'Ewa, you're free to go wherever you want, you know that. If you find a job in Agarpara, all well and good, I will be very happy for you. And if you stay with us in Rowland Road, that will make me happy, too.'

This said, we unlink our arms and join the picnic at Riverwood once more, heading towards the other refugees, finding our place amongst our own. As I eat a cucumber sandwich I have this realisation: Ewa won't be with us indefinitely. She is going to go away and make a life for herself. Believe it, Benjamin, she's not yours. Maybe she never was.

Later on in the afternoon we go to the Agarpara clubhouse and Daniel plays tennis outside with a Hindu boy he's just met, called Krishn. Inside, an American GI is playing a few notes on the piano, and some people gather around to sing. We wander up to join them. I am standing next to some other American soldiers from the Barrackpore headquarters. One of them is a spiky-haired man called Joel Krieger, who comes into our lives with this song that he learnt from the British soldiers:

Hitler has only got one ball,
Goering has two but very small,
Himmler has something sim'lar,
But poor old Goebbels has no balls at all. Tra la la la.

Joel has his hand on the shoulder of another American soldier, called Barnaby, who taps away at the piano keys. Joel holds the crowd with a perfect smile and an easy presence, waving his lit cigarette around in the air, trying to rouse everyone to an even higher pitch.

How strange life is, that we can find ourselves here, singing loudly about Hitler in a small club that's been cut out of the jungle in a corner of India. I sing cautiously at first — these names do not slip easily from my lips — but there is no fear in Joel's eyes as he sings about these sinister warmongers on the other side of the world. I am thinking: he is lucky, this American, that he can sing about it. So lucky.

Ewa, like myself, sings cautiously at first, but is soon fully engaged by Joel and his command over the audience. She starts to sing louder, with her perfect pitch. He notices and their eyes sing together for a few minutes. I have a flash of anxiety as

Barnaby continues to tap the keys and another chorus echoes around the room. Why am I upset?

Before long a band starts up in the corner of the hall and Joel asks Ewa if she would like to dance. As they glide onto the dance floor I can see their lips moving. They are talking to each other over the music, but I can't even start to imagine what they're saying. I have to remind myself that it is no business of mine, really. This is what Ewa wants, no? She deserves to have a new life. To be free of me. And why on earth not?

I go to find Daniel. His tennis partner, Krishn, looks as if he has taken a shower under a stream of coloured powders. There are pink beads of sweat on his forehead above green eyebrows and orange cheeks. His eyes look unnaturally brown amidst all of this colour as he smiles at me and starts telling me about their game.

Throughout this conversation with the children I am thinking about how I can rescue Ewa from the dance hall. I am thinking: how wonderful that Daniel now has a friend in Agarpara. We'll come and visit Krishn lots if Ewa ends up working here.

I take the boys back to the verandah to eat potato chips. All the while I am trying to stop myself from going back to the party, because I don't want to disturb Ewa, and neither do I want to watch her, but my curiosity won't allow me to sit and talk with two seven-year-olds, so what do I do? I go back in, of course. The music has slowed down now and there is a crowd of couples on the dance floor, holding each other close. Somewhere in the middle of the crowd I see the familiar blonde hair that I can recognise anywhere, and I make out Ewa's face. She has her eyes closed and I can see the contrast of Joel's spiky dark hair as he leans over her. She is in his arms, listening to him crooning into her ear, and she is smiling at his unfamiliar touch while the band plays *Wish Me Luck As You Wave Me Goodbye*.

I feel like going up to the band and telling them to stop playing, but I know I will make a scene, so instead I convince myself that a little bit of romance is in Ewa's best interests. Why not? Look, she has a handsome GI to dance with, and I am just an old friend from back home, soaked in a hotchpotch of unhappy colours.

I am thinking: what's the point of watching them? Why should I punish myself? So I get up and go to talk with Daniel and Krishn again, who are in mid-conversation outside on the verandah.

'If you don't cut all the other kites out of the air,' Krishn says, 'then you've lost the competition. The battle is over!'

'How to cut string when kite's in air?' Daniel asks, in his best Polish English.

'Glass. You rub glass flakes onto your own string and then the wind will pull your kite across the other boy's kite and then his will fall down. *Patark!* Bang, out of the sky, and finally only one kite left!'

I try to engage myself in their conversation about kite warfare. I try to think about kites falling out of the sky, but all I can feel is my own kite, cut down, a diamond falling through the air. The boys hardly notice me sitting there. They're not interested in me and why should they be? They've found each other. What do children need with an adult anyway? I sign the chit for some more potato chips and then I go back to the clubhouse so I can torture myself some more. I cannot stop this punishment. Why am I doing this to myself? Why should I even need to see Ewa and Joel together to know what they are doing on the dance floor?

The happy couple are on the edge of the dance floor when I go back, so I can see them more clearly. His hand is around her waist and his mouth close to her ear. His other hand holds his cigarette down by his side. Now he is turning his head away from my Ewa to bring the cigarette up to his lips. She is laughing as they move slowly. She is laughing! How can I not be pleased for her? I must force myself to be pleased, no? This is what Ewa deserves, isn't it? She needs to be appreciated and loved, surely; who doesn't? But what if Joel treats her badly? What if he leaves her? And who the hell am I in all of this? I am replaying their whole relationship as if they've met and loved and parted. Already, in the space of a few songs! Stop thinking like this, I tell myself. They are dancing together, that's all. What right do I have to stand and stare and curse the poor man?

Ewa catches my eye, says something to Joel and then comes up to me, smiling warmly, beckoning me to come over and dance with her. Joel has wandered off to stub out his cigarette and find his friend Barnaby, and now I'm in his place, with my arm around Ewa's waist, smelling the coconut shampoo in her blonde hair. I cannot help but notice: she feels radiant from the warmth of Joel.

'He seems nice,' I say.

'He's lovely,' Ewa says.

'I'm glad.'

'Are you having a nice time?' she asks me.

'I'm glad that you are,' I say, and I smile as I hold her, just like Joel did a few seconds earlier. 'I love you, Ewa. You deserve the best, you know.' I don't want to add that the best is not me. She knows that, I hope.

The band plays 'A Little on the Lonely Side' and we continue dancing. Joel is watching us and, although he's smiling, I feel as though I'm dancing in somebody else's shoes. So I say, 'I must go and check on Daniel now.' I walk towards the verandah and when I look back Joel is already in my place.

Outside, the two seven-year-olds are talking about sickness. 'My father is a doctor,' Daniel says proudly. I am thinking: thank you for reminding me. Nothing could be further from my mind than medicine and I feel totally unworthy of Daniel's pride. 'But my mama sick and nobody make her better,' Daniel continues.

'Mama will get better, my darling,' I tell Daniel in Polish, sitting down next to the boys on the steps. 'Don't you worry. She'll be healthy and running around just like before.'

Thinking of Rivka, even though she is sick in bed back in Calcutta, gives me some consolation through all of this torture. Losing Ewa should not matter, because I have Rivka, the woman whom God has given me. So why this foolish desire for Ewa still? Why can't I just let go of all the ideas we had about each other? Somewhere I am thinking: because she is the only person you have from your past. Because she is the only one who can bridge the distance to the time in your life when there was nothing more important than love.

'When will Mama get better?' Daniel asks.

I say, 'In a few weeks, just wait and see.' How could it take any longer? After all, we're talking about a woman who was prepared to hold up a farmer at gunpoint to get food and soap for her child. How could she lose her strength now, when times are easier?

'I want to go home and see Mama,' Daniel says, and I feel relieved that we finally have an excuse to go back into the clubhouse and talk to Farha about leaving.

As soon as I whisper into her ear that Daniel wants to go home, Farha gets one of the bearers to go and find her driver, and I go up to Joel to apologise for taking his beautiful dance partner away. He smiles, because he knows that he is going to see her again. This is just a temporary separation; the permanent separation is reserved for me, this is what I am thinking. Joel will see Ewa again, no problem, because that's the way things are and that's the way they're meant to be.

It's dark by the time we climb into Farha's car to go home, and I watch the shadows pass our windows, feeling the leftovers of this dreadful day in the pit of my stomach, along with the potato chips. Daniel lays his head on my arm and falls asleep through all of this misery of mine. Ewa looks out of the window at the dark shapes of Bengal: black buffaloes wallowing in lotus ponds, and the faces of villagers walking along these roads in the night. No doubt she is thinking about her dance partner.

Farha sits in the front seat next to the driver, asking him about his family and instructing him not to give too much money to his 'goodfornothing' brother-in-law. After a while, listening to her talk, I find myself thinking of Rivka. I so want her to get better. We'll go up to Darjeeling together when it gets too hot in Calcutta this summer and collect basketfuls of apples, just like Ewa and I did when we were children in Poland. Rivka will get better, and then our lives will return to some kind of normality. This is all that I can wish and hope and pray for.

CHAPTER 24

The morning that we leave the Warsaw ghetto, I put on my coat, with my father's sidelocks sewn into its hem, and I have this strange feeling of protection once more.

As we leave the house, Ewa looks anxious and I try to reassure her, because my experience tells me that anxiety is like a beacon, calling for trouble. The rest of us seem more prepared. Daniel is on his best behaviour as we walk down the street, and he listens calmly when we give him his instructions to go ahead and knock on the door of the fire station.

'Are you going to be scared?' I ask him, and he shakes his head. 'When you meet the firemen,' I ask, 'what are you going to say?'

'I'm going to tell them I'm on an errand for Zegota and they must leave their door open for a few minutes so that we can all get through.'

I pat him on the head and put some coins in his pocket. 'Give this to the firemen from us,' I tell him. 'Even if they say they don't want it, you must leave it behind, alright, my darling?'

As we walk down the street I check to see that there are no 'greens' or 'blues' nearby, and send Daniel off in the direction of the fire station. While Daniel runs ahead, we three adults stop where we are, as if we're having an ordinary conversation in the street. Ewa and Rivka have their arms interlinked, and I can tell by looking into their eyes that Ewa is by far the most nervous, finding it hard to act naturally or even think about the words she is saying. A short distance away I see Daniel knock on the fire station door, and I look behind me to make sure there are still no police or soldiers nearby. Then I look ahead again and see him pulled inside by the shoulder. The door shuts and I laugh as I say, 'I'm going to get my son an ice cream, because he's been so good.'

Rivka looks back at me, understanding this code, and smiles with Daniel's eyes, stopping herself from turning her head and looking down the street to see what I've just seen. Then I take another casual glance down the street and I see the door of the fire station slightly ajar, unnoticeable to anybody except me.

I take Rivka's arm and we start to walk towards the open door, and I can feel that door, believe me. Feel that it's open. Getting nearer I drop a coin, and then bend down to pick it up, looking behind us at the same time to check if we're still safe. Then, when we're right next to the door, we take our leap into the dark. A sideways shift, the three of us, and we're inside the fire station. Within seconds we are all together again, with Daniel, who, believe me, looks so excited it worries me.

There are four firemen on duty and one of them is looking out at the street on the other side. 'We have to do this quickly,' he says gruffly. 'The prison in Gesia Street is filling up with you people escaping.'

'Sir, you have no idea how grateful we are,' Ewa mumbles.

'It's our duty as Poles,' one of them says, and I feel so relieved to hear this and know that there are Poles in Warsaw who are willing to risk their lives to help Jews, but there is absolutely no time to stay and thank them properly.

We leave the fire station in two groups and arrange to meet at the café down the road on the free side. I take Daniel's hand first, without looking back. We continue walking and I don't turn my head until we're at the café. Then and only then do I walk slightly ahead of Daniel so that I can guide him by the shoulder inside, glancing back casually as I do so. There is no sign of either Rivka or Ewa behind us, so I sit down and order some tea.

The waitress has already brought the tea essence, together with water, and milk for Daniel, and still there is no Rivka or Ewa. I have to stop myself from getting up and walking back to the fire station. I am thinking: just shut up and drink your tea, Benjamin, and look as if you're enjoying it. How strange it feels to be sitting in a café after months of deprivation. To be wasting our money like this and sipping tea as if we have partied our way through the war.

'Drink up your milk,' I tell Daniel, and he finishes it in one gulp, he is so nervous, my poor boy. I soon finish my tea and before long it's given me a stomach cramp. I am just about to get up, pay our bill and take a casual walk back up the street, when I see the two women at the door, Ewa with her brow furrowed, and Rivka smiling fakely at the waitress as they come and sit down next to us. I don't ask them why they took so long. I don't ask them if anybody saw them. I just say, 'What would you like to drink, ladies?'

This is how we finish off this terrifying trip to the café. I look at my watch. 'My goodness, the train will leave soon, we'd better get going,' I say, and signal the waitress for our bill. I do not rush as I pay her, but when I take Daniel's hand afterwards I wonder if she noticed the sweat on my palm as I took my change.

We go by tram to the station, and show our papers when we buy our tickets. Still not a single hitch. This is miraculous. All we need to do now is cover some distance, but the train stands painfully still for far too long, while soldiers pace the length of all the carriages and even more passengers climb on board. When the train finally pulls out of Warsaw station, Ewa says quietly, 'Now that we're out, I can believe that we'll make it to Japan.'

'Just act natural,' I tell her. 'We don't want to look too excited,' and I smile at them and change the conversation. 'Maybe we can buy some food at the next terminal. What do you say?'

As the train leaves Warsaw I bid a silent farewell to the city where I was born and raised. I suspect that I may never set foot here again. I say goodbye to the Vistula River which heads towards the freedom of the seven seas and the world beyond. As I hold my coat tightly around me, I pray that our journey away from this place will be just as smooth and fluid. That we will survive this terrible ordeal and find somewhere more peaceful, far, far away.

CHAPTER 25

As we trek eastward out of Poland and into Lithuania, with the help of a guide, we still feel as if we are sitting on the tongue of a lion, waiting for it to snap its jaws shut at any minute. We are leaving Hitler, but we are also travelling directly into the arms of Stalin, there is no doubt about it. This experience of being on edge at all times is so familiar from our time with the partisans, believe me. We have to walk quietly through the forest, alert to the smallest rustling of branches. We bathe only at night, always on the look-out for people through the trees. Everything is so familiar, really: the same smell of the birch trees, the mushrooms and berries, the ground and the sound it makes when we walk.

Throughout our journey I keep feeling the gold coins in my pocket to check that there's still something there to pay the Lithuanian peasant who has agreed to take us over the border and into his country. Where would we be without this man? Groping our way in the dark, no doubt, or worse still, travelling on the road and serving ourselves up for questioning to Russian soldiers. This man is safe, this much I know. He is strong, with a broad face, a couple of gold teeth, short ginger hair and a shirt that doesn't quite reach the top of his trousers. He says he's helped a few groups now since the Russians annexed Lithuania and closed the borders. He knows the way and, more importantly, he knows the people he can trust, as well as the dangers.

As we're making our way through the forest I am thinking: why didn't we just get up and go when the Russians retreated? Why did we risk staying in Poland all this time? The reason, of course, I know. How easy is it to leave the country of your birth, really? To leave everything, your family, your friends, and know that you may never see them again?

We stay one night in a farmhouse, and in the morning I wake up thinking: thank God we haven't been turned in. This guide of ours is honest. We're going to make it to Kovno. Still the lion has not shut its mouth … yet.

After a long journey on foot, carrying Daniel most of the way, we arrive at a small town and our guide buys train tickets to Kovno, where he has agreed he will leave us, once we have found the Japanese Consulate.

Kovno is beautiful, even though it is raining when we arrive. Our guide takes us through the old town with its baroque buildings, past the cathedral and town hall, and eventually to the wrought-iron gates of the Japanese Consulate in Vaizgantas Street. By now the rain has stopped and a rainbow is in the sky above us. Surely a lucky symbol, no? This is our guide's final destination after a successful mission. This is the point at which he will turn around and no doubt go and pick up another group of Poles hoping to escape the tragedy of their country. How impatient he must be as we ring the bell.

So, I am standing there, ringing and ringing, but nobody answers. The gates are locked so I call out, hoping to get the attention of somebody inside. Still no answer. After I call some more, a window opens on the second storey and a woman leans out to talk to us. 'The Japanese Consulate has closed,' she tells us, just like that. 'No more visas.' Can you believe it? After coming all this way?

Before she has a chance to shut the window, I ask her, 'Where did the Japanese diplomats go? How can I find them?'

The window closes and we all look at each other, certain that this is the end of our hopes. This is as far as our guide is obliged to take us, yet he is too polite to ask for his payment and be done with us. Disappointed, I feel for the coins in my pocket once more while I think about what we can do next, now that we have arrived at the rainbow's end and our destination is slipping further from our sights.

'Maybe we can find a small hotel,' our guide suggests, and just as we're making plans to leave, we see the woman who spoke to us a few minutes earlier walking towards the gate.

'I'm just the landlady,' she calls out, rattling her keys. 'Are you Jewish?'

None of us says anything. Why is it that somehow these words always sound like an accusation, even when spoken so gently? I look at her for a second and wonder what this lady could do to us if she knew we were Jewish. Maybe she knows of some other place we can get visas?

'Are you Jewish?' she asks again, and I say, 'Yes, yes, we are Jewish.' I feel Rivka gripping my hand, tighter than before.

'The borders are all closed,' the woman says, 'but there's an American in Vilna helping Jews get through to Japan.'

We talk some more and Ewa asks her, without sounding too desperate, 'Do you know where this American lives?'

'Ask somebody in Vilna,' the landlady replies. 'That's where all the Jews went after the Japanese Vice Consul left. Then she adds, 'You know, he was writing those visas and handing them out even as his train was leaving.'

When I hear these words I am thinking about that rainbow above us; thinking there may still be some hope. So when the gate is shut once more and we're standing on Vaizgantas Street, I ask our guide, 'Will you need extra money to take us to Vilna?' He looks a little embarrassed. 'If you can spare some,' he replies, and we make the following deal: I give him the three gold coins I have left in my possession, and in Vilna he will find some rubles to give me in return so that we can afford the train to Japan, as well as a few nights in Vilna. Having struck our deal, this ginger-haired man smiles, and I see his two gold teeth shine the same colour as the coins in my pocket.

Let me take you back to the night we spend in a Jewish hotel in Vilna's old town, near the Dominican church which they say is haunted, like so many other buildings in this gothic city. The hotel is run by a man called Yoram, who warns us of the dangers ahead of us in Siberia. 'Lithuania is not Poland,' he tells us. 'It's far safer for Jews here, even with the Russians.'

This evening I will always remember, because we gather so much information about the journey ahead of us, and in turn we tell Yoram about some of the things that are happening to the Jews we left behind in Poland. 'From the first day the Germans invaded I knew that there was no hope — no hope at all. You must pray that they never invade Lithuania,' I tell him, at which point Yoram waves a hand and dismisses the idea that they ever could.

'Let me show you one of these transit visas,' he says, after supper that night. 'Not even written onto a passport. So easy, you know.'

We learn about the people who are still copying these visas that were written by the Japanese Vice Consul, and discover that the landlady at the Kovno consulate was right to send us here. One of the places where they do good forgeries is actually at the Jesuit church. 'There's a very good man called Father Andreas Gdowski. He's been helping Jews,' Yoram tells us. 'Then there's also a man I know called Jakob — he doesn't live so far from this place.'

It is at Jakob's house that I discover how useless my rubles will be on our journey across Siberia. Imagine: all this time I have been thinking that money alone can solve our biggest problems. Here I am believing that I can buy us all tickets to Vladivostok, and to my horror I discover that we need dollars, not rubles — one hundred and eighty dollars to be precise. I am thinking: so what are we going to do? Go back and finish off our money and our lives in Poland? We have to get on the train, even if we have nothing. We are going to leave Vilna by train, no matter what.

It is at this man Jakob's house that we meet Mosze and Lewek, both of them Polish Jews who have recently escaped from the ghetto in Krakow. They show me their beautifully forged visas and I feel as if I have been allowed into the inner sanctum of the temple to see the most holy of documents.

Jakob invites Yoram and me into his house, with its low ceilings and wooden beams, and we watch him get to work copying four visas for us, in the same elegant handwriting of Chiune Sugihara, the Vice Consul who wrote visas for the other Jews in Kovno. 'So many Jews came to him without passports,' I am told, 'he was just issuing visas on slips of paper in the end.'

The two Polish men, Mosze and Lewek, watch as intently as I do while Jakob finishes the forgeries, marking the visas for the women with a tiny red dot, because there is no way that we can read the Japanese inscriptions and know which ones are for which sex. 'I don't know what your name is on these papers,' Jakob says, 'so it's best not to understand anything the customs officials ask you. Others have done the same, so don't worry.'

It's at Jakob's house that I draw a copy of a map of Japan, which I still have today. It looks like a mythological island on the edge of the world, beyond the steppes of Siberia — a magical place that has just become our destination. Really, I cannot quite believe that it even exists, until Jakob shows us a letter sent by somebody who made the trip over to Japan and lived to write back to describe the journey. You cannot believe how encouraging this is — the fact that a Polish Jew has made it all the way over there is enough for this trip of ours to seem possible. For the rainbow above Vaizgantas Street to follow us here, and touch the roof of Jakob's house.

The three of us listen to every word spoken by Jakob, so that we don't miss a single piece of information — information that could cost us our lives. 'Travel at night and talk as little as possible, and be careful in Vladivostok,' he tells us. 'They've been arresting people there just for the release money they get from the American Jews.'

He brings out a map of the Trans-Siberian Railway and shows us the stops that will be good, should we need to get off the train. 'Buy a pillow each in Vilna,' he tells us. 'You'll be sleeping on hard planks for days. And if you can't afford the ticket, you can lie down under the seats when the conductors come on board.'

'But where is the best place to board the train?' I ask, and he tells me, 'Cross over the border on a milk train, and make your way to Moscow. There, it's easier to pay for your ticket in rubles.'

After discussing the journey some more, Mosze, Lewek and I decide that we should travel together, at least to the border. 'There are some more people travelling with me,' I tell them. 'Two ladies and a small boy.' I wait for them to back out of this journey with us, but then Yoram helps out. 'You never know, you could be safer if you're travelling as two families,' he says. 'Who would throw children or ladies off a train?'

I remember our discussions at the hotel later that day. We decide that Mosze will be Ewa's husband for the purposes of this journey, and Lewek, with his paler skin and wider eyes, will be Mosze's brother. 'Nobody will believe I could have such a beautiful wife!' Mosze jokes, and Ewa smiles, no doubt thinking the same thing herself.

The following morning we begin our long journey towards Vladivostok, as if we're some sort of biblical exodus party. We even have our very own Moses — Mosze — in our midst. The only difference is that there seems to be no God guiding us, and the only instructions on what lies ahead have been given to us by a young Lithuanian Jew who's probably never even travelled out of Vilna. It feels as if we are being sent out into the wilderness with nothing but a few rocks and bushes to guide us, yet this exodus of ours has to work, because we have no alternative but to go forward and find our Jerusalem, wherever that might be.

At the border we get on the milk train, as Jakob suggested. The train belches its way forward into the night, and I can breathe again. We have really started our journey now, and I feel a sense of relief, but with it some fear of the unknown regions we are heading towards.

Somehow, the presence of new friends gives us new hope, a feeling that we are facing the unknown in greater numbers. We are on our way now, thank God. Aboard a train with a track that travels in two directions: towards Hitler or towards Stalin. Nonetheless, I sense that whatever lies ahead of us cannot possibly be as terrible as what lies behind.

CHAPTER 26

God told Moses: 'Nobody can see my face and live.' So instead He sent his voice to the prophets, He sent visions, He sent revelations. But what has He done for us now? He has killed our prophets. He has hidden His voice and withdrawn from the world. He has flipped over our lives and shown us that there is zero on the other side. Are we to give praise for such useless information?

We are in the desert of Siberia, pretending to be Russians, even though we have no more than a handful of Russian words between us. We have no right to be here at all, on God's earth, it seems. We are not wanted anywhere and we have nowhere legitimate to go. We have to rub out our presence, virtually crawl along the earth's surface so that we're not noticed.

Mosze, Lewek and myself travel under the seats in our train carriage most days, to escape the eyes of the ticket inspectors, because we bought our tickets in rubles, or rather asked a

Russian man to buy them for us. We have no right to travel here, as I said, no right even to exist. As I lie here under the hard seat, squashed flat in the semi-darkness, I am thinking: how on earth can we be expected to believe in God? How on earth?

So, we are under the seat, Mosze, Lewek and myself one day, when I see four shoes enter our carriage and voices start shooting a round of questions at Rivka and Ewa. The women do not answer, obviously not wanting to give away their Polish accents, until finally one of the Russian inspectors gets very angry and starts shouting. Now I can hear Rivka, in broken Russian, saying, 'Good sirs, we do not speak well Russian. We are on our way to Japan — look, we have visas.' She is trying her charming best, but these men are aggressive and I can hear them discussing what to do with the women in our party. I am listening to the conversation, understanding a little, and thinking quickly about what I should do next, all the time feeling like an idiot lying like this under the seats.

Then I hear Ewa shouting, 'They're taking our bags down, Benjamin. Come out, quickly!'

I see the bags shift along the floor in front of my eyes. Mosze and Lewek stay absolutely still, and it is clear that they will not give themselves up just because the rest of our party is being forced into the corridor. They will stay to the end of the line, all the way to Vladivostok, in this horizontal position if needs be.

I also do not move, until I hear Rivka swear at the conductors in Polish, saying, 'Get your *kurva* hands off me, you bastard, I'm not a criminal.' Then I hear the train slowing down, and I am thinking: what if they're stopping the train to throw Rivka, Ewa and Daniel out into the steppes of Siberia? If the inspectors kick them off we may never meet up again. This thought sends a bolt of panic through my horizontal body and I do not hesitate: I push my body sideways into the passageway between the seats, even though I know I am drawing attention to Mosze and Lewek who are hiding with me. What choice do I have, really?

When they see me coming out from under the seats, these two inspectors are so stunned, I'm telling you, that they start pushing me in the chest and forcibly emptying my pockets. They find my ticket and take it from me, swearing in Russian. Then they look under the seats to see who else is down there. Needless to say, Mosze and Lewek come squirming out, like worms. The humiliation continues and, worst of all, we have no words we can use to defend ourselves or our intentions. No way of describing our predicament, and little sign that these men would even care. We are herded down the carriage to the nearest door and our whole party is pushed, like a troupe of gypsies, out of the train.

I take one look at the godforsaken little platform in the middle of nowhere and my heart sinks. We have reached the outpost of human existence. Here there is no sign of human existence whatsoever, just plains and plains of fruitless earth, no village, nothing. Vladivostok has suddenly become a dream, and the map of Japan an unbearable fantasy. Really, I feel as if we have travelled to the edge of the world, only to find that the place is empty.

As we watch our train disappear into the distance without us, Lewek cracks a joke about how this will give us all a bit of time to get to know each other. He is the only one who laughs, for goodness sake. All through the journey he has been trying to impress Ewa — how could I fail to miss it? Even Mosze said to him back in Minsk, 'She's my wife, you *schmuck*, leave her alone.'

By nightfall another train still hasn't come, and even Lewek can't think of anything to laugh about. There is nothing for us to do here so we settle down to sleep, huddling next to each other for shared body warmth, all of us together on the cold Siberian earth, in a wooden shed near the railway station. I am on the outside, next to Daniel, who lies next to Rivka. On the other side of Rivka sleeps Ewa, and then Mosze and Lewek. Two thin blankets cover all of us, and even Daniel, who is surprisingly good at falling asleep through the most incredible ordeals, is awake in the cold. I move even closer to Rivka so that there is no space between our skins for the air to chill our son. He keeps me a little warm, although my back still freezes. I don't want to add my complaints to everyone else's, but I'm hoping, even willing, that a train will stop here before the night is up.

Sleep is the least of my expectations, but nonetheless I find myself drifting in and out of consciousness. I am not in my body, but above us, looking down. I cannot feel the cold, but I can feel the vastness of the land we lie on, and I know that there are stars above us, making this place vaster still. I can see all of us huddled up together, with the blankets tucked under our feet.

Mosze is holding Ewa tight, and Ewa is snuggled against Rivka's back. I feel no jealousy, just reassurance that we are all as warm as we can be.

I'm still watching over everybody in this dream of mine, when I hear a note being sung. It is the most beautiful sound I have ever heard in my life. I do not know where this note is coming from, but this much I do know — I am still asleep. There are some Hebrew words, too, spoken in my voice as if I am the one reading them: *Bishvili nivrah halolam*; For me the world was created. And the mysterious note is held — sung, but without any human breath.

I startle myself awake, to see if this sound really exists, and immediately reach over to Rivka to tell her what I've just heard. The first thing she says is, 'Why did you wake me? I was listening to the most wonderful music!' Believe it or not, this is the absolute truth, and as soon as she says this I feel certain that something significant has just happened.

'It was a revelation. We are here in the presence of angels,' I tell her.

'Let me go back to my dream,' Rivka says, and I, too, try to get back to sleep, to that beautiful state, but it has slipped away as mysteriously as it arrived. The moment is gone and I feel cold again, but I do not feel the discomfort of that cold, because I'm still flying on the joy of having heard what I did, and having that same revelation shared by Rivka.

I stay awake and think about all the revelations I remember from my studies in *cheder*, back in Warsaw. They all took place in the desert. Why? Because there are no distractions there. Not even a train goes by. No birds in the sky. No people or nations or religions claiming the God of revelations as their own. Nothing but space and quietude to receive the epiphanies. Wasn't Joseph, too, on the run and in the desert when he dreamed of the angels that went up and down the ladder to heaven? Wasn't Moses in the desert when he saw the burning bush?

For me the world was created. I repeat these words to myself, thinking: we have forgotten about the divine gift of life — forgotten to acknowledge it, forgotten to recognise its magnitude, forgotten to give thanks for it or to sanctify it, to live life knowing that it is holy. In this moment I feel guilty for denying the presence of God, because while I am still alive and while I am still a Jew, I should honour this God who gave us this sacred gift — the God of armies, the God of prophets, the God who created everything in this world and gave us the power to bless it.

For me the world was created. If this is the truth, then surely I had better show some appreciation for this life of ours, so I pray — and, you know, as I lie there in that shed next to the railway station, I feel as if I am receiving blessings for hearing this message. I feel as if there is a God in the world who wants good to prevail and believes in this most basic right to live and let live. That this God is the God of the desert, unclaimable by any single religion. The One God, who by that very token must be present within us: omnipresent. Maybe I am kidding myself, but I feel as if I am connected to this force of life once again. As if God has postponed our happiness, but not forgotten about it entirely.

CHAPTER 27

When another train finally arrives we board it as if we are humble Siberian peasants and take our customary places under the seats. Ewa, Rivka and Daniel befriend some Russians in our cabin who defend them loudly and passionately whenever a conductor asks for their tickets, and so we make progress, day by day.

At the end of the Trans-Siberian Railway we arrive in Vladivostok and fall into the same trap as every other Jewish traveller — held up for not paying for our tickets in American dollars. Of course, we have no money left for bribes, but the official 'deposit' for our release is paid by an American Jewish organisation and we're sent on our way.

From the moment we arrive in Japan we're looked after by the Kobe Committee for Jewish refugees, who pick us up from Tsuruga, where our freighter docks. And when we get to Kobe, what do we find? Around three hundred students and teachers from the Mir Yeshiva, one of the great rabbinical colleges in Belarus! How could this place so far from anywhere be so full of refugees, travellers and traders?

Here we meet Russian Jews and Sephardic Jews — in fact every sort of Jew you can imagine — as well as a Japanese man called Mr Kotsuji, who isn't Jewish at all, but graduated in Semitic Studies from Berkeley, California. This wonderful man has put up his own money to petition the government so that all the refugees can stay in Japan.

A few weeks after our arrival we meet him through one of the committee members and we show him the visas that were copied for us by Jakob in Vilna. He laughs when he reads them. 'You and all the others like you are called Rabinowitz. No wonder the border guards think all Jews are called Rabinowitz!' I am thinking: who cares what we're called? Who cares now that we're out of Poland? I'm only too happy to be a Rabinowitz, or anything else for that matter.

So we have reached this mythical island where our troubles are meant to end, but, would you believe it, everybody here is trying to get out. To Palestine, to China, to anywhere but Europe. Yes, we are very welcome here, but who's to say the Japanese will always be so friendly towards Jews? There is little doubt about it — Japan will soon enter this war. And so once more we are forced to think about how we are going to escape.

Rivka, Ewa and I have been given separate allowances from the Joint Distribution Committee in New York. We sleep with other refugees in long wooden sheds. We are safe here, because there are no enemies or collaborators, but every night when I close my eyes I am back in the lap of danger. Any small sound, even the sound of a door opening, and I'm sitting up shouting before I know it. Of course Rivka gets cross and tells me to be considerate, but I'm not the only one who loses control when we're sleeping. In the night, this fear can take a grip on any one of us. There's so much wakefulness in this building, really. Even though I lie down with my eyes closed, some part of me is awake. There is always coughing and whispering from behind the flimsy partitions — the sounds of a group of people who are so conscious of danger that they can see it even through closed eyelids.

In the daytime we seek out information. Mosze and Lewek come with us, because now we're a family of sorts, at least for the purposes of this journey, and after some enquiry, it appears that Hongsew in Shanghai is to become our destination, because the British are not releasing visas for Palestine. 'There are many Jews being resettled in China,' one of the other refugees tells us. 'It's not so bad. They have a ghetto for Jews there that's quite safe.'

At the mention of the word 'ghetto', Ewa is absolutely certain that she is not going to this place. 'Hongsew? Where the hell is that?' she says. 'I've never heard of it and I'm not going there, that's the end of it.'

So we go back to Mr Kotsuji, the Japanese man who is assisting the refugees here, and we ask him to help us get a visa for Palestine. 'This lady has been in the Warsaw ghetto and she refuses to go to another one in Hongsew,' I explain. 'Is there anybody you can talk to who will be able to organise some visas for Palestine?'

He looks at me with great sympathy, this Japanese man, and says, 'If she doesn't want to go there, nobody should force her. I can help, but you must give me time. Just stay in Kobe for a while and see what happens.'

Stay here and do what? There is nothing for us to do in Kobe. Nowhere to go, except the synagogue and the few centres that have been set up to help the refugees. We have nothing to do but wait for answers from various governments of the world. Our lives have been suspended while authorities all over the world focus on battle plans and borders, artillery, ammunition and what have you. There is no thought for people at all.

Daniel keeps saying, 'I'm bored, can't we do something?' Of course, there is nothing for him to do here, either. We are trapped between two worlds — between the living and the dead — and here there are no entertainment halls. Time passes, that's all. We walk and walk in the daytime, exploring this trading town, and sometimes we go a little further into the countryside, with its pretty storybook scenery, its abundant groves of bamboo, small thatched houses with rush-matting floors and smiling Japanese people. All so different for us, you have no idea, and of course most of the Japanese people here cannot understand a word of what we try and say to them. How strange it must be for *them*, to be invaded by so many foreigners.

One day we find ourselves walking in the Jewish part of Kobe's cemetery, and we read some of the inscriptions on the stones. We walk past one that reads: 'Moses Cohen. Born in

Aleppo, Iraq on such and such a date. Died in Kobe in 1936.'
Looking at the inscription Rivka says, 'Please, whatever else we
do, let's not die here in Kobe. Anywhere but here.'

Just when we think we should be booking our plots in the
Kobe cemetery, because our lives are all but finished, our visas for
Palestine come through and we are allocated places on a migrant
ship. Thank God for the *Asama Maru*, we are thinking. Maybe
next year we will celebrate Passover in Jerusalem, after all.

There are so many people boarding the *Asama Maru* with us,
and even more expected to board in Singapore, Hong Kong and
Penang. Too many people, with so many suitcases, bundles and
attaché cases I am worried that we could sink the boat before
we even leave the port. Really, it seems as if half of Kobe is at
the docks, on the way to goodness knows where.

Rivka, Ewa, Daniel, Mosze, Lewek and myself all board
together, not wanting to be separated, but as soon as we talk to
the officer organising the dormitories, it seems that separation is
inevitable, as Rivka, Ewa and Daniel are directed to a women's
dormitory and I am directed to a room full of bunks, with
Mosze and Lewek. Immediately, Lewek takes the bunk closest
to the porthole, and Mosze takes another lower bunk, leaving
me a bunk on top of two others that knocks my head when I sit
up. I say to them, 'If I bow my head the whole way to the
Promised Land, they'll have to let us in!'

Hearing me speak in Polish, another man, Jankel, who is
moving into our dormitory, gets up, says hello and introduces

his cousin, Zalman. It turns out that the two of them worked in a textile mill together in their home town, Lodz, and escaped from the ghetto there with the same idea that we had, to get out through Lithuania towards Japan. As Jankel stretches towards me to shake hands, I have this sense that we are strengthening in numbers and somehow this has to work in our favour.

After these introductions we go out on deck to meet the rest of our party, and we all hang onto the rails and stare back at the dock, with the gulls circling above us and this feeling in our stomachs that we're going back into the unknown. After a while the number of passengers boarding the *Asama Maru* trickles down to just a few latecomers and coolies, and there are more passengers behind us, pushing against the rails, speaking in so many different tongues it seems as if we are all aboard Noah's ark, representing our various different nations on a journey towards some kind of new world. Then the ropes are thrown back on board and there's no turning back. 'Bye, bye Japan,' Daniel says, as if he is bidding goodbye to a new friend.

Soon Japan starts disappearing into the distance, and the country that we were so determined to reach a short time earlier vanishes from our view altogether. By the afternoon we are surrounded by an expanse of water that seems to stretch out to the ends of the earth.

Once we are at sea we spend a lot of time exploring the ship, which is like a treasure trove for Daniel. He takes my hand and makes me look at every toilet, every cabin and deck area, and even manages to get us entry into the kitchen and engine room. The next day, and the day after that, we discover more levels and more little areas of our floating world than we ever imagined could exist. Of course, once we have discovered virtually every piece of this ship, the novelty of a life at sea soon wears off and I cannot help feeling cooped up, acutely conscious of the ship's small boundaries. Really, apart from talking to all the people on board, what is there to do on this ship?

Then one day the monotony is broken when some whales start herding their young, not far from our boat. Rivka, Daniel, Ewa and I are on deck watching this incredible sight, and Daniel is leaping up and down with excitement. 'Mama, let me jump into the sea and swim with them,' he says, with his usual disrespect for safety. Without thinking, I put my arm around Rivka and she pushes her body against mine, and we kiss. Really, we are just innocently holding each other and admiring these creatures that we've never seen before, but within a few seconds Ewa starts sobbing and saying, 'I hate you. All of you! You treat me like I don't even exist!' Then she runs back to her cabin without another word.

I have to say, I am quite taken aback. What have we done for goodness sake? Nothing, except show a little affection towards each other.

'I'll go and talk to her,' Rivka says.

Daniel stays with me, looking at the whales with fear in his eyes now, and I am thinking that what we need more than any captain is the grace of God to guide us over these rough waters.

I do not let Daniel go back to their cabin, and he stays with me until suppertime when we file into the dining hall to sit down with all the other travellers on board. Rivka and Ewa arrive separately, and both look like they've been crying; worse still, neither is talking to the other. Trying to ignore the situation, Mosze, Lewek, Jankel, Zalman and I talk, and Lewek tells of how he was supposedly married to Ewa for the entire period of the train journey. 'Unfortunately, by the time we got to Vladivostok she had decided to take out a divorce.' We all laugh, but both women remain painfully silent. I look at the two of them with their red eyes, then look out the small window where the only landmass we can see is the surface of the distant moon. My stomach starts to churn, and while my guts are in motion like this I cannot put any of the ship's sloppy food down my throat.

Later that night, when we are back in our dormitories, Daniel comes in and tells me, 'Mama is outside and she wants to talk to you immediately. She says it's very important.

Daniel is looking worried again, so within a few seconds I'm out in the corridor, where Rivka is pacing, rubbing her hands together as if she's preparing some long speech for me. She turns to Daniel nervously and tells him to run off back to the cabin. As he darts off, she shouts out, 'Don't talk to Ewa. Play with that other little girl instead.' My heart sinks as Rivka then takes my hand, with more affection that she has ever shown, and reaches forward to give me a passionate kiss, saying, 'I love you, Benjamin.'

At this point I have to pull back from her and say, 'Rivka, you didn't call me out to tell me this. What's going on between the two of you? How's Ewa?'

'Why don't you ask how I am?' she sulks.

'This is not like you,' I say. 'We have no choice but to get along, all of us. And you, of all people, are the most practical I know.'

'But it's impossible stuck here on this boat together,' she wails. 'I don't know what to do. None of this is my fault. I didn't force you to marry me. It's just awful.'

By now Rivka is crying and crying, without telling me anything about what's going on. Eventually, I calm her down and she says, 'Why did you ask Ewa to come with us? She hates you.'

I take a deep breath and tell my wife, 'Even if this is what she says, she is like family and I love her, Rivka. We have to get along.'

'But we can't be a family,' she sobs.

How can I make Rivka understand that we have no choice? How can I turn this situation around so that we are sailing our boat on friendly seas once more? I feel at such a loss, not knowing how to intervene in the affairs of these women. All I can say is, 'Rivka, I made my choice in marrying you, and now you have to make some decisions in the interests of everyone. You can make Ewa feel better, I know you can.'

'But she's trying to control your feelings towards me, can't you see? She doesn't want you to even touch me.'

'Nobody can control us,' I say. 'We have no country, we're at sea: we have no rules except for the ones that we make for ourselves. Can't you see, Rivka, that we have to make the kind of world we want to live in, because nobody else is going to do it for us?'

Rivka is quiet for some time. We sit together on the deck until I am exhausted from catching tears and she has emptied her buckets full of them.

For some days we continue sailing in this uncomfortable climate, and I try to spend as much time as possible in the cabin so that I don't upset anybody accidentally. Then, after several days, we hit some rough weather and the *Asama Maru* starts swaying heavily in the water. Passengers, who have already organised themselves into various ethnic groups, desert the decks, and I, too, take to my bunk. However, once I have emptied my stomach I can walk around the cabin again and the feeling of seasickness subsides.

Just as I am starting to feel better, Rivka comes into the men's dormitory and tells me, 'Benjamin, I'm going to have to call the ship's doctor for Ewa.' What disaster has struck us now? I am thinking. I follow Rivka back to her cabin and no sooner do we open the small door then we are hit by a stench of vomit that's far worse than in any other area of the ship. Ewa is lying there, so sick she can hardly talk. All she says is, 'I'm so sorry,' and then she groans and groans like someone who is being slowly tortured. Together, Rivka and I go and search for the ship's doctor, who is busy seeing to several patients up on the top deck. We go back to wait with Ewa, and Rivka keeps saying, 'I hope she gets better soon, poor thing.'

When the ship's doctor has assessed the situation, he offers to move Ewa to a private cabin on the next floor up and enlists Rivka to look after her. Two cabin boys take Ewa up one floor on a stretcher, and Rivka, with all the informal training she has received from her father, nurses Ewa over the next week, day and night.

Once they are settled, I ask Rivka if I can talk to Ewa, and she tells me, 'You must,' so I go and see Ewa at least twice a day to hold her hand and talk about my life since we were together. I tell her all about Rivka's father, about Piaski, and about our lives with the partisans, and she tells me about how her father was taken by typhoid and her mother by the Gestapo on suspicion that she was lying about her Catholic identity. Ewa is so frail, and her head is swimming with these memories, combined with this nausea of hers, but I feel as if we are making some kind of progress. I don't expect anything from her in this condition, believe me, but nonetheless I feel there has to be some good come out of all this talking.

This is how our lives on the *Asama Maru* continue and over the next few days we meet more and more Polish Jewish men who are travelling on this ship with us, and they swap bunks with other passengers until our cabin is almost filled with Poles, as well as a couple of Czechs. Daniel moves to the men's cabin, too, and shares my bunk with me, and I can see that he loves it here with us, because he is the centre of attention, being the only child. We pass our days in good company, and eventually the *Asama Maru* enters quieter waters once more, on our approach into Hong Kong.

It is the eve of Rosh Hashanah when we arrive at the dock, and Jankel has this idea to telegram a man called Lawrence

Kadoorie, one of the leaders of the local Jewish community whom he has been told to contact. In this telegram, Jankel asks if we can disembark to celebrate Rosh Hashanah in the local synagogue, but the captain says that the police do not allow disembarkation. Nonetheless, we receive a telegram back saying that Lawrence Kadoorie has offered the police a personal guarantee to return us to the ship, and we must be ready to go ashore in the afternoon!

None of us have any smart clothes, but Jankel organises to borrow a few garments from some of the other passengers who are remaining on board for the night. Then, when we are looking as smart as we can, all ready to leave, Rivka and Ewa come out of their cabin. Rivka, it seems, is insisting that Ewa comes with us to celebrate Rosh Hashanah.

'I think it would be very good for Ewa to walk on some solid land,' she says, and when I hear my wife say this I know that Ewa is somewhat better, and so too is the relationship between the two women in our party. There is something quite wonderful about getting off the ship. The land below our feet is so firm that I am thinking: how can anybody really appreciate stability until they have experienced its opposite?

There are a number of Hong Kong Jews who have come to welcome us at the docks, and they embrace us as if we are long-awaited family members. They take us to a market to shop for supplies for the next part of our journey, without asking for any payment. And how different this market is! Once more we are strangers in a strange land. For instance, turning a corner I see a bucket of water snakes for sale — and one of these snakes at the top of the bucket gets a chance to slip away down the street, before being caught by the shopkeeper and decapitated in front of us! None of this is familiar, believe me.

Then our hosts take us into a fancy Jewish club, where we sit down for the first proper meal we have had in months, served to us by beautifully dressed Chinese bearers, and we dine as if we are kings visiting from distant shores. I drink more wine than I should, and become quite overwhelmed by this heartbreaking generosity of the Hong Kong Jews, because it could not have come at a more crucial moment. Rivka and Ewa are engrossed in a conversation with each other, and Ewa seems to have regained some of her health as well as her optimism. All this time I am thinking: thank God that this part of our journey together is over. At last, it seems, we have come to some sort of understanding that is worth celebrating.

CHAPTER 28

When Naomi arrives at a crossroad on her way back to Israel, she asks her two daughters-in-law if they want to follow her back to the land of her birth. Their husbands are dead, so there is no need for them to accompany their mother-in-law back home. They are princesses, after all, and could stay in the land of Moab and enjoy their birthright, rather than go back to a land where their futures are uncertain.

One daughter-in-law goes home when Naomi presents her with the two paths up ahead, but Ruth? No, not Ruth! She says that God will have to strike her dead to stop her going back to Israel with Naomi; so they leave together, and Ruth gives up everything when she leaves the land of Moab — her family, her country and her royal status. Everything except her faith in God and the hope that circumstances might improve.

When I first told Ewa this story she was a young girl, promising to convert to Judaism for me. Now when she tells me she is converting, I know it is not for me, but for Joel Krieger. And so it was with Ruth. Her first husband was dead, so she went elsewhere and married again.

Ewa knows what it means to be Jewish, even though we would never describe her as such. She has worn the Nazi armbands bearing the Star of King David, and withstood the taunts of Germans. But the girl I remember lit candles for the dead on All Saints Day, and went regularly to Mass with her parents to the sound of all those bells.

When Ewa sat down with the Beth Din and told them of her desire to convert, the Calcutta Council asked her formally: 'Are you prepared to throw in your lot with a doomed people?' And Ewa said, 'I already have.' So here in Calcutta they are letting her learn the Torah and prepare for the time when she will dip herself in the mykwa and become formally Jewish, just like the Nazis always said she was.

I suppose at this point I should say that Ewa no longer lives with us in Calcutta. There is plenty of work for her in the offices of the tobacco factory at Agarpara, which is apparently doing a roaring trade to provide American soldiers like Joel with their generous cigarette rations. These soldiers and their needs have conspired to take away a fair few of the Calcutta girls, I am told.

Still, Ewa comes regularly to visit us from Agarpara — whenever she comes for conversion classes, in fact. She has come alive again, too, what with her work and her Judaic studies. She knows more than I do now about Judaism, or so it seems, and now I understand why the Gemara claims that converts are like the plague: because they make the rest of us Jews look bad, that's why.

Sometimes Ewa asks, 'Papa would have been happy to know that I am converting, no?'

'He was a convert to Catholicism,' I say. 'Who knows whether he would be pleased or not.'

Sometimes I wonder whether Ewa is so devout only because she wants to meet her father, somehow. Is it naivety or loss that makes her feel so strongly about this religion of ours? I think this, but I have to admit that there was a time when I could have been accused of the same enthusiasm.

'It's just a passing phase,' I tell her, 'because you're doing all of this study. Do you think that this excitement over what you're learning can really be sustained? Do you think that the people of Israel could prolong the state of revelation after Mount Sinai?'

Really, Ewa is a convert who puts the rest of us to shame. On her last visit here she asked me about Amos — the part where it talks about the Jews being the chosen people. 'You alone have I singled out,' she quotes, 'that is why I will call you for account.' Then she adds, 'We have to be held to account. I am not willing to do a halfway conversion. If I am going to be Jewish I will take full responsibility for my actions as a Jew. I will become a better person, too — if we're supposed to be different or better, or whatever ...'

'There is no better,' I tell her. 'How on earth can we say that we're better than anybody else? Goodness is not something that's dished out to one people alone. There's so little of it, and it's scattered all over the place, here and there. Don't you think?'

I feel a little uncomfortable hearing these Jewish ideas repeated to me straight after her classes, but when I tell Rivka about my concerns in private, she reminds me that I wanted to be a rabbi once upon a time.

'Yes, but that was long before the war,' I say. 'How can anybody become a rabbi after all of this business has started in the world?'

Rivka tells me to take it easy on Ewa. 'She's Jewish, alright. Her soul would have been there at Mount Sinai, no doubt about it,' she says, but I tell Rivka that she's wrong, because I have seen Ewa light candles in front of Mary and her baby. 'She is a Catholic, what are you talking about?'

Then Rivka says, 'Why are you making it so hard for her? What's your problem? You should love the convert; it is written fourteen times in the Torah. The Israelites were strangers in a strange land, and we, too, were converts after we left Egypt. Remember that, Benjamin.'

The truth is that I do love the convert, but I don't tell Rivka this. When Ewa goes back to Agarpara I miss her and I miss talking about the important things that I scoffed at in front of her. We have come so far from the truth of our teachings; concentrated only on our survival. We have forgotten to sanctify the ordinary in our daily lives, our obligation as Jews; instead we live through the days one at a time, pleased to have food and shelter. Yes, we could learn a lot from Ewa. She is entering the covenant so inspired it's embarrassing for the rest of us Jews getting by on the small amount of faith we have left in us. It's plain to me that what I need is a spiritual revelation of one sort or another, really. If I could give myself a shot of something at the clinic that would bring about this transformation, believe me I would do it, but nothing is quite so easy when you have a spiritual sickness, this emptiness.

Of course, you can always talk about these things, and that can help a little. In fact, nowadays I find myself talking about God with anybody who wants to have such discussions, and here in India everybody is willing to exchange ideas on the subject. There is absolutely no shame in talking about your Maker over a cup of tea. No shame whatsoever.

'Mitra,' I ask one day after the clinic, 'what about your Hindu gods? Why so many of them?'

My doctor friend looks at me with his doubly large eyes, and with great seriousness corrects me on my false understanding. The next day he has a book with him which he reads from.

He who lives as our guide, who is one, and yet appears in many forms; in whom the hundred lights of heaven are one, in whom the Vedas are one, in whom the priests are one — He is the spiritual atma within the person.

'There is only one God,' he says as plainly as possible, making me feel stupid for my childish assumptions. 'But your God of the Bible, is he always consistent? Does he always behave the same way?'

'No.' It is true: there are many faces of God. I think about the God of Armies, the God of Angels, even the God known simply as *Rock*, the God of Infinity, and all the other descriptions...

'So these Hindu gods are just the same. They express the various personalities of God, that's all. The singular divinity that is in everything, including us.'

Ha! If only I could feel this within myself, I am thinking.

'Why do you worship statues, though?' I ask, tentatively, because I have centuries of suspicion behind me over the worship of idols and I do not wish to sound too judgemental. 'In my religion we believe that no man can see God's face and live.'

'Aha. So we are in the same predicament. Isn't that strange?' Mitra says, clapping his hands together, delighted that we are both stranded on the same boat. 'Neither you nor I can see God; so we have only stories!'

The next day he brings in another book — his Torah — and he reads it to me.

Eye cannot see Him, nor words reveal Him; by the senses, austerity, or works He is not known. When the mind is cleansed by the grace of wisdom, He is seen by contemplation — the One without parts...

'See, we have an invisible God, too, how strange is that!'

'But what about the statues on your prayer table?' I ask.

'Well, how else am I to understand the infinite? It's a very big saucepan, no? And I need to have a handle on it somehow!'

Mitra pulls out an old silver coin from his pocket and gives it to me. 'See, this is a Ganesh on one side and a Durga on the other. I'd like you to keep it.'

'But it has an image of God on it, and we are not allowed —'

'Nonsense! It's a coin. Money. Are you allowed to have money?' He is laughing now, and I keep my special coin in my pocket.

'It will bring you luck,' Mitra tells me.

'Money-back guarantee?'

'Of course, of course,' and he is laughing now so hard at having tricked me into accepting his beautiful idol that I am glad to have made this concession and to have a lucky coin. It was the goddess Durga who welcomed us to Calcutta, and so far Calcutta has been a fortunate port of call. I am thinking: I must have an open mind here in India and learn more of Mitra's Torah, because we cannot live forever with our isolated beliefs, knowing nothing of the diversity around us.

When Ewa comes to visit us in Calcutta next time, she asks Mary about the churches in the city. She has a task, it seems, and that is to say goodbye to the religion of her birth. I ask her if I can come along, just like I did sometimes back in Warsaw. She agrees and so we take the car to St Thomas's, past Flury's and on towards Loreto College.

It's early in the morning when we arrive at the church. The porch in front has rush mats rolled down between the columns, so we lift them to go inside. Ewa leads the way, because even though she has never been here before, through birthright this is her familiar terrain. She lifts the heavy iron clasp on the thick wooden door and turns it to let us inside. She crosses herself, and we go down the aisle together past the tall columns on either side of us, to the front, where she kneels.

For a minute I wish I had not come. I feel awkward about whether or not I should be bowing down towards an image. I feel like a cheat being here, because I want to do the right thing, but I don't have the correct papers, or traditions, or whatever. I am an imposter in this House of God. I don't know how to manage myself here, for one thing, and my religious training has not prepared me for any compromises.

Yet at the same time I feel the need to find some common ground, so I sit on this long hard wooden pew, a Jew in a Catholic church, contemplating the Unity of God and waiting for some inspiration. It's the Shema that immediately fills my head: 'Hear O Israel, the Lord is our God, the Lord is One. Blessed be the Name of His glorious kingdom, for ever and ever.' And you know what, the Shema suddenly feels like a Catholic prayer! Why not, if the Lord is truly One?

I pray with my eyes open in this church, and looking around I have to admit there is a feeling of *kadosh*, of holiness, and I remember that it is in our power to make everything holy; in fact, it is even our obligation, as Jews, to do so. Yes, the space in this church feels holy: the very stillness of the air, the columns, the gallery above with its large open windows and birds flying in and out under the high arched ceilings. In its holiness it feels as familiar as Maghen David Synagogue.

I need to tell these thoughts to Ewa, so I put my arm around her and whisper into her ear, 'You're not saying goodbye to anything. God will follow you out of this church and into the next one.'

She opens her eyes, and they look as if she has been some place far away, somewhere in between these two religions of hers. She smiles at me and closes her eyes again. This time I don't disturb her, because she has to make her own rituals for this ceremony, for surely there are none that already exist. She must make her own peace and feel comfortable with her choices.

I continue with my Shema, and I have to say, it hasn't stirred me like this for quite a long time. Until recently it's been hard for me to feel any kind of divine inspiration, and it feels especially odd when it comes at me all in a rush, in a Catholic church of all places. Ewa is sitting next to me, but I am hardly aware of her. She is freeing herself from her past, and I have an instinct that I should do the same, so I take my arm from around her and contain myself. I close my eyes, and if I am praying before graven images, so be it. This feeling is coming from the inside of me and soon I am not even aware of the benign statues ahead of me.

I pray for Ewa and for myself, and I pray that the strings that bind us are undone. If this is a time of endings, let it be an ending for me, too. Oh God of mine, please, please take away the burden of this desire. Take away any expectations I have ever had and allow forgiveness, if that is necessary, for my feelings and actions.

I swear, once I have announced this intention, I have the sensation that everything around me is gone. I am dead — as dead as Ruth's husband. It is not as if I don't care for Ewa or for anybody else, it's just that I feel as if I am beyond any experience, any religion, any desires at all. I have arrived at a place that is too rich in feeling to have any compartments for people, places or religions. My eyes are closed and I don't want to open them. I stay like this, feeling totally whole, entirely still, just inside myself.

Ewa says something like, 'I've finished. We can go now,' — just like that. And I slowly open my eyes to find myself here in a chapel in Calcutta. I see the painting of one of their saints to one side of me, and the pew feels hard beneath me once more. I look at Ewa, and she, too, looks composed and resolved. I thank her for letting me come with her, and we get back in the car to go home without needing to say anything much to each other at all.

CHAPTER 29

Some months after Ewa's conversion, she and Joel get married, Calcutta style. Farha and her effervescent sister, Leah, organise the whole affair so that it will be in keeping with the customs of the Baghdadi Jews of Calcutta, but we are officially the hosts, it seems.

The night before the ceremony, Joel is told to send sweets, wax candles and shoes to our house in Rowland Road, along with henna to ward off the evil spirits. Our house is full of people making preparations for this event — servants from other households, and a few others from the Jewish community. Even Rivka is helping, with the little strength that she's recovered. Looking over at me and seeing that I'm not really involving myself in the preparations, she takes me aside to our room to confront me about Ewa.

'Why aren't you helping?' she asks. 'Why aren't you at least pretending to be happy for her?'

'There are so many others helping,' I tell her. 'Why would I want to get in the way?'

'Tell me the truth, Benjamin, you wish it was you, don't you?' Rivka says this with such harshness in her voice and her chin held up so high, really, I am wondering if she has been preparing this little confrontation.

There's a silence, because I don't want to encourage this conversation any further.

'Rivka, I have tried my best to be a good husband. If you think I haven't ...'

'That's not what I asked you.'

'So?'

Then she asks me straight out: 'So, do you still love her?'

What can I say? She asks me again, and still I don't want to say anything that will get me into trouble with my wife. Then she asks the same question even louder. 'I've always tried to make concessions for you, Benjamin, but it's about time you told me the truth. Do you still love her?'

I'm worried that the others will hear us now, so I tell Rivka, 'Be quiet. Of course I love her.' I say this as if I'm telling her that trains arrive in stations, or stars can be found in space. It would be stupid to lie about it. 'But Rivka, I love you, too, can't you see? Everything I've done in Calcutta has been for you and Daniel. What is love if it can't be demonstrated? Ewa is no longer my responsibility, that's all.'

Now Rivka is silent as she holds her head in her hands and I can't even read her expression.

'Rivka, you love Ewa, too, you know that. You've crossed the world with her. We've all shed our tears together. Should I stop loving her just because she's getting married? I've loved her all my life, for goodness sake, but you're my wife, and that's more important to me than anything.'

I take off my shoes and lie down on our bed, totally exasperated, because I never wanted to say this; because these things should not be said. Rivka lies down next to me. We don't touch, but she starts to cry, taking my hand to wipe her tears. How it breaks my heart to see her this upset. Why did I tell the truth, for goodness sake?

'When I get better,' she says through her sobs, 'I'm going to make you forget all about her.'

We hold each other, and my face is wet from her tears. 'My sweet darling, I don't know what I would do without you, Rivka,' I tell her. 'Daniel will grow up and leave us, but you're my life, you have to believe it. We'll always be together, and I'll always love you.'

We are interrupted by Leah, who tells us that our guests have started arriving, along with the *dakaka* — the traditional entertainer she has organised to sing bawdy songs in Arabic and balance glasses on her head as she thumps her tambourine. What a party it's going to be, and what a messy time for the two of us to fall apart, this is what I'm thinking.

'Come.' I take Rivka by the hand. 'We have to do our best for Ewa's sake, Rivka. We're her only family. If we can't celebrate her happiness, who is going to do it in our place?'

I see that Rivka has enough compassion to understand that what I am saying is the only truth that matters at this moment in time. It is much more important than our own feelings right now. I pull her up and she takes her hand away to wipe her tears.

There is great cheering outside our bedroom. Ewa has arrived from Agarpara for her celebrations — this *Khadba* — and she is surrounded by well-wishers. Rivka makes her way through the small crowd to give her friend a big welcome and a long hug. Then they both start crying, as if Ewa has witnessed everything that has just gone on in our bedroom and there can no longer be any secrets between the three of us.

It's a good half an hour before I have a chance to talk to Ewa and wish her all the happiness in the world. No sooner have I wished her, she tells me, smiling sweetly, 'Rivka told me you still love me.'

I am quite taken aback, I'm telling you. Then Ewa gives me a kiss and tells me, 'Whatever you do, don't tell Joel!' I laugh, embarrassed, and she gives me another hug and says, 'I'm going to miss you, Benjamin, more than you'll know.'

Later in the evening Farha and Ewa are hugging tearfully again, while Ewa's toes are being painted with henna and her mouth sweetened with *baklava*. They are crying together even though the party is in full swing and Arabic music is being played at top volume, announcing to the neighbours and the Calcutta crows that a wedding is soon to take place that will finally end any slight fancy I might have had that Ewa and I could one day be together.

One Saturday just before Ewa and Joel leave Calcutta to take up a posting in Delhi, Joel and I go to the races together. This day, really, has to be one of the most enjoyable days I remember in Calcutta during the war. There are a fair few other Jewish friends there, all of them breaking the *mitzvah* like we are, and none of us mentioning it. We are having a fine time, and I have to say, I'm surprised to realise how much I like Joel.

It's at the races that Joel asks me about Ewa's parents, and I tell him about our lives together and the closeness of our two families.

'You and Ewa were going to marry, she tells me.'

I shrug my shoulders and smile. 'But things don't work out the way we plan, do they?'

Then he asks me, 'I hope you don't mind that I'm taking her away,' and I find myself laughing. 'I have no right to mind, she's a lucky woman.'

Joel places his bet on a horse called Sweetheart and I place my money on Playtime. Neither horse wins, which doesn't bother either of us. 'You win some, you lose some,' he says, and the two of us go off for consolation to the bar. How strange it is to find myself liking Joel now, especially when we are on our own together and I'm not coloured with this insane jealousy.

He tells me how much I would love America, and I believe it, because I like him. He tells me about pine forests and bears, and I think of Poland. He tells me about the moose and the silver birch trees, the canyon lands and the snow on the quaking aspen trees in the west — all these stories about the country that he loves and misses. How nostalgic this makes me feel. There was a time, too, when I would have talked with the same passion about my homeland, but I have nothing I can say to him now. America is like a fairytale: no wonder so many of our people are trying to flee there, this is what I am thinking.

'You must come and visit us as soon as we're settled back in New York,' Joel tells me, and I promise him that one of these days we will come. When this war is over. When peace has come and all the wounds have healed, we will visit America.

'I give you my word.'

CHAPTER 30

Ewa's departure has given me an unexpected peace of mind. In all the times that I sought to be with her as a boy, I could never have imagined this sense of relief I have now that she is gone and has a life of her own. I finally feel as if our journey is over. Our trip from Japan on the *Asama Maru* was our last voyage together. There is no more need to settle down, because our home is here now and our lives have become less complicated since Ewa left. Really, this is a time of beginnings and endings.

And you know what? Like a miracle, Rivka has fully recovered, too. We are a family once more, and in some ways we are a family for the first time. Rivka, Daniel and I go for long walks together on the Victoria Maidan, eat ice candy and go to the movies, like normal people here do. We have come to terms with the fact that this war could go on for the rest of our lives, and if there is fighting in the world, we will have to find peace of mind within ourselves to carry on our lives.

Daniel is ten and doing well at St Xavier's, and there are moments when we would like to share these simple achievements with other family members, but that will never be possible, so what to do? In spite of this, everything is running smoothly in our lives now and we have to be grateful for what we have, especially when there are so many villagers still living on the streets after the recent famine.

Even this verandah clinic of ours has become so popular now that Mary has to turn people away, which feels horrible, absolutely, but the good thing is I no longer have to disturb Mitra to ask questions or get a second opinion, which makes everything so much easier. In fact, we're working so well together that we've decided to start a full-time clinic in Sovabazar Street.

Rivka and I go to look at Sovabazar Street often. Such an interesting area, really. Nearby are all these crumbling palaces belonging to the old Bengali families, their verandahs with the kinds of columns and elegant plasterwork that you could find in Paris or Rome — but here the facades are falling apart in this weather, making exotic new shapes and patterns that are unique to Calcutta. Some of the buildings near our new clinic even have trees growing out of them where the cement has eroded.

I love this area of Calcutta and always have, ever since we came here first. In Sovabazar the decay has its own beauty, its own unique fungus and discolouration. This part of Calcutta sums up the Almighty's desire to express everything about the whole truth — the entire passage of time. Even the trees look ancient, yet still full of a dark green life in their leaves. You can see how the banyan roots have grown around the shrines that were once placed beside their trunks. Yes, there are shrines here that look as if God has poured a tree over them!

Our premises are on the ground floor of a four-storey building with large wrought-iron balconies. On the top storey sit two angels that hold their hands up towards the skies, and crows sit on their crumbling fingers. Such a beautiful old building, believe me. We have permission to turn the whole place into a small hospital if we're to expand, and these plans keep me alive and well and happy to be a part of this wonderful city.

The hard part of these small successes, though, is leaving Nayar Babu, because we have become such good friends over the past four years. When I tell him I'll be going off to work elsewhere, he says, 'Didn't I tell you that you should be doing this work all along?'

Still, my feelings are very mixed when I actually leave the offices in China Bazaar for the last time. I am relieved that I will no longer have to pretend I know something about business, yet without this job, where would we be now? I assure myself that they will find someone much better than me. What makes me so good at shipping, anyway? The fact that I caught a boat once to Japan and another to come here? For sure there will be someone else to replace me at Bose Paper Mills, somebody else who will come along and try to understand Nayar Babu's filing system and sit next to this wonderful man who does all their work for them.

When our clinic in Sovabazar Street has been painted and prepared, Mitra organises a prayer ceremony. 'Come to the *puja* and leave your religion aside just for a while,' he tells me. 'Let us bless this clinic together.'

Rivka does not feel comfortable coming to the ceremony, so I go with Daniel and we meet Mitra there in Sovabazar. The *pandit* arrives and we take him to the main area where patients will wait. We sit around a small, square metal bucket and this priest of Mitra's starts to recite his blessings in Sanskrit. He lights the fire and I watch it, hypnotised. Mitra closes his eyes and I notice that those eyes of his even look large when they're closed. He rocks gently and joins in with the word '*swaha*' every now and then, and looks very peaceful. I close my eyes and listen to this rhythm, this chanting, while Mitra leans over every now and then to translate. 'This is where we're giving the blessings of peace to the world,' or, 'We are saying here — I do this not for myself.'

This ceremony is so beautiful. So colourful, really. In front of me, Daniel leans forward to receive the vermilion and rice mark on his forehead, just like an Indian would, and I take pride in the fact that he has grown up without any suspicion or hatred of other beliefs. When we've finished the ceremony a coconut is opened and we are all given sweets. I know that many of the other Jews in the community accept these sweets graciously, only to put them aside later, but what do we do? Eat them, of course, because they're far too delicious to waste! After all, why should only Hebrew blessings be worthy of the One God? This is what I am thinking.

On the wall of our clinic is a photograph of Mitra's father, framed in a garland of sandalwood flakes. It makes me feel as if I should put up a portrait of Rivka's father, my first mentor, but how would we get hold of such a picture now? A small altar is also set up in the clinic where our patients will walk in. There are some deities here, which have been installed in a kind of box, and offerings are made to them. I do not offer any sweets, because that is not our way, but I have no problem with Mitra's prayer table being in our clinic. India has taught me to accept so much, and taught me, too, the privilege of receiving acceptance. For this I will be grateful, till the end of my days.

After the ceremony we continue the celebration party at home. Rivka has made a tableload of Polish food — cabbage pancakes, *latke* and *kreplach*. Farha and Aaron have brought some Arabic food like *humeen*, as well as *baklava* and *mulfoof*, and Mitra has brought some Indian *namkeens*, some *bhajis* and *mithai*. None of this odd mixture is accidental. Rivka and I asked everybody to bring something different, because we wanted to celebrate this strange combination of people who will gather around this table of ours.

The party is in full swing, and in amongst the chatter of friends, children and Tota's chirpings, Farha proposes a toast. She says this: 'I have known Rivka, Benjamin and Daniel since they first arrived here in Calcutta and I have never seen such goodness come from so little. I have learnt so much about the human spirit from their own indomitable spirits, and I wish them every success in their future. God bless their clinic, may it prosper and may they always stay in Calcutta, with us!'

'Hear, hear,' the others join in, and I start feeling awkward with such praise. All we have done, truly, is try to survive, and try to do the best we could once we had arrived somewhere safe. I stumble to my feet, wanting to respond, knowing that this is the most appropriate time to give something back, even if it is just in words — yet before I have told them what I want to say I have tears in my eyes. Why is it that I cannot control myself at times such as this?

'Friends,' I say, 'friends,' and the small crowd falls silent again and I try to gather myself together to express my gratitude with strength. 'I want to thank everybody in Calcutta for being such good friends. You have taught us the true meaning of friendship and given us hope when we thought that it was something we would never again enjoy. I want to propose a toast to all of you here for making our lives worth living again. For your friendship, your love and your wonderful and most generous support. I want you all to know that it is something we can never forget. Finding a home so far from our own homes, and finding such good friends, too, is more than we could possibly have expected. Thank you for sharing our home today, and an especially big thank you to Doctor Mitra for making all this possible.'

Late in the evening, when everybody has gone home, Rivka and I are alone and we decide to continue our celebrations in private. I find a record for the gramophone I bought last year in the Thieves Bazaar. Believe it or not, this is the first time I am playing it, because Rivka is well and we have so much to celebrate. From now on there will be music in our lives, I am thinking.

Rivka kicks off her shoes and comes close to hold me, slowly moving her hips to the rhythm. I take her in my arms and we glide around the room. I am a good head taller when she has her shoes off, which brings out something else in me. 'Look, you can dance again, you're beautiful!' I tell her and she smiles, because she knows it and it makes her feel so smart. There is such grace in this simple fact. Rivka is well now and we can dance together and forget about everything. There is no war while the gramophone plays. No war at all.

'I want another child,' Rivka whispers in my ear, as if she's telling me a secret, with such intimacy that I cannot feel any reservations. I want to say, wait until the war is over and we'll have a dozen children, but I don't. She is in my arms and we are dancing, so it doesn't matter, she can have anything she wants from me. We have each other back, and we have our lives back: that is the main thing.

Tota is watching us. She squawks, stretches out a leg and winks at me as I sing along to the words of the song on the gramophone, *When the Lights Go On Again*.

Rivka whispers again, 'This time a little girl. Can you give me a little girl, Benjamin?'

It seems like the easiest request in the world. How I would enjoy giving her a little girl! She is laughing softly as she talks into my ear. It is so wonderful to hear Rivka laugh, to feel her body free from anxiety over her health or Daniel's wellbeing, and to see her so beautiful, enjoying her power over me.

'I'll give you a baby any time you want,' I tell her, but I am not thinking about any baby being inside her, I am thinking of how much I want to be inside her, moving to the rhythm of the music. Rivka's hips are so close to mine and she is enjoying this seduction of hers. She moves them closer still and watches my face to see my satisfaction. I love to see her like this. She is so alive! She is kissing around my neck and it is too much; I cannot stop myself from taking her by the hand to our bedroom. We walk quickly and purposefully to the bed. I pull back the mosquito net as fast as I can, but I am not very patient and it rips a little. Let those mosquitoes bite, I don't care. I can think of one thing only and that is the completion of this task of mine.

'If you want a baby, you'd better take off your clothes,' I say and I help her, taking them off as fast as I can. 'I have a million babies, my darling, and they're all yours.' How we are laughing now.

Rivka naked and healthy and wanting me is a combination that is too much, really. Maybe I am too impatient, not wanting to lose a minute, but my clothes are off now, too, and we are touching each other as if we are on the honeymoon that we never took. It feels as if she is holding me for the first time and I have never felt so wanted in my life. We are kissing and kissing like young lovers and I feel her eagerness to please me. This feeling of loving and being loved is so warm, so sweet and precious, I want it to last and last. I want to keep this feeling of love, to give Rivka the child she wants, and to make her happy. I give her everything of myself, and my seed is inside her, for her to do with as she pleases — make triplets if she wants — I am all hers, and we are kissing each other, feeling so, so good.

'Don't ever let me forget how nice that was,' she says, and I nuzzle into her body.

Thank you, Rivka, I am thinking, for giving yourself to me after you thought you had nothing more to give. I feel young again and you look radiant. So radiant, with your healthy flushed cheeks and tangled long hair after making love. I want this love to grow and stay with us. There is no need for us to be separated by anything, ever again.

CHAPTER 31

Since she became pregnant, Rivka is more interested in life than ever before. She does not let Mary take Daniel's tiffin to school at lunchtime, but goes herself. She has organised the painting of the house, and there are constant teams of men in loincloths, wiping their faces and smoking their *bidis*, squatting and chatting on the marble porch at the front of our house. She has ordered a beautiful cane cot that swings from the ceiling, and she has given the tailor instructions to make lace sheets and pillows, for she is certain that this child will be a girl.

'Do you think that I could love another child as much as Daniel?' she asks, and I say, 'You love your second husband as much as your first, so what of it? Surely it has to be the same with children.'

Rivka has more affection towards Daniel and me than I ever thought she was capable of. Her fear has lifted and this new life inside her uterus has been the start of a new era of life for the whole family. She sees me differently, I know this much. I feel her admiration and trust as I never did before. I am discovering new dimensions to this wife of mine, really. This playful side of hers is a big surprise.

What's more, the growing child has brought with it a growing swell of patients, all of them making the practice healthy from its first days. Mitra and I are already talking about employing a few more staff to cope with the influx, especially as we want to keep our free clinics for three days a week and have facilities for a couple of simple operating theatres for minor surgery. These are grand ambitions, but it feels just fine to have them. It is a sign of health to be able to plan for the future, that's what I have always said to my patients.

It's not just my life that is going ahead so smoothly; Daniel's life is, too. He excels at all his studies, he speaks fluent Hindi and Bengali now, and he's made so many friends that he's always off somewhere or other after school. For us it would be enough that he is happy, but the fact that he is happy and making us proud is much more than we could expect from him.

I asked him the other day, 'Do you still want to be a rabbi?' and he tells me that he has given up that desire long ago, and wants to study medicine at Calcutta University. I think he will make a good doctor, if he does decide to become one. He has a microscope and collects all sorts of things to examine, including lice from the sweeper's son's hair! He has a sympathy that he must have learnt from his grandfather, and a warm and loving nature, too, which will take him a long way.

'What do you think you're going to have,' I ask him one day while we're waiting for this baby of ours to be born, 'a sister or a brother?'

He agrees with Rivka that the next child born into this family will be a girl. How can he be so sure? I have seen too many women decide on the sex of their children before they're born and it worries me — all this knowing so much about nature. But Rivka says she knows, that's all, even though she doesn't mind what she has, 'so long as it's healthy'. Healthy or unhealthy, I tell everyone, I am going to love this child. Boy or girl, it is going to be the most precious gift imaginable, for no place is truly a home, they say, until it has seen a birth.

There are a few moments when Rivka looks unwell in her third trimester and I worry about whether she was quite ready for pregnancy after her extended illness. When she gets breathless, I have to remind myself that this is common for women at this stage of pregnancy.

'You didn't see me when I was pregnant with Daniel,' she says. 'I stopped breathing for a whole month before he was born.'

What sort of reassurance is that, I am thinking.

Rivka tells me that she wants to have the baby at our clinic, but she wants an obstetrician present to deliver her. Mitra knows of a man called Doctor Bannerjee, who is reputedly one of the best, and he's agreed to come on board, not just to deliver our baby, but for other births, too. No sooner is this organised than Doctor Bannerjee has a surgery two afternoons and one evening every week, and there are four babies born at the clinic before Rivka is ready to deliver ours.

It's so exciting I have to tell you about it — that first birth, I mean. On this night I see Mitra lighting incense at the small altar, I hear the patient moaning, and I find myself saying my prayers, too. There is a new human life about to start in our surgery — in the next room. I cannot believe it, a new life! I feel like dancing while that poor woman wails! I want to go in there and tell her that it'll all be over soon and she'll have the baby in her arms, but I don't. I stay outside and watch the incense burn, until it is too late to wait any longer. When I go home to Rivka and tell her about the first delivery that has started at our clinic, she says, 'I wish I'd been there, just to hear the sound. It would remind me.'

Even though it's been a while since Daniel was born, she is confident about this birth; more so than I am, in fact. In spite of my medical training I have a problem understanding how a feat such as birth can be achieved. With the help of angels, yes maybe, but could it take place without Divine assistance? I don't quite believe it.

Rivka is in bed, heavily pregnant, and can hardly move the morning that my copy of *The Statesman* arrives with the news that the war has ended and the Japanese have finally surrendered. Tariq has brought me my breakfast in the living room and I have to stop him before he leaves. 'The fighting has stopped!' I cry out to him, my tea spilling in the excitement. 'The war has ended!'

He replies, 'Very good, *saab*,' and leaves with my morning tea tray, smiling. Then I read the whole story and about the deaths from the two deadly atomic bombs and my heart sinks to know that the world has come to this. What would have happened to the wonderful people in Japan that we met, Jews and Japanese alike? Could any of them have left Kobe to travel to Hiroshima or Nagasaki at the time the atomic bombs were dropped?

I run to our bedroom to tell Rivka, feeling sick with excitement and overwhelmed with confusion about the bomb. What if Hitler had used something like that to destroy us in Poland? What would the world have said?

'Rivka,' I say, 'Rivka, look at this, the war is over!'

'No, it couldn't be. Show me!' Like me, she has always felt that there will be wars for the rest of her life. How unprepared we are for peace!

'It's over, look. Finished after the bombs the Americans dropped.'

She is starting to read and cry at the same time now and I wish I hadn't shown her the newspaper. 'What about that man, Chiune Sugihara, who helped so many of us? What about the people who saved our lives in Japan?' She is sobbing helplessly now, even though neither of us knows the full implications of the new bomb that has just been unleashed on the world. 'Look here,' she says, 'the American President is saying that the bomb was dropped on the military base of Hiroshima. Benjamin, how can he say that? Hiroshima is a city, for goodness sake. There are people living there. Ordinary people like you and me. Didn't they even know this much? Haven't they killed enough people in Japan already?'

'But, darling, there's going to be peace now. Everybody will
be safe. First peace in Europe — absolutely unimaginable — and
now in India, too. We'll be safe in Calcutta forever. There will
never be another war like the one we've just been through. We
can even go back to Poland if we want. We'll write to everyone
we know. They'll all be back in their own homes by now.'

She starts crying again and I know why. What family do
either of us have back in Poland? We have found happiness here
in a place that seems so far from the rest of the world, and it is
too precious to give up now.

'Don't cry, my darling, it's not good for you and it's not good
for the baby. We should be happy. We were so happy up till
now. Come, we will have a celebration tonight, light candles
and say prayers for the world.'

By the evening Rivka has cheered up. The sadness I've
known her to carry for years at a stretch lifts fast nowadays, in
an afternoon even. Daniel has a school friend, Vikram, home to
dinner, and they light fireworks on the front porch. Mitra
comes round with a big bunch of roses for us, and somehow
Aaron, Farha, Zek and the girls also think to visit us on this
night, the last day of the war. They bring some kosher wine and
a box full of pastries from Nahoum's, and all our children play
together out in the garden that is now so full of greenery and
life. How sweet it is that people think of us on a day like this:
this is what I'm thinking. I feel so blessed to have come through
the war, and so relieved for the world. As the news travels there
are hundreds of candles lit around the city and songs being sung
in all areas of the neighbourhood.

After our guests have gone home, Rivka and I go for a walk on our own down to Circus Avenue, to the market in Karaya Road. Everywhere, people are celebrating. The streets are alive. The mosques are full, the Hindu temples in the small rooms off the street are lit up and the statues are adorned with flowers. Everywhere there is such hope.

Two weeks later, Rivka tells me that she is getting pain shooting up to her stomach. It doesn't take much to work out that the labour has started, so I call Doctor Bannerjee and drive Rivka down to the clinic. Mitra is already there and waiting by the time we arrive. 'How often are the contractions?' he asks me and I tell him, 'Too often for me to time, I've been concentrating on Rivka.'

He is looking pleased, this wonderful man. He doesn't come into the operating theatre with us, but I know that he is lighting his incense on the other side of the wall, because I can smell it, even above the smell of antiseptic that hangs in the air. Although I have never understood how those statues are meant to work, I am hoping now that they do, and am filled with affection for my friend in the other room.

Rivka is in such pain I cannot even start to understand what she is going through, but I hold her hand and offer all the words of encouragement I can. I cannot think about the baby; I can only think of her, and about how I can help her to get through this. I am worried about how her body will cope with this much pain after her mysterious sickness, but the worrying isn't doing any good. I tell myself: stop it! I have to stop thinking that her body will fail her. I have to think positively. I have to know that she is going to get through this, otherwise the sound of her suffering will have too much power over me. I have to remind myself of Rivka's strength; her bravery in the forest when we lived with the partisans.

She can hardly see me, because her eyes are half closed, but she turns her face to me and says, 'Help me, please.' The sweat is rolling off her face, and I help her all I can, pulling her upwards when she says, 'Up.' But then she stops giving instructions altogether, because the pain is pushing her beyond her senses. 'Help,' she says again, weakly, between contractions, and I realise that the only power I have as a man through this process of childbirth is to give her some support with my words, so I whisper into her ear, 'Rivka, you can do this. You're so strong. You could run with Daniel in your arms through the forest and you could hold a farmhouse up at gunpoint. Don't forget it. This is nothing for you.'

Somehow, after these words, she seems more rested in the few seconds between contractions, and then rises to them. Before long she has started to push, making the brave roars of a warrior as she exhales. I hold Rivka's heaving belly under the sheet and feel our baby, curled up tight and still in preparation for its passage into the world. Soon this child will be out, because I can feel Rivka now at the height of her powers; this child's mother has the strength of a dozen armies!

Our child is born within ten pushes. Such a miracle in medicine I have never seen before, believe me. A heart-melting universe of a child is in my arms and I am given the honour of smacking her bottom! I cannot bear to hurt her, so I hold her upright as she takes her first breath, and she looks at me through swollen slits for eyes from a wise and crinkled face. She does not deserve to be smacked, poor thing. Her lungs fill up naturally with air and she takes her first breath of life without any violence being taken out on her, even in love. She is our beautiful, beautiful baby girl, our reward and our gift. Conceived in the war and born in peace. May her whole life be lived in peace and may she never have to experience anything that her parents did, as a child or as an adult.

I give her to Rivka, who takes me into her arms with our baby and kisses us all together. 'My little darling,' she says in the sweetest and most charming voice I have ever heard. She speaks to somebody she has known only by her movements and by the dreams they have shared together over the past nine months. Nothing of the pain remains. Just the strength of her love and our happiness together at the birth of our child, Hannah Sarah Rahabi.

CHAPTER 32

Who would have thought, when we first came to India, that we would still be here when the British started to make plans to leave? But we have stayed here this long, and now it's actually starting to happen, believe it or not. Certainly, this is a time of endings as well as beginnings, and it makes us question our purpose here in India — our right to remain.

For Rivka and me, it hardly makes any difference whether the British stay or go, and Hannah is too small to care, but Daniel, he's all for it. He and his friends from St Xavier's believe that the British should quit India now. He is truly Indian, this boy of ours. I say to him, 'Why get rid of the British? The war is over. They have no power any more. Their empire is gone. Finished.'

'But they haven't gone yet, and they should have, Papa. Can't you see?' he tells me stubbornly, like some young partisan.

I say, 'The Indians have never truly lost their freedom, believe me. They don't know what it's like to live under an occupying army. The British are just businesspeople. They're not like the Germans. They don't want to get rid of any us, particularly. Look at how they let Ghandi carry on. He doesn't need to go with his gun into the forests, now, does he?'

'But what about Colonel Dwyer?'

'Yes, yes.' People are still talking about this fellow, but really, his shootings were the work of one man. I tell Daniel about the terrifying massacres of many, many men — the annihilation of whole groups of people — all committed on orders from the German army. Sometimes I worry about reminding him so often about all of this, but there is a part of me that wants to keep this information alive in our son, because he is the one who will outlast us, and he must understand that there are degrees of everything.

The British are leaving now, it seems, and what of it? It's this partition business that worries me more than anything else. Why all this talk of it? What for? This is how it always was for Poland — continually being divided between the different nations. But India? It has been united all this time under the British, so why are they dividing it just as they are leaving?

At the time I am thinking all these things, the Chief Minister, Mr Suhrawardy, declares August the sixteenth as a public holiday and day of agitation for a separate Pakistan. I put this date in my diary, because I know where agitation can lead us. That same day, our Muslim cook, Tariq, asks me in his cross between Bengali and English, 'May I please be going to visit my family?'

Farha always says, 'Don't give the servants too many holidays — they will start to take advantage of you,' but I don't want to have resentful servants, so I always let them go. What saddens me this time, though, is that I am agreeing to his attendance at the rally. This much I know.

So I let him take off before lunch, let him go to the Ochterlony Monument and scream nonsense at the top of his lungs, but before he goes I tell him, 'Tariq, great crimes are committed by people who do as they are told by their leaders, so please be careful and listen to your conscience.' He looks at me as if he doesn't quite understand what I'm saying and I know that I have not managed to get my message across, so I say, 'Whatever you do, don't hurt anybody and don't get hurt yourself.' He nods politely and says goodbye.

It's a public holiday, but nonetheless it's a Friday and both Mitra and I have patients that we cannot let down, so we don't take any time off for this whole business of unnecessary agitation. Instead I make my way down to the clinic in the afternoon, as usual.

The shock that awaits me is beyond belief.

Everything about Sovabazar has changed, just as the streets of Warsaw changed within a few hours of the German invasion. Riots have begun and people are running down the street — Muslims, Hindus, everybody. Some are running with looks of fear and others with uncontrollable anger. Somebody has cut off a dog's head and pierced it with a stick, hanging it in a window of the grocer's shop, which is hardly a window any more, except for some shards of glass. When I see the broken shop windows, I cannot help but think of the stories we heard about the shattered glass of

Kristallnacht, the night when Jewish shops and synagogues were ransacked all over Germany and Austria. A familiar sick feeling grips my stomach. It is happening again. All of it. The suspicion, the hatred, the violence. I get out of the car and go straight inside the clinic, thinking: why, why, why? Why all this again?

Mitra is already there and he is dismantling his small altar.

'You should be praying,' I say, 'not pulling down your altar.'

'This is civil war, Benjamin,' he says. 'One war finishes and another starts — what is going wrong with our world?' He looks at me with exasperation in his huge eyes and I have no answers for him.

'Should we be working or should we get away from here?' I ask.

'What did you do during the war in Poland? Did you work or did you hide?'

'Both.'

Mitra is even more disturbed than I am. Outside we can hear screams and shouting, and the last thing I want to do is go onto the streets again right now. He stops and thinks, and then he starts to place his statues of Ganesh and Lakshmi back onto his altar. 'We might be needed,' he says and gives me a long, desperate look. 'Will you stay?'

'I'll stay, and you go. This fighting is about Hindus, Muslims and Sikhs, not Jews.' For once, it is not about Jews. As I say these words I realise what a tragedy this world is, that there will always be an enemy, no matter who that enemy is.

Someone is banging on the door and I walk up hesitantly and ask loudly, 'Who is it?'

'Doctor *saab*, please, open the door, my wife … my wife … please just open the door and take a look!' The voice is desperate, and there is definitely a woman with him, sobbing and screaming hysterically.

I look at Mitra and he nods for me to open the door, so I do. I could be opening the door for the partisan who came to see us at Piaski in the middle of the night. It's alright to be doing this, I tell myself, but I cannot stop thinking of Rivka, Daniel and Hannah back at home, and I'm wondering if the fighting has reached South Calcutta. Should I go back to them, or is it alright to be here helping these people?

When I think about it, the answer becomes clear. My life was saved during the war because I was a doctor. It is my duty to help people now, whoever they are. Even if things get as bad as they were in Poland.

I open the door and I see a Muslim man with his wife in his arms; one of her breasts is half severed and bleeding profusely. He is covered in blood and I feel like throwing up, in spite of all my experience, because the work we have to do now is not about medicine. We are not dealing with any disease of the body; we are dealing with the hatred and sickness of the whole of humanity. This is the work of a city gone mad, out of control, acting in absolute ignorance, abusing the sanctity of life.

'Did you know the person who did this?' Mitra asks.

'No, *saab*,' the man weeps. 'They came inside our house, the whole mob. My wife was in the bedroom.' He starts wailing so loudly his voice chokes out to a rasp. 'I couldn't get in to stop them …'

As we listen to this poor man I am painfully aware of the fact that there is no time for his sorrow. As much as I would like to give him my sympathy, it is his wife who needs the most urgent treatment — so Mitra and I help to carry the woman to the surgery, leaving a trail of blood through the waiting room.

We are on our own; there is nobody to help with the work. Nobody to administer the anaesthetic, so Mitra fixes the needle himself, while I hold the woman's pulse and close my eyes, praying as I feel the rhythm of life that taps on persistently, thank God.

When she is fully unconscious, her husband is struck with panic as he sees the deep laceration on his wife's breast; his eyes are wide with fear as he watches Mitra staunch the flow of blood with his artery forceps and put ligatures on the bleeding points. When the breast has been sutured back to the thorax, I swab away the rest of the blood. As I touch around his wife's breast I glance up at the man and see a look that I can never forget. He is staring at his wife's body as if he has murdered her himself, and when I see his face I pity the fact that it is not he who is under anaesthetic. I feel so angry, so powerless and so deeply offended that this could happen to anybody. What if I were doing this for Rivka? Then what? How would I feel?

The thought of Rivka makes me panic. What are they doing right now back at home? I look at the devastated man and his tears are my own, his wife could be my own. As soon as we are finished, I excuse myself, because I am panicking too much now about Rivka. I go for one minute to the telephone in the waiting room and make a call home.

'What's happening?' Rivka asks me, and she sounds distraught. 'There's all this smoke coming from your side of the city.'

'Don't worry about me. Is everything alright over there?' I ask.

'Everything is just fine at home, but I'm worried about what's going on in Sovabazar. Is it serious? They've called for a curfew tonight.'

I tell her about the procedure we've just performed, and she says, 'How could they have done such a thing? Benjamin, what on God's earth is happening? Will you be alright?'

I know what she is thinking. She is thinking that she cannot afford to lose another husband, but her sense of charity is still gloriously alive and she is thinking also of the woman in the operating theatre whom she has never met before. When I ask Rivka if I can stay, she says, 'You must stay and do whatever you can to help.'

I am so touched by her words, I cannot tell you, because they make me realise what a wonderful woman I have married. She is the child of the biggest-hearted doctor I have ever met, and her father would have wanted me to stay as well, this much I know. So I make her promise to lock the gates and all the doors of the house in Rowland Road. Tonight is the Sabbath and she will be lighting her candles without me. Whatever prayers she says will help us, if we are not beyond help altogether.

So I get off the telephone and there's another knock on the door. This time an old Hindu man arrives, with a few fingers that have been severed. He has been punched so severely in the mouth that whatever teeth he had before have fallen out, leaving a sunken hole of an orifice. He is brought in by somebody who does not even know him, but says he has come to this clinic before for treatment of a skin condition. The old man continues to wail, for he cannot speak any words, and no words are necessary to see the damage caused to his face. Why this old man, I am thinking. What sort of a fight could he have put up? I feel like weeping, but I know that it would be selfish to think of my own reactions to the violence outside.

There's a spare table in the operating room, so Mitra and I sedate this poor man and start to trim his finger bones to complete the vicious amputation of the mob, finally sewing the skin edges together, then cleaning and dressing his injuries. Before long he is mumbling incoherently again through his bloody mouth.

Throughout this procedure more people are coming and delivering patients, Hindus and Muslims alike, and even one Sikh man arrives, unable to walk on one leg. He has been gashed by a knife that has opened an artery. The wound is pouring blood as if it were a tap. The clinic is in chaos. Never before have I worked in such crowded and desperate conditions, but the people continue to flood in. Before long our whole surgery is full of injured people, on every bed available, and there are many lying down on the floor. I am thinking: thank goodness this place was cleaned this morning; but already it looks a mess.

I call out to Mitra, 'There's blood all over the floors — what about infection?'

He looks over, his eyes doubled in size with distress, and he says, 'What to do?'

We cannot help everybody ourselves, so we are handing out scissors, bandages and antiseptic to the people who have taken refuge in our surgery. We don't even think about our own safety until the door bursts open and a few wild and furious-looking men stare into the waiting room for a few seconds. Good God, I am thinking. What the hell can they do? There's enough blood here to quench their thirst for it. How much more do they want? One of the Muslims inside puts his hands together and asks the men to go away. Amazingly, they do, and I get back to the task of administering medicine — mostly pain relief, because it is not in my power to reattach limbs.

We work all night, and the shouting and screaming continues, sometimes louder, sometimes quieter. When it is quiet for a minute, I open the door and look outside. My car has been ransacked and all the windows smashed. I don't know if it will get me home and even if it could, a night's sleep is out of the question.

However, in the early hours of the morning I do manage a few hours of sleep on the hard polished cement floor. My bed for the night is bloodstained; the blood of Hindus and Muslims mixed together. There is no sheet spare to cover me, and no privacy to be found, but I am so exhausted it doesn't matter. My eyes close for a few minutes and I slip into the kind of deathly sleep I experienced when we were escaping through the forest. During those few minutes I dream about another world where these things were possible, back home. There are Hindus and Muslims, together with Nazis and Poles, all mixed up in a place that is both Poland and Calcutta. Everybody is fighting, and I am carrying a small child, who is Hannah, perhaps, I don't know. I am trying to save her life and escape from the bloody murder all around.

Just as I am making my escape, Mitra wakes me to ask if I can help him administer anaesthetic to a patient who's just been brought in with a pierced lung. For a moment when I open my eyes I am still dreaming. Then I get up to help this poor man. I don't know what we'll be able to do for him. I would like to say that I'm offering him my best, but I don't think that I am capable of my best right now, because I'm so dizzy with exhaustion and nausea. I look around after my dream and I feel as if I am hallucinating all of this bloody chaos. Everybody is sleeping on the floor, no doubt dreaming up spectres of the madness outside, just as I was.

I step around all these people and follow Mitra into the operating theatre. We do our best, but the man dies on the floor that is the operating table while I am administering anaesthetic. I feel his pulse fading out to nothing as the needle goes in, and I tell Mitra, 'There's nothing more we can do. I'm going to stop the anaesthetic.' When I pull out the needle all the anxiety I had about treating sick people when I first arrived in Calcutta comes rushing back to me. I feel hopeless, really, but I try to persuade myself to carry on, telling myself: Benjamin, you are not to blame for this man's death, any more than you were to blame for Tomasz's death in the bunker that time.

We work all through the next day, and some patients manage to go home, so there are fewer people in the clinic. One of the women, an old Hindu without even a sari blouse, bends down and clings to my feet as she leaves. I cannot explain how strange this is for me. They touch feet here out of respect, but I've never before seen such desperation. I know this feeling myself. I would have kissed the feet of some people in my past, believe me, but here I am having my feet kissed while this elderly woman mutters something in a language that can't be Bengali, because I cannot understand even a few words of it.

There are still half a dozen patients who are unfit to walk, so we cannot turn them out onto the streets, even though the riots seem to have slowed down. We are stuck here at the clinic, so we continue to administer pain relief and stay inside, sleeping and waking at odd hours, so that after a while my perception of time has completely altered.

Finally, when the noises of suffering inside our clinic are quieter, I go outside to get some air and to see where this madness is coming from.

What I see is beyond description. I have walked out into some kind of hell. All around are lifeless bodies. Believe it or not, one man is lying dead with a knife in each hand. There are rows of burnt-out shops and buildings, and at the Grey Street—Chitpur Road crossing, I see the same sight I saw back in Warsaw: military tanks, pulling up to meet the debris.

This is surely a hallucination.

I see those tanks and I scream. I don't know how, but the scream is leaving my mouth before I can stop myself. Even though there are no swastikas on the tanks, my body feels as if it has gone into some sort of seizure, caused entirely by my memories of Warsaw. I see the Indian troops get out to move the debris that's blocking the crossing, and even though they have come to keep the peace, my heart is racing, as if they were the Nazi army coming to stake their claim here in Calcutta.

The war is over, the war is over. I have to remind myself, because it is replaying in front of my eyes with such intensity that the fear is swelling in my stomach and blacking out my reason, giving me these random, crazy thoughts. I am frozen on the spot while I watch the soldiers pulling away burnt wood and bodies. Thankfully they are not interested in me — a Jewish doctor, covered with blood, immobilised in the midst of the chaos — and they go about their business without more than a glance in my direction.

Somehow I manage to stumble back to the clinic, and soon after the telephone rings. It is Rivka, telling me that *The Statesman* reported that there have been nine hundred fires over the previous days.

'Are you scared?' I ask. 'Do you want me to try and come home?'

'How will you come home?' she asks. 'You could be killed.'

'How are Daniel and Hannah?'

'They're fine,' comes her answer, without giving anything of her own troubles away.

Only later do I find out that four families were in hiding in our Rowland Road house during the time of the riots. A Muslim family, the Iqbals, whose son Shabbir goes to St Xavier's with Daniel, and three Hindu families, who live in Karaya Road and are all somehow related to Girish, our sweeper.

When I finally get home to Rowland Road, the Iqbals are still there, ready at any time to disappear into one of the back rooms that locks. I am so exhausted, but I try to appear sociable regardless.

'They live in a Hindu area, Papa,' Daniel explains. 'Shabbir is my friend from school.'

'Don't worry your father about us,' Askander Iqbal says. 'Just look at him, he's exhausted.'

I haven't thought yet about my appearance, but before I go to have a bath and rest, I tell them, 'Please, stay. My home is yours. It's not safe outside, even now, believe me. I've been through the city.'

Askander and Ayesha keep apologising for being in our house, and their apologies sound familiar — like our own when we received any kindness on our journey to India. I explain to them that there's no problem, no problem at all. Shabbir and Daniel are busy playing together, and their young daughter, Jameela, is delighting in kissing Hannah and helping her walk around the house. Everybody is getting along just fine, so what's the problem? But needless to say, Askander and Ayesha are feeling uncomfortable about imposing on us, and their discomfort reminds me of the Schreibers and Kaufmanns back in Piaski. The last thing I want is another situation like the one back then, so I go out of my way to welcome them and insist once more that they stay with us as long as they wish. 'We had to rely on safe homes, too,' I tell them. 'We know your situation, really.'

After a short rest, Askander and I have time to talk. Over a whisky I tell him about what was going on in our clinic and, like myself, he is distraught that anybody — be they Muslim, Hindu or Sikh — could do such things to each other. Meanwhile, Ayesha and Rivka start blaming the politicians and the men in this world for bringing about all this fighting. Hearing the women talking like this, Askander and I look at each other and laugh. Then he starts telling us how their home was looted.

'It was Daniel who called and told us to come over,' he says. 'Your son. You should be proud of him.'

'I've always been proud of Daniel,' I tell the Iqbals. 'Daniel knows how to behave in an emergency. This much I know.'

And so it is that we make new friends here in Calcutta — amongst the best friends we've ever been blessed to have — once more in a time of terrible trauma.

In the aftermath of those Calcutta killings we tell the Iqbals everything about our time in Poland, and somehow it feels good to talk about these very personal losses of ours to people who have just been turned out of their home. It feels good to hear Askander take offence on our behalf. To rage with us against the insanity of this world we live in. And you know, while we're talking about these things I can't help thinking: why is it that we humans always need a crisis to bring us closer together? Perhaps this is the only benefit that can ever come out of conflict — this desire for unity afterwards.

By Tuesday the army has helped to bring some order back into the city, but still there are random killings taking place all over Calcutta. Only later do we discover that the death toll has gone up to reach several thousand; the people that Mitra and I were able to help is so small in number compared to the massacres that have taken place in Calcutta to date. Now *The Statesman* is even publishing the names of staff who have gone missing and asking for information about their whereabouts. Can you believe it?

The news continues. One Muslim has been retrieved from a sewer nine days after having been thrown in there, and for many days afterwards bodies are still being cleared by the army and the untouchables, before the vultures have too much of a feast here at our expense. Yet even with all this clearing, bodies keep appearing — sometimes in the Hooghly, whitened so that the skin looks like bone, as only this river seems able to do. There are bodies in water tanks around the city, and cadavers in canals. Everywhere: bodies, bodies, bodies. There has been a war in this city, no doubt about it. And the stench, you would not believe.

Mahatma Ghandi arrives, and I watch carefully to see if this man's magic can work, and you know, somehow it seems to help. Gandhi says he has come with a blank mind to do God's will. Thank God it is blank — without the imprint of any religious bias. Crowds gather around the house where he stays on the outskirts of this city, and people are calming down, it seems, and starting to see some sense in the old man's words.

But still this question remains: what do people do once they have satisfied their blood lust? How do they settle back into their ordinary lives and justify their acts, when their vengeance is lukewarm and their deeds are an embarrassment to them? This is the question I keep asking myself. And another thing I am thinking: what lessons did we forget to learn, through two great wars? When are we ever going to say 'enough fighting' and be done with it all?

CHAPTER 33

Aaron tells me that there was once a maharaja by the name of Ranjit Singh, who bought a diamond to Shalom Cohen, his ancestor, the distinguished jeweller from Allepo and founder of the Jewish community in Calcutta. The diamond was one hundred and ninety-one carats, and known as the Kohinoor. When Shalom Cohen was asked to value it, he inspected the diamond carefully, returned it to the maharaja and told him, 'This stone has no value.' Naturally, the maharaja was outraged. What stupidity! How could such a renowned jeweller — a jeweller to kings, no less — not know that this stone was valuable beyond description?

Shalom Cohen's explanation was simple. He said, 'This diamond can never be bought by anybody, so it has no price. It can only be acquired as a gift or through the shedding of blood — so how, good sir, do you intend to put a value on that blood?'

Ranjit Singh understood the meaning of these words and praised Shalom Cohen for his wisdom. Some years later, this same stone was stolen from the Peacock Throne in Delhi, and was taken to England to become the Jewel in the British Crown. There it remains to this day. Nobody has yet risked letting blood to take it back. Neither has anyone tried to buy it back, for that matter.

I always think of this story when I look back at what happened in Poland. There was never any price that the Germans could pay to have our country. They could only have it through the shedding of blood. And what value did it ever have to anybody if this was the case?

As for the British, they still have India. They took it even though they had no right to it, with the same motives of envy, greed and ambition driving them on. And of course Daniel and his St Xavier's friends still want them to go. They talk about it as if they are young warriors — you should hear them. Whenever Aaron hears them talking about the indecency of the British occupation, he mumbles the usual line: 'None of us would have the comfortable lives that we do here if it weren't for the British.'

Maybe Aaron is right. You couldn't say the same about the Nazis.

But who am I to have any strong feelings on the matter? I am not a passionate schoolboy any more, and I have never had any troubles with any of the British people I've met here. I know this much only: they are on their way out. Believe me. I'd be surprised if they even last to the end of next year.

It is New Year's Eve and there's a feeling of freedom in the air. Rivka and I are going to celebrate the end of 1946 at a dinner dance being held at Firpo's Restaurant, and by the time she has finished preparing herself for the evening, she is positively glowing. She wears a new green dress that sets off her eyes, and her hair is shining as it catches the light. What we are saying goodbye to and what we are welcoming, I do not know, but we are surely at a turning point now. I don't know how or why, but this will be an important year for all of us. Rivka is healthy, and more beautiful than ever; everybody is energised, excited, about something, goodness knows what. Really, I've never felt much exhilaration on New Year's Eve, but this year it's different. Firpo's seems to have absorbed the atmosphere. The bearers are smiling more charmingly than ever, the chandeliers glimmer more brightly and the mirrored walls reflect back a picture of Calcutta society at its most optimistic.

Askander and Ayesha Iqbal, as well as Farha and Aaron, meet us at the restaurant, and it seems that they, too, have this feeling that everything is about to change. We toast this new feeling, all of us, lifting the rose-tinted glasses to our lips. 'L'chaim,' I say, 'To life'.

After we have eaten our dinner, and danced till Farha has lost a heel on her shoe, we sit down at our table again and listen to Askander's prediction for the New Year.

'This year we witnessed the last race for the Viceroy's Cup,' he announces confidently.

'What makes you say that?' I ask.

'The British will be leaving before December. They're out. I have it confirmed by some people I trust.'

Aaron says, 'Bye-bye,' and waves at an Englishman at the other end of the restaurant, who waves back, not quite knowing why his attention has been caught.

'So what will happen? Nothing. They'll just leave,' I say. It's not as if they're going to take the whole population on a death march with them; what's the problem?

'It will make a huge difference,' Farha says. 'Just you watch: the Jewish people will start leaving, for sure. If India is going to be for Indians, what place will we have here?'

I cannot believe I am hearing this. It is like being back in Poland and hearing about Poles marching to Czestochowa shouting 'Poland for Poles'. How could India be the same?

Farha says, 'Just wait and see. The men will start leaving to study abroad and there'll be nobody left here to marry our girls. We'll all have to leave.'

The band slows down as Farha says these words, and for a split second it seems as if the night's optimism has lulled. As if this fear of the future has hushed the crowd. The uneasiness is in everybody's eyes as they look towards the musicians, as if they have the solutions. But then the ships on the Hooghly all blast their sirens to mark the passing of the year and the stroke of the midnight hour. The New Year has begun, the band starts up again and we all get up to dance, even Farha, this time barefoot. We have made it! We have survived! All the way through to 1947! The war is over, we are alive, Rivka is well and happy, and from now on surely only wonderful things can happen.

The day we find out that India will be given her Independence, Daniel decides to hold a small party. We celebrate with the Iqbals, but Farha and Aaron are not celebrating, because they're worried about whether or not India will be safe without the British. I tell them later, 'Poland was a lot safer without the Nazis,' and Aaron laughs, but Farha remains silent, and I know that she is thinking about the future of her children.

So it seems just a few days ago that we celebrated the end of the year, and now we find ourselves celebrating the end of an era. Another passing of the midnight hour: this time on the evening of the fourteenth of August.

Daniel has asked if he can stay up late to hear Nehru's speech, which will be broadcast from Delhi, and we've given him permission, because this is the moment that he, more than anyone else in this house, has wanted to witness. It's a Friday night, so we light the Shabbas candles, offer blessings for the food and wine for the last time in a British India, and put Hannah to sleep. Then we stay up late into the night with a very excited young son who is timing the minutes left before India becomes an independent nation.

'Ten minutes to go,' he says triumphantly, with the pride of a true revolutionary.

And then Nehru starts one of the most brilliant speeches I have ever heard; one that captures the Zeitgeist and brings tears to all our eyes. It has some power over me, not just because it is soulful and inspired, but also because it makes me think about how my parents would have felt when Poland was given her Independence in 1918.

'Long years ago,' Nehru's voice crackles over the radio, 'we made a tryst with destiny, and now the time comes when we shall redeem that pledge, not wholly or in full measure, but very substantially. At the stroke of the midnight hour, when the world sleeps, India will awake to life and freedom. A moment comes, which comes but rarely in history, when we step out from the old to the new, when an age ends, and when the soul of a nation, long suppressed, finds utterance.'

Looking at Daniel, I have that same feeling I had at New Year — of breathless excitement mixed with anticipation about this substantial stretch of future facing us all like an unknown blank corridor.

Nehru continues: 'The appointed time has come — the day appointed by destiny — and India stands forth again, after long slumber and struggle — awake, vital, free and independent. The past clings on to us still in some measure, and we have to do much before we redeem the pledges we have so often taken. Yet the turning-point is past, and history begins anew for us, the history which we shall live and act and others will write about ...'

Then it happens. 'It's midnight. IT'S MIDNIGHT!' Daniel shouts, jumping up and down. 'We're free, the empire has finished! The whole world will be free now!'

There is no going to sleep now, because we would be shutting our eyes to history. It's a giddy feeling for me, as if we are being given a new life — a time when the clocks all start afresh, not just for us, but for everyone in this country. We are sharing a monumental moment with India — the country that has taken us in and taken us to its heart. Before I hadn't cared if the British stayed or left, but at this moment, believe me, I feel elated.

By the time the sun rises we have had no more than two or three hours of rest, but nonetheless Daniel wants the two of us to go and see the Chief Justice, Sir Arthur Trevor Harries, hoist our new flag for the first time. So we go down to Calcutta's grand British courts, with their cloisters and corridors, and I am trying to work out why the place looks so different today. 'Look,' Daniel points out, 'all the lawyers are in national dress instead of their coats and trousers!'

I have never before seen such a frenzy of excitement. Daniel is looking around for his friends from St Xavier's, and whenever we find one of them we carry on looking for more through the crowds. Then Daniel finds Shabbir and I have a chance to talk to Askander.

'Farha and Aaron are probably rather sad to see these people go, no?' he says.

'But it's better that they're going, don't you think?'

'Of course. Just look at how happy everybody is.'

A group of men rally around chorusing, '*Hindu, Muslim aykh ho.*' Muslims and Hindus are one.

Daniel joins in our conversation. 'How can they be upset? Look, for once there is no fighting. The whole country is coming together.'

There are men giving out sweets to anyone in the crowd. Others, all well dressed for this important occasion, cheer and wave flags. Somewhere, too, I detect a feeling of disbelief, as this freedom is so new and heady, and there are still these British people walking around in our midst. Where else could they go? They're not going to turn into smoke and lift off the ground just because the British flag has been pulled down.

But by the time we walk past Government House, I realise that truly the British are never again going to come back as rulers, because the Indians have burst onto the sacrosanct lawns and there are literally thousands of them wandering across the turf that was once reserved for the British alone. Nobody is stopping the people of Calcutta, old and young, as they stake their claim to their own earth.

This feeling of Independence is so exciting, you cannot imagine. Daniel insists that I take him into the grounds of Government House. 'I want to walk on some free soil!' he says. So I take my Indian son and we walk on these beautiful lawns that have been taken in this moment as common land for the common man. We walk like kings, greeting the other kings, feeling such a sense of ownership that I can hardly believe we have been here only six years. Yes, we are indeed Indians, and what a pride I feel when this fact finally dawns on me.

A few days later and this moment of freedom is over, finished, along with our short spurt of peace. The division between India and Pakistan has started — and the bloodshed, you would not believe. Why, why, why did the British chop up India like that? What the hell did those British people think — that the people would happily pick up their things and move, just because the government tells them to, by the million? Really, what on earth did they think? That there would be a peaceful reshuffling of people? A grateful surrender of homes? What insanity! Now I am really beginning to see Daniel's side in all of this. How could the British have done this just to please a few shrewd politicians?

When the news comes through that lunatics are attacking women on trains and severing their breasts, I feel sick with disbelief. I remember the woman who was brought to our surgery during the riots in Calcutta. Her name I will never know, but her eyes, half open under the anaesthetic, I will never forget. Neither will I forget the agony of her husband — the poor man who had to watch it all, without any anaesthetic at all.

Every day, every single day, the most horrific stories are reported. Not so bad in Calcutta, but a nightmare in the Punjab. We listen to the news on the radio every evening after work and things simply don't improve. When is this fighting going to stop? This is the time for peace, no? The time to start up again as one nation.

In the middle of all the violence we get a letter from Ewa and Joel, asking us if we want some help to get papers for

America, land of peace and equality. Ewa has not been on my mind for a long time, so this sudden invitation takes me by surprise and gets me thinking about how things would be for us if we were to live out there. Reading their letters I think of the bears and silver birch trees that Joel described to me. The canyons and the giant redwood trees. It's strange — I see them with a house in the forest, even though I know they live in New York.

'Would you like to go and live in America?' I ask Rivka, and she says, 'I can live anywhere in the world if it's with my family.'

'But how would you feel about leaving Calcutta?' I ask.

'No, no, no, pleeeease let's stay here,' Daniel cajoles us. 'I never want to leave India.'

I ask Hannah, 'Do you like India, baby? Would you like to stay here?' Of course she cannot understand me yet, but I take her smile as a yes.

'What's the point?' Rivka asks. 'How can we move Daniel again?'

Daniel echoes his mother, with even more defiance: 'How can you move me again? Don't you think I've been moved enough?'

As he says this, I hear his voice — the voice of an Indian boy — which makes everything clear. We haven't been talking in Polish together, like we used to, because Daniel's languages are now English, Bengali and Hindi. He is the one we have to consult for the correct Bengali words to express ourselves. He is the sugar that fell into the milk in India, and he has immersed himself here in the cream of it. How would we be able to take the sugar out now and move elsewhere, for goodness sake?

Later, when I talk privately to Rivka about this, she agrees that we should stay in India. Poland is out of the question, and America is a distant dream. I sleep peacefully after our conversations on this subject, knowing that we will be able to stay in this land where the milk and sugar flows, albeit along with blood. And, more importantly, I will not have to find a place alongside Ewa in yet another new country, so far from the one I have grown to know and love.

CHAPTER 34

Now that the armed forces have left Calcutta for good, the synagogue seems empty. The rabbis that came with the soldiers have left, too. We go to Maghen David less frequently now, but when we do I can still hear the echoes of a larger congregation when I sit there; only the faces are fewer.

Some people have come from Israel, too, and they are setting up meetings which are very well attended. 'Your spiritual homeland is now opening up,' they're telling us, 'and it should be the mission of every Jew to go and make a home in the Promised Land.'

I think about it, I really do. I try and imagine living on a *kibbutz*, and wonder how Daniel and Hannah would manage in one of their tent cities.

'Let the young go first,' these Aliyah people say, 'and then all of the rest of you should follow.'

All this talk of Jerusalem makes me think of my father and the patch of missing plaster on the ceiling of our apartment in Warsaw. My dear God, I miss him now that the State of Israel has been created. Why, he would have been on the first boat there.

I remember him reading passages from the Tanakh about Jerusalem. His favourite psalm was the one that the Israelites sang by the rivers of Babylon:

If I forget you, O Jerusalem,
let my right hand wither,
let my tongue stick to my palate
if I cease to think of you,
if I do not keep Jerusalem in memory
even at my happiest hour.

Our lives were comfortable and prosperous during my childhood in Poland, but at the back of my mind I always felt that one day my whole family might just pick up and leave, against my will. They would go to this place with rolling hills and sacred sites where our people would be welcomed home with rejoicing and merrymaking. We would arrive in this idyllic land like a few tribespeople who had found their way back to Israel through the calamities of the centuries. We would see the flat roofs and domes of the holy city of Jerusalem, at first from a distance and then closer. When we arrived we would visit the site of the temple and rebuild it, so that it became even more glorious than in the time of our ancestors! Ah, what a story I was being sold ... A house would be given to us to honour our return — a home with cool ceramic urns of water at every entrance. We would be served spiced wine and pomegranate juice. There would be figs and vines growing in the courtyard. All these images I had of Jerusalem, would you believe, and still I didn't want to leave Poland!

It was my father who put these ideas into my head. If he were here now, he would be right up in the front row of these meetings, watching the films that the Israelis are playing. He would have finally arrived home. And my poor mother? Why, she would be right there behind him, complaining about moving, but following him nonetheless.

Now the gates are wide open and where is my father?

All those years ago I wondered how it would feel to end up in a strange place and have to learn everything from the very beginning. I hated the idea of leaving my home town. Yet if I had known back then what was going to happen, I would have insisted that we all leave Poland together, while we still could. I would have forced us all to leave, no doubt about it.

As it turns out, I was the only one who almost made it to Palestine, without either of my parents. And the biggest laugh of all is this: I never get there. What is it about this Israel that stops me from ever setting foot there? Here I am, watching a film on the bright future that awaits us in the Promised Land, and I am guaranteed passage on a ship that will not break down from engine failure. Our whole family is being called out on a special invitation, and this time it is not me, but Daniel, who wants us to stay. And who am I to uproot us all? I was forced to leave the country where I grew up, so why should Daniel be forced to do the same? This is what I am thinking. No, we will stay here in India, because this is the place that gave us a home when we most needed one. This is the place that I have grown to love. The place where our bodies, minds and hearts have settled. There is no doubt about it: now, more than ever, Calcutta is our home.

At about the same time as people start making Aliyah, Aaron's father falls sick, and it soon becomes clear that he is not going to survive.

Rivka and I are with Aaron when he is reading the Shema by his father's side for the last time. The old man lets out a long groan and I am the first to recognise this sound: it is the last breath, being expelled by a body that no longer requires it.

Aaron looks to me, too choked to speak, and I reach forward to feel his father's neck and pulse, then pull up his shirt to see that there is no longer any rise and fall with his breath. Then I go and stretch my arms around both Aaron and Farha, and say, 'Aaron, your father's time has come.' I don't need to say any more.

It's sad enough just being there at this moment, but then a Muslim call to prayer starts up in the nearby mosque. We all listen as the haunting tones reach their plateau and then drop off into the lonely regions between notes. Aaron is weeping by his father's bedside and Farha, for once, is unable to do a thing. We are all comforting each other and Rivka rings the Burial

Board, making sure that preparations commence. Then this wife of mine takes all five children to our house to play and I stay with Aaron.

'Will you help me place my father on the floor?' Aaron asks, and so I take the feet and we lay Aaron's father, Jacob, out next to the bed. 'I'm so glad you're here,' Aaron says, his tears falling on his father's body. 'Not as a doctor, but as a friend.'

If there is anything to be glad for, it is this: that I can be of some service to the Isaacs, who have done everything in their power to help us while we have been here in India.

The servant comes with small earthenware pots of water, which Aaron starts to pour over his father's body. I help him, and continue when he can no longer bear to do this himself; it is my privilege, really, to be able to do this. If I could not perform the last rites for my own father, at least I can do them now for Aaron's. I finish pouring the water and afterwards the pots are broken. Soon after, other people start arriving, which I am grateful for, because I do not know the correct procedures in these parts. They wail as they busy themselves putting white garments on the body, covering it in a shroud and sprinkling it with rose-water. After a short while a wicker carrier arrives for the body, and to stop myself from thinking about my own father, I muster all the medical instincts I possess to see the body as a body, not as a Somebody.

There is more wailing, and prayers are said as we leave the apartment and the body is carried through the streets for some distance. Muslims, Hindus, everyone, turns to watch and offer their respects to us, which is so touching. We have gathered quite a crowd of onlookers by the time we reach the hearse and make our way to the Jewish cemetery.

I climb into a car with Aaron, and he tries to cheer himself up, wipes his tears and tells me, 'You know, the cemetery we're going to was bought by my ancestor, Shalom Cohen, for the price of a ruby ring.' He laughs in the way people do when they're distracting themselves, and I'm thinking: it's strange that in all this time in Calcutta we have never needed to go to the cemetery, even once. How fortunate we are to have stayed in such a safe haven for Jews through these years.

Rivka meets us at the cemetery together with all the children and Mary, who no doubt is attending her first Jewish funeral. The prayers by the graveside begin and I look over at Rivka, who is watching that hole in the earth with a face of shock and disbelief as the body is lowered. Then Aaron lowers himself into the grave alongside his father, believe it or not, and Rivka looks away and covers Hannah's eyes. At first I am surprised and think: why is he climbing into the grave? This is not something we do in Poland, believe me, and I am almost too taken aback to look, but then I see Aaron touch his father's body with such love that I have to continue watching the next religious obligation, which I have never seen before, anywhere. He pulls down the shroud and lifts his father's eyelids, slowly and gently, to fill them with earth. I am transfixed. My eyes are as wide as that of the corpse as I watch this last exchange between father and son. I cannot look away, but I am glad that Rivka has made all the children stand back a little, and I am hoping that they haven't seen this.

After our shirts are torn as a sign of mourning we are reminded to go home via a shop or some place else so that the bad luck does not go with us. Goodness knows why we still keep these superstitions, but on that day we do end up going home through the Army and Navy store in Chowringhee, just in case! Whatever bad luck is left there, I trust it does no harm to their business, for they continue to operate as normal for quite some time to come.

A few weeks after the funeral, Aaron comes for a check-up at the clinic in Sovabazar and I am immediately suspicious that something is wrong. Not with his health, because I have never been a doctor to him, but I know that something is wrong, regardless.

He sits down at the desk opposite me and says, 'Just check that everything is okay.'

I ask, 'Have you been feeling sick? Is there something wrong?' I have to say he is looking as young and healthy as ever.

'No,' he says, but just as I'm about to lift my stethoscope to his chest, he comes out with the real purpose of this visit. 'Actually, I wanted to come here to tell you that we're planning to leave Calcutta.'

This throws a completely different light on his visit. I drop my stethoscope, sit back at my desk and we take a long, serious look at each other. I understand the difficulty that Aaron has in telling us this news. He knows that he and his family have been our lifeblood here in India. We have received the support of the

Isaacs as if through transfusion. They have been our heart, kidneys, liver and lungs until we could find life in ourselves to revive and set up on our own here in Calcutta.

'I am so, so sorry to hear this,' I tell him, and that old feeling of loss comes back. It must be written all over my face, because he says, 'Farha and I want you to come with us.'

'Where are you going?' I ask, knowing that we will not follow. Daniel will insist otherwise, even if his best friend is leaving the country.

'Israel or Australia,' Aaron says. 'We're having difficulties proving that we're not Indians for the Australian government, but if permission comes through, Australia will be our first choice.' Then he continues: 'There'll be better opportunities. Who knows how long the jobs will stay open here for minorities? You should seriously consider coming out there with us.'

'And start all over again as a doctor? How on earth? I don't think I would ever make it.'

'But you're still young. You should get out of this place while you still can.'

'How many times can you transplant a tree, Aaron?'

'As long as there are roots,' he answers, 'and as long as the sun still shines and the rain still falls down. Remember, you once told me you were like a turtle, with your home on your back?'

I have to laugh; that was in another lifetime. 'I have a home now. Your wife helped me to find it. So I gave my back a rest!'

How could I just pick up and go? I would be walking out on all the people who have grown to trust me here in Calcutta.

Aaron can leave his job running Bose Paper Mills and find something much better overseas, but how could I start up all over again?

There is a knock at the door and Chitra, my assistant, reminds me that there is a queue outside waiting to see me. 'We didn't get to do the check-up,' I tell him. 'Do you still want to book a time?'

'No, no, my body is in perfect condition. It's my mind,' he says, tapping his head. 'That's the problem. I love this place ... and it hurts me to leave ...'

I can see that this friend of mine is trying so hard to hold onto his emotions, and I, for one, know how it feels to walk away from a whole lifetime of memories.

'Aaron, you know the kindness you have shown to us will be returned to you many times, and wherever you go you will have your whole family with you. You are leaving in a time of peace and that much is a blessing.' This is all I can say.

In spite of my sense of loss, I know that this will be a hard time for Aaron and Farha; a time when we can return some of the support that they gave to us on our arrival as refugees here in Calcutta. This is the only thing that makes me happy after the sad news that our best friends in the world will be leaving as they had often planned to do, once and for all.

CHAPTER 35

It's been ten years since Independence and the emigration hysteria in Calcutta has reached epic proportions. We, though, are not planning on going anywhere; everybody is so settled, so what's the point? Daniel is now at medical college, and Hannah is a young schoolgirl. However, with the passing of time, it seems as if most of our closest friends are living elsewhere. They go to places like America, Israel, England, Australia — these are the new destinations for the Jewish community here in Calcutta.

I thought the synagogues were empty when the armed forces left, but look at them now. We stand and *doven* in the same places where we used to sit shoulder to shoulder and there are gaps between us where once stood a full congregation. The charity box remains at the back, with its many different slots to choose from. Money for widows, money for orphans, money for Israel, money in the names of the different prophets, but nowadays there are so few people to drop a coin in any of these slots. The great charitable deeds of the Jews of Calcutta are dwindling now that there are so few of us left to help.

Letters from Ewa and Joel keep arriving, every one encouraging us to emigrate to America. Ewa is running a jewellery shop in New York, with great success, and Joel is working as an architect, building their growing city. They have a daughter called Frieda, who is twelve, a year younger than Hannah, and they are prospering in their land of the free.

Frieda and Hannah have become pen pals, and Hannah always writes letters to entice Frieda to come and visit us in Calcutta. She tells her about her school, Loreta, and the nuns. She tells her pen pal stories about the festivals of Calcutta, and Frieda writes back saying that she wants to visit us one year for Holi. She is intrigued by our lives here, this daughter of Ewa's. She writes Hannah a letter saying: 'Are there really beggars walking freely around the streets in India?' Hannah writes back saying that there are lots of them, and she tells Frieda about her favourite one, an old man called Paran. Frieda's letter comes back and she's outraged, so the next time Hannah writes a tame story that she thinks won't shock Frieda — a story about our pet parrot. On receiving this particular letter, Frieda writes back from New York saying: 'Teach Tota to sing the American national anthem and I promise I will come and watch her.'

Hannah is desperate to meet Frieda in the flesh, so she sits down with Tota, who is not so young any more, and sings this song she has learnt about the American flag flying in the early light of dawn. It's the funniest sight — seeing this Tota of ours stretch her legs and squawk back. Of course Tota is a creature of habit and far happier saying things like 'The Germans are coming', but Hannah doesn't give up. She keeps singing this American national anthem until even Mary and Tariq are singing it. In fact, everybody sings this anthem of theirs except Tota. 'She is loyal only to India,' Daniel tells Hannah, when he comes back from medical college one day. 'She's an Indian parrot. Even if her wings worked, she wouldn't want to fly to America.'

But Hannah? She wants nothing more than to emigrate to America, like everybody else. She is the opposite of Daniel. India is all very well and good, but she has this feeling that she should explore the whole world, instead of just sitting in her little corner of it. 'Let's go and live with Aunty Ewa and Uncle Joel,' Hannah tells me one day. 'Then I can go to Frieda's school.' I say, 'Won't you miss your friends here?' and she says, 'Of course not. There'll be plenty of new friends for me in America.'

So easy. Just like that. She wants us all to live together, even Ewa and me, so that she can be with her pen pal. 'It's not so easy leaving the country where you were born,' I tell my daughter, and a few days later Daniel tells her the story of how we all left Poland. Of course, Hannah doesn't quite believe us. How could she?

'Why don't you take me to Poland?' she asks, this daughter of mine. You can imagine my reaction. I am thinking: yes, we can all go back on a happy family holiday, trying to find where I used to live in Muranow, Warsaw. It's unthinkable, really. The stories are starting to come out now about what has happened to our people back in Poland, and what happened to our beautiful city. A whole section of society wiped out. A whole city razed to the ground.

Three million Jews slaughtered in Poland alone.

With this slow unveiling of news I know that I will never go back to the place where I grew up and loved so dearly. Daniel shows me pictures of Warsaw after the war, and there is absolutely nothing left standing, except St Augustyn's, the church at Nowolipki where Ewa went to get our papers. I've kept a photo of this church, standing like a tombstone over the area where I grew up. It's the only recognisable sight of my childhood. One day, my beautiful daughter, you may go back and see this church, but it is a journey you will have to make on your own. This is what I am thinking every time Hannah talks about holidays in Poland.

As all the news starts coming out, we finally receive a response to one of our letters, from an old schoolteacher in Piaski. Absolutely unbelievable, after all these years. We open it up with great excitement, but this excitement lasts only a few minutes, because we are both completely devastated after Rivka finishes reading even the first page. The schoolteacher starts off complaining about the communists, before telling us about the horrors we managed to escape. 'More than ten thousand Jews were taken to the Piaski ghetto,' he writes. 'Even the Jews who were marched to Poland from Germany and Czechoslovakia.'

I look at Rivka and I can see that her stomach is turning. 'Benjamin, you read it,' she says, and passes it to me, her hands shaking.

I read some more out loud, about the headmaster in Piaski, Jerzy Drylski, who instructed his students to form a home-baked resistance movement they called Zemsta. 'These boys collected guns left behind by the retreating Polish army in the fields and hid them in a coffin in the cemetery. They put Zemsta newspapers into the pockets of everybody in church, and one postman who was a member of Zemsta even intercepted letters from people in Piaski telling the Germans to arrest people they didn't like. These letters were buried in bottles around Piaski, but they've all been dug up now.'

Then this schoolteacher starts writing about how the young boys in Zemsta were all arrested. 'So young they were, when the gendarmes came with their lists and took them off to the Zamek (the castle in Lublin) where they were beaten with iron rods and had needles pierced under their fingernails, then killed or sent to camps, to write sad letters home asking for more woollen socks to be sent in the mail.'

This letter goes on to tell us about Majdanek, the death camp that the Germans set up near Piaski after we left. 'You have no idea how terrible this was. They have left it standing, just to remind us all of the hell we lived through.' The schoolteacher writes: 'There were Jews who were hiding in the nearby mines. They covered themselves in white sheets one day when it was snowing and they crawled along the ground to Majdanek to cut the wires and save some of the prisoners.'

Really, this is an unbelievable story, and I feel a sense of relief when I read it, but then I think: what about the three million that weren't saved? This thought is too sickening to bear.

We continue to read this shocking letter and the schoolmaster tells us more about the killings that the Germans carried out in Piaski. 'On the third of November,' he writes, 'they took about two thousand of the Piaski Jews to the *Kirkut* (the cemetery) where they were all shot. I saw them walking. They looked calm. One man was even eating some bread. I don't know if you know Honig,' his letter goes on, 'but he survived.'

I feel like tearing up the letter, not just because I don't know Honig, but because I feel so outraged that only one Jew from Piaski still lives in the area where once lived thousands. How did they do it? How did they actually, physically, mentally, manage to kill so many people?

This one letter finally closes the chapter for me on Poland. We can never go back there, ever.

But can we go anywhere else, at this stage of our lives, with everybody so settled? Letters also arrive from Aaron, Farha and family who keep inviting us to go and live with them in Australia. They are doing extremely well in Sydney, living in a place called Bondi Beach, which makes me think of palm trees and monkeys throwing coconuts at each other. One of these days we will go and visit them and eat coconuts together on their Bondi Beach, but will we stay? I don't think it's possible.

Aaron has found a good job in shipping, and Ezekiel writes long letters telling Daniel about mountains that are blue and heroes who save people from drowning in the sea; stories about picnics on beaches and people lying in rows to get suntans. He also tells his good friend Daniel about Australian girls, but I know that this won't interest our son, because he has already become friendly with a Bengali girl called Sangeeta, a wonderful young art student here in Calcutta, and his loyalty could never be tempted elsewhere.

I should say, at this point, that Daniel is going to marry Sangeeta. Other people here are asking me if she is going to convert, but I do not pass on these concerns to Daniel. Some of the Jews left here in Calcutta ask, 'What about the children?' I say to them, 'What about them?' Then they say, 'Well, they won't be Jewish!' at which point I shrug my shoulders. There are greater crimes in life, and Daniel is a free spirit living in a free India. Of course Rivka would have preferred it if he found a Jewish girl, but as Sangeeta says, 'Marriages are made in heaven.' She does not know this, but our Talmud says the same thing: that a voice from heaven announces the wife of a man — his *bashert* — forty days before the boy is even conceived.

When I tell Mitra he is delighted. 'They are mixing the blood. It will make a wonderful cocktail!' Then he asks me quietly, 'Do her parents mind that she is not marrying a Hindu?'

It's strange, but I hadn't thought about whether or not *her* parents would mind. In the face of this concern Mitra gives me some very 'Mitra' advice: 'Tell them that their Abraham is our Brahma, and Sara is the same as Saraswati! See, they're even called the same names — you can't tell me that these two religions don't have the same origins somewhere back in time.' He lifts his eyebrows above those enormous eyes of his and I have to laugh. Then he adds some more useful advice. 'When you leave the house of Daniel's in-laws, don't say *Shalom*, just say *Om*. It's much shorter and easier!' He is falling about laughing at his own joke now. 'Same words, same religion, same everything, ha, ha, ha.' He cannot stop himself, my dear friend, so taken is he by his own wit.

There is no dissent over this marriage, because it does seem to be 'made in heaven'. There is no question of telling young people here to 'live some more' before getting married. Besides which, Daniel has done all the living and staying alive that he needs to do. The only suggestion I make is that he finishes his practice in the hospital. Everybody involved agrees that this is the best course of action, including Daniel and the heavenly Sangeeta, so the marriage is set for two years from now. It will be a Vedic wedding, where the priest will sing and the fire will be lit and they will sweeten each other's mouths with the delicious milk cakes that the Bengalis make. It will be underneath a wedding canopy made out of garlands of flowers, as is their custom, and we will come through the streets with our Jewish 'boy' to be received like royal guests outside Sangeeta's home.

All these things to look forward to now. Already it feels as if our lives are less important, and the next generation will make a better job of their world than we have of ours. The world is turning faster than ever, it seems. One day soon Hannah will find somebody, too, and then Rivka and I will be able to say that we have completed all our responsibilities in life, just as the Hindus say when they have married off all their children. Then, God willing, we will be able to watch the future unfold in a world of peace, from our home here in Calcutta, where we will stay, even when the last Jew has left, because this is where we have made our lives and been able to live them, in freedom. Calcutta has become our Jerusalem, no doubt about it, and no amount of emigration can take us to a better place than the one we are in right now, in our hearts and in our minds.

CHAPTER 36

I didn't want to end this story in New York, but what to do? For years Daniel received invitations from Ewa and Joel, persuading him to come out and visit them, and he always said he had no interest, telling me that he'd prefer to go and visit Zek and his family in Australia any day. But then Sangeeta wanted to meet an art critic called Greenberg, whom Ewa knew, and what did Daniel do? He went running to the airline to buy a ticket, of course.

After that first trip they both wanted to move out to America, so who was I to stop them? Then when Hannah asked Daniel if he would pay for her to study medicine in New York, Daniel jumped at the opportunity. No doubt in order to force us to come over and join the two of them.

Oh, I resisted at first, believe me. 'You were the one who wanted to stay in Calcutta all along,' I told Daniel, 'so why this talk of emigration?' Still Daniel kept talking about this better standard of living, and I always thought: what nonsense has got into his head? Meanwhile, all Rivka could say was, 'Oy *vay*, another time creates another people.' Really, who were we — two old people who knew nothing?

Then Daniel came to India on a trip and told me, 'It's become too dangerous to live in Calcutta.' I reminded him that we had survived the Great Calcutta Killings and even the Naxalbari movement that started up in the hills around Darjeeling, propagating armed struggle for the workers. We had survived the revolutionaries, the political rallies, the summers and the pollution, and we still didn't want to leave.

Then Daniel started having children and they were so far away. Our grandchildren, Sonya and Rahul, were born, and all we got were the photographs. Hannah, of course, then went to New York to study medicine, and she too became seduced by this place of theirs. After only one visit home during her three years of study, she announced to us in 1972 that she would be marrying an Italian surgeon called Graziano. That was quite some time ago, and now they have two children as well, Chico and Maria, and we were lucky to see them once a year when they came home for the holidays, all of them together. We took the children to Alipore Zoo and to the Calcutta Club, but within a few days they had to go home again and all our conversations came to an end.

Every time they were about to leave, Rivka said to me, 'Maybe we should go and live over there, just to be with all the children, before they grow up and have children of their own.'

Then Daniel joined in, saying, 'How can you stay here when all of your family are living elsewhere?' So what was I supposed to do? Was it my idea to send them all off?

I suppose I should tell you about how we are picked up and dragged over here once I'd retired, to this New York. It is Daniel's idea, I'm sure, although he has Hannah making him do this thing. Like I said, I resist their offers. I tell them that they don't have servants over in New York and we'll be useless without them. I ask, 'Who will look after us when we finally become totally hopeless?'

'You won't need servants, Papa,' Hannah tells me. 'You'll have washing machines instead, and we'll come and help out every day.' Really, they say everything to try and persuade us, and maybe we are bullied into leaving Calcutta in the end, but in the sweetest possible way.

Daniel and Sangeeta ask if they can come with us to ensure a smooth passage and I tell them not to bother. Both Rivka and I have picked up and moved countries before. 'Yes,' Daniel says, 'but last time you didn't have so many possessions.'

I tell him, 'Do you think it was any easier coming here with nothing?'

He says, 'Last time you were younger.'

'Okay, okay,' I say, 'you think we haven't noticed?'

They don't ask us again whether or not we want the help. They simply tell us that Sangeeta wants to come over to see her family, and they'll just drop by and pack us up while they are at it. Believe it or not, in the short three weeks that they are here, they actually manage to pack up our whole house and organise the shipping of *everything*.

So we have this easy emigration — only the goodbyes are difficult. At this age you never can tell when you will see someone again. Saying goodbye always seems so final, and saying goodbye to our oldest servants, Mary and Tariq, is the hardest task of all.

We are by the familiar door of our home in Rowland Road, standing at the top of the stairs under the porch of the house we've lived in for nearly fifty years, when we hug Mary and Tariq goodbye. They touch our feet, and cry like we do as the car pulls out from our driveway for the last time ever. As we turn the corner into Ballygunge Road I am thinking about one passage from the Book:

> *A season is set for everything, a time for every experience under heaven:*
> *A time for being born and a time for dying,*
> *A time for planting and a time for uprooting the planted . . .*

So, the time for uprooting is happening once more, it seems.

Only a few things I take with me in my hand luggage: my walking stick, and my father's sidelocks tucked into my top pocket in a small box. When we are on board the aeroplane, I hold Rivka's hand as we listen to the instructions about escape exits and life jackets, knowing that there will be no need for any 'escape' this time, because we are making the journey from our homeland in safety and comfort. We are happy and we are together. The world is at peace and we are moving of our own free will — almost. I hold Rivka's hand and the air hostess notices. Always people notice when we are doing these things, because no doubt they think we are too old to be showing our appreciation for each other.

Then the plane leaves and we are high up in the air above Calcutta, both of us crying as we say goodbye to the city that took us in and became our home when we had none. We sit and drink our orange juice hundreds of metres up in the air, looking down at the paddy fields and ponds of Bengal, maybe for the last time. Yes, we are comfortable, if you compare this trip to the one we took on the *Asama Maru* from Japan. Not a hiccup the whole way, and within the space of a day we've landed in New York and everybody is there to greet us. Hannah and Graziano and their two children, all adults now; Daniel and Sangeeta with their two. So settled here, they are, really. Such a large family we have now, after living on our own for so long.

We are taken to our new apartment on 82nd Street, uptown Manhattan: a much smaller home it seems, but so comfortable, and filled with life — children, grandchildren and now Rivka and me, two old refugees in a new city, who have come all the way from Calcutta to the centre of the world.

I have to admit, at first I am determined not to like it, because I don't want my children to feel as if they've done the right thing. I don't want them to think that this New York is better than Calcutta. However, I make a few concessions and, fortunately or unfortunately, I can see that New York does have some attractions.

Coming here at this age is like having a holiday away from real life, but whatever New York is, it can never be Calcutta. Somehow there is a gap that stays unfilled — I cannot explain this feeling exactly. The place itself is much more perfect than Calcutta. Such a tidy city, yes — and they complain about the graffiti on the trains, would you believe? There is so much order over here, really; no street processions; nothing that I would call a traffic jam; such a nice clean city, but people still talk about pollution. What is wrong with them?

Daniel tells me that New York is the Calcutta of the West, but the only thing that reminds me of India is the smoke that comes out through the grids in the pavements. Sometimes I see this and I can imagine the pavements of Calcutta steaming after the monsoon rains. Through the steam I can almost picture a few drenched trees with their thick, dark green leaves, and an altar or two on the sidewalk. But instead of the barefoot men in *dhotis* pulling rickshaws and ringing their bells nearby, there are men of every skin colour driving taxis. Instead of the *saris* and *dhotis* in elegant cottons and silks, there are young people wearing hardly anything — girls with their *tuchus* hanging out.

Yes, everything is different over here. What is Daniel thinking? Instead of the crumbling colonial mansions with their pillared entrances, there are canopied red carpets leading into the mouths of skyscrapers. We live in one of these — Daniel's choice. Instead of our *durwan*, or gatekeeper, in Calcutta, we have a doorman who sits on the ground floor of our building. He helps us up the lifts with our shopping and tips his hat whenever he sees us. 'Treat him well,' Daniel tells me, 'you cannot live without a doorman in New York.' I ask you, is this boy the son of Farha? Does he even remember living without a gatekeeper?

So, we are here now, and we have to make the most of it. Like Calcutta, they say that New York is a 'melting pot', but how many of us come here who have already been melted down before our arrival? Over here people are always asking me, 'Where are you from?' because my accent sounds a little Polish, a little Indian. Where am I from? Even I don't know the answer any more. In this city it seems as if all parts of my life have come together. One minute I look around and I see the New York Hassidic Jews dressed in their black hats and coats, just like they wore in the old towns of Poland. The next minute I see elegant Indian ladies, strikingly dressed — Punjabis mostly, taking their daily constitutional in their *salwar chemises* and sneakers. How strange is life that everybody could end up in the same place — this New York.

Whenever I see one of these Indian ladies I want to go up and start talking about India. To tell them that I am Indian, actually, but would they believe me, or would they even be interested? After all, they have made their lives here in America. Would they care to talk to an old man who is missing their homeland probably more than they are? And the Hassidim in their black coats — what of them? I tried talking to one of them in Polish some time back and he walked down the street as fast as possible to get away from me! I don't think he could even understand what I was saying.

One more funny thing I notice about this melting pot — no matter what people look like, you can never know where they are from. The kings, queens and superstars look ordinary, and the beggars are dressed in the smartest of clothes. Let me tell you this story. One beggar comes up to me when we first arrive here and says, 'Excuse me, sir, my wallet's been stolen and I need five dollars for a taxi home.' So what do I do? I give him his five dollars, of course. But then another beggar comes up to me, and then another. How many people have had their wallets stolen in this city? I hate to say it, but I'm used to seeing beggars who are dwarves, beggars with limbs missing, beggars who talk to you as if they are using their last breath to ask you for a few rupees. Beggars who tell you, 'May God bless you, *saab*: my mother has died, my father has died, I don't have any food to put in my belly.' So, you must understand, it is hard to listen to a beggar say, 'Please give me five dollars for a taxi,' in a smart suit and speaking with a perfectly polite, prosperous American accent.

'You don't know anything about this place,' Hannah tells me. 'You know the old immigrant's joke here? They say: I was a stranger in a strange land and I was taken in. You've been taken in, Papa, well and truly, yet again.'

She gives me strict instructions that I should not gaze into the eyes of strangers here, but I cannot help myself. I am curious — and where will I see the world if not in their eyes? On CNN television? So, I am a stranger in this land, and I am taken in a few times, but what of it?

I suppose I should tell you how it was to meet Ewa and Joel for the first time after so long. No doubt you are curious.

It was a moment I had imagined many times while we were living in Calcutta. I knew that one day all of us would meet up again and we would probably say nothing about the things that we went through together. Say nothing, but feel everything all the same. I thought that it would be the same as always, but somehow things change. Our lives change us; our experiences bring us together, and then take us apart again.

Still, the day before we go and visit them, I get Daniel to take me to Bloomingdale's and I buy a new bottle of aftershave; don't ask me why. Maybe I'm a little nervous, I don't know, but this much is a fact — a little aftershave is not going to bring back even a minute of my youth. There is no disguise for my age, but somehow I feel obligated to be the person I always was, and that person is frozen in time, a young man in Warsaw.

So we go to their apartment, with Daniel and Sangeeta, and Rivka is looking at me as they ring on the doorbell. I am sure she is thinking: why the new aftershave, Benjamin? But she doesn't say anything. We are all nervous, even Daniel and Sangeeta, who see Ewa, Joel and their daughter, Frieda, all the time. We are nervous because we are going to have to make a giant leap over so many years, with so much behind all of us, for the sake of friendship and forgiveness.

Ewa opens the door and I clutch Rivka's hand tighter, expecting this to be something too overwhelming, but you know, the minute I see her I know that we'll be great friends once more. She is so much older, I don't believe it. I don't know why I expected to see someone much younger than myself. Why should she be under obligation to stay the same while the rest of us are allowed to age, really?

'Benjamin!' she cries out. Her voice is the same. We hug and we don't let go of each other, because it is a meeting of lifetimes and there is a lot to say in this one welcome. Then Rivka and Ewa hug. We all hug, and wipe away our tears.

And Joel? I was expecting a handsome GI, goodness knows why. I couldn't see him any other way than in his smart American uniform — the sort that was always more shiny and elegant than the rougher khaki ones worn by the British soldiers. But no, he's wearing pants and braces and his figure has a completely different line from the last time we saw him in Calcutta. Ewa says, 'Joel has lost weight, you should have seen how much he put on while he was still working.'

We laugh at ourselves, and I find myself searching Ewa's face for the young girl I once knew. It is still there, in the eyes, this youth of hers, I'm telling you. What they think of Rivka and me, who can say? Ewa and Joel are probably shocked at the sight of us two old cronies from Calcutta.

We spend a lot of time together in New York: Ewa, Joel, Rivka and I. We are oldies together, we four survivors. Relics, actually, if you want to be blunt about it. We don't talk about those days much, because we live in a new world now, and the stories have to be saved for those who have the inclination to hear them. Only sometimes, when there is somebody else to talk with, do the stories of Poland and Calcutta come back. For example, one time we are sitting with Ewa's friends, and this one fellow tells us how he went back to Poland after the war, and was too scared to stay there after the massacres of Jews that took place at Kielce.

'We were right not to go back to Poland,' Rivka says. 'What would we have gone back to, really?'

I say, 'What for to go back? Everybody is here, for goodness sake!' Ha ha, very funny, but the truth is, I don't want to go back because I am neither young enough nor strong enough to relive those memories on the very soil where they took place.

'Go back now and they'll think you're after your old land and the Poles will hate you,' this fellow tells us.

'Let them have the land, if it's worth that much to them,' that's what I say. 'I am never going to fight another battle on Polish soil.'

We must live in the present. This is what I think whenever these things come up. Nobody can take the past away from us, even if they take away the properties and the possessions we owned. The memories never disappear, this much I know.

No, somehow the memories of Calcutta are easier to return to. One day we are talking — Ewa, Joel, Rivka and I — and I tell them, 'You only need to wave a curry under my nose and I feel like catching a taxi to the airport and going back to visit our home.'

Joel listens as I say this, and it is he who comes up with this plan — this idea to go back to Calcutta. 'We'll make it a nostalgia trip. Heck, we'll all go back together.'

The four of us laugh. We look at each other. Of course I am thinking: we are all far too old for this nostalgia business, but still the idea doesn't go away. We keep on talking about it, and then — what do you know? — this idea starts to take form! When we tell Daniel and Sangeeta they're as excited as we are about the idea. Hannah and Graziano are less so, but all it takes is a suggestion for Daniel and what does he do? Why, he goes out and buys tickets for all of us, without asking us for a cent. Then Daniel and Sangeeta go ahead and do all the organising for this trip, just like they did for our move out here to New York, and I am thinking: we raised this son of ours well. He went through misery, but look how he came out of it, and look at what a good boy he's become.

Even as we get into the stretch limo to go to John F Kennedy airport, I know that this will be my last visit to Calcutta — the place on this earth I most call home. There are six of us this time, including Daniel and Sangeeta, all of us a little nervous, I must say, to be treading these paths together after so long.

As we get on the plane I am thinking: whatever happened to Mosze and Lewek? Did they ever make it to Palestine, or are they living in New York now, like the rest of the world, just a few blocks from us? How strange to think of them, now that we are about to arrive in India again after all these years.

When we finally arrive at Calcutta's Dum Dum airport I feel waves of excitement as I watch the metal staircase being wheeled up to meet our plane. Then they open the doors and I get my first lungful of the air here — thick and warm and organic — and everything comes back to me.

We all help each other down those metal stairs, because our bones don't move so freely now, and when I find myself standing on the tarmac I bend down slowly and touch the ground beneath us. Can you believe it? We've made it back. Yes, it really feels as if we have come home.

Daniel organises coolies to help with our bags in his still perfect Bengali, and we get into two black ambassador taxis, asking their drivers to take us around for a while so that we can say hello to our old city. I cannot tell you how it feels. Rivka and I, Ewa and Joel, all in the same taxi, and not a single word from any of us.

For me it could be that same trip we took to the Jewish Girls' School from Kidderpore Docks. Almost, but not quite, because I am not a stranger here. I feel such a fondness for the things that were all once ours. I notice small things, like a brick wall half painted in blue and then fading to pinks, whites, then bare bricks at the top. Not the work of indecision, but the work of someone who wanted to use up half a tin of paint to improve the gully. I think of that person and a rush of love for the people here comes out and makes me start pulling at my handkerchief. I look around and both Ewa and Rivka are wiping tears from their eyes, as well. What is it about this place? What is this love affair all about?

There's that same chaos in the streets, as always. The chaos that we know only too well. The same old houses of the Raj with their stained yellows, their Venetian shutters unhinged now, luxuriously decadent, framing windows that once had grand views of horses and carriages and Calcutta streets that were washed clean every day.

This drive through Calcutta for the first time since we left — *wah!* I cannot tell you how excited we are to smell the air; see people in *dhotis* and *saris*; the children and their parents washing under the taps in the streets; the policemen in their white uniforms, standing on canopied stage posts in the middle of the road. Then we pass The Strand and all the buildings have crumbled even more than they had before. Now it seems as if the old British buildings have turned into pots for trees, right there next to the docks.

I observe everything so intensely, more so than our first arrival here. Noticing the plants more than ever before: the peetle trees growing from cracks in houses, vines straddling bushes and grasses, nature piggybacking nature, and of course the beautiful banyan trees growing around the pretty little shrines that are installed at their feet.

We drive through the avenues of banana trees and coconut palms, streets filled with deep orange flame of the forest trees and bright yellow Indian laburnum. Hanging above us, from telegraph pole to mango tree to wrought-iron balconies and pillars, are all the familiar political messages, flying in the breeze like prayer flags. I look up, and above us are the roof gardens that poke their bushes and pink frangipani trees up at the sky, in the place of New York skyscrapers. I cannot tell you how I feel, to see this home of ours.

When we drive towards the Maidan the taxi driver announces, 'This is Victoria Memorial,' and I feel like saying: of course it is. Do you think we're stupid? But instead I tell him to stop and let us out to walk for a while. We flag down the other car and Daniel and Sangeeta stop, too. How incredible to be here, all together, in Calcutta's huge Central Park. 'Do you remember how the planes took off and landed from Red Road during the war, Daniel, or were you too young?' I ask.

Daniel says, 'Of course I remember. This is where Zek and I caught the Victorias to go out on our adventures.' As he says this it all comes back to me, and I remember one afternoon when the two boys went missing to the Kalaikunda airstrip to get chocolate from the GIs.

After our walk we get back into the taxis and drive along Chowringhee, and there in front of us is a sight that has my eyes popping out of their sockets. Firpo's, where we used to spend every New Year's Eve, has gone. It's simply burned down, along with the market that had taken over in its place. Rivka and I look at each other in amazement, and once more we tell the driver to stop, and Rivka takes photographs of this sorry sight. What would Angelo Firpo have said if he could have been there, looking at his elegant restaurant with its wide verandahs and mirrored walls all reduced to piles of charcoal debris? Looking at Firpo's, strangely enough, makes me realise that nothing will ever be the same again. I realise how much this world of ours has changed in our lifetimes, and it makes me wonder how different Poland would look to us now, if we dared go back there after all these years. How many of the Jewish areas would have been burned down, just like Firpo's is now?

I am thinking these things and looking out of the window. Thinking about how the past can be found in a place, in a smell, in a smile, and I am looking at this sorry sight and the same old

Chowringhee further down the street. I am feeling the shock and the familiarity of being in Calcutta once again. Nothing can describe it, believe me.

Finally, after our 'tourist ride', the driver takes us up to the Taj Bengal Hotel where we will be staying on our visit to this beautiful city. What a far cry from the Jewish Girls' School where we first arrived, here in Calcutta. There are palms and waiters and a swimming pool; bearers at the door who look like princes in their immaculate starched traditional white suits and turbans. They salute us as we walk in and I am thinking: what a strange life this is. How quickly the world turns full circle.

How much has changed since 1941, when we first came to Calcutta. Now we sleep in our elegant air-conditioned bedrooms, with the comfort of bathrooms attached. Anything we want to eat, they'll cook up for us, we just have to reach over to the button under the lampshade and press it. There is no rolling out of mats on the floor, no collecting of coins to pay for bread. All of these changes in this one lifetime — how is it possible?

It is at the Taj Bengal Hotel in Calcutta that the most unlikely scene imaginable takes place. Daniel has sent for Mary and Tariq, our old *ayah* and cook, and they both arrive together to meet us for dinner. The hotel staff, meanwhile, take one look at the pair and tell them to wait outside. Would you believe it — so rude! Minding our own business, we wait in the dining hall for our dinner guests, who have promised to be on time. You see, this was Daniel's plot — some idea he had of repaying his *ayah* and Tariq for all their years of service — but I am thinking: of course they're not coming. Why would they want to come here? They'd feel so uncomfortable, no? By the time we realise that this instinct of mine is correct, it is too late to do anything about it. Daniel's plan has failed. Tariq and Mary are both sitting on the outside steps, feeling terrible. Tariq refuses to come in, and Mary is too embarrassed to make a second attempt, even if she comes in this time with official guests of the hotel.

So what do we do? We go to Mary's house — the house that Daniel and Hannah helped her to buy some years back. It's a small house in Kumartuli, near the streets by the river where craftsmen prepare thousands of goddesses for Durga Puja every year. Here we have a beautiful meal, all of us together, sitting down on the floor and enjoying being guests of our long-time servant, for the first time in our lives.

There are some other beautiful things about this trip. Rivka and I go to our old clinic in Sovabazar Street, and the whole area is even more crumbled than ever, but somehow it is not without its glory. The grand buildings with their ornate porticos and decorative plasterwork, the high ceilings, the pillars standing tall for the Raj, the beautiful wrought iron, the buildings where every layer is different, like a wedding cake — they're all still there, just older now, like the rest of us. The big difference, however, is that Mitra is no more. He died on a Sabbath, peacefully in his sleep, and standing here looking at the clinic we started together makes me miss him so badly I cannot stop myself from crying.

After our trip to Sovabazar we meet Askander and Ayesha Iqbal at the Calcutta Club, and in that building absolutely nothing has changed, except that a few more names of Club Presidents have been inscribed in the reception area. Since we've been in New York we've kept up with the Iqbals and heard all their news through their son, Shabbir, who lives in Connecticut.

'Did you ever consider going to live with Shabbir and his wife in America?' I ask Askander, and he says, 'Why on earth would I want to go and live in a place with such a low standard of living? Nobody to work for you, nothing!'

Ha, it is so strange to hear him saying the same things that I used to say to Daniel and Hannah. 'No, no, there are washing machines. Machines, machines, everywhere, machines,' I say.

'But who brings you your *chai* in the morning? A machine?'

'Yes, yes. There are tea-making machines in America believe me!' I have to laugh at myself as I say these words. Who am I trying to persuade, really? Already I'm sounding like an American, you see, even though my heart is here.

'The real problem with America,' Askander starts up, 'is that too many of our children are going to live there now. We're always worried that the boys who go over are going to come back with a Susan or a Hilary.'

'Making cocktails,' I say, repeating my old friend Mitra, and do you know what Rivka says? She surprises me completely by saying: 'There's nothing wrong with that.'

After the Calcutta Club we go and visit Farha's sister, Leah, because she is one of the few remaining Jews we know here in

Calcutta, and how I miss the rest of the Isaacs when we see her. Leah is bedridden and smiles benignly at everyone in the room. I tell her how shocked I was to see Firpo's burnt down and ask her about the other changes that have taken place since we left.

'Changes?' She thinks for a while and then tells me, 'Now that the British are back, at least it's a little cleaner.'

I am not joking, this is what she says, and this lady is only five years older than me, so I am thinking: how much longer will my marbles hold out, for goodness sake?

Our next excursion we take early on the Saturday before we leave. On this day, before even the hawkers are awake, we go to Maghen David Synagogue. We've driven past it a few times during the week and I've noticed how the rows of trinket sellers have now expanded over the pavements outside. It is almost impossible to get a car inside the compound during trading hours, they say, but today, at this time of the morning, there is nobody here.

The bearer lets us in and we wait under the old red porch, sitting on the steps next to the marble plaques that name some of the community benefactors who helped us when we first arrived here. We wait for a short while, and then a few familiar faces appear. So few of them, though, that even with Joel, Daniel and me, we are not enough to make up a *minyan*. Apart from the sad loss of faces, everything else is the same as that first time we came here from our dormitory at the Jewish Girls' School. The same gold stars on blue skies on the ceiling. The same seats made of Burma teak. The same Ladies' Gallery, only now there isn't a single woman looking down on us. What for to sit upstairs when there are only five ladies present? No, now everyone sits and prays together in the main hall. Hardly a person to read, when once we had so many Jews here we could auction the rights to read from the Book.

We start the service, and the prayers are as familiar as the smells, as the walls, as the fans above us that spin circles in time, taking us back to our first visit here, when we came to give thanks for being alive.

There is no doubt about it that this time, too, we are coming to Maghen David Synagogue to give thanks for being alive. To give thanks for having lived a full life in a place where we could grow old, look back on our history and have some hope for the generations that will come after us.

EPILOGUE

Grow old along with me!
The best is yet to be,
The last of life, for which the first was made:
Our times are in His hand
Who saith, 'A whole I planned,
Youth shows but half; trust God: see all, nor be afraid!'

ROBERT BROWNING, from *Rabbi Ben Ezra*

So you see, I did not know where to start this story and neither do I know where to finish it. Everything I have told you is within living memory, and still no hand has turned off the switch to put that memory to sleep.

True, I am very old, but I do not want to sit and wait for my funeral. We are a people, after all, who celebrate life. It is to life that we raise our glasses. If we cannot make our lives sacred, well then how can we celebrate the existence of God on earth?

Many centuries ago, it was declared that we should be a light unto the nations. How well we have achieved that, I do not know. What I do know, though, is that a light shines brightest in the darkness, and if my people have known anything at all, it has been darkness. We have grown accustomed to seeing through the darkness, and witnessing the power of God, even on the darkest and cloudiest of nights.

The Lord said, 'As long as you are my witness, I am God,' and I believe that as long as we can still witness goodness, we have hope in this world of ours.

I have been a witness as best as I can. I have been a witness to the goodness of many peoples — be they Muslim, Hindu, Christian, Jewish, whatever. I have been a witness to harmony between religions. I have been witness, too, to the saddest conflicts imaginable in the name of God. And the conflict does not stop. This city of New York is now playing host to this hatred in the name of religion. Since the planes crashed into our buildings, I have heard some prophets of the streets announce that the end of the world is nigh. I, too, remember feeling that way many years ago, and yet the world keeps turning, as sure as anything. The goodness of people, be they Muslim, Jewish, Catholic, anything, comes to the surface and we remember what it means to be human. We remember that there are more parts to the story than our own, and it is these stories that lead the way forward to unity.

Now I see altars to the human spirit on the streets of New York — a vision you could never have imagined a few weeks earlier. In Warsaw, I hear, they are lighting candles all over the city in memory of those killed in New York, and here, too, they do the same. When a million candles light up the darkness, what power can it have over us? We see each other all too clearly, and even start to enjoy our differences. We see that a spiritual life is not only valid, it is necessary. Personally, I have never quite trusted a person who does not have one, be they Jewish-Shmewish, Catholic, Muslim, anything.

Nowadays I spend some time as a volunteer at the Holocaust Museum in Battery Park City. It is there that I will continue to be a witness, not just to the hatred that this world has known in recent times, but also to the spirit of hope. I am lucky to be alive: nobody needs to remind me of that. I am fortunate to be able to tell stories like the one I have told just now, and really, I believe that these stories have the power to save us.

I do not tell these stories out of pity for myself or moroseness about the fate of my people. For we do not simply share a fate, we also share a destiny — the same destiny as all of humanity. If we are to make this journey together, I believe, all hatred should be brought to light as soon as it arises, for we cannot allow it to fester. No nation should feel that it is the owner of moral purity, for none of us knows the whole Truth, and no country can be sure that it lives by it. We see through the glass darkly, as the Christians say, and must act as best we can with our vision impaired and our knowledge compromised.

The legends say that we knew the whole Truth before we were born, but at birth an angel came and took it from us by wiping its finger above our lips and leaving a dip above the cupid's bow. I know this is only our legend, but still it must be clear to anybody that we, as human beings, don't know the whole Truth. So who are we to wave sticks at each other in the name of truth? Not just sticks, but knives, guns, bombs, everything. In the name of the One God, the time has come to live and let live. Here in America, in Poland, in India, in the Middle East, everywhere.

To this day I have not made it to Jerusalem, and I do not know if I ever will. Neither did my father, although it was his dearest wish. Perhaps he is there now, who knows. If so, I hope that the Truth is with him and that we will see peace there and in Palestine for the future generations. It is my dearest wish that there is peace in the world, and that the politicians who hold the power over people and their ignorance find the sense to stop the antagonism and put an end to all the bloodshed.

I hope, too, that my father is able to sit down with the priests who saved our lives, as well as the priests and nuns who saved the lives of so many other Jews in Poland. I hope in this conference of his he can also sit down with some of the bishops and cardinals of Poland, whom he believed incited violence against the Jews, and work out a comfortable agreement of how things were and how they could have been, in a place where nothing can be denied and forgiveness is infinitely available.

For my children, grandchildren, great-grandchildren and their families, I hope that they too will live to be a light unto the nations, no matter what religion they are brought up to believe in. That they will strive to create peace in the world by peaceful means, and continue to celebrate the incredible gift of life in every way they possibly can.

As long as we have a future here on earth, this is my prayer.

Shalom — or *Om*, as Mitra would say, if he were still with us, here on this earth today.

ACKNOWLEDGMENTS

This novel is a story that tells of real events. The characters may be fictional, but there are many who can justifiably take credit for the story. Firstly, Olek, the father-in-law I never met, whose escape from a Nazi transit camp and life with partisans is told here. Secondly, to all the people who arrived in Calcutta on the *Asama Maru*, and the people like Bolek Rembaum who decided to stay.

My love and gratitude goes to my mother, Pramila, for starting me off — for giving me the picture of Durga in the Hooghly and so much more. Also, to my father, William, for listening enthusiastically to my early chapters and for being my dad. Thank you to my grandmother, too, for looking after us all in India and for being such a huge part of our lives.

To Wojciech Dabrowski I owe my title. Thank you so much, Woj, for your insights and encouragement during the years I took to write this book. Thank you, Kathy, too, for sharing Olek's stories with us, and thanks to Dr David Miller for your expert medical advice. To Jan for love, and to Tally and Rishi for being so enthusiastic and proud of Mama's writing. I love you all so much.

Thank you, Niki Zubrzycka, for nudging me in the direction of this story by lending me your book *Jews of the Raj*. To Ruth Max, for putting me in touch with David Nahoum, and to David Nahoum for taking time away from your bakery to tell me stories from Calcutta's golden days and for introducing me to the Jewish community. Thank you to Ian Zachariah, too, for your wonderful hospitality in Calcutta.

My gratitude must also go to Rabbi Ninio and Esty Gutnick for letting me attend those inspirational classes on Judaism. Yours was an open-hearted invitation to explore further.

Thank you to Kasia and Marek Zielinski for hospitality in Warsaw; to Janusz Ostrowski for stories from the fire station; and to Zofia Garczynska for your inspiring wartime stories. A huge thank you to Joanna Golaj for the gift of your translations in Piaski, and to Marius Golaj for your hospitality in Gardzienice. Thanks must also go to Lucjan Swietlicki for all the heart-wrenching memories of Piaski during the war; to Marian and Danka Grinberg for sharing stories of the Warsaw ghetto; and to Diane Armstrong for checking my Polish.

For financial and moral support, I wish to thank Asialink for the residency in Calcutta. My residency was funded by the New South Wales Government — Ministry for the Arts, as well as the Australia-India Council and the Australia Council for the

Arts. Amanda Lawrence and Asha Das made my time in India unforgettable, along with the wonderful Dr Bannerjee at Burdwan University. I also wish to thank the New South Wales Government — Ministry for the Arts for my literary fellowship.

The support of my publishers, HarperCollins, was inspirational. Thank you, Linda Funnell, for connecting so deeply with the heart of this story and offering your wonderful insights throughout the journey. Thank you, Nicola O'Shea, my editor, for bringing out the best in me and in this book, and thank you, Catherine Day, for seeing this book through to its birth. Thanks must also go to Fiona Inglis, my agent at Curtis Brown, for being such a loyal supporter.

I read dozens of books to research this novel, guided by my wonderful librarian, Denise Syme, but the two that stand out in my mind are Leo Cooper's *In the Shadow of the Polish Eagle* and *Turning Back the Pages* by Esmond David Ezra. The first brought home some devastating facts, which I was careful to include, and the second transported me to another time and place that inspired me beyond words.

Finally, I should say that this was an unbelievably difficult novel to write. I wept on countless occasions as I researched and wrote it, yet none of the tears I shed can even touch the suffering of those who lived through similar experiences. This book was written as a prayer for those people who could not live to tell their tales. It was written, too, as a prayer for the future of our world, in the hope that stories like this have the power to save us.